ghost

A novel by Helen Grant

Ghost
Helen Grant

Published by Fledgling Press, 2018
Cover Design: Graeme Clarke
graeme@graemeclarke.co.uk

ISBN 9781912280094

www.fledglingpress.co.uk

Printed and bound by:
MBM Print SCS Ltd, Glasgow

MIX
Paper from
responsible sources
FSC® C117931

For Ann

Prologue

Langlands House is haunted, but not by the ghost you think.

It's the ghost of a girl who died here during the War, that's what they say.

The house is difficult to get to – in the middle of a private estate and surrounded by forest. But if anyone does make their way up the winding track under the dark canopy of trees, they eventually find themselves on a gravel area in front of a big grey stone building topped with slate-roofed turrets. Langlands.

Although rare, this does actually happen. People travelling across country by foot stray from the usual routes and stumble across the house. Once, a census taker came to knock in vain. And occasionally, people come especially to look for the ghost.

Any of these people may find themselves standing on the gravel staring up at those grey walls, streaked with patches of damp and lichen, and the windows which are always darkly reflective, like jet, because there is never any light behind them. They may glimpse her at one of those windows, looking down, or perhaps gazing back at them from a patch of deep shadow under the trees that ring the house.

Sometimes they doubt their own eyes. They stare and stare, and sometimes she goes away. She drifts away from the window or vanishes into the darkness under the trees. Other times, she gazes back at them, not going anywhere. That always frightens them off. They back away, or they just turn right round and make a run for it, skidding on the gravel, stumbling on the ruts in the tracks. I've seen this happen.

A rational person would say, how can this be, considering that there are no such things as ghosts? And they would also say: how did you see this happen?

The answer to both of these questions is: it's me they see. I'm the one they run away from, round-eyed, sometimes screaming. The Langlands ghost is me.

chapter one

In an instant my eyes were open, staring into the dark. My heart was thudding at the deep rumbling that swelled until it seemed to fill the sky above the house. There was one brilliant flash that traced the outline of everything in my room for a split second: the iron bedstead, the wash stand, the bookcase. Then a terrible splintering crash which reverberated through the entire house. It was so loud that I thought the entire roof must be coming down on my head.

I threw back the covers and slid out of bed, the wooden floorboards cold under my feet. From somewhere within the ancient house I heard a series of minor shocks, as though something were crumbling and falling in. I imagined a widening breach, cracks running through the aged structure, a sudden and final collapse. I ran for the door.

The moment I wrenched it open I knew my mistake. Langlands House had neither gas nor electricity; the passage outside was pitch dark, lacking even the moonlight that seeped into the bedroom between the shabby velvet curtains. The candle, unlit, was by my bed; instinctively I felt for the matchbox I always carried in my pocket, but of course I was clad only in a nightdress.

No time to go back for it. I was thinking about the one other person in Langlands House – the person who was also in danger if the building came down.

"Grandmother," I shouted.

Light bloomed at the other end of the passage as my grandmother came out of her bedroom, carrying a brass oil lamp with the flame protected by a glass chimney. She too wore a long nightdress, but she had sensibly thrown a warmer robe over hers. Her white hair hung over one shoulder in a loose plait, giving her a strangely ethereal look.

"Are you all right?" I wanted to drag her downstairs that instant, to find safety, although I could hardly think where that would be – under the stairs, outside in the grounds?

Grandmother was remarkably composed. "Perfectly all right," she said calmly. She looked at me carefully, with no sign of urgency in her manner.

"We should go downstairs," I said urgently. "We're being bombed."

"I very much doubt it," she said drily.

Now it was my turn to gape at her. "But did you hear it? It sounded like something fell on the house,"

"Yes," she said. "But listen. Do you hear anything else?"

She raised her hand, and in spite of myself, I did listen.

Nothing. No further reverberating crashes; no droning of engines overhead. A window rattled in its frame from a sudden gust of wind. That was all.

"But what was that crash?"

Grandmother said, "We had better go and see what it was. But you must put a robe on first."

I was amazed that she could be so sensible at such a time. But my teeth were beginning to chatter. I went back to the bedroom and wrapped myself in my dressing-gown before we went to investigate.

The subsiding, shifting noises I had heard had stopped. Instead, there was a curious rushing sound that I could not at first identify; it made me think first of the sound of a distant river flowing, and then of loud whispering.

2

The first two rooms we looked into were seemingly undamaged. We looked into the third, on the east side of the house, and even Grandmother was shocked; a soft sound escaped from her, as though she had been winded by a blow. There was a hole in the ceiling, and through it we could see the night sky. In fact, we could feel the night on our upturned faces, because the wind was coming in, and it was carrying drops of rain with it. You could see the whole structure of the roof in a brutal cross section, the ragged-edged plaster and the shattered beams and beyond that the broken edges of tiles.

Apart from the rain and the wind's doleful howling, which was producing the rushing noise I had heard, there was no sound from outside that I could detect. Nor was there any light except that of the moon, half hidden behind the scudding clouds. If this was an attack, it was over.

In the middle of the worn Persian carpet was a mess of plaster – whole chunks and pale dust – and broken stones. I approached it with caution, looking for pieces of the bomb that must surely have done this. At first, I saw nothing, but as I circled the heap of rubble, the light from Grandmother's lamp picked out the dull gleam of metal.

"Look at this."

I craned over, straining my eyes in the low light. Grandmother came closer to look for herself, but after a moment she shook her head.

"That's not part of a bomb, child. It's the weathervane. The storm has brought one of the chimneys down. That was what we heard."

I didn't think a person of seventeen could possibly be considered a *child*. But I let it pass because I was digesting what she had just said.

The storm.

Was it possible that the tremendous crash that had ripped me out of sleep was simply a chimney coming down in the wind and rain?

I glanced up to check that no more debris was about to fall from the ceiling, and then I put out a hand and brushed plaster dust off the metal object. Sure enough, it was the weathervane from the topmost chimney, bent and twisted beyond repair.

I suppose I should have been relieved. For the War to have reached somewhere as remote as Langlands would have meant something very serious indeed. That the skies above the house were lit up with nothing more sinister than lightning was a *good* thing. We were safe. Langlands was safe. So why was I disappointed?

chapter two

I used to dream of someone from the outside coming to Langlands. I dreamed of a friend before I even knew what that was.

I didn't lack company. Grandmother was always there, except on the rare occasions when she went into the nearby town for things we couldn't make or grow or find for ourselves at Langlands. She was never too busy to talk to me; in fact, sometimes I had the feeling she pushed herself to do it, to amuse me or to tell me things she considered educational. She told me about the assassination of Julius Caesar while kneading bread dough so forcefully that it might have been the assassins' heads she was pummelling. Another time, I remember listening to her describing the life of Mary, Queen of Scots while we pulled up carrots and potatoes from the earth, shaking them to loosen the clinging soil.

It wasn't as though I was always alone, or never heard the sound of another voice. I simply felt that there could have been something else. The idea was somehow shapeless; I couldn't think how or why things would be different with a friend to the way they were with Grandmother. They just *would* be.

I would daydream about someone being there with me – someone my own age. Sometimes when I had no chores to do and was free to roam around the house and grounds, I would imagine that this someone was with me, keeping step but a little way behind, so they were just invisible, even out of the corner of my eye. It was understood that I was too polite to turn around suddenly to catch them unawares. Since we never entertained, I had no idea how I was *supposed* to amuse a guest. So I would show them Langlands, as a way of showing them my life.

Langlands was a fortress and a labyrinth and a treasure chamber all rolled into one. There were bedrooms and sitting rooms, dressing rooms and store rooms, and funny little circular rooms in the turrets that were no use for anything because you couldn't put furniture against the walls. It had a grand main staircase, with newel posts carved into stylised thistles that looked more like fat artichokes, and other, hidden staircases once used by servants. There were servants' passages, too, so that the long-vanished staff of Langlands House could move about discreetly. I wondered whether their footsteps had been audible. I thought so, because in every part of the house the ancient floorboards creaked and groaned under passing feet. It must have been strange, I thought, to hear the sound of someone pattering from one end of the house to another, without being able to see them. Perhaps that was how Langlands had acquired its reputation for being haunted.

Some of the rooms were not in a state to be used – they were full of lumber, or empty, or closed up completely. Two of us could hardly use so many rooms, after all, let alone heat them all properly. We had a bedroom each, furnished with some of the best things in the house, although the rooms themselves had been selected on the basis of which held the best beds, since it was completely impossible for the two of us to move anything so heavy by ourselves. A long time ago, back in a time my memory could not reach, I shared Grandmother's room, but as soon as I was old enough to have my own, I had moved to my current one at the other end of the passage because I liked the iron bedstead and the green velvet curtains.

In addition to our own rooms, there was a library containing thousands of volumes, and we had a piano, which Grandmother played beautifully and I less so. There were other, fascinating things all over the house – paintings and portraits, and stuffed creatures and exotic souvenirs brought from overseas by adventurous ancestors. It was easy to lose an afternoon sorting through strange seashells or faded postcards or coins worn smooth by age.

There was even a little stone mausoleum hidden away in a tangle of overgrown bushes in the woods, where former inhabitants of Langlands House had been laid to rest centuries before. The path that had once led to it was almost entirely overgrown. Grandmother discouraged me from going there out of respect for the dead, but sometimes when I strayed close to it, I would glimpse the grey walls, disfigured with growths of lichen. It had never bothered me, solitary child that I was, to have the long-dead nearby. There was something almost reassuring about it; if I had no wider family circle than Grandmother, at least I had these historical forebears.

I'm making it sound like a museum, but Langlands was a working house, even if we couldn't keep up every part of it with only two of us to do the work.

We had nearly everything we needed. There was plenty of firewood for the winter, and we grew a lot of our own food. We had a vegetable garden, chickens, and aromatic herbs in pots. There was a water pump in the kitchen. It took a fair amount of effort to keep things running: to tend the vegetables, to bring in the wood, to draw and heat water for a bath. I preferred the work to studying, though. As well as Mathematics and Botany, Grandmother made me learn Greek and Latin, but I could never see the point of those. It wasn't as though I even had anyone to talk to in *English* apart from her. If outsiders ever came to Langlands, I always had to hide.

And that is my very earliest memory: hiding.

I don't recall who came to the house, or why. I remember someone knocking at the front door, the blows brisk and loud on the weathered oak panels. I remember toiling up the wooden staircase to the first floor, holding up my skirts in my fists. At the turn of the stairs, I looked down at the hallway below with its black and white chequered tiles and saw my grandmother staring back at me, her brows drawn together and her jaw thrust forward, her eyes blazing an urgent message. She gestured at me, abruptly.

Go.

She couldn't shout it – the person outside would have heard.

I reached the top of the stairs before I heard the bolts being drawn back on the oak door. In a corner of the upstairs landing there was a stuffed bear standing on his hind legs, his jaws frozen in an eternal snarl. I was not afraid of him; his savage expression was belied by the moth-eaten patches in his fur and the bluntness of his claws. I squeezed into the space between his hairy back and the panelled wall and crouched down, hugging my knees. I waited, breathing in the dusty scent of fur.

I don't know how long I hid there, nor what my grandmother said when she came to find me. What I remember is just that: having to hide myself.

You don't question things like that when you are really tiny. But later, I did. *Why* did I have to hide? Why couldn't I leave the estate? Where was my mother, Grandmother's daughter, of whom she spoke so seldom and so sadly? And eventually: who was my father, of whom she never spoke at all, and what had become of *him*?

The answer was always the same: the War.

Far away, on the other side of the dark forest that surrounded Langlands House, War was raging. Aeroplanes flew in formation across the night sky, showering the cities below with incendiary bombs. Great metal machines with caterpillar treads instead of tyres rumbled through the ruins of towns, crushing everything in their path. Even the oceans were infested with deadly submarines that cruised back and forth, stalking the ships. Those who were not called up to fight had to work for the war effort. Grandmother was too old, she said, but I was not; if I were discovered, we would be separated.

"You'd be taken away."

I remember her saying that to me, perhaps for the first time, perhaps for the tenth. She held me by the shoulders, shaking me a little, and her grip hurt – it was too tight. I wanted to pull away. A strand of white hair had shaken loose from the knot at the back of her head, and hung down over her face; she looked a little wild.

"You'd never come back, do you understand?"

I did understand; she made me understand all of it. I would have to go into the city and work in a munitions factory, under constant threat of bombing. No more hours passed curled on the window seat in the library with a book open on my lap; no more picking my way silently through the forest, to be rewarded with a glimpse of a young deer lifting its head to look at me, or a rabbit dashing away with a flash of white tail. Just endless, grinding work, with the stink of hot TNT in my nostrils and the constant danger of accidental explosions in addition to the threat of enemy attacks. Grandmother talked and I listened until terrible visions filled my head, of girls my age whose skin and hair was dyed yellow from incessant contact with sulphur, of girls crushed flat in the bombed rubble of their apartment houses. And supposing my curiosity about the world outside Langlands was so persistent that it overcame my fears? Well, there was the guilt.

Alone at Langlands, Grandmother would be unable to keep things running by herself. A practical problem like being unable to chop enough firewood could make a harsh winter lethal for someone her age. When the War finally ended, then assuming I had survived it, I might tramp back to Langlands and find that it had become a tomb. I imagined myself walking up the track in winter, the frozen earth black under my feet, white flakes of snow drifting slowly down; finding the house dark and cold, the front door locked, no answer to my knocking. Walking around to the back door; glancing into the chicken run and seeing a few pitiful heaps of feathers lying still and silent. Seeing those tiny deaths; knowing I don't want to go inside the house because death is there too.

That – that was why I had to hide, and why I could never go outside the estate. It didn't mean my mind didn't want to go there.

Sometimes I would go down to the very edge of the Langlands estate, where the forest ended. There was a track leading away through the fields, eventually meeting a road. The road was too far away for me to see very much of what passed up and down it, but I could pick out the larger vehicles. Everything seemed to be moving about very peacefully. Now and again I saw an aeroplane, but there never seemed to be anything sinister about that, either: no dropping bombs, no distant fires.

So, I said to myself that Grandmother had chosen our hiding place well, and Langlands really was too remote to be affected by the War. What else could I believe in, if not in her? Who else did I have in the whole world but her?

chapter three

The morning after the storm, we went into the damaged bedroom to find more rainwater coming in through the hole in the ceiling.

The room was never slept in, and the carved oak bed once used by a previous occupant had been dismantled, the large wooden sections propped against a wall. It had escaped damage, but the ancient Persian carpet that covered most of the floor was sodden, its faded crimson threads darkened to the colour of blood.

I glanced at Grandmother and her face was grim. It was already nearly the end of October; with winter coming, we could expect more rain, and worse. I imagined opening the door on one of those glacially cold December mornings and finding the room a dazzling white cavern of fallen snow, the skeleton of the bed almost buried in a drift of it.

Now that the savage Scottish weather had breached the old house, it would gnaw its way more and more deeply into the open wound. Damp would seep into the rooms below; timbers would rot and collapse. Like a festering injury, untreated, it would be the death of Langlands.

Grandmother looked at the ragged hole in the ceiling for a while, her lips set in a tight line. Then she said, "This is more than we can repair ourselves." She shook her head. "I shall have to drive into the town and ask someone to come."

It was a good thing she was looking at the hole in the ceiling and not at me. *Ask someone to come.* I could have danced around the room. I glanced up at the hole in the ceiling, willing the damage to be even worse than it looked.

"You know what this means, don't you, Augusta?" Grandmother was saying.

Her calling me that, *Augusta*, snagged my attention. She only ever did it when she had something serious to say. The rest of the time she called me *Ghost*, a nickname I'd had ever since I was tiny and hadn't been able to say my own name properly. '*Gust*, I used to say, and somewhere along the line it had turned into *Ghost*. It was apt really, considering that that was what the few people who saw me thought I was.

I knew what was coming.

"I have to hide," I said. I did my best to sound resigned. If she realised I was dying to see whoever came to the house, she would make it her business to see that I was out of sight. Would she go so far as to lock me in my room? I didn't *think* she would, but I didn't want to risk it.

"I'm sorry," Grandmother said. "It will be very dull for you. The work may take days."

She looked at me. Grandmother had eyes the colour of summer skies, but the impression they gave was anything but sunny. There was an intensity to their gaze; it was nearly always useless lying to her. This was important though. I made myself hold her stare, my expression carefully neutral. I tried very hard to look as though it had not occurred to me that having someone come to Langlands would be anything but very, very boring.

"You really cannot be seen," she said. "You understand that?"

"Yes," I said. "I'll go up to the attic and stay there the whole time, Grandmother."

"You'll be terribly uncomfortable up there," said Grandmother, doubtfully. She looked down at the sodden carpet, strewn with chunks of stone and plaster. "But we simply cannot leave this as it is. It's out of the question."

"No," I agreed. "It's all right, Grandmother. I'll be perfectly fine. I can take some bread and cheese and a lantern and a stack of books," I added.

"You'll be so cold," she objected, but I could see that she was weakening. There wasn't much else she could suggest, anyway.

"I'll put the old bearskin from the library up there, and wrap myself in blankets," I said. "I'll go and make a space, right now," I added and slipped off before she could protest. I ran to the end of the passage, where there was a green baize door. On the other side of that were the steep narrow stairs that ran up to the attic; I went up them as fast as I could, hearing the door slap shut behind me. I had to suppress the urge to whoop out loud, in case Grandmother heard me.

I didn't really need to clear a space in the attic. There was a space there already, behind all the trunks and shrouded picture frames, and close to the only window. I went up there sometimes when I wanted to think about something in peace. The window had a view out over the gravel drive and the forest; I could imagine myself skimming away over those treetops like a bird. Now, I picked my way over the trunks and boxes and settled myself by the window.

Outsiders were coming to Langlands. Never mind that it would probably be ancient workmen, too old to be called up to fight. It was still the most interesting thing that had happened for ages. New people. New faces. And I would see them; I was resolved about that.

chapter four

Grandmother drove into the town in her black Austin. The car reminded me of an enormous black beetle, with its darkly gleaming body and rounded lines. It had two big headlights like protuberant eyes.

Grandmother did not think that the workmen would come back with her that day, but she told me to make myself scarce anyway. After she had left, I dragged the bearskin up to the attic, and then went back for some books. I spread out the bearskin and tried lying on it, experimentally, with my head close to the window. There was a very clear view of the drive, although I wasn't sure how much detail I would be able to pick out from that distance – and I wanted to see *everything*, even if the workers were gnome-like old men.

I was still staring down when Grandmother's Austin reappeared, coming up the drive from the forest. I watched the car turn the corner, and waited to see whether a second vehicle would follow. There was none.

By the time I had run downstairs, Grandmother was already in the kitchen, unbuttoning her sober navy coat. There was a cardboard box full of groceries on the big pine table. Normally, I would have fallen on it, to see what she had brought back with her; today, I had other things on my mind.

I suppose I showed it too clearly, because Grandmother said

rather sharply, "Stop dancing about, Ghost. Whatever is the matter with you?"

"Nothing."

"If you have so much energy, there's plenty of work to do." Her expression softened. "I mean it, Ghost. You may as well use some of it up, because you're going to be stuck in the attic for the next few days."

I made myself stand very still. "A few days?"

"Probably. I spoke to Mr. McAllister. He's coming to assess the damage tomorrow morning, but he doesn't think he can repair it in a day."

"Oh dear," I said gravely. I didn't miss the glance she shot me. There are dangers in living for a long time with only one other person; eventually, you can more or less read each other's minds. Something in my tone of voice had hit a false note. She was wondering whether I could be trusted to stay out of sight. I was asking myself the same thing, only I already knew the answer.

She didn't pursue it, though. What else was there to do? We couldn't mend the roof ourselves; we would have had no idea where to start. Leaving the room open to the elements wasn't an option, either. Grandmother had no choice but to trust me.

Early the next morning I took what I needed up to the attic: the blankets, the bread and cheese. I took a couple of apples from the kitchen too. At twenty to nine I slipped downstairs one last time, hoping that Grandmother wouldn't hear me. There was a room on the first floor that we used to call "the study", although it didn't look as though it had been used as one for a very long time; too much furniture had been put inside, so that you had to weave your way around it to get from one side of the room to the other. I went straight to a tall oak press, the dark wood shiny with age, and opened the door, turning the key with exquisite care to avoid making any sound. I was just reaching inside for the thing I wanted when I heard something from outside the house: the distant rumble of an engine.

"Augusta!" My grandmother's voice sounded brittle with anxiety.

I grabbed what I wanted and slipped out of the room, closing the door behind me as I quietly as I could. Then I went to the head of the stairs and looked down. Grandmother was standing in the middle of the hallway, like a queen on the black and white chessboard of a floor; her hands were clasped in front of her, and she was rubbing them together compulsively.

"I'll go," I called down in a low voice, keeping the hand with the precious object in it out of sight. When I saw that she had understood me, I flitted away along the passage. I was halfway up the back stairs when I heard tyres crunching on the gravel before the main entrance, and by the time the slam of a door closing reached my ears, I was in the attic, pulling the door shut behind me.

There were voices below, already inside the house, I thought. My heart sank a little. It was no good if the visitors were already inside; I wouldn't see a thing.

I glanced down. Perhaps it had been a mistake going downstairs again for the field glasses; it had cost me just a little too much time. I'd probably have to wait right until the end of the working day for a glimpse of anyone coming out of Langlands now.

Still, I couldn't resist looking. I got down onto my hands and knees, and then onto my stomach and elbows, inhaling the dusty scent of bear fur, and then I wriggled forward until my breath was misting the window glass. There was a vehicle parked in front of the house. It was nothing like Grandmother's. This was something altogether more functional, like a big box on wheels. I supposed that was what it was: a container for transporting things from place to place. It was somehow sleeker than Grandmother's Austin, but I thought it was uglier. There were letters painted onto the side of it, scarlet against the white background: *Neil McAllister*. Underneath that was a string of numbers.

I put the field glasses to my eyes. They were heavy, and the little screw you had to use to adjust the focus was stiff; first I struggled to turn it, and then it came loose and went too far, and the view swam out of focus again. I managed it in the end, though, and now I was able to see the vehicle in sharp detail.

It was then that I caught a flicker of movement at the front of it. I held my breath, waiting, and for a moment I thought I had imagined it, or that I had simply seen the motion of the tree branches in the wind at the other side of the drive. Then someone stepped out from behind the vehicle, out into the open, and I saw him.

chapter five

He was *young*, like me.

It was a shock, realising that; I felt it as sharply as an indrawn breath of freezing air. Someone the same age as me, or just a little older. And he was...he was something I didn't have words for, or words I would not have dared to say, even to myself.

I gazed down from the attic window with a kind of stunned fascination, watching him strolling about the gravel drive, scanning the front of Langlands with casual interest, his breath visible on the cold autumn air. I felt the warmth in my skin as the blood rose to my face, but I didn't stop looking.

The weight of the field glasses was already beginning to make my wrists ache but I couldn't put them down; instead I tightened my grip on them. He had brown hair, not quite dark enough that you could call it black. Even with the field glasses it was impossible to see the exact colour of his eyes at this distance, but I thought they were grey or hazel, light-hued under dark brows. He looked around him in a way that somehow suggested wary interest. Perhaps he had heard the stories about Langlands – about the ghost.

Once, he glanced up towards the high window behind which I lay full length on the bearskin, gazing down, and I froze, my heart thumping, not daring to move in case I drew attention to myself, but he looked away without reacting. I suppose my face was invisible, so high up, behind the reflections on the glass.

He wore a dark jacket of some thick material, blue cotton twill trousers and heavy boots. Nothing as smart and elegant as the costumes displayed in the oil paintings at Langlands, which included tailcoats and frock coats and military braid.

Clearly, people on the outside had no time or energy to spend on fancy clothing.

Why hasn't he been called up? I wondered. *What he does, rebuilding things, maybe that's considered important, like being a doctor. Grandmother said they don't get called up. Maybe this is the same.*

I touched the glass, feeling it cool under my fingertips. I watched him lean against the side of the vehicle, obscuring the lettering. *Neil McAllister.* Was that his name? His face was turned towards the house; I suspected he was listening to or watching something. A moment later his posture changed, and he pushed himself away from the van, standing to attention.

Grandmother appeared on the gravel below with a second stranger, whose shiny bald head pronounced him old and therefore less interesting.

Something about the way Grandmother moved suggested that she was not happy. She moved stiffly, her shoulders raised, her head a little to one side, as though she were turning away from bad news. I thought I knew what the problem was. It was the younger man. She didn't want him here. She probably judged, quite rightly, that I would find him interesting – assuming I ever laid eyes on him, which she was evidently determined I wouldn't.

I watched the three of them – Grandmother and the two men – moving around the gravel drive as though they were taking part in some formal dance that none of them liked performing. Grandmother gesticulated several times, and then I saw the older man shake his head. I guessed that she was objecting to the younger workman, though I couldn't imagine on what grounds. She could hardly say that she didn't want young men around her granddaughter, since they weren't supposed to know I was here. At any rate, whatever she was saying, it wasn't working. The older man had his cap in his hands, standing politely bareheaded before a lady, but he evidently wasn't giving way. Several times I saw him shake his head very slowly.

After a while, some kind of agreement seemed to have occurred; all three of them began to move towards the stone porch which overhung the main door of Langlands House, and they vanished from my sight. I knew what was happening now. Grandmother would take them to the bedroom with the ruined ceiling so that they could assess the amount of work required to repair it.

I knew better than to go downstairs and try to eavesdrop or even peep out through a crack in the door, although I was dying to. Grandmother would be on her guard; the merest creak on the attic stairs would land me in hot water. All the same, I came down three or four steps and sat there for a while, listening. I knew those stairs, like I knew every other part of Langlands; the creaks they gave when you went up or down them was like playing a tuneless harmonium. The top ones weren't too noisy so long as you kept to the right-hand side, so I did that and then I sat and waited.

Langlands was never truly silent. Even at night, when I lay motionless in my bed, I could hear the house creaking. A change in temperature as day broke or night fell would make the ancient boards expand or contract. Sometimes you would have sworn that someone was moving stealthily about. The slightest breath of wind would make the old windows rattle in their frames, or shake the branches of the trees that clustered close to the back of the house, so that they would tap on the glass. I wasn't frightened by these noises. My ear was finely attuned to them, so that now I could pick out the discordant notes, the sounds that told me people were moving along the upper floor of the house. Not just people: Grandmother, the old man, and...him.

I hugged my knees and tried to hold my breath, the better to hear the tiniest sound. I heard the brisk sound of a door closing; that would be Grandmother, shutting off one of the rooms from the visitors' view.

She must hate this, I realised. I couldn't remember any outsider ever coming into the upstairs part of the house. No work that the house had ever needed had required it – until now.

What was his name, the one my age? I supposed it was reasonable to assume that the older man was the one in charge, so presumably he was the *Neil McAllister* whose name was painted onto the vehicle. Was the younger one his son? Sons were sometimes named after their fathers; I knew that from the dusty novels in the Langlands library. He might also be *Neil* – but he might just as easily not. I tried to imagine what name might suit him instead, and in this way, I amused myself for some time, until the door at the bottom of the stairs opened and Grandmother appeared.

It was just as well I hadn't been sitting at the bottom with my ear to the door. I had been too preoccupied with my own thoughts to hear her coming.

She looked up at me, and although half her face was in shadow, I could see the disapproval on it.

"You shouldn't sit there, Ghost. If someone were to open the door, you would be plainly visible."

I knew whom she meant by *someone*. The thought of coming face to face with him gave me a sharp pang that was both thrilling and guilty.

I took a risk and said, "I heard them leave, so I was just waiting here for you."

"Hmmm," she said. "Well, you had better come down now. They *have* gone, and they're not coming back."

"Not at all?" I couldn't keep the note of alarm from creeping into my voice, and I saw her frown. "I mean, what about the repairs?"

"No," she said. "Just not today. Mr. McAllister has some materials he has to buy." She went on for a minute or two after that, telling me what the workmen had to get and what they were going to have to do both outside on the roof and inside in the bedroom, but I was only half listening to that; I was too overwhelmed with my own relief. I couldn't have stood the disappointment if the outsiders had gone without my having more than a glimpse of them.

I went down the stairs to where Grandmother stood and followed her down the landing. I wasn't thinking at all about where she was going, but I should not have been surprised that we went back to the bedroom with the damaged ceiling. Of course, she would want to examine it again and satisfy herself that she trusted the workmen's opinion, and she would want to tell me about it.

I hoped half-heartedly that the men would have left some sign of themselves in the room. There was a certain thrill in knowing that they had been here, on this exact spot – that *he* had been here. The room wasn't one I had visited very often, but now I looked around it with new interest, trying to fix everything in it in my mind: this was the environment in which the men would be working, these were the things that they would be seeing every day they were here.

Grandmother talked, gesturing at the ruined ceiling, holding out a chunk of fallen plaster. Meanwhile, I wandered about, giving as much of an appearance of rapt attention as I could whilst taking in everything for myself, and after Grandmother had finished and taken herself off downstairs, I still lingered in the room.

It was the middle part of the day now, and for once it was clear and dry; the light coming in through the windows was cold but very bright, showing the contents of the room with crystal sharpness. That was how I came to see it – a small sliver of silver glinting on the dusty floorboards. I knelt and picked it up. It was flat and thin and I had to use my fingernails to do it. I held the thing in the palm of my hand and stared.

A key. It was obvious what it was, but I knew immediately that it didn't belong to Langlands; there was nothing here it would have opened. Grandmother had a great bunch of keys, although we rarely bothered to lock anything up, and all of them were of a much more robust design, with cylindrical stems. Nor were any of them silver-coloured; they were mostly made of dull brass.

It belongs to them. One of them dropped it.

chapter six

Tom

It's like we're being watched. I had the same feeling yesterday when we arrived. It's a dark day, because of the rain, and inside the house, it's so gloomy you can hardly see what you're doing. The air feels *thicker* in here, like something invisible is pressing in on us.

Well, I say to myself, *perhaps it is thicker, there's that much dust in it.* You can *smell* the house – a smell of old furniture polish and dead flowers and mould. Like something decaying.

We go up to the bedroom we saw yesterday, and right enough, the rain is pouring through the hole in the ceiling. Dad asks Mrs. McAndrew whether there's any other way we could get at the roof so he can take a closer look – a ceiling hatch leading into the space between the ceiling and the roof, maybe? While they're discussing that, I wander over to the window to look out.

There's something on the window sill. A shiny silver key. It looks newer than anything else in this room. It looks like my door key, the one on the keyring in my pocket. I put my hand into my jeans and pull out the keyring, and my door key's not on it. There's just the key for the bike and another one I never use, a locker key I was supposed to give back when I left high school.

I glance behind me. Dad is following Mrs. McAndrew out of the room. She's still talking, in that voice that makes it sound like she's telling him off, and waving her hands around. I suppose they're going to look at ceiling hatches.

It's definitely mine. How did it get here? I didn't miss it yesterday, but Dad let us in when we got home. Okay, so I could have dropped it in this room, but I didn't come over here to the window. Someone's picked it up and put it here, and if it was old Mrs. McAndrew, why didn't she just give it back to me? And it's not just my key that's sitting here on the window sill. There is something else with it. Until I picked the key up, the two things were side by side, like they were put there on purpose.

It's a coin, an old one, now brown and dull. There's a man's head on it. There are words around the edge of the coin, but they don't make a lot of sense: what does IND IMP mean? The only one I can recognise is GEORGIUS. I guess that's *George. King George*. When was that?

I turn the coin over in my fingers. On the back there's a woman in a helmet with a thing like a pitchfork. ONE PENNY, it says. Underneath the woman's feet is a date. The date is 1944.

1944, that was the Second World War – we did it at high school. I think about the *other* thing I heard about back then, only it was from the other local kids, not the teacher, who came from Edinburgh. The Langlands ghost. The girl who died in the War.

I tell myself I'm being stupid. It's just an old coin, old like everything else in this house. The old lady must have left it here.

But why? I think. *Why would she do that?*

I have a strange cold feeling about this. The back of my neck prickles; I think I have my hackles up, like a dog at bay.

I think: *What if it wasn't Mrs. McAndrew who left that coin there where I would find it, if I looked around for my key? What if it was someone else?*

chapter seven

Ghost

A coin – that was what I decided on. I gave the matter a lot of thought. I had to leave *something*, to show that the key had been put there on the window sill on purpose. It couldn't be anything as obvious as a note. Supposing Grandmother went into the room before the men did, and found it? Or supposing they showed it to her? No; a coin was safer. If Grandmother saw that on the window sill, she might reasonably conclude that one of the men had found it lying about and put it there, or even that it had been there all along, overlooked. There were bits and pieces all over Langlands house – things put down and forgotten by former inhabitants, decades ago.

If they found the key and the coin and said nothing to Grandmother, then–

Then what? I said to myself, as I sat at the top of the attic stairs, listening to the rain drumming on the roof and wondering whether anyone had gone into the damaged room yet. It was a question I couldn't answer. I didn't know who would find the things I had left. Didn't it all depend on that?

For a while, there was nothing to hear except the rain; then I heard the groans that meant that the landing floorboards were protesting under the weight of people moving about. I heard muffled voices, but I couldn't pick out any individual words.

I hugged my knees, shivering. I was used to Langlands House with its unheated corridors and ill-fitting windows, but it was hard to stay warm sitting still in one place. I dared not move about, though. I imagined the men working in the rooms below under Grandmother's watchful eye, pausing to listen to the sound of light footsteps overhead. They would glance swiftly at Grandmother: *isn't she supposed to be the only one in the house?* Then they would look at each other and wonder...

The men weren't the problem, though. Grandmother would tell them it was the boards expanding or rats in the attic. The trouble would come later.

No. Better to stay still and silent, at least while I knew they were all on the first floor. I did my best, although by the middle of the day I was so chilled that I crept across the attic and opened one of the trunks that were stored there to look for another layer to put on.

Every single piece of clothing I owned had come from these trunks. Whenever something had become too short or too tight for me to wear, or latterly, when I had worn something so long that it was beyond our powers to repair it with sewing and darning, Grandmother and I would come up and select some new items from the trunks and boxes stored in the attic. There were a great many things, ranging from tiny silk robes edged with lace to fit a young baby, to a sombre dark greatcoat of heavy wool, with a cape over the shoulders. Grandmother tended to pick out the plainest, most hard-wearing things she could for me; it was no use, she said, my wearing a tulle dress when I had to collect firewood or pump water or pull up carrots from the kitchen garden. This hadn't prevented me from seeing some of the treasures folded away neatly in the trunks, with lavender bags that had long since lost all but the faintest trace of their scent tucked between the layers. As well as the tulle, there were high-necked lace blouses and delicate white lawn frocks, and a beautiful violet silk dress with dozens of tiny buttons up the back. There were gloves and underthings and pretty fans, although these last struck me as useless: I could hardly remember a single occasion when it had ever been hot enough at Langlands that I might have needed to fan myself.

The trunk I opened now did not look promising: the first thing I found in it was a black bombazine mourning dress, the fabric stiff and heavy. After I had burrowed down through several layers of gloomy-looking clothing, however, I found something that looked deliciously warm: a thick velvet cape decorated with tiny jet beads and trimmed with black fur. I didn't care that it looked funereal; I wrapped myself in it and luxuriated in its warmth, rubbing my nose against the soft fur.

Late in the day, when the light was fading from the attic window, Grandmother opened the door at the bottom of the stairs and looked up to find me still swathed in the black cape.

"Goodness me, Ghost," she said. "You look like a very young widow."

I was stiff from the cold and sitting so long, despite the cape. I went carefully down the stairs towards her. "Have they gone?"

"Yes," said Grandmother. "A few minutes ago."

I hesitated, wondering how to ask what I wanted to know. I didn't want to seem too eager.

"Have they finished the work?" I asked in the end. I knew they couldn't possibly have, but it seemed a safe thing to ask.

"No, it's going to take a couple of days," said Grandmother. She looked directly at me as I reached the bottom of the stairs, and for a few seconds we were staring into each other's eyes.

Then I shivered, and she said, "You look chilled. Come down to the kitchen and have some cocoa."

I followed her along the passage. It would be time to light the lamps when we got downstairs; already Grandmother was little more than a dark shape moving ahead of me. We passed the room where the work was being done; the door was ajar but there was no time to do more than glance through the crack.

It was not until much later, after we had eaten and I had warmed myself by sitting close to the kitchen range, that I was able to come back upstairs by myself to look. By then, it was completely dark both outside and inside the house, so I had to take a candle with me.

As I made my way upstairs, the flame flickered, sometimes streaming out almost horizontally behind the wick. Langlands was a draughty place; sometimes it seemed as though the old house was sighing. I paused at the head of the stairs and looked down, just in case Grandmother should have decided to leave the warmth of the kitchen and follow me up. But all was still and silent in the hallway below.

I pushed open the door of the room and stepped inside, holding up the candlestick. It was colder in here than it was in the rest of the house, because of the hole in the ceiling. Overhead I could hear something billowing restlessly in the wind, and guessed that the men had put up some kind of temporary covering.

I stood for a moment, eyes straining to see in the soft yellow candlelight, nostrils flaring in the cold air. There was not much to see. The pile of broken stones and twisted metal that had been in the middle of the carpet had been removed; all that remained was an outline in pale dust on the darker background of the Persian carpet. I went over and stood looking down at it, and I could feel the yielding dampness of the carpet under my feet. Once the work was finished, we would have to light a fire in here, to try to dry it out. I looked up at the ceiling, but the light from the candle did not reach far enough to show me the state of the repairs.

I found myself putting off going over to the window where I had left the key and the coin. Now that it came to it, I was afraid I would find that they were exactly where I had left them, unnoticed. Or perhaps the key would have been found and pocketed without any further thought. I lifted the candlestick again, experimentally, and I thought I saw something gleam on the window sill. *Oh no. Still there.* My heart sank.

Now was the only time to look, though, so I picked my way carefully across the room.

The coin was there on the window sill, that was the first thing I saw. It wasn't exactly where I had left it – at least I didn't think so – but it was still there.

I stepped closer and saw that the key had gone. I glanced all along the windowsill and it was not there. Then I looked at the floor and there was no sign of it there, either. So it had really been taken.

I looked more closely, and I could see the tracks of fingertips in the dust on the sill, where someone had picked up the things I had left, then pocketed one and put the other back. I put out a hand and touched the track marks with my forefinger, tracing them. Behind me the covering in the roof shivered in the wind.

Then I saw what I had not seen before. Among the faint marks on the dusty sill with their abstract sweeps and arabesques, one stood out very clearly.

Someone had drawn a question mark in the dust.

chapter eight

It was not such a big thing, a shape drawn in the dust on a window sill; it was gone in an instant when my hand passed over it. But I had stepped over a boundary; I had exchanged messages with someone from outside. It felt as strange as if one of the bewigged and bejewelled ladies in the oil paintings downstairs had suddenly come to life. Writing in the dust was a brilliant idea. Easily executed, easily erased, and if Grandmother happened to see it, it could be passed off as a piece of idle amusement.

What shall I say in return?

Of course, I was going to reply; it never even entered my head that I wouldn't. But as I stood there with the wax from the candle slowly running down the candlestick and congealing on my fingers, I wondered what my answer should be. If I committed myself so far as to write my entire name on the windowsill and Grandmother saw it, I would have incriminated myself quite clearly. No; I dared not do that, not yet.

After some further thought, I reached out and wrote *A* with my fingertip – simply that, the letter *A*, for *Augusta*. I wrote it at the side of the window sill, close to the shabby brocade curtain, where it was only obvious if you were looking for it. Then I rubbed my dusty fingers clean on my dress, feeling vaguely guilty.

It was time to leave. No point in risking being caught in here when Grandmother came upstairs. It would only make her suspicious. I took one last look at my handiwork, the initial drawn out in the dust. Then I shielded the candle flame with my free hand and slipped out of the room as silently as I could.

The passage outside was completely dark. The blackness at the head of the stairs was so absolute that it was clear Grandmother was still shut up in the warm kitchen; otherwise I would have seen the faint glow of the lamp she carried when she came up to bed.

I went to my own room and closed the door. I set the candlestick down on the bedside table and began to get ready for bed. It was never a task I wanted to linger over – the room was high-ceilinged, and even if we lit the fire, it rarely became properly warm. The moment between taking off my clothes and pulling my nightdress over my head was always gruesome. I put on a robe too before I started undoing my hair from its long plait. Unbraided, my hair fell to below my waist and it took some time to brush it out. Sometimes this task irritated me, but tonight I brushed mechanically, hardly aware of what I was doing.

All I could think about was that question mark drawn in the dust. Did *he* write it there – the younger one? I imagined him standing there by the window, head bowed, tracing out the shape with his forefinger. Thinking about it made me feel hot and cold with a strange guilty excitement, as though I had been caught eavesdropping on someone.

But was it him? Or could it possibly have been the older man? I wished I knew more about the way people behaved. It seemed to me that Grandmother was more serious than I was, and less tolerant of anything unexpected. I could not imagine someone old exchanging cryptic messages with an unknown person for the fun of it. This didn't mean that every older person was like Grandmother, though, nor that every younger person was as consumed with curiosity as I was.

I went on thinking about it after I had climbed into bed and blown out the candle. It was the last thing I recall thinking about as I gradually became warm in my cocoon of blankets and drifted off into sleep, and it was the first thing I thought about when I opened my eyes the next morning.

I awoke to the sound of rain rattling against the window panes. The downpour had not stopped.

From the attic window I saw the men arrive again, but this time they parked close to the corner of the house, out of my line of vision. I watched for a long while after that but saw nothing more, and heard nothing but the rain on the roof.

Eventually, driven by frustration, I crept down to the bottom of the attic stairs and pressed my ear to the door. You could never say that Langlands was entirely silent, with all the creaks and groans the old house made, but it was as silent as it could ever be. I pulled the door open and stepped out into the passage.

The damaged room was empty, as expected. I approached the window from the side, keeping behind the curtain where I could not be seen from outside. Then I looked out.

I could see Grandmother's umbrella below me. In front of her, and evidently conversing with her, was a bald-headed man, clearly the one I had seen from above the day before. He was old, but not as old as Grandmother, I judged. It was difficult to form an opinion about his appearance though because the rain was coming down very hard on his bare head; his exposed skin shone with wet. I saw that he was holding a hat or cap clutched in his hands; his knuckles were white and glistening in the cold rain. Grandmother, of course, would be dry under her huge umbrella.

Until now, I had gained most of my understanding about the way human beings treat each other from Grandmother –

and from the books in the Langlands library, which were an unreliable source of information; the people in those were constantly having surprise proposals of marriage or discovering mad spouses in the attic or encountering other situations which seemed to have no relevance to me at all. Grandmother insisted on doing things "properly", even in our limited world; we said "please" and "thank you" and on special occasions – which were rare – we dressed for dinner. There were a good many other little rules and regulations. Generally, Grandmother had given me to understand that she was a pattern of propriety and good breeding.

Now, however, I looked down at the broad span of the umbrella protecting Grandmother from the elements, and the man standing in front of her with his hat off and the rain streaming in torrents down his exposed face; I waited for her to tell him to stop or come indoors, or at least for her to conclude the conversation and let him finish the work as quickly as he could. Still she stood there talking, and the cold rain ran down so that he blinked against it, and licked his lips.

This is wrong. Grandmother is wrong.

I would not have done what she was doing. I would have said, "Forget the hole in the roof, come inside and get dry."

I would have been kind, and Grandmother was being *unkind*.

I stood and watched until at last she became tired of whatever she was saying, and the umbrella moved away towards the front of the house. The man had already turned back to his work, and so I dared to come forward, right up to the window, and look down.

The younger man was there, standing with his head turned in the direction Grandmother had taken. His head was covered, so it was impossible to see his expression, but I thought I could read his thoughts from the way he was standing staring after her. I thought we *agreed* about Grandmother's behaviour.

I stepped back behind the brocade curtain, and stood for a

few moments in the shadows. I had the strangest feeling and I couldn't even give a name to it. It wasn't guilt exactly, though I could feel the warmth in my face, nor was it confusion, because I knew exactly what had happened, even if I didn't know what to feel about it. For the first time ever, I had agreed with someone else *against* Grandmother.

I didn't dare stay where I was any longer. I went over to the door, listened to be sure that Grandmother was nowhere about, and then slipped away down the corridor. A couple of minutes later I was back at my post by the attic window, hugging my knees and thinking about what I had seen. What had really happened? Nothing. Neither of the men had even seen me. And yet I still felt strange.

I had to stay in the attic for the rest of that day. The men finished what they had been doing outside, which was to clear away the bushes and overhanging branches and build scaffolding against the side of the house. Then they came inside for a while, although I couldn't tell what they were doing. Once, I heard the door at the bottom of the attic stairs open and close softly and guessed that Grandmother had come to check that I was safely out of sight. I did not risk any more excursions that day.

That night, when the men were long gone and it was dark inside and out, I went back to the room again with a candle. The candlelight didn't penetrate far enough to let me see the state of the ceiling, but I guessed that some progress had been made because although the rain was still pattering against the windows, I could no longer feel it on my upturned face.

I went slowly across the room. It wasn't just that I was being careful not to make a sound; it was also that I was a little afraid of what I would find – namely, that it would be nothing at all.

But there *was* something. It was right at the end of the window sill, even beyond the spot where I had drawn my letter *A*, and hidden by the curtain. In the dust, someone had written: *TOM.*

chapter nine

I looked at that name, *Tom*, written in the dust, for a long time before I smoothed it away with my fingers. There was something unreal about seeing it there. It was an intrusion from another world altogether. I was afraid that if I didn't fix it in my mind, I would think that I had dreamed it when I got up the next day.

There was no doubt in my mind that the younger one had written it. I'd seen the way Grandmother dealt almost exclusively with the older man. Even if he hadn't been so obviously the senior one, he was clearly the owner of the business, the Neil McAllister whose name was painted onto the side of the vehicle. So that meant the other one was Tom.

I turned the name over in my mind as though it were a puzzle to be solved, but it did not tell me very much. He might be the older man's son, in which case he would be Tom McAllister, but he might simply be an apprentice. What else did I know about him? Only that he hadn't told Grandmother about the things I had left for him to see. If she had had the slightest hint of what I had done, I would know all about it. So, he hadn't said anything. All the same, I couldn't immediately decide what my next move should be.

What's the worst that can happen if I speak to him – to Tom? I asked myself. It gave me a funny little twinge of self-consciousness to call him that, even in the privacy of my own head.

The answer came promptly to mind, as grim as an omen. *You can't trust people not to talk.* Grandmother had told me that often enough. If it once got about that the reclusive old woman at Langlands wasn't alone, that she had her granddaughter living with her, there'd be no more hiding. All the terrible things Grandmother had described to me passed through my imagination: the planes that bombed Edinburgh, killing people in the open street; the factory explosions that tore the workers to bloody fragments, that painted the blasted walls with a fine red mist. Even the desolate homecoming I had imagined for myself if I survived the War.

He hasn't told anyone so far, I argued to myself. Then I thought: *All I've given him is the letter A. What is there to tell?*

I stared down at the streaks of dust where I had erased Tom's name.

What now?

It was impossible to say or ask anything more complicated by scrawling letters in the dust, although there was plenty of dust in Langlands. To do that, I would have to find a way to speak to Tom alone, or else leave a proper message – a written note, left where he would find it. If I did either of those things, I was committing myself, offering proof of my own existence here at Langlands.

A distant creak from the staircase alerted me to the fact that Grandmother was coming up. There was no time to decide what to do now. I slipped across the room and looked out of the doorway. Yellow light was faintly visible from the lamp Grandmother was carrying. Swiftly, I wetted my fingers and snuffed out the candle. Then I flitted across the passage and into my own room.

Grandmother passed the doorway a minute or two later.

"Goodnight, Ghost," she said softly, perhaps thinking that I was already sleeping.

"Goodnight, Grandmother."

I was relieved when she continued on to her own room without stopping. I waited until I heard her bedroom door close. Then I climbed back out of bed, still in my clothes, and began to undress. It was not easy getting changed into my night things in the pitch dark, and by the time I got back into bed, I was shivering. It was not the cold that kept me awake long after that, though. It was that question.

What now?

chapter ten

The following day was clear and bright; the autumn sunshine picked out every detail visible from the attic window with crystalline sharpness. The good weather evidently lifted Grandmother's spirits because she came to find me halfway through the morning, looking less fretful than she had for the past two days. In fact, she brought me a cup of tea and called me down to the bottom of the attic stairs to fetch it. I sat on the stairs and sipped it gratefully while she told me that the work was going very much better now, an unwelcome piece of news.

The men were working on the broken chimney that day, and leaving the damaged roof so that the damp timbers could dry out in the fine weather before they sealed it all up again. I saw that the work had a schedule and that it was progressing through to an end point, after which the men would clear up their things and go, and my chance would be lost.

After Grandmother had gone, I made up my mind. I would write a letter to Tom, and leave it where he would find it. I was dizzy with the sense of my own daring, but it was now or never.

It was easy enough to slip down the passage to my room to find a pen and paper. As well as the pencils I used for my lessons, I had a fine green-and-gold fountain pen. Paper was a little more difficult; since I never wrote letters to anyone, I had no writing paper. I did however have several exercise books with blank pages. A leaf taken from the back of one of those would have to do. More difficult was the question of what to say.

Even beginning the letter was problematic. I had read plenty of examples in the novels in the Langlands library, but there was nothing to tell me the best way to address a stranger. Simply to write "Sir–" was too cold, and anyway, I knew Tom's name. On the other hand, to begin with "My dear Tom" was impossible. I wrote it out carefully once, just to see how it looked, but tore it up almost immediately, feeling hot with embarrassment. At last I settled on "Dear Tom". It still seemed a little familiar, but since I was not sure of his surname, it was the most sensible option.

I spent a long time on the rest of the letter, writing drafts which were defaced with crossings-out. Eventually, I judged that I had done the best I could. I had written:

Dear Tom,

What would you do if someone wanted to speak to you? Supposing it was someone you had never met – someone you didn't know – would you still let them speak to you?

Supposing it was someone who was not supposed to speak to you, someone who would get in terrible trouble – perhaps even danger – if anyone found out that you had spoken to her? Would you agree to speak to her without telling anyone else – not anyone at all, not ever?

Supposing it was someone whose questions were strange to you, who seemed to know too little of the world – would you promise to tell her the truth?

I hope and believe that the answer to these questions is yes. If it is, please leave me a message in the place where you found this. "Yes" is enough.

If the answer is no, please destroy this letter and forget that you read it.

Tom, if you can, please say yes.

A.

I copied the letter out again so that it was perfect, and then I folded it very carefully, until it was small enough to be hidden behind the curtain. I thought I might tuck it into the crack between the window and the frame, where Tom would find it if he looked, and it could not flutter to the floor where it risked being seen by Grandmother. Then I slipped the letter into my pocket and went down the attic stairs to listen at the door at the bottom. I did not really expect to hear anyone moving about; I knew the men were working on the chimney. After a few moments, I pushed the door open.

The passage was empty and silent. Late afternoon sunlight slanted through the open doors, across the polished boards and the worn runner.

I stepped out into the passage.

I could feel a pulse beating rapidly in my throat; I shivered with excitement. In my mind's eye, I was already running lightly across the bedroom to the window, I was pressing the folded letter into the crack of the window frame. I imagined Tom finding it and plucking it out of its hiding place, his brows drawn together in concentration as he read the contents. What reply would he leave me? Would he reach into his jacket and draw out a pen, and scrawl that single word I longed to read – Yes? The idea consumed my thoughts, and that was why, for those few moments, I forgot to be as cautious as usual.

I passed Grandmother's room and barely registered that the door was standing open. It was not until her quiet voice said, "Ghost?" that I froze in my tracks, horrified.

I didn't want to turn and look. For one instant, I was tempted to continue down the passage as though nothing had happened, as though I had not been caught in the act. But even before I did turn my head, I heard a creak as Grandmother rose from the chair where she had been sitting, the brusque click of her shoes on the floorboards.

"Ghost?" she said again, and this time her tone was unmistakably grim. "What do you think you are doing?"

There was nothing I could say that would not make things worse.

Grandmother didn't waste time interrogating me then, either. That would come later. She grasped me firmly by the upper arm and walked me back the way I had come. Her grip was so tight that it hurt, and I winced, but said nothing. I could hardly have spoken anyway; I was choked with disappointment and shame at being caught. I let her push me, unresisting, through the doorway that led to the attic stairs; I stood silent and unprotesting as she locked the door behind me.

As Grandmother's footsteps receded away down the passage, I sank down onto the bottom of the stairs. I had my hand in my pocket, holding the letter I had written to Tom.

If Grandmother had found it—

The idea made me feel almost sick. My fingers curled into a fist around the folded paper, crushing it. Then I crept up the stairs into the cold attic and waited for nightfall.

chapter eleven

I expected Grandmother to be furious with me when she came to let me out of the attic that evening; I expected her to rant and scold. In fact, it was worse: she was cold with me, frozen hard by anger. I tried to say that I was sorry for disobeying her, that I had meant no harm, I had only wanted to peep out of one of the windows for a glimpse of the outsiders who had come to Langlands. Perhaps she believed me about that, because she never gave any sign that she knew about any of the other things – the key, the coin, the messages scrawled in the dust. It made no difference, though. She was inexorable. The following morning, she took me to the attic earlier than before and locked me in again.

When I heard the key turn in the lock, I was tempted to bang on the door, to shout at the top of my voice, to try to force her to change her mind. But I knew that Grandmother would send the men away without finishing the job before she would risk them hearing me.

I was angry too, unreasonably.

Why can't I ever speak to anyone? Why do I have to hide myself away all the time?

I knew the answer, of course: the War, the wretched, never-ending War. I saw, though, that there was more than one way of ruining a life – doing nothing with it, for example. Supposing the War dragged on and on, and I grew old, never seeing anything outside Langlands, never speaking to anyone new? I might as well go to the old mausoleum in the woods and lie down there right now – buried alive.

Anyway, I said to myself, *Tom wouldn't have told on me.* I called him that boldly in my head, *Tom*, as though we were already friends. The angrier I became with Grandmother, the more convinced I was that I could have trusted him, if we had only been able to speak.

I thought about the little I had seen of the world beyond the borders of the estate: the countryside, the road with vehicles moving peacefully up and down it, the aircraft that crossed the skies as harmlessly as migrating swallows. Sometimes it was difficult to believe in distant horrors. Certainly, there was nothing to say that life out here in the country was as desperate as it must be in the city. Why should Tom give me away? What could he possibly gain from doing so?

The chance was gone, though. The door stayed locked all that day, until the men had left. Grandmother came to let me out then, and if she noticed how stiff and cramped I was, she said nothing. She led me down to the kitchen and made me a cup of cocoa while I warmed myself at the iron range.

While she was preparing dinner, she said, "The work will be finished tomorrow."

She looked at me, to see that I had understood what she meant, which was: *the men will be going for good.* I said nothing. There was nothing I wanted to say to her.

The next morning it was the same story. Grandmother took me to the attic early and locked me in. I considered simply refusing to go. I was as tall as she, and certainly as strong. She couldn't force me. But she must have seen my thoughts in my face because she said, "Ghost, the work is very nearly done. If you will not stay in the attic, I shall simply tell the men to go without doing any more."

45

I climbed the attic stairs and contented myself by lying on the bearskin and watching from the window for the men to arrive. I saw the strange, box-like vehicle draw up; I saw both of them get out. It was another dry, bright day and with the help of the field glasses I could have seen the minutest detail, but after a few moments my vision was too blurred to see clearly. I had never said goodbye to anyone before. I wiped my eyes with the heel of my hand, and when I looked again, the two men were gone.

Early in the afternoon, I heard Grandmother unlocking the door.

"Ghost," she called, and I went down the stairs to where she stood. I knew that they had left, Tom and the older one called Neil McAllister. I didn't want Grandmother to tell me so; I thought I should scream if she did.

I came to the bottom step and Grandmother opened her mouth to say something, probably the very thing I was willing her not to say, but before she could do so, we both heard a distant hammering. Someone was knocking at the front door, and energetically, too.

Grandmother frowned. "They'll have forgotten something," she said. "Stay here, Ghost."

Before I could say anything, she had closed the door and turned the key in the lock. I heard her footsteps moving briskly down the passage; she wanted this over and done with, she wanted the men gone for ever.

I stepped off the bottom step and onto the floor. There was a strange sensation inside my chest, a fizzing, tingling feeling, almost unbearable in its intensity. The door was not locked. Either Grandmother had failed to push it fully shut in her haste, or the old lock was worn. At any rate, it was not closed. I could see the thinnest line of light outlining the edge of the door.

Another few moments and I heard Grandmother on the stairs; the creaks the boards made were distinctive. Cautiously, I pushed the door right open and stared down the empty passage. Disappointment and resentment made me reckless. Tom was going; I would never see him again. Why shouldn't I take one last glimpse from one of the front windows, if I could?

I could hear voices downstairs now; they were talking to Grandmother in the hall.

Now or never, I said to myself. I didn't waste time thinking about it. I made my way down the passage as swiftly as I dared, moving cautiously to avoid the places where the boards creaked the loudest. I was not far from the head of the stairs when it happened: I heard someone coming up.

Grandmother, I thought, panicking. I turned my head, looking for the nearest open door. But it was not Grandmother. If it had been, I probably would have managed to hide myself before she reached the top of the stairs. It was Tom.

He came up the stairs at speed, taking them two or three at a time, and I was still standing in the middle of the landing when he reached the top. The moment he saw me, he stopped dead. We could not have been more than ten feet apart from each other.

I could see the individual strands of dark hair that fell across his forehead, the texture of his skin, the firm lines of jaw and cheekbones. I could see the flare of his nostrils, the way his chest heaved from running up the stairs, the involuntary parting of his lips when he saw me standing there at the top. Every detail was clear and sharp. And it was all wrong.

The feeling of constriction in my chest was so intense that I thought my heart was bursting, that I was dying. I didn't care; there was nothing for it now but to die. I had broken my secret, Grandmother's secret, all our safety, all of it gone, for something I had hoped would be one way and which turned out to be something entirely other, something terrible.

Because he wasn't looking at me the way I'd hoped and imagined he would if we ever properly met – with friendly interest, or even with neutrality. He looked horror-struck. The colour drained out of his face. He stared and stared at me, and the eyes which I was now close enough to see were a pale blue-green, fringed with dark lashes, were round with shock.

Abruptly he put his hands over his face and I understood that the sight of me was something he could hardly bear. I terrified him.

I should have turned and left then, and there might perhaps have been some tiny chance that he would think he had dreamed me, that he had seen a trick of the light or a reflection or nothing at all. I didn't do it, though. I had not meant to do this, but now I had thrown myself into the situation anyway. There was no way back.

I kept my voice low, so low that Grandmother, down in the hallway below, could not hear it.

"Say something," I whispered. "Speak to me."

But he said nothing. My words seemed to strike him like a slap; he shuddered back from them.

As the silence drew out it became like a gulf widening between us. At last I turned away. I had just enough self-control left not to run from him down the passage. Instead, I went into the nearest room and stood behind the door, where I was invisible from outside. I held my hands over my mouth to stifle the tiniest sound, the smallest sob.

Tom did not come after me. For a time, I think he did nothing at all. I didn't hear him go along the landing. He didn't call out, to me or to anyone below. At last, I heard a series of creaks that meant he had started back down the stairs, but with none of the energy that had propelled him up them. He trod slowly and heavily, as though descending with reluctance.

Would he tell the others what he had just seen? I had no idea, but I thought he would find it hard not to let the shock show in his face. Whatever he did or didn't do, I dared not be caught out of the attic by Grandmother. Before the sound of the heavy front door closing had reverberated through the house, I was already at the attic door. I drew it closed behind me. A few moments later I had reached the top of the stairs.

I threw myself down on the dusty boards. I couldn't even cry. The pent-up tears had vanished. Instead, I felt a pain so crushing that it was like imploding. I lay on my side and curled myself into a ball, my hands into tight fists. I squeezed my eyes shut, but it was no use. I knew that even if I plucked them out altogether I would never be able to stop seeing the look of horror on Tom's face.

chapter twelve

Tom

What just happened??

I walk back down the stairs, going slowly so I have time to pull myself together, so they won't see it on my face. The shock.

Did I really see a ghost?

Maybe there's some other explanation for what I just saw, but I can't think of it right now. I'm stunned. I ran up the stairs and when I got to the top, there she was. A girl. She was wearing a long dress that was so old-fashioned I've only ever seen anything like it in films, and she had very long dark hair: it went right down past her waist. Her eyes were dark, too, and very large, and her skin was very pale, so she looked sort of faded, like an old photograph. She was beautiful, but in a strange way, like she belonged to a different time.

1944. The thought just popped into my head.

I stared at her and I blinked hard, twice, but she was still there, I was still looking at her, and she – she was looking at me. You can tell when someone is looking at you, really looking. And she was as stunned as I was. I saw her mouth open, forming a silent O of shock.

I cannot be seeing this.

I put my hands over my face and blotted her out. I said to

myself: *When I take my hands away, she'll have gone.*

And then something happened that made my blood run cold. I heard her whisper: *Say something. Speak to me.*

I didn't reply. I couldn't. It creeped me out too badly, hearing her whispering to me like that, like she was trying to crawl into my brain. I stood there with my hands over my eyes until I realised there was nothing but silence. Then I looked and she had gone. Another shock, finding myself alone.

So now I'm going back down the stairs and Dad and old Mrs. McAndrew are looking up at me. Dad looks like he's waiting for an answer, and the old lady just looks pissed off. She'd have stopped me going up there if I hadn't been so quick.

"Find it?" says Dad.

I shake my head. The truth is, I didn't even look for his spirit level. It's probably up there all right, in the bedroom where we did the work, but I'm not going back again. Anyway, how can I explain what I was doing up there all that time if I admit I haven't already looked?

Mrs. McAndrew gives me a hard stare as I go past. She can't wait for the pair of us to be out of the house. When the front door shuts behind us, I can hear the scraping noise as she puts the bolt across.

Dad keeps complaining about his spirit level as we get back into the van. I don't say anything at all. I'm concentrating on doing what I have to do: open door, slide inside, fasten seatbelt. I do all of it like I'm in a dream. I feel strange, maybe a bit sick. Disconnected.

As we're bumping down the track away from Langlands House, Dad glances at me.

"What's up?"

"Nothing," I say.

"You look—"

"Tired," I say. "Just tired."

I look back over my shoulder as we follow the curve

51

of the track and see the house vanishing behind the trees. Mrs. McAndrew wrote Dad a cheque for the full amount while we were packing up. I won't be seeing that place again.

I put my head back against the rest and close my eyes. *What just happened?* The question nags at me, but I can't answer it. One thing I do know. I'm never going to tell anyone about this.

chapter thirteen

Ghost

"Ghost?"

Grandmother was calling me from the foot of the attic stairs.
I stood up, rubbing at my face with my fingertips. I hadn't
been crying, but I knew she would see from my expression
that something was wrong. I couldn't hide it; the pain had been
etched into me. I dragged myself reluctantly to the head of the
stairs and looked down.

"Come down, Ghost."

Grandmother was looking up, but her face was hidden in
the shadows. I could not tell whether she was angry or even
suspicious. I went slowly downstairs. When I was nearly at the
bottom, she said, "This door was not locked."

"Wasn't it?" I said. Even to my own ears, my tone was
dull. Perhaps Grandmother took my apparent lack of interest
for innocence. Then the light slanting in showed her my face.

"Good heavens, child, whatever is the matter?"

"I have a headache." This was not entirely untrue. I had a
heavy feeling in my temples, like the pressure before a storm.
I could well believe that it would have developed into a full
blown sick headache by evening.

"You seemed perfectly all right just now," said Grandmother,
but it was concern I heard in her voice, not suspicion.

"It started suddenly." I turned my head, not wanting to look into her eyes. "I think I'd like to lie down."

Grandmother touched my hand. "Goodness, you're half-frozen. Come down to the kitchen first, and warm up."

I didn't have the energy to argue. I let her lead me down to the kitchen, where she made me sit close to the stove. Then she made me a cup of sweet tea, which I liked, and a cold compress for my forehead, which I didn't like, but submitted to anyway. It was easier to let her fuss over me than to resist.

I suspected that she felt guilty about locking me into the attic, especially that last time, when she had pushed me back inside and shut me in so peremptorily. Grandmother was strict but she was not *cruel*. And clearly she had absolutely no idea what had just happened with me and Tom. She thought I was simply chilled and low in spirits after being confined in the attic so much.

As I sat cradling my cup of tea and watching Grandmother bustling about, it began to occur to me that I had done something very bad, even if I hadn't meant to. Someone had really seen me now, someone from outside Langlands. Clearly Tom hadn't said anything to Grandmother, but that didn't mean he wouldn't tell *other* people. And then...

All the things with which Grandmother had terrified me over the years came crowding around me like leering demons. The worst of this torment was, I couldn't talk to Grandmother about my fears, not without admitting what I had done. And since I couldn't undo it, there seemed no benefit in confessing. Instead, I would have to live with knowing that our safety was dependent on the actions of a stranger. Would he tell or not? I had no idea.

The compulsion I had had to communicate with Tom seemed pitiable now. Whatever I thought I had seen in him based on mere appearances, he hadn't seen the same in me. He had seemed utterly horrified by the sight of me; he wasn't interested or sympathetic. It was never going to be like the books in the library, the novels in which the hero was strangely taken with the heroine the very first time he saw her. It wasn't even going to be like the ones in which he *wasn't* impressed by his first sight of the heroine but later came to realise how interesting she was, because the work was done; Tom wasn't coming back. And for this mirage I had endangered our life here at Langlands.

That night I lay for a long time staring wide-eyed and sleepless into the dark. It was a very quiet night, windless and dry, not at all like the night of the storm, when the chimney had come down through the roof and caused the damage that had led to all this trouble. Now the roof had been repaired, and the weather had become so calm that you would hardly believe such a thing could have happened. The only thing that had really changed was me. Before that night, I had longed for contact with the world outside Langlands; now I was sickened at the idea of it, and judging by the way it had reacted to the sight of me, I was just as repellent to it. Things felt hopeless. Perhaps I slept in the end, but long before the light came I was lying awake again, and I was not aware of having been unconscious at all.

chapter fourteen

In the morning, Grandmother took me up to see the bedroom where the work had been done. You could tell where the ceiling had been repaired if you looked. It was the same with the chimney stack when we went outside to look at that; it had been repaired enough that rain wouldn't come down the chimney, but it looked lop-sided because the stack hadn't been rebuilt properly. That would have taken a lot longer, and cost more, and Grandmother would have tolerated neither.

"Not terribly pretty, is it?" said Grandmother.

I still felt wretched and couldn't bring myself to care very much either way, but I didn't want Grandmother to notice that and ask me what the matter was. So I said, "I suppose it's difficult, with the War on."

I wasn't looking directly at her, but out of the corner of my eye I saw her head turn towards me. It seemed important to keep the conversation going, to make things normal, so I added, "It gave me such a shock when the chimney came down. I really thought we were being bombed."

Grandmother said nothing to this, which was unusual. I would have expected a short instructive homily about not panicking when something alarming happened, or some such thing. Instead, she was silent.

I couldn't think of anything else to say. The events of the

previous day were pressing in on me like a miserable fog, but in spite of this, I couldn't help seeing that Grandmother was preoccupied. She didn't appear to have taken in what I had just said; she had something else on her mind. After another minute or two of silently following the byways of her own thoughts, she seemed to come to herself. She looked at me and said, "I am so sorry you have to be shut up here, Ghost, with only an old woman for company."

So had I been, until yesterday's catastrophe. Now I simply said, "I know it's for the best, Grandmother."

"For the best," she repeated, more to herself than to me. "Yes, I've tried to do whatever was for the best."

She turned her back on the view of the ill-repaired chimney and began to lead the way back into the house. I was not sorry; it was a bright dry morning, but the air was bitterly cold. Soon winter would properly sink its fangs into Langlands; only the kitchen, with its ancient range, would be warm enough to tolerate, and our routine would shrink to the span of its four walls for most of the day.

"Grandmother," I said, "Do you think there's any chance at all that the War will end soon?"

We were entering the shadow of the stone porch at the front of the house; now Grandmother paused for a moment, looking at me.

"The War will end?" she repeated, and again she sounded preoccupied. She didn't answer the question. She seemed lost in thought for a few moments and then she replied with another question of her own.

"When will you be eighteen, Ghost?"

"April 12th," I said promptly, although the question surprised me a little. Grandmother knew perfectly well when my birthday was. It wasn't as though either of us had a whole range of anniversaries to remember, just one each: mine in April and hers on 15th July.

"Less than half a year," she said thoughtfully. We resumed our walk into the house and made our way down the passage to the kitchen, where Grandmother set the kettle on the range to make tea. Then she came over to where I was standing. I hadn't sat down; instead I was over by the window, gazing out. There was a patch of bright sunlight on a grey corner of wall that jutted out from the house. That patch of light would move up and over the house as the day passed, shortening in the middle of the day and lengthening as evening approached. Then darkness would come, I would have been at Langlands another day, and nothing would have changed, at least, not for the better. The days seemed to stretch out in front of me, and I no longer knew what to wish for.

Grandmother glanced out of the window too, and then she said, "Ghost," so that I turned my head to look at her. I had to force myself to meet her gaze; I was still afraid she would see in my eyes that I had something on my conscience. But she noticed nothing, and it was not until much later that it occurred to me that perhaps she had something on *hers*.

She put out her hands and touched my shoulders, and said, "I want you to remember, whatever happens in the future, however things may seem, that I have always, always, had your best interests at heart."

"Yes, Grandmother," I said, though I was mystified by her words. Did she think she had been too severe, making me hide in the attic? I could not think what else she could have done.

Then she kissed me lightly on the forehead and went back to whatever she had been doing, perhaps embarrassed by this unusual display of sentiment. I turned my gaze back to the window, and when I sighed, it was too low for Grandmother to hear.

chapter fifteen

The winter was very harsh that year. We had snow before Christmas, and much more of it afterwards. Once, we ran really low on supplies and had to wait a week before Grandmother could take the car into town, because the track was so thickly blanketed with snow. Many times, I had to go out in the early morning to clear away the snow in front of the chicken coop and replace their water that had frozen solid; carting in firewood for the range meant a nipped nose and chilblains on the hands.

During those months there were no repercussions from the day when I had seen and been seen by an outsider. No visitor came to Langlands – not that there was any need, since we had no more accidents – nor was there any other sign to indicate that the outside world had noticed my existence. The guilt and anxiety that had gripped me after the incident occurred began to slacken off, although I was still sore about Tom's reaction to seeing me. *As though he had seen a ghost,* I thought. Well, perhaps he thought he had.

The odd thing was, that Grandmother seemed to have been affected by the storm damage and the presence of the men at Langlands, even though she knew nothing of what had happened to me. I couldn't account for this. We couldn't have fixed the roof by ourselves, so she had had to call them in; they had done the work and gone, and our life had resumed as before. There was no reason for her to dwell on any of it, and yet it seemed that she did.

More than once she made some apologetic reference to my having had to hide in the attic, as though it were a much greater hardship than it had really been.

Every time, I made the same reply: "It wasn't really that bad, Grandmother," but I sensed that this wasn't easing her mind. Those days in the autumn really bothered her, and I couldn't understand why.

I remember one morning in February I found that the first snowdrops had come through and called her outside to see. It was freezing outdoors but bright all the same, and I was grateful to feel sunshine and fresh air on my face after spending so much time inside. I suppose it was that that made me chatter on so cheerfully; after the monotony of winter days, any new thing was interesting, including the appearance of a cluster of tiny flowers. Even the misery and disappointment I had felt after the disastrous encounter with Tom had faded to a dull ache rather than pain. I found myself almost happy again, at last.

My enthusiasm did not infect Grandmother. She came outside all right, and looked at the snowdrops, pulling her winter coat close around her, and she listened to me talking, but she said very little herself. If anything, my happy mood seemed to depress her.

Eventually we went back inside, to the kitchen. I had some studying to do, so I sat down at the table in front of my books, and was rather surprised when she came and sat with me. Then she actually took my hand in hers, and I was really mystified; evidently, she had something serious to say, but what?

Tom, said my conscience, but I dismissed it easily. If anything had been going to happen about *that* it would have happened ages ago.

"Augusta," Grandmother began, "I have something to say to you, and I hardly know where to begin." She hesitated, and a clouded look came into her blue eyes, as though she were listening to some silent call that I could not hear. Then she went on. "I ask myself very often whether I have done the right thing, keeping you hidden here for so long, without the company of any other people. No, don't interrupt me, my dear. It's true, I do ask myself about it. I've told you before that I have tried to do everything for the best, and so I have, but you may not always agree with me."

It was certainly true that I hadn't always agreed with her, but I tried to say something reassuring anyway. She hardly seemed to hear me.

"In two months' time you will be eighteen years old," she said, "And no longer a child in anyone's eyes. A great many things will change then, Augusta. A great many things," she repeated.

"What things?" I asked, but she shook her head.

"In good time, my dear."

I gazed at her in perplexity and then confusion hardened into an unpleasant suspicion. "I'm not going to have to go and work in a factory, am I?"

I saw her give a little jump at that; had I hit upon the truth?

"No," she said. "Not that."

"But the War–" I began.

"The War won't always – won't always affect you the way it does at present, Ghost."

"You mean it's going to *end*?" I was stunned.

"I suppose..." said Grandmother, and hesitated again. Then she said, "Yes, I think we can say that it may end."

I seized the hand that she had laid over mine. "But that's amazing! You really think it's going to end? So we won't have to hide here any longer – we can just go out – and go into the town and–"

"Augusta," she said sharply, and with difficulty I reined in my excitement. "Nothing has changed yet. Until it does, we have to continue as we always have. If we need anything from the town I shall go. If anyone should have to come here again, you must stay out of sight. Nothing can change *yet*, you understand me?"

"Yes, Grandmother." In truth, I was barely listening to what she was saying; I was too preoccupied with the idea that our solitary life here at Langlands might be *about* to change. We might be able to go out; others would be able to come in. We could visit all the things I had read about but never seen: the town; Edinburgh, the capital; the sea. Amazingly, out of this maelstrom of exciting ideas, one question suddenly thrust itself forward into my consciousness.

"But Grandmother, what does the War ending have to do with my being eighteen?"

A brief flicker of emotion passed across Grandmother's face. I would have said it was dismay, but I could see no reason for her to be alarmed at the question, which seemed quite reasonable to me. She said, "Only this, my dear – that there are certain truths that will be easier for you to cope with once you have become an adult." She put up a hand. "No, don't ask me anything else today. Please just remember what I have told you. Will you do that for me?"

"Yes," I said, rather unwillingly, since there were a thousand other things I would have liked to ask.

But Grandmother said, "Kiss me," so I kissed her gently on the cheek that was so soft and papery, and then she got up and turned to preparing the vegetables for lunch as though we had never had any conversation at all.

I had so much to think about that it did not occur to me until later that although she had said she had something to tell me, she had not really told me anything at all. Things would change when I turned eighteen; the War *might* end soon; I should remember that she had always acted for the best. What did that add up to?

I resolved to wait for a suitable moment and ask her some more questions, starting with *what makes you think the War is going to end soon?* That was the burning question, because if she was right, and it was coming to an end, everything about our lives here was about to change. But I never got to ask her any of these questions, because a few days after the conversation in the kitchen, Grandmother drove into town and never came back.

chapter sixteen

I remember it was another of those clear bright February mornings, with brilliant sunshine but so cold that it made your lungs ache to breathe the outdoor air. We were starting to run low on a few things – sugar, soap flakes – and since the track through the forest was clear at present, Grandmother had decided to stock up before the snow came again.

When she left, I was sitting in the kitchen with my books. I didn't take any particular notice of her departure. I was still very preoccupied with thoughts of what would happen if the War ended, and how we might possibly predict such a thing; an ordinary trip into town for soap flakes seemed comparably uninteresting. I didn't go out to the gravel drive at the front of Langlands to see her off.

I worked until lunchtime, and then I put the books away and made myself something to eat. I boiled a brown egg from the long-suffering chickens and cut myself a slice of Grandmother's home-baked bread. Then I made tea and stood by the kitchen window with the warm cup cradled in my hands, watching a robin hopping about outside. I wondered when Grandmother would be back, and whether she would bring anything more interesting than the essentials.

After that, I went out to the log pile and lugged some firewood inside in a basket. I never liked that job very much anyway, but it was worse at night when I couldn't see properly and would bark my shins on piles of cut wood or the chopping block; better to get it over and done with by daylight.

I peeled the vegetables for dinner and left them on the range in a pan of cold water. Finally, I fetched the mending basket and embarked upon the tedious task of sewing on buttons and repairing rips in various articles of clothing. After some time spent on this, I realised that the strong light from outside had gone. The sun had moved and the shadows had lengthened. I was starting to struggle to see what I was doing. I cast off the thread on the petticoat I was mending and stuffed the whole thing back into the mending basket.

I was beginning to feel a little impatient for Grandmother's return. Where was she? I would have expected her to be back by this time.

I wasn't alarmed – just a little frustrated. We hadn't agreed anything about cooking the evening meal if she were late back.

When the sun sank behind the trees however, and twilight closed in on the house, I began to be really concerned. I fetched my coat and went out to the front of the house, shivering in the freezing air. The gravel area where Grandmother would normally have parked the car to unload the shopping was empty. Pulling my coat more closely around me, I went to the place where the drive passed under the trees and gazed down the track, straining my eyes for any sight of headlights approaching through the gloom. Nothing. I listened, too, hoping for the sound of the car's engine purring up through the forest, but all I could hear were the wind moving lightly in the trees and the occasional sounds of birds.

I went back to the house, troubled. I told myself that there was probably no cause for alarm. Perhaps the car had developed a fault and Grandmother had had to stay in town for a few hours while it was repaired. Or had she had to go further afield than usual, and I hadn't taken it in when she told me? I racked my memory until I wasn't even certain myself. And all the time night was coming closer, and the Langlands estate was becoming darker.

Eventually, I couldn't fool myself any longer. The sun had gone down; it was pitch black outdoors, the moon a mere sliver obscured by clouds. Something was really wrong. I was afraid Grandmother would not be back that night at all. Several times I went back to that spot on the edge of the forest to look and listen again, but there was still nothing. It was so utterly dark under the trees that gazing into them was like being struck blind. I had never really been afraid of the dark – how could I be, when so much of Langlands was unlit at night? – but now it began to play on my nerves. I began to think of the ancient mausoleum buried in the undergrowth and its ugly contents, and to imagine how terrible it would be if the shades of the dead were walking out there among the damp black tree trunks.

I went back into the house, closed the door behind me and leaned against it, thinking. The hallway was lit by a single candle I had left burning on top of one of the pieces of heavy old furniture. Shadows danced over the panelling and the paintings, the pair of silver pheasants on the hall table and the stuffed stag's head on the wall. The stag's glass eyes gleamed dully. I could hear the sound of my own breathing, and other things: the tiny creaks and groans that came from the old house itself.

So far as I could remember, I had never in my life spent the night alone in the house. Grandmother had always been in her room at the end of the passage; if anything had happened, such as the night the chimney had fallen through the roof, she was close enough to hear me call. Now she was not here, and I had no idea why. The unlit passageways and echoing rooms of Langlands House no longer seemed friendly; they felt like a series of cold dark caverns in which anyone or anything might lurk.

At last, I made a decision and locked the door on the inside. I would spend the night in the kitchen, in the comforting warmth that at any rate suggested safety. If Grandmother did come home and found the front door locked, she would try the back one and I would hear her, and open it.

I fetched a blanket from my room, and I drew an old wooden settle that stood against the wall of the kitchen closer to the iron range. Then I wrapped myself up as snugly as I could and did my best to sleep.

I awoke the next morning with a headache and stiff limbs from spending the night on the settle. I felt cold, too. I put out a hand and touched the range. There was still some warmth in it, but not the heat I expected; usually Grandmother would have packed the wood carefully to keep it going overnight and fed it again in the morning before I was downstairs. I had not imagined it; she really hadn't come home, and I was still alone.

I unwrapped myself from the blanket and did my best to get the range going properly again. It would be a while before there was any hot water for tea, and my fingertips were waxen with the cold. I made myself some breakfast with the last of the loaf and some of Grandmother's blackberry jam, and then I set about the usual morning chores: feeding the chickens, fetching in more firewood. I went about these tasks mechanically, trying not to think about the situation. These things needed to be done; I must do them. There was nothing else to do but to wait and see; perhaps Grandmother's car had broken down so catastrophically that she had had to stay in the town, and she would simply turn up later today. It was not as though there was any way she could let me know if such a thing had happened after all; Langlands had no telephone. I tried not to dwell on the other, more sinister possibilities.

The day seemed to pass with agonising slowness. At a little after two o'clock I went to stand at the bottom of the gravel area again, and gazed down the track that led through the forest. There was a savage bite in the air and the sky had taken on a lurid shade that meant snow. Under the trees was only earth and mud so far, but out in the open, fine white flakes were already drifting down. If enough snow fell, Grandmother would be unable to get back to Langlands, however much she wanted to.

By nightfall she had not come home, and the snow was inches deep. With the darkness came wind, and the snow banked up against the walls and inside the stone porch.

I spent the night in the kitchen again, although I barely slept. I fed the stove while hot tears splashed onto the backs of my hands as I worked. There was no denying it now: something very serious had happened to Grandmother. Even if the car had broken down, she would never have spent two nights away. She would have paid someone to bring her back to Langlands. She might even have abandoned the provisions and walked back. She would *never* willingly have deserted me.

It was hard not to conclude that her disappearance was to do with the War. Perhaps she had been mistaken; perhaps the War was going to end all right, but not with Peace, with conquest. Perhaps the enemy had landed on our shores at last, and finally made it as far inland as our lonely corner of nowhere. What was going on out there, beyond the border of the estate? I felt sick thinking of the possibilities, but I was desperate to know.

On the second morning alone, I tried to open the kitchen door to go and feed the chickens, and couldn't; the snow was too deeply piled against it. I went out through the front instead, where the stone porch had given at least a little protection, into a cold white world. It was a struggle to wade through the snow and go around the house to the chicken coop.

I had wondered about going down the drive a little way, to look for clues as to what might be going on in the outside world, but I could see that it was really impossible. Instead, once I had finished the necessary chores, I climbed up to the attic and looked out of the window, kneeling at the very spot where I had lain on the bearskin and caught my first glimpse of Tom, months before. I could see nothing but the black and white of trees in the snow. There were no tell-tale plumes of smoke rising beyond the forest, no ominous shapes in the pearlescent winter sky. This told me nothing useful, of course; Langlands was so remote that the city of Perth itself might have been burnt to the ground and we would have seen nothing. All that I knew was that I was now utterly alone.

chapter
seventeen

The snow lasted for a week, and then rain cleared much of it. When the rain had finished, everything was sodden. Even when the sun reappeared it had a pale, watery look to it.

I had taken to living almost exclusively in the kitchen during that week. Now I looked around me and saw that I was living in a mess. Cups and plates were piled up, waiting to be washed; at first it hadn't seemed worth heating water for one person's things and then there was suddenly so much to wash up that I couldn't face it. The table was littered with bottles and jars and the sticky spoons with which I had scraped out the last of their contents. The floor was a gritty mess of gravel and mud that I had trodden in from the grounds.

I looked down at myself. The hem of my dress and my shoes and stockings were spattered with mud. Even my fingernails were grimy.

Supposing Grandmother came home now and found you like this? I said to myself. I had virtually given up hope that she would ever do that, but the thought stung me. It was no use going on like this. I had to do *something*. But what?

In the end, I tidied and cleaned the kitchen, and then I heated water so that I could wash myself. I dressed in clean clothes, selecting everything for maximum warmth, and then I put on my coat and a knitted hat. There was a single apple left in the bowl on the table; I put that into my pocket.

I secured the kitchen door and then I let myself out of the front one, locking it behind me. It felt strange doing that; I couldn't recall ever having done such a thing in my life. I had never been far enough from the house to lock it up.

There were muddy leaves in the porch. It looked as though nobody lived here at all. I stepped over them and went out onto the gravel. A few days ago, when everything had been covered in snow, every step I took would have been marked by footprints; now my passing left no trace.

I followed the sweep of the drive until I came to the place where the gravel ended and the track began, winding its way into the forest. Under the trees, the atmosphere was dismal. Trees had fallen, and as long as they were not obstructing the way, they had simply been left to grow green and mossy. Near the place where the track began was the crumbling remains of a wall, and that too was growing a damp-looking coat of moss. Further down were rusting metal posts and curled wire where stretches of fencing had been. Water dripped from the branches of the trees, leafless, dank and black. There was no wind today. All I could hear between the trudging of my own feet and the sound of my own breathing was the drip-drip of that water.

I was used to being alone, or if not alone, to having the company of only one other person. I had never been in a *crowd* of people in my entire life. And yet now the isolation bore down on me. The quiet in the woods seemed ugly and expectant, like the silence of a tomb waiting to welcome an occupant. I began to mutter to myself under my breath, trying to reassure myself.

"Cold in here...very cold...What will I see when I reach the end of the forest...?"

After a while, I lost heart and fell silent. I tried whistling, but my lips were unaccountably dry. It seemed to take a long time to get down to the edge of the estate.

At the edge of the forest, there was a straight piece of track leading straight to a kind of gateway: the gate was open, but you couldn't just walk right through because there was a shallow square pit with a series of bars laid across it. It was not entirely impassable to people; if I had wanted to, I could have balanced carefully on the bars and crossed like that. However, there was a small gate at the right-hand side with no such obstacle, so I went through that instead. Then I stood under the shelter of the trees at the forest's edge, and surveyed the land in front of me.

In spite of the recent rain some of the distant hills were still ghostly white with snow. The fields were dotted with compact shapes that I identified as sheep, but I could see no human figure anywhere in the landscape.

Everything that I saw was still and peaceful; even the sheep moved slowly and gently, cropping the wet grass.

What did you expect to see? I said to myself. Then it occurred to me: supposing I had seen Grandmother's black Austin with its gleaming nose buried in a hedge or ditch, a still figure slumped behind the wheel? I shivered. But there was no sign of anything untoward anywhere in that whole peaceful view: no discordant sounds, no more traffic on the distant road than I had ever noticed before, no column of smoke anywhere on the horizon. All the same, I hesitated to leave the cover of the trees.

I guessed that the distances I could see from here would take me hours to cover by foot, and as I could not see the town Grandmother talked about, it must be further still. I would be exposed out there, once I was too far away from the forest to dodge back into the safety of its deep shadows; I would be like the rabbit that streaks across an open space, heedless of the watching buzzard.

You'll have to go in the end, I reminded myself. I knew that was true. But which way, exactly?

I stood there for a while, simply staring, and at last I heard something that roused me from my deliberations: a droning sound, the sound of an engine. I knew it was that because it reminded me of the noise Grandmother's Austin made. But there was no car coming up the road towards me. The sound was coming from overhead.

I looked up and saw an aircraft high above me, moving parallel to the border of the forest. Instinctively I backed into the undergrowth, away from the treeline.

Did it see me?

The droning sound intensified; it was right over me. I stayed perfectly still, my heart thudding. Then the sound changed in tone and I realised that the plane had flown on; very quickly it left me behind, the sound of the engine diminishing as the distance between us lengthened. When at last I dared step out into the open and look for it, the plane was a mere black speck in the sky, and soon after that, it had vanished.

It was enough for me, though. My nerve was broken. There was something sinister in the way that the one thing to interrupt the dead quiet of the scene was this machine with its monstrous drone. Was it possible that it had actually been looking for *me*? At any rate, it must have been looking for *something*. I could think of no other reason that it would patrol this unpopulated landscape.

At last I turned back into the forest and began to trudge back to the house. My hands fidgeted and burrowed like rodents in my pockets; I chewed my lip until I felt the coppery taste of blood on it.

Grandmother, nagged my conscience relentlessly.

Think first, said common sense. *Find a map in the library – at least know which way the town is, and how far, before you try again.* I walked on, my head bowed.

73

An unexpected voice spoke up from the recesses of my mind. *Arm yourself next time.*

That idea took me by surprise, but as I considered it, I could see the sense. Amongst all the other things stored at Langlands there were several hunting rifles. I knew how to load and fire one, because Grandmother had shown me. She had had some idea of supplementing our diet with game, although we had never carried it through; her eyesight was no longer good enough to shoot, and I had flatly refused to kill anything. Frankly, I didn't believe I could shoot a person with it. It might, however, deter anyone from attacking me.

With these and other thoughts, I occupied myself as I toiled my way back up through the woods to Langlands House. It seemed to take very much longer than the walk down had done. I ate the apple without very much enjoyment; I was starving now, but it was rather soft. As I came within sight of the house, I threw the core into the undergrowth, and as I turned to walk on, I heard the sound of a vehicle approaching.

chapter eighteen

Grandmother, I thought immediately, with a great rush of incredulous relief. I turned to look down the track behind me, eager for a glimpse of the familiar black Austin. The car was not visible yet, but even as I moved back and forth to peer past the clustered trees, another thought occurred to me.

Maybe it's not Grandmother.

I thought of the aircraft I had seen following the line of the forest border. The feeling of joyous relief drained away in an instant. I stood for a moment in the middle of the track, torn between the desire to stand my ground and see who it was, and the urge to run. The sound of the engine grew louder; the vehicle must be in sight any moment now.

I broke and ran for the house. I was tired after walking for so long in the freezing air, but now panic gave me a new energy. Gravel crunched under my feet as I sprinted for the front door, my winter coat flying out behind me. I dared not glance behind me. I was afraid of what I would see.

My boots slapped on the flagstones as I raced into the protection of the stone porch. The sound of that engine was so close now that I knew it could only be seconds before I heard tyres on the gravel in front of the house.

The keys, the keys!

My hands were numb with the cold; fishing the keys out of

my pocket and fitting the right one into the lock was a fiendishly difficult manoeuvre, made worse by the shrinking time frame left to complete it. I could have screamed with frustration as the key jittered uselessly around the keyhole, my fingers refusing to obey me.

The key turned just as I heard the crunching sound I dreaded. I opened the door just far enough to slip through the gap, then closed it again as slowly and carefully as I dared; the sound of it slamming now would be fatal.

Outside, the engine died. A moment later I heard the crisp sound of a car door closing. I turned to race for the staircase and then I thought:

Lock the door.

I slid the key into the inside lock, by some miracle managing it first time, and turned it, praying that the click it made was not audible outside.

There were footsteps outside in the porch – more than one set of footsteps. I heard voices – unmistakably male ones. Now I knew this wasn't Grandmother. I didn't try to move; the sound of the boards creaking might give me away. Better to stand stock still, barely breathing for fear of making a sound.

I nearly didn't lock the door. The thought made me feel sick with horror. I imagined the occupants of the car pushing the door open easily and invading the house. I couldn't have hidden from them; every step you took inside Langlands House made the boards shriek under your feet. It would be as bad as running the gauntlet of a thousand tell-tales, all screaming *There she goes!* Wherever I'd gone, they could have followed me easily.

A thunderous knocking on the door almost made me jump out of my skin. I'd known they would try it, but there was a vehemence in the blows that made me quail.

I didn't move. I was invisible behind the door; as long as I stayed silent they could not know I was there unless they actually broke it down.

"Hello?" shouted someone, and after a pause: "Is there anyone there?" There was a muffled consultation, then more knocking and shouting.

My mouth was dry, my legs felt weak beneath me and I longed to sink down onto the floor but dared not. If they did think of breaking the door down, I would have to try running for it.

Eventually, I heard their footsteps recede away through the porch and crunch onto the gravel, but it was too soon for relief; there was no sound of car doors opening and closing nor of the engine firing up again. Evidently, they had not given up. More probably they would try the kitchen door, or peer through some of the ground floor windows.

Who are they?

That was the question. Whatever they were doing here, I thought it had to have something to do with whatever had happened to Grandmother. It was too big a coincidence that she should vanish and that strangers should come calling as soon as the track was clear of snow again. After all, nobody ever came to Langlands–

I put a hand to my mouth then, to choke back a gasp. We had had visitors, of course. Supposing the two outside were Tom and the older man, Neil McAllister, come back again? It seemed more likely than that two strangers would come and bang on the door so boldly. I remembered that last day they had been at Langlands, the day Tom and I had so disastrously confronted each other. After the men had gone, Grandmother and I had found an instrument left in the room where they had been working; Grandmother said it was a spirit level. Perhaps they had come back for that, although it would be very strange to come for it after all this time.

Now I *had* to know. It occurred to me that I could see them. On the first floor there was a turret window that the architect of Langlands had fancifully designed to look like an arrow slit, even though the house had been built long after bows and arrows had been abandoned as a means of defence. It was narrow enough, and the turret itself dark enough, that I could almost certainly look out without being seen from outside. I could at least settle the question of who was out there, and then decide what exactly to do about it afterwards.

I crossed the tiled hallway soundlessly and then began the hazardous task of climbing the wooden staircase without making too much noise. Every long drawn out creak and groan of the ancient timber made me cringe. If anyone were standing right outside the front door, he must have heard me; there was nothing for it but to pray that the men were still walking around the drive. But there was no reaction, no further knocking.

At last I reached the safety of the turret and looked out through the window. From here, I could not see the vehicle parked outside. All that was visible was a section of Langlands' grey outer wall, and a slice of the gravel drive bordered by trees. I waited for what seemed like a long time, and then I detected a flicker of movement right at the very border of my line of vision. A moment later the men stepped into view, and I saw with a cold thrill of horror that they were strangers, and both of them were in uniform.

I stepped back smartly from the window, into the shadows. It didn't matter that the window was too narrow and dark for them to see me inside it; I didn't dare risk it.

Soldiers.

The uniforms were black, and bulky – armoured against injury. The faces beneath the peaked caps were grimly unsmiling. I had not noticed weapons but I guessed they must be armed, and I was certainly not going to hazard another look.

Grandmother was right, I thought. *It's not safe out there.*

I was not sure if I was safe in here, in the house, either. The doors were solid oak, but there were plenty of windows that would be easily broken if someone really wanted to get in.

I waited in silence for one of two things: either the sound of the car engine as the men made to leave, or the sound of breaking glass downstairs. I waited for so long that I was able to track the motes of dust that I had disturbed when I entered the turret as they drifted lazily down through the strip of sunlight from the window. At last, I heard the car doors closing, and then the engine start up; moments later the vehicle had crunched away over the gravel and was gone.

It was a long time before I went downstairs.

chapter nineteen

Tom

Christmas passes, then January. We're into February now and I still think about Langlands a lot more often than I'd like. What I saw up there – or *thought* I saw. The girl in the weird old-fashioned dress.

There are no such things as ghosts.

That's a fact, right? There are people who believe in them, but there are also people who believe in astrology and Elvis still being alive and doughnuts being found on Mars.

But if I didn't see a ghost, what did I see? That's the question, and there's no good answer. Hallucinations are not a good thing to have. They're either a sign of your brain giving way or else taking too much of something. It wasn't the second one, so that leaves something wrong with my brain.

Nothing else has happened since that day. I haven't seen zombies shambling down the High Street or anything, so I'm hoping nothing's seriously wrong with me. Still, it's there at the back of my mind. She looked so real. As real as I am.

I try not to think about it, because it's a mystery I'm not going to solve, but it still bugs me. Then something happens that makes me think about it all over again.

I'm in the town, paying in cheques at the bank for Dad, and when that's done I start walking back up the street towards the spot where I've left Mum's little car.

About a third of the way up the hill, the street opens out into a square. A couple of months ago the town Christmas tree was here, and the whole square was lit up with coloured lights. Now all that's gone, and since it's a freezing day, you'd think people would be in a hurry to get from one side of the square to the other and into a nice warm shop, but looking ahead I see a small group of people standing around something.

As I get level, I see someone's on the ground. I can't help looking. It's a small town, the same old faces, so there's a good chance it's someone I know. And it is. Only it's not someone from the town.

It's old Mrs. McAndrew, from Langlands.

I stop and stare, and right away I'm sure: she's dead. She's not injured or anything, not that I can see. She just looks totally still and lifeless. Like a block of something, wood or stone.

Or meat, I think, revolting myself.

Her eyes are slightly open but all you can see is white, like the white part of a fried egg. That makes me feel slightly queasy too.

I guess I've made some kind of sound, because a woman turns around and looks at me.

"I've called the ambulance," she tells me.

A couple of other passers-by slow down to see what's going on, and eventually the same woman starts telling them to move on and stop staring, to give the old lady some room. She's one of those people who like to take charge; she'll probably tell the ambulance crew off when they get here for not managing it in a shorter time. There's nothing I can do: in fact, there's plainly nothing anyone can do for Mrs. McAndrew, so I walk on in the end.

Inside I feel strange. I've just seen a dead body. I expect they'll say she died in hospital or dead on arrival or something, but anyone could see it was all over.

I have no reason to mourn Mrs. McAndrew. I worked for

81

her for a few days but I didn't really know her. And it's not like she was tragically young. She was *ancient*.

Still, it's sad that she was all alone in that big gloomy house, that she didn't have anyone to share her life with. I wonder if there was anyone she loved, or trusted. If there was, she died without them. Nobody holding her hand, just a bunch of strangers standing around staring.

Langlands, I think. *What will happen to that?*

I suppose someone will inherit it, though they'll have to be found first. Hard to imagine anyone being thrilled about it: a crumbling old place with no proper heating or lighting, not even a phone line. In the meantime, though, the old house will just sit there, cold and silent, rotting away in the middle of the forest.

And that's when I decide to go there.

chapter twenty

Ghost

I was afraid for a while, and then I was angry. It was a strange, all-encompassing anger, like the droning of a cloud of wasps. I was angry with Grandmother, unreasonably, for leaving me alone; I resented the uniformed men who had trespassed in the grounds and forced me to hide; I hated the War – the bloody, bloody War.

I was angry with myself, too. My foray to the edge of the forest had done nothing but endanger me. I had been afraid to go further, and I had achieved nothing.

Next time, I would go armed.

I found the hunting rifles and a box of cartridges. I loaded one of the rifles as Grandmother had taught me, but I didn't dare practise firing for fear of drawing unwelcome attention to myself.

It was a beautiful object, made of highly polished wood and finely engraved metal, but it was also deeply ominous, a work of craftmanship designed for death. It felt like a dangerous intruder in the house; to handle it was to risk being infected with the desire to kill. I hoped that if it ever came to a confrontation between me and someone from the outside, it would be enough to show them the weapon – that I would not have to fire it.

Later, I searched the library for maps of the area. There was nothing that showed the Langlands estate *and* the town, so I spent some time poring over different maps and trying to work out where they overlapped. It was a difficult task, because the maps were frustratingly inaccurate. The best one of Langlands, for example, the one with the largest scale, showed things that did not exist at all, such as a small lodge down by the gate on the edge of the estate. There was no building there. This made me wonder whether I could trust any of the information on the maps.

I found the town and deduced that if the map were accurate as regarded distances if not details, it would be possible to walk there. It would take me some hours but I thought it could be done, if I left at first light and went quickly.

Should it be done, though? That was the question.

I had no idea what I would be walking into. For Grandmother to go to the town and not come back said that whatever was happening there was *not* good, and she herself had urged me to continue with things as they were. On the other hand, I was running out of all sorts of things; I could manage without sugar if I had to, and I could wash my things with ordinary soap instead of flakes, but once all the flour was gone, that was an end of making bread.

There was something else, too. It wasn't as though my happiness depended on being with other people. It had always just been Grandmother and me, apart from stolen glimpses of the very rare visitors to the estate, and the awful encounter with Tom. But I thought that if I spent too long entirely alone, never hearing another voice, never seeing a face that was not painted onto canvas or framed by the gilt edges of a mirror, I would begin to lose my mind. Already I felt as though parts of my inner self were fragmenting, crumbling away; I was lingering too long over the maps and plans, not making a definite decision about what to do, my energy dissolving into apathy.

I let a day pass after my excursion to the edge of the forest, and then another. Rain came, and then biting wind. It was not a good time to go, but if I did not make a move soon, there would never be a good time.

Tomorrow, I said to myself as I stared out of the kitchen window at trees buffeted by the wind. *Put on your warmest things, take the gun and some food to keep yourself going, and walk to the town. Don't bother trying to decide a plan now; keep to the trees and hedgerows; keep away from busy roads; don't be seen until you come to the edge of the town. Watch, see what's going on, and make up your mind then.*

This self-delivered advice made sense, so I roused myself to prepare for the expedition. There were no more apples and no cheese; the best I could find to take with me was a packet of biscuits. The maps were still in the library. I would have to fetch them. I also thought of the field glasses I had used the day the men came to Langlands; so far as I knew, they were still in the attic, on the boards close to the window, where I had lain on the bearskin and watched Tom through them. So up I went, to the very top of the house, and it was on the way back down, when I was on the staircase that led down to the hallway, that I heard a car approaching.

It was unmistakeable. I could even hear the change in engine pitch as the vehicle struggled up the curving incline to the front of the house. People who have been in great fear say *my blood ran cold*; for me fear was the tempering that hardens steel. I knew that the confrontation had come. If the men in the black uniforms had returned, it was because this time they meant to get in. If it was someone new, it was as bad, because it meant the outside world was becoming interested in Langlands. I did not panic. Instead I felt a strange and terrible excitement, the compulsion of the cornered animal to fight for its life.

The loaded rifle was on the upstairs landing, leaning against the wall. I ran for it, not bothering to be silent on the stairs; things were past that now.

Outside, the familiar crackle of tyres on the gravel came to an abrupt halt and the purr of the engine died. I picked up the rifle, and heard the sound of a car door slamming; whoever it was wasn't bothering to hide their presence.

As I descended the staircase, trying to fit the polished stock against my shoulder as though I meant what I was doing, I wondered how badly they wanted to get into the house, what lengths they would go to in order to do it. And it was then I remembered something that gave me a jolt worse than the sound of the approaching car had done. I had been out of the front door that morning, just to get some sunlight on my face for a few minutes.

The door was unlocked.

chapter twenty-one

Tom

It's a while before I do anything about my idea. Snow comes, and for a week it's a pain going anywhere, let alone Langlands with that steep track. Then there are a few days of heavy rain. It clears the snow all right, but after a day of working outdoors in it, I'm ready for a hot bath, not a drive through dark wet woods. So a bit of time goes by, but the idea doesn't go away.

Eventually, I get a free afternoon with nothing much else to do and it's not pissing it down any more, so I borrow Mum's car and off I go. I tell her I'm going into Perth, then get out the door before she can ask me to bring a load of stuff back from Tesco. I don't want anyone knowing where I've gone.

Why am I even doing this? I guess I'm hoping I can get into the house somehow, now the old lady's not there. I want to take another look and see if it comes out another way, if I can stand in the same spot on the landing and *not* see her. That girl. Then maybe I can convince myself I didn't really see her last time. There's nothing there now, so there was nothing there before, right?

And what if I do see her? I tell myself that this time I won't close my eyes. I'll speak to her. It. Whatever it is, I'll try to work it out. But that isn't going to happen, because there isn't going to be anything to see.

I get to the cattle grid at the edge of the forest and start up the drive. Mum's car struggles up the hill, bouncing over the ruts. Everything looks the same as ever: dark and gloomy and overgrown. If nobody ever manages to trace old Mrs. McAndrew's relatives, the forest will probably just close up around Langlands House. A tree will fall right across the road one day and that will be that.

I drive up onto the gravel in front of the house and park the car in front of that big stone porch. I slam the car door closed, and the sound is very loud in the silence hanging over the place.

I stand on the gravel and stare up at it for a moment. There's no sign of movement anywhere. No creepy dead-girl face at any of the windows.

There's no point in hanging about; it could take me a while to find a way inside without doing too much damage. The doors are probably locked, of course, but there's no harm in trying them anyway; it'd be stupid to break a window if old Mrs. McAndrew forgot to lock up properly. So I go into the stone porch, which is full of leaves and stuff that blew in during the bad weather.

Just as I'm reaching out for the door handle, I hear something: little creaks, like someone has run over some of those dusty old floorboards in there.

What was that?

I listen for a moment.

Wind in the trees, I tell myself, and right enough, I can hear a faint creaking from the forest as the branches sway in the breeze. I don't think the sound I heard just now came from out there though, I think it came from *inside*.

Rats, I say to myself. *Or maybe the old lady had a cat.* If so, it will be glad to get out of the house.

I grab the handle and turn it, expecting the door to be locked, and when it opens easily I'm so surprised I just stand there for a moment, with my mouth hanging open like an idiot. Then I pull myself together and go in.

It's dim in there, so it takes a minute for my eyes to adjust until I can pick out the ugly old bits of furniture and the moth-eaten stag's head on the wall. And then I hear it.

A long creak on the stairs, as though someone has put down their weight very deliberately.

Slowly I turn my head. There's a sick feeling in my stomach. She's there, on the stairs. The girl I saw before. I couldn't mistake her, not with that long dark hair, that cold, beautiful face. The gaze of those big dark eyes is fixed on me. There is nothing friendly about her expression.

She's dressed differently from before, in warmer clothes, as it's February now, and colder, though God knows whether ghosts care about that, if that's what she is. I don't really notice that until later, though. What I notice right now is the thing she's holding in her hands, braced against her shoulder. It's a rifle, and it's aimed at me.

chapter twenty-two

Ghost

I nearly shot him, right then. I was halfway down the stairs, at the point where the staircase turns, when the front door opened. It opened stealthily, and there was a moment before he actually came inside, a moment when I raised the rifle and put it against my shoulder, doing my best to aim although my hands were trembling. I was so nervous that it was a miracle I didn't just pull the trigger when he came in.

I was expecting the men in the black uniforms, or others like them, so when I saw it was only one person, and then his face turned towards me, still it took a second for me to understand whom I was seeing. Then the shock was so acute that it was like being struck.

It was him. The intruder was Tom, who had hurt me so much by looking at me with horror that other time. Now he was staring at me again, and there was that same expression on his face, as though I was the most appalling thing he had ever seen, as though he couldn't believe his eyes. And it was worse this time, because I thought I had healed but now it was like carving the wound more deeply.

The rifle felt like a live thing in my hands. Suddenly I was intensely aware of the power within it, craving to be released.

The gun *wanted* to shoot him, it wanted to blast away the pain he had given me – or perhaps it was the trembling of my own hands that made the barrel shudder in eagerness.

I saw him flinch at the sight of the rifle trained on him.

He opened his mouth to speak, and at first nothing at all came out. When he managed it, his voice sounded hoarse, rusty.

"Don't shoot."

I stared at him, but I didn't lower the gun. I couldn't make sense of this: what was he doing here now?

"Please," he said. "I'll go, okay?"

He took a step backwards, slowly and cautiously, as though he were backing away from a dangerous animal.

I found my voice. "Stop."

I came down a step, the gun still trained on him, and then another, but I took care not to get too close.

I said, "What are you doing here?"

He didn't answer the question. He looked as if he were finding it hard to breathe. His gaze met mine for a moment and then it darted about, looking for a way to escape. His mouth opened and closed.

At last he did manage to say something, but he didn't tell me what he was doing at Langlands. He blurted it out.

"Are you Ghost?"

Something seemed to clench painfully inside my chest at the sound of the pet name Grandmother had given me. It cost me a great effort to keep my expression neutral, and to keep the gun barrel level.

"Yes," I said, as firmly as I could, and saw shock pass across his face. When it became apparent that he was not going to say anything more, I said, "You're Tom."

He nodded, swallowing.

"Is the other one here?"

"What other one?"

"Neil McAllister. Is he here too?"

91

"You mean my dad?" He shook his head. "No. Just me. I came on my own."

"Why?"

"Because..." He stopped, looking confused.

"Why?" I repeated. "Why did you come here?" I wasn't feeling inclined to shoot anymore; the longer we stood there, mere yards apart, looking at each other, the less I believed I could fire at him. But I had to understand what was happening.

"I saw you," he said eventually. "Before, when we were here mending the roof."

"I know," I said.

I saw him lick his lips, nervously. "You...Are you really here? I don't..." His voice trailed off.

"You can see me, can't you?" I said. "You can hear what I'm saying."

"Yes, but..." I thought he looked a little sick. "Dad said Mrs. McAndrew lived here on her own. Nobody else, just her. And everybody says Langlands is–" He stopped.

"Haunted," I supplied. "And you thought I was the ghost."

Tom said nothing. He didn't even nod or shake his head. I guessed that he was afraid: afraid that saying it, *the ghost*, would make it real. Or perhaps he was afraid that it would offend me, and provoke me into using the rifle. He was wrong if he thought that, though. It was almost a relief, knowing that was the reason for his utter horror when he had seen me – he thought I was the Langlands ghost. In fact, he still wasn't sure I *wasn't*. *Are you really here*? he had asked.

None of this explained what he was doing here now, entering the house like a thief.

"So why did you come back?" I demanded.

"Can you put the gun down?"

I thought about that. Eventually, I took a few steps backwards, so that I could react if he tried anything untoward,

92

and then I held the rifle across my body, the barrel pointing harmlessly at the ceiling.

Tom exhaled slowly.

"Why did you come back?" I asked him again. I wasn't going to give up.

"I couldn't understand what I'd seen." He looked at me pleadingly. "I thought I was – I don't know – ill. Seeing things. I thought if I came back and looked again and there was nothing there, I'd stop thinking about it. I wasn't going to take anything, or do any damage. I swear."

He was looking at me with those blue-green eyes, appealing to me, and it was tempting to accept what he said. It made sense, after all. I knew Grandmother had encouraged the idea that Langlands was haunted, to discourage people from coming up here, and to make them doubt their own eyes and ears if they *did* come and they saw anything.

All the same, he wasn't telling the whole truth. He knew my nickname – *Ghost* – and that was hardly possible unless Grandmother had told him. I could think of no reason why she would do that. She had insisted that things must stay the same, that I must continue to hide, right up until the day she had got into her black Austin and driven out of the Langlands estate and seemingly out of my life. True, she had said that things were going to change, but not yet. I was still not eighteen. And that was not the only thing...

Ugly suspicions crowded in on me.

"You came because you thought the house was empty, didn't you?" I said. "How did you know Grandmother wouldn't be here?"

"Mrs. McAndrew?" he said, sounding surprised. "I was in the town when she..." He stopped. "Mrs. McAndrew was your *grandmother*?"

I didn't reply to that. I said, "When she *what*?"

"Look, I don't think–"

"When she *what*?" I was nearly shouting now. I was almost unbearably tempted to point the gun at him again, to *force* him to speak. "What happened to my grandmother?"

He looked at me for a moment in silence, and then he said: "When she died."

chapter twenty-three

Tom McAllister told me how Grandmother had died. None of the things I had imagined had happened. The country hadn't been invaded. She hadn't been attacked by criminals emboldened by the state of war. She had simply had a heart attack in the street, and died, there on the pavement.

I had known, really, that she wasn't coming back after the first couple of days. Grandmother would never have gone off and left me alone on purpose. Something awful and final had happened to her. But that kind of knowing was different from this one.

Suddenly, I didn't care that Tom McAllister was there, that he had seen me properly, even spoken to me. He could have walked out of the house and gone into the town and told everyone he met that the Langlands ghost was a real person and that everything in the place was theirs for the taking if they wanted it enough – I didn't care about any of that, either. All the spirit drained out of me. I sat down on the stairs with the rifle across my lap and grief overwhelmed me, dragging me down into a terrible place inside myself. I don't know if I even cried. I felt as though I had shrunk into a dense knot of pain.

After a while, he came up the stairs and sat down near me. I thought later that that was brave of him. He didn't know for sure that I wouldn't use the gun. He sat a little apart and spoke to me, and I remember he touched me lightly on the shoulder, comforting me or perhaps bracing me up. That was the first time I remember anyone other than Grandmother touching me. My parents must have, when I was tiny, but I had no recollection of that. It surprised me, shocked me even. I looked at him, and I thought I saw kindness in his expression, but I was not an expert reader of faces, having seen so few.

"You shouldn't be here on your own," he said. "Is there someone I can call for you?"

"No," I said immediately. The question brought me back to myself. I *did* care whether Tom told the outside world about me or not, or at any rate, the things that Grandmother had taught me were too deeply ingrained to be thrown away in an instant, however upset I was. "You mustn't tell anyone I'm here. You mustn't!"

"Why not?" asked Tom.

"It's not safe." I pushed back my hair from my face and made myself look Tom in the eyes, trying to show him how serious this was. "Please, you mustn't say anything. Promise me."

Tom stared back at me. His brows were drawn together, although I couldn't tell what he was thinking – whether he was irritated at being pressured, or just puzzled. He didn't promise, but nor did he refuse to promise. After a moment, he said, "But don't you have some other family? What about your mother?"

"My mother's dead," I told him. "In the War."

I said it matter-of-factly. It was something I was used to, after all. I thought about her sometimes, of course, or rather, I thought about the mother-shaped hole in the fabric of my life. I wondered whether she would have been as strict as Grandmother, or more affectionate, or simply different. But I had no memory of her at all, so I didn't miss her in the same way I missed Grandmother. Tom couldn't know that, though.

He said, "I'm sorry," and I thought he really did sound sorry. Then he said something that shocked me. "Which war was it?"

I could hardly understand him asking something like that.

"The war that's on now," I said.

There was a long pause, and then Tom said, "Sorry, I don't really keep up with foreign news that much."

In spite of my grief over Grandmother, I flared up at that. "How can you say that? Men are dying, *thousands* of them. How can you not care what's happening?" Something else occurred to me then, a question I had asked myself when Tom first came to Langlands. "And why didn't you go off to fight yourself?"

"I'm not really the type to become a soldier." He came out and said it just like that, as though it wasn't really that important.

"You're an objector?" Grandmother had told me about those: conscientious objectors, people who refused to fight on their own moral grounds.

Tom just looked at me and shrugged.

After a moment, the anger drained out of me.

"I suppose I'm no better," I said. "Hiding here, when I could be helping with the war effort." It was true, of course. I had no right to criticise. Grandmother and I had been so safe at Langlands that sometimes I had found it hard to believe in the War at all.

"War effort?" repeated Tom. My words seemed to strike him in a strange way, as though he hardly understood them. He looked down for a while. It looked as though he was studying his own hands, but I thought he was actually thinking something through. "Look," he said eventually, raising his head again and looking at me very earnestly, "Just tell me which war this is. I know I *should* know, but pretend I don't, and just tell me anyway."

Was he making fun of me? I didn't *think* he was, and it was hard to imagine anyone making a joke of such a serious topic.

"World War Two, of course," I said, very carefully.

I saw Tom's eyes widen, and his lips parted as though he had drawn in a breath very sharply. I could not guess what he was thinking. Why had he even asked the question, and in that way? It flashed across my mind that perhaps the War really had ended, as Grandmother had said it might. But Tom would still know about it, wouldn't he?

Perhaps it isn't that, I said to myself. *Perhaps he thinks there's something wrong about me, and he's asking these questions to find out, like in books, when someone has a bump on the head and you ask them what their name is and who the prime minister is, to see whether they can remember.* There were other possibilities too, but those loomed in the recesses of my imagination with such murky enormity that I hardly knew how to examine them.

At last, Tom broke the silence. "All right," he said slowly, "I know this seems like a – an obvious question, but what year is it?"

Now I thought he really must be testing me; it was such a strange thing to ask.

So I said, "1945."

"1945," said Tom, and there was a sort of flatness in his voice.

"Yes," I said.

I thought he would say something then, but he was silent for a very long time after that, seeming to be lost in thought.

At last I said, "Why did you ask what year it is?"

He didn't answer the question. He looked at me and then he asked one of his own.

"Is there anyone else living here, besides you and–?"

He was going to say *Mrs. McAndrew,* but he stopped when he realised that she wasn't living here anymore.

I shook my head. "It's always been me and Grandmother."

"Always?" he said. That seemed to impress him in some

way, good or bad, I couldn't tell. "You mean you've been here...a long time?"

"Yes," I told him. "Ever since I can remember. Since I was a baby."

"And how long ago was that?"

"Well, I'm seventeen. I'll be eighteen in April."

He thought about that. "So where did you go to school?"

"I didn't go to school," I told him. "Grandmother taught me."

"She home-schooled you?"

I nodded, a little uncertainly. I'd never heard Grandmother call it that. "She taught me everything. Reading, writing and arithmetic...and later on, Latin–"

"*Latin?*"

"Yes," I said. "And Greek."

He seemed so surprised at this that I said, "Didn't you study Latin and Greek?"

"No. I–" He hesitated. "My school didn't really do those."

"Oh." There seemed nothing I could say to that that wouldn't sound critical. It couldn't have been a very good sort of school.

He didn't seem concerned. He was more interested in other questions.

"Didn't you get lonely? I mean, if you were home-schooled, how did you make friends?"

"I don't have friends," I said, truthfully.

It was strange but not unpleasant, talking to Tom McAllister like this. It was a new experience, being asked so many questions. Grandmother did ask me things sometimes, like how the weather looked today or whether I had fed the chickens yet, and she used to test me on things I was supposed to have learnt as part of my studies. But nobody had ever asked me questions like these before – about myself, and my life. There was no reason for Grandmother to ask me those questions because she knew it all already, and there had been nobody else to ask

99

me. Perhaps, I thought, if I had had friends that was what they would have done.

I began to feel something new and warm towards Tom. I couldn't say that I was happy, not when I was grieving for Grandmother. But it was good to be sitting here with him. I hoped he would stay longer. I wished he would keep looking at me. His eyes were the colour I had always imagined the sea to be, a soft shade between pale green and blue. I wanted us to keep talking, so I went on.

"I couldn't have friends," I explained. "Grandmother said it wasn't safe for people to know that I was living here, because of the War..."

I stopped. I knew that I wasn't good at working out what people were thinking from their expressions, because I'd only ever had Grandmother to practise on, but even I couldn't miss the look that crossed Tom McAllister's face when I mentioned the War again.

"What?" I said. "What is it?"

He seemed very reluctant to say anything.

"It's something about the War, isn't it?" I said. "Just tell me."

"Look," he said eventually, "Your Grandmother told you it's 1945, right? And there's a war on. World War Two."

"Yes," I said. I waited, but he looked away. He seemed to be having problems putting whatever he wanted to say into words.

"Grandmother said it might finally end soon," I said. "There'd be peace. Is that it? Is it ending?"

He glanced at me, but the gaze of those blue-green eyes couldn't hold mine for long; it danced away, over the dusty staircase and the chequered tiles below.

"Sort of," he said at last.

I wondered if he was trying to be diplomatic, to break a very great piece of news to me slowly, so that it would be less of a shock.

I just came out with it and asked, "Has it already ended?"

"Yes," he said.

"Well, that's–" I began to say how wonderful this news was, and it was, of course it was, but then I remembered that Grandmother was gone. She had not lived to see the day we had both longed for. There was a terrible irony in the fact that her death had come such a short time before it.

"When?" I asked instead. "When did it end?"

This time, when Tom didn't reply right away, I began to feel impatient. He was undoubtedly trying to be kind, but now I really wanted to know.

"When?" I repeated. "A week ago? A month?"

He made a strange face, a kind of grimace.

"Tell me," I persisted.

"Look," he said, "I'm not sure I should be the one to explain all this. Don't you have anyone else, anyone at all?"

I shook my head. "No. I've always lived here, with Grandmother. Nobody else." I hesitated and then I added, "You're the first person I've spoken to, apart from her."

"What, *ever*?" He seemed thunderstruck by this information.

"Yes." I didn't count people I had only seen, from a distance. "I don't know anyone else. You'll *have* to tell me."

"Oh shit." He put his head in his hands.

I had no idea what that meant – I'd never heard Grandmother use that word and I'd never come across it in books either – but it didn't sound like a good thing to say.

I put out a hand and touched his wrist. It was another first; reaching out and touching someone other than Grandmother. His skin was warm under my fingertips, and I felt the heat come into my face.

"Please," I said. "Tell me."

And he did.

chapter twenty-four

"Look," Tom began, "You're not joking, you've only ever spoken to your grandmother before?"

I nodded.

"So everything you know about – everything – is what she told you?"

"Yes."

"Well, um, what she told you is mostly true, I mean, *partly* true. There *was* a war and it *did* end in 1945. Only...that was a while ago."

"A while ago?"

Tom's gaze slid away from mine, as though he were looking for a way out.

"A long while ago," he said, eventually.

I opened my mouth to say that that couldn't possibly be true, because Grandmother wouldn't have lied to me. Not *that* much. Saying the War was coming to an end soon, when in fact it had just ended, wasn't such a big lie; she might have been breaking it to me gently. She wouldn't have lied to me for *years* though.

Then I thought about the trips I had made down to the edge of the estate. Everything was always so peaceful. I had seen no actual proof of what Grandmother had told me. Perhaps Tom was telling the truth. Perhaps Grandmother had lied to me.

Thinking like this was horrible. It was as though the truth I had always lived with was guttering like a candle flame, plunging me in and out of darkness.

It's only Tom's word, I said to myself. *I don't have to listen. I could tell him to go.*

I couldn't do that, though. Even if it were Tom who was lying, I had to know what his story was.

"How long ago?" I said, and even to my own ears there was a cold hardness in my voice.

There was a very long pause before Tom answered.

He said, "Seventy-two years." When I didn't reply, he sighed, and said, "It's 2017."

I found my tongue. "I don't believe you." I really didn't. It was too much to take in. I wasn't so much shocked as numb. What Tom was saying was utterly impossible.

"Why would I lie to you?" said Tom. He didn't sound annoyed. He sounded sort of sad.

"I don't know," I said with sudden anger. "I don't know you – I don't know anything about you. You might have a reason of your own." Something occurred to me. "You haven't gone to fight. You might not be an objector – you might be a deserter."

"That's ridiculous," said Tom. Now *he* sounded angry. I had virtually accused him of cowardice. "You can't be a deserter if there's no war to desert from."

"*You* say there's no war on," I pointed out. "Why should I believe you? If you were telling the truth, Grandmother would be lying, and she wouldn't do that."

Even as the words came out of my mouth I felt a chill stab of doubt that I tried to suppress.

"But she did, didn't she?" said Tom. "There's no war because it ended seventy-two years ago. And she knew that, because she'd been in the town, so you can't say she didn't. She deliberately lied to you." Then he seemed to relent; his voice softened. "Look, she probably had her reasons. Maybe she thought she was doing it for the best..."

I couldn't look at Tom any more. I put my head down, hugging myself, and let my hair fall forward over my face, hiding me.

"I don't believe you," I said again. I wanted that to be true. I wanted to keep on believing in Grandmother. And s*eventy-two years*? That was impossible. It was a whole lifetime. Thinking about it was terrifying; it made me feel as though I were crumbling into fragments inside. It went through my head that perhaps there was a Langlands ghost after all, and it was me. How else could time flow so differently in the outside world, so that it had passed the point where I was fixed by *seventy-two years*?

Tom was silent for a few moments. Then he said, "Look, I'll prove it to you. I've got my mum's car outside, that's how I got here. I'll take you into the town and I'll *show* you."

I was shaking my head before he had even finished speaking. All those years, wondering what it was like outside the Langlands estate – the people, the cities. I had longed to see the sea, that expanse of water they said was so great that you could faintly see the earth's curvature on it. Now suddenly I didn't want to go, not then, not as abruptly as that. At that instant, it felt as possible as hurling myself from the highest tower of Langlands house, knowing that I would be shattered to pieces when I hit the ground.

"No," I choked out.

"Well..." Tom hesitated. "If you don't want to come out, I guess I could go, and come back with something that'll prove it. I could get a newspaper and show you the date."

His words sent that chill doubt stabbing more deeply into me. *Why would he offer to bring proof if he's made all this up?*

I had a brief impulse to tell him to go away and not come back at all. I could try to forget the hurtful things he had said about Grandmother lying. Then I thought of my last trip down to the edge of the estate. If I sent Tom away, I would eventually be driven there again when supplies ran out completely, facing a long trek into an unknown situation. Whatever the truth, I had to know it. And if Tom said he could bring proof–

"When will you come back?" I said.

"Tomorrow. Or maybe the day after. It depends when I can get the car. It's not mine, it's Mum's. And I have to work, with Dad. I'll come back as soon as I can." He paused. "There's one thing. I don't want you shooting me by accident when I come back. Can you leave that thing somewhere?"

He nodded at the rifle.

"It's not safe," I told him. "Other people came before you did. Soldiers. The door was locked then, but they might come back."

"Soldiers?"

I nodded. "Two of them."

"That's not–" Tom stopped. He put up both hands and rubbed them over his face, massaging his temples with his fingertips. Then he looked directly at me, with a strange expression on his face; he was smiling but his brows were drawn together in a sort of frown.

He said, "I'm starting to think I'm off my head after all. You're living in 1945 and you say there's a war on. And *soldiers* have tried to get into the house. And you say you're a ghost. If I come back, are you even going to be here, or am I imagining all this?"

"I didn't say I was a ghost," I said, although the idea gave me a little ripple of unease. I had been thinking almost exactly that a few minutes before – that perhaps *I* was the Langlands ghost. It seemed no more bizarre an explanation than anything else I could think of.

"Yes, you did," said Tom. "When I came into the house. I said, *are you a ghost?* And you said, *Yes.*"

"Oh," I said. "I thought you said *Ghost*, not *a ghost*. That's my name."

105

"Your *name* is *Ghost*?"

Something in his tone stung me. "It's a nickname. My real name is Augusta."

"Augusta?" Tom put his head back and stared up at the ceiling, but he was smiling. When he looked back at me again, he said quite gravely, "Ghost is better."

Then he stood up. "I'll come as soon as I can. When I drive up, I'll sound the horn three times, okay? Then you'll know it's me, and not to shoot me."

I nodded. I watched as Tom descended the stairs. He crossed the hallway with its black and white tiles, and when he got to the front door he paused for a moment with his hand on it, and half turned, as though he had forgotten something. But then he changed his mind. He left without saying another word, and the door closed heavily behind him.

chapter twenty-five

2017, Tom McAllister said.

After he left, and the sound of the car engine had faded into the distance, I sat for a very long time on the staircase, with the rifle across my lap. I had a strange dull feeling inside me, a heaviness in my chest like the suffocation of burial.

Grandmother was dead. That was the one stark and terrible fact. Whatever the other truths, she would never explain them to me. I wanted to grieve for her, but the other things, the unanswered questions, seemed to stand in the way. Was it possible that she, whom I loved and trusted, had lied to me all my life, and that I was hearing the truth from someone I barely knew and had no particular reason to trust at all?

Seventy-two years.

It seemed impossible. I would consider the possibility that Tom McAllister was telling me the truth, and then I would stumble against that monstrous claim, the years that amounted to over seven decades, and I couldn't believe it. It *had* to be a lie.

I'd have known, I told myself.

How? said an insistent little voice at the back of my mind. *You've never left the estate.*

After a while, this internal argument overtook the miserable heaviness I felt. I wanted to believe Tom; I didn't want to believe Tom.

It seemed strange now to remember how I had hidden in the attic and watched him and his father arrive at Langlands. I had been so desperate to set eyes on a new face. Back then, just a few months ago, the idea that I could sit beside someone my own age and talk, that we would sit close enough to each other that I could put out a hand and touch him, that we would look into each other's eyes – that would have thrilled me. Now I looked back at that time and it was as though I was seeing it through the wrong end of a telescope. It seemed so far away that it might as well have happened to someone else. Losing Grandmother had taken the joy out of everything.

It wasn't just that. I didn't know whether to trust him or not. It was the same as with Grandmother – I didn't know whether I should be grieving for the person who had protected me all my life, or raging because she had deceived me all that time. I didn't know whether Tom was my saviour or the perpetrator of the most preposterous lie ever, with his own sinister intentions. And the worst of it was, I couldn't believe in both of them. It was one or the other: the dead woman or the living man. I swung from one extreme of belief to the other, and while the pendulum swung, I dared not give in to any emotion. I choked them all down, and felt as though I was suffocating myself.

I can't wait until he comes back. I have to know.

I thought there was perhaps an hour of proper daylight left, and I knew better than to think that I could go very far in that time. If I dared try for the town again, I would need to make a morning start. But I could think of one thing I could do.

Five minutes later, I was bundled up as warmly as possible, and running down the track. There was no need to pace myself, because I knew I would only be going as far as the gate. I ran, too, to try to outpace the feverish thoughts that kept running through my head.

When I got to the gate and that strange grille that lay across the road, there was still enough light to see what I was doing, but only just.

The map in the library had shown a building here, some kind of lodge or gatehouse, much smaller than the main house. As I came down the hill, it should be to the left. The map, like everything else at Langlands, was dated no later than 1945. I thought, in fact, that it had had *1938* marked on it. I had never seen any sign of a lodge there when I had been down here before, and I had assumed that the map was wrong; now I wondered whether it was the *time* that was wrong, not the map itself. If over seventy years had passed, anything might have changed.

There was nothing to see from the track. I stepped off it, onto a spongy surface of moss and rotting leaves. The desiccated remains of brambles looped across the ground and caught at the hem of my coat as I picked my way through them.

There's nothing here. No lodge. It was just a mistake.

But there was. I suppose someone had carted the masonry away years ago, because there really was nothing to see from the road – no walls, no chimney stack. There were still foundations though, hidden under the moss and brambles.

I felt rather than saw them first. I took a step forward and there was a solidity under my feet instead of the yielding earth. I probed with the toe of my boot and found a flat stone surface.

After that, it was easy to follow the line of the long-vanished walls. There was nothing to say what kind of building this had been any more, but it was exactly where the map had shown it. It had been here in the 1940s, and now it was gone. There was no way to tell exactly how many years had passed, but the forest told its own story. Tree trunks had thrust up through the spaces that had been rooms.

I stood there for a while, although the sun had gone and the shadows were crowding in. With the setting of the sun, the temperature dropped, and I could feel the bite of the cold even through my warm coat.

I thought about Grandmother, but it was like reaching out to touch her and finding only an empty space. I had known nothing true about her. What I remembered was all false.

She was right about one thing, anyway, I thought bitterly: *I can't trust anyone.*

I turned away, and trudged back to the house. It was fully dark before I got there; if there had been no moonlight I should have struggled to find my way at all. I went inside and locked the door behind me. Then I went to the kitchen to warm myself. There seemed no reason not to spend another night there. Who would care, after all, if all those other rooms, so cold and dark, stayed empty?

I lit a lamp, and by its yellow glare I made myself a cup of tea with the last of the sugar and no milk. I wasn't hungry at all. I sat at the pine table with the tea in front of me, listening to the tick of the kitchen clock. It was a while before I realised I was crying.

chapter twenty-six

Tom McAllister came back the next day. He drove up to the house and sounded the car horn three times as he had said he would.

I had wondered whether he really would come. The whole of the previous day seemed strangely unreal, as though I had awoken from a fever dream. If Tom had never come back, I might have thought that that was what it was.

Grandmother is dead.

That was the least difficult thing to swallow. I knew something terrible must have happened for her to desert me.

Grandmother lied to me.

I was still trying to comprehend that. Even after seeing the ruins of the lodge under the mulch in the forest, I couldn't completely believe it. A day was too short a time to unravel seventeen years.

I talked to Tom.

That was the strangest one of all. We had sat so close to each other that I could see the pulse in his neck, I could see the colour of his *eyelashes*. I liked the way he looked, when he had got over the shock of seeing me, the shades of expression that passed across his face.

That morning I was restless, waiting to see if he would come. He had said it might not be that day, it might be the one after, but I was impatient. So I braided up my long hair and occupied myself with the things that always needed doing at Langlands: I washed up my breakfast things and scrubbed the table and swept the kitchen floor. Then I put on an old greatcoat to keep out the cold and went outdoors to feed the chickens and fetch more wood for the stove. It was a clear, dry day and it was pleasant to be outdoors, but if I was honest with myself, I really wanted to listen for the sound of a car engine. And sure enough, late in the morning he came. I heard the car coming and watched from the stone porch until I could see it was Tom. Then I stepped out and went over to him.

"Ghost," he said, and grinned. The name seemed to amuse him. He had his arms full of things, but he wouldn't let me look at them right away. He said he wanted to put them down, so we went into the house and I took him down the passage to the kitchen.

"Do you want some tea?" I said, and then added, "I'm afraid there isn't any milk or sugar left."

"I could get you some more from the town if you like," said Tom, and then looked a little surprised at his own suggestion. He'd said he'd come back a third time, without thinking about it. He didn't want any tea, though. I couldn't say I blamed him; it tasted pretty horrible like that, plain and unsweetened.

Tom put the things on the table. There were magazines, three of them. I knew what they were because there were copies of *Country Life* in the library, all of them very thin and brittle and with nothing but black and white pictures in them. These had very shiny colourful covers.

There was also a box of chocolates, and the moment I read the words on the side, my mouth began to water. I had not realised I missed having sweet things so much. Or even the feeling of being full after eating. I was hungry a lot of the time since Grandmother disappeared, because I forgot to cook or because all the best ingredients had been used up. I looked at the chocolates longingly, hardly able to believe they were for me.

"I went down to the gate last night," I said. "You know, the one at the edge of the forest. There used to be a building down there, a lodge or something."

"Yeah?" said Tom.

"I found a map from 1938. There was a building there then. But now it's just a few stones in the ground."

I stretched out a hand and touched one of the magazines, feeling the smooth glossiness under my fingers, looking at the bright images on the cover rather than at Tom.

"A lot of time has gone by, hasn't it?" I said.

"Yeah."

I still couldn't look at him. There was something else I wanted to ask.

"Where will my Grandmother be?"

There was a pause as Tom thought about it. "I don't know," he said eventually. "They'd have taken her to hospital in an ambulance in case...well, in case there was anything they could do." He hesitated. "And I suppose then they'd put the body in the hospital morgue until they'd managed to contact her family to sort out the funeral."

"She didn't have any family," I said. "Except me."

"Well, someone should have come up here to check, I guess," said Tom.

"There were those two men," I pointed out. "The soldiers."

"It wouldn't be soldiers. The War is over, remember?"

"They *did* come," I said. I knew what I had seen.

Tom considered. "What did they look like, these soldiers?"

"They had black uniforms on."

"Were they kind of bulky, around here?"

I nodded.

"That was the police, not soldiers. They probably came to see if Mrs. McAndrew had any family living here."

"And I hid from them," I said, softly. It was disorienting, the feeling that Tom knew what I had seen better than I did. Suddenly, I wanted to sit down. I slid onto one of the kitchen chairs, put my elbows on the table and my head in my hands. I was used to having no experience of the outside world, but now my ignorance seemed to extend terrifyingly in all directions, a vast swamp full of traps and hazards. Was it true that the men I had seen were policemen, and not soldiers at all? Should I have opened the door to them? But if there was nothing to fear from them, why had Grandmother insisted that I keep myself hidden? Nothing made any sense at all.

Tom pulled out a chair and sat down across the table from me. "Look," he said, "Don't worry about that. You can sort that out later. It's not against the law to be out when the police come round."

"But what will they do?" I asked.

"With your grandmother? I don't know. I suppose they hang on to people with no family for a while, and then they bury them, or cremate them. I could try to find out, if you want."

"No," I said suddenly. "I don't want to know." I knew I sounded petulant, and probably later I *would* want to know, but right at that instant I really didn't. I didn't want to make decisions about burial; I wanted Grandmother here in front of me, alive and well. I wanted to grab her by the shoulders and demand that she tell me *why* she had done this to me – *why*? She had left me alone in a world I didn't understand, and I had no idea what she had done it for.

I was angry with myself, too. The more I thought about it, the more naive and unquestioning my own behaviour seemed to have been. The night the chimney had come down through the roof I had instantly thought that Langlands had been bombed; I had imagined aeroplanes droning over the roofs and turrets. I had thought of War, and yet Grandmother had not seemed afraid of that at all. She had been dead calm.

I very much doubt it, she had said when I blurted out that we had been bombed. Why had I not seen then that she was not afraid because she knew we had not been bombed, that it was altogether impossible?

Stupid, stupid, I berated myself. It made me wonder whether I was right to trust Tom, but then, what choice did I have? I knew nobody else in the whole world. And he had said he would bring proof that what he had told me was true.

I drew the magazines towards me. It wasn't difficult to pick out the dates printed on the covers. *March 2017*, said two of them, the third, *February 2017*. I could not imagine how anyone could create such things just to support a lie. These had to be real.

The first I opened was called *National Geographic*, and it was full of the most beautiful photographs I had ever seen, all of them in colour. They were so vivid that they seemed more like the loveliest of the paintings in Langlands House than photographs.

I looked at a series of pictures of a great city, and then some of a kind of sleek and gleaming machine whose purpose I could only guess at. It seemed to me that life in this world was as different from life at Langlands as the coloured photographs were from the sepia ones in the house. Nearly everything in Langlands had the soft shades of age. The woodwork was worn, the carpets and curtains were faded, the rooms we rarely frequented were covered with a fine layer of grey dust. Even the pages of the books in the library were yellowing.

Outside, though, the people who thronged the streets wore a dazzling rainbow of different colours, some of them so bright that they seemed to glow. Everything was lit very brightly. Streets, cars, buildings – from all of them light streamed out in such prodigious amounts that I wondered how the people were not blinded by it. And how did any of them ever sleep? It seemed as though night had been banished completely out there. It was also plainly impossible that a war should be going on in such places. How could anyone hide from bombs dropped from the air, when every building revealed its existence with such brilliant lights?

I finished looking at the *National Geographic* with a strange hard feeling like a knot in the centre of my chest.

Lies. All lies.

Somehow the lie about the War seemed the worst of all. I had dreamed of men wading through mud, tangled in barbed wire, mown down by gunfire; I had imagined gas and blood and screaming. But those things were history; they had long since ceased to be. I felt as though Grandmother had tried to make me behave myself by pretending to have some terrible disease. It was not right to say such things unless they were true.

I opened the second magazine, which was full of pictures of houses with people in them. These were the insides of those fantastical light-filled buildings I had seen in the *National Geographic* photographs. The rooms were decorated in bold, jewel-like colours. Some were puzzlingly stark and plain, but one house was clearly an old one, made beautiful with all the materials and techniques that the modern world could offer. On the mantelpiece at the back of the sitting room were two silver pheasants like the ones that faced each other on top of the cupboard in Langlands' hallway. I stared at that photograph for a while. It was strange seeing something so familiar in such a setting, but it proved the link between my life here and the life outside. The things in the magazine were not imaginary, they were *real*.

"What's that?" I asked Tom McAllister when I came to a series of photographs of kitchens filled with unfamiliar things.

He came around to my side of the table and I was conscious of his nearness as he leaned over my shoulder to look. I could hear him draw breath.

"It's a dishwasher," he said. "You stack the dishes and all the rest in it, and it washes them."

"And that?"

"That's a washing machine. For clothes."

"There's two of them."

"The other one's probably a dryer – for drying them."

"And that?"

"That's a microwave." He must have realised that meant nothing to me because he added, "You cook food in it."

"How? There's nowhere to light a fire."

"With electromagnetic waves." He glanced at me. "That doesn't mean anything, does it?"

Irrationally, I found myself becoming angry. Tom was just trying to be helpful, I could see that, but–

"You think I'm stupid," I said.

"No," he said, far too quickly. "Of course not. If you've never seen one before, how can you know?"

"Is it unusual?" I asked, pointing at the object. "Is it new, I mean? Or does everyone know about it?"

"It's not really that new," he said. "Pretty much everyone has one of those."

I stared at the pictures and it occurred to me that not only should Grandmother have *told* me about these things, she should have *got* some of them. *A machine for washing dishes! I need not have hand pumped water and heated it on the range every time we had to wash up. We could have had a machine to wash all our clothes and dry them too, instead of doing it all by hand.*

I was becoming too angry; I was afraid I would lose control. I closed the magazine with its alluring pictures and pushed it away from me.

I shouldn't have picked up the third magazine. I could have told Tom I was tired, I'd read it later. But there was a certain sort of bitter recklessness welling up inside me now. I wanted

117

to know the full extent of it, how very far out of step with the world I was, how deeply Grandmother had betrayed me.

This magazine wasn't cities or houses. It was all people. Women and girls. They were wearing coats, dresses, even trousers. I saw a photograph of a girl about my own age wearing tight-fitting trousers, made of the same blue cotton twill as the ones Tom McAllister was wearing, and a shirt that seemed to be made of tiny overlapping silver scales. There were shirts that seemed to show an alarming amount of shoulder, and dresses that skimmed the thighs. One set of photographs showed nothing but older women, dressed in clothes that were more colourful and more revealing than anything I had ever put on. All of them had beautiful, flawless faces and every single one of them, without exception, had short hair – short, that is, in comparison to mine. Some – shockingly – had hair cut as short as Tom's, but none of them had hair that came lower than their shoulder blades. None of them had hair like mine, that cascaded over my shoulders and down past my waist and hips so that I seemed to be forever swimming upstream in a great gush of it. I saw myself suddenly, in Tom McAllister's eyes; I saw that where I wished to be interesting or at least normal I was ludicrous, and at last I lost control.

chapter twenty-seven

Tom

When it happens, it catches me unawares. She's sitting there, leafing through the last of the magazines, when suddenly she just goes berserk. Her hands tighten on the pages until she is holding handfuls of scrunched-up paper in her fists, and then she's ripping at the magazine, trying to tear it in half. That doesn't work, so she starts pulling out the pages. All the time she's making these terrible sounds, sobs that are almost screams.

I'm still standing right by her, but I don't think she even remembers I'm there. She rips the magazine to shreds and then she sweeps it off the table, taking her tea cup and saucer with it. The teapot is the next to go, and that smashes on the flagstones. There's a wooden box full of cutlery on the table and when that hits the floor there's a massive crash as all the knives and forks and spoons go everywhere.

It's when she reaches out for the tea canister that I come to my senses. She's already run out of sugar. If she throws that around she'll be drinking nothing but hot water. I reach over and pick it up myself.

Then she puts her head on her arms and cries.

I put a hand on her shoulder, very carefully. At first, I don't think she's even noticed, but then she sits up a little and leans against me and cries until she's worn herself out.

At least, I think she's worn herself out. She stops crying and wipes her eyes, and then she gets up from her chair, moving away from me, down to the other end of the kitchen, where there's a kind of wooden dresser with plates stacked on it. I think for one moment that she's going to start throwing the crockery around too, but she opens one of the drawers instead. When I see what she takes out of it, I'm so shocked my jaw drops.

"Don't," I say, and take a couple of steps forward, but then I stop because she's holding the scissors up. They look huge in her hand. These aren't wee scissors for cutting paper, they're great big shears with sharp points to the blades.

"Put those down, Ghost," I say, feeling a bit sick thinking what she might do. "Don't hurt yourself. It's not worth it."

She looks at me, calm as anything. Then she grabs the thick plait of hair hanging over one shoulder, opens the blades of the scissors and hacks into it.

"Don't do that," I say, horrified.

"Why not?" she says. "Nobody has hair like this anymore."

"I know, but..."

I stare at her. It's too late. She's halfway through it. She keeps going, struggling a bit because the plait is so thick it's hard to get the blades of the scissors around it. Then she's through it, and the whole lot slides to the floor like a snake. She's standing there with the scissors in her hand, breathing hard like she's been running.

She puts down the scissors on the table and combs out her hair with her fingers. It's still long, below her shoulders, but the ends are all uneven where she's hacked at them.

"You can close your mouth, Tom," she says, and I realise it's hanging open.

She looks down at the jagged ends for a moment or two and then she says, "I can't finish it myself. You'll have to do it."

"What?" I say. "I don't know how to."

"You have to do a better job than I would. I can't see the ends properly to do it, not at the back."

She brings me the scissors and holds them out. "Go on."

If the day was getting strange, now it's completely unreal. I have a girl asking me to cut her hair for her with kitchen scissors. I can't imagine any other girl I've met asking me to do that.

I take the scissors, reluctantly.

"Turn round, then," I say, and she turns her back to me.

I look at her hair. There's still a lot of it despite what she chopped off. I touch it gently, trying to smooth the ends so that everything lies flat before I cut it.

"I've never cut hair before," I say to her.

"Neither had I," she says.

She waits. The ends of her hair look as though someone cut it with garden shears. It'd be hard to make it any worse. I line up the blades of the scissors and make the first cut, gently.

She moves slightly.

"Stay still," I tell her. I go along the bottom of the hair, doing my best to cut in a straight line. This is probably all wrong. A real hairdresser would do that thing where they hold the ends in their fingers and cut along them, but I don't know how to do that.

I go along the hair once, and then I go back and try to trim any uneven bits. I lean back and look at my work. Not as bad as I thought it would be. I put down the scissors, and then I put my fingers into her hair and comb it gently. My fingertips graze the back of her neck and she shivers. And that is when I think about kissing her.

Suddenly I'm clumsy and my hands snag in her hair, which has to hurt.

"Sorry," I say awkwardly. I free my fingers carefully. "I think it's finished."

She turns to face me, putting up her hands and running them through her hair.

"It feels light," she says.

I don't say anything. With her shorter hair she looks more like a normal girl, less like the ghost of Langlands. She looks like a normal, very pretty girl.

She turns her head from side to side, feeling the hair move.

"It looks good," I say eventually.

"It's better," she says. For the first time I see a smile on her face. Then it's gone, as quickly as it came. Her face is serious again. "I'm sorry," she says. "About just now. I just...I lost my temper."

I shrug. "No harm done – except your teapot and cup."

She thinks about that. "I'll have to look and see if we have another pot."

"You could just get teabags," I tell her. "If it's only you you're making it for, you might as well."

"Will you get me some, Tom? As well as the sugar?"

I'd forgotten about that. "Yeah," I say.

"When will you come back?"

"I don't know. I can't always get the car. It's not mine, it's Mum's."

As it happens, I've got a back-up, but I don't mention that. I want to think a bit first, about that feeling of wanting to kiss her. I'm thinking it might be wrong to do that, even if she wanted me to, kind of like stealing something from someone without them even knowing. Does she even understand what her grandmother has done to her? I think about her losing it, smashing things in the kitchen. That was after looking at a few magazines. What about when she gets outside and sees the real world? She's going to need help, not kisses, and maybe more help than one person can give.

I tell Ghost I'll try to come back some time in the next few days, keeping it vague. I guess she gets the message, because she comes with me to the front door of the house and just as I am about to get in the car she says, "Tom, I'm sorry I lost my temper. You will come back, won't you?"

I nod. "Of course I will."

As I drive off, I look back, and she's standing there by the stone porch, with the new shorter hair blowing back in the wind, watching me go.

And I think: *Will I?*

chapter twenty-eight

Ghost

The next day, Tom didn't come, nor the one after that. I told myself that I couldn't really *expect* him to come back so soon. He had his own life, one I could hardly begin to imagine. But there was a persistent worry at the back of my mind that he wouldn't *ever* come back again, because of what had happened in the kitchen. I had torn the magazines he gave me to shreds right in front of him. I'd screamed like a banshee. What he thought of having to help me cut my hair I couldn't imagine, but I had no regrets about *that*.

And then there was the question of what I thought about Tom. What should I believe about him – what should I feel?

After he had gone, and I had gone back to the kitchen, I saw the chocolates he had brought me. I'd forgotten about them because I had been focussing on the magazines; I hadn't even thanked him. I opened the box, and they were all set out in a little tray. I meant to try one and save the rest for later, but once I had put the first into my mouth and felt the explosion of sweetness on my tongue, I realised how badly I missed having sugar. I couldn't stop myself after that. I ate all but two, and the only reason I left those was that I was beginning to feel queasy. After that I felt guilty, and somehow uneasy, wondering whether everything in Tom's world was as irresistible as that, whether it would drag me into itself like a craving for laudanum. In spite of that, perhaps because of it, I longed to see him again.

Being alone at Langlands was harder now than it had been before. Every part of the house was haunted by the invisible presence of Grandmother, but now I did not know whether to mourn her or rage at her. I would go into a room to find something I wanted and see something of hers: a book that would never be read to the end or a set of glass jars that would never hold the jam they were intended for. A terrible sense of loss would wash over me, and then I would remember the shock of hearing Tom say *seventy-two years* and grief would dissolve into a hard, bitter anger that felt as though it would poison me. The worst of it was, I didn't know *why* Grandmother had done this to me. Grandmother was gone; much as I longed to seize her by the lapels of her coat and shake the truth out of her, I was never, ever going to be able to do that. She had made me a stranger to the rest of the world, and perhaps I would never know why. And yet there had to be a reason. What was she so afraid of? What did she think would happen if I came into contact with the outside world?

There were times when that world I had glimpsed in the magazines Tom had showed me seemed unreal. Langlands was there, just as it had always been, full of familiar things and requiring me to carry out the same tasks I always had: chopping wood, heating water to wash clothes. Believing in Tom's world of brilliantly-lit cities and labour-saving domestic machines while continuing to live at Langlands was like trying to believe in Heaven while going through the grind of daily life. It was very hard not to believe in what was in front of me instead.

By the third day, I had made up my mind that Tom would never return to Langlands. It was now a matter of when the lack of supplies would drive me out by myself, to take my chances in the outside world. When I heard the pre-arranged signal of three blasts on the car horn and came out of the house to find Tom getting out of the car, I was so pleased to see him that I *ran* to him across the gravel, and he was either pleased too or taken unawares because he opened his arms and I ran into them.

I had thought it was bad doing without sugar; it was far worse doing without human company. I was so thrilled to see Tom that I didn't think about the rightness or wrongness of embracing him. I just did it. He folded his arms around me and I leaned in to him, resting my head against his shoulder. He smelled good; he had some kind of cologne on and it smelled as intoxicating as the chocolates had tasted.

Tom held me as long as I clung to him, but there was a kind of stillness about him; I felt it and assumed he was stunned by my boldness. Perhaps he was actually shocked. I made myself pull away.

"I'm sorry," I said, trying to smile at him to show it wasn't such a big thing. "I was just so pleased to see you. I thought maybe you weren't coming back."

Did some shadow of an expression flicker across his face when I said that? I wasn't sure. Then he gave a half-smile.

"I brought sugar and tea. And this."

He reached into the car for something and held it out to me.

"What's that?"

"It's a drink. No, don't shake it."

I held the thing doubtfully. The brightly-coloured metal container was very cold in my hand. I thought it looked strange, more like a can of paint or Brasso than something you would drink.

Tom had brought other things too: grapes, a loaf of bread, a carton of milk. He carried everything into the house and through to the kitchen, where he set it all down on the table.

I watched him doing this, turning the metal can over in my hands.

"Here," he said. "You open it like this."

He handed it back to me.

"Should I put it in a glass?"

He shrugged. "Just drink it out of the can." He watched me, and then he laughed. It was the first time he had done that, and it was a good sound. I smiled back, tentatively.

"It's strange."

"It's fizzy," he said. "Don't drink it too fast."

There was no danger of that. I thought the drink was interesting but I couldn't make up my mind whether I actually *liked* it or not.

Tom had a can of it too, so I supposed he *did* like it. He began to wander around the kitchen with it in his hand, looking at everything: the dresser with the plates, the range, the pans hanging on the wall. I couldn't help it, I followed him with my eyes. He looked at everything except me.

Then he said, "I nearly didn't come back."

"Oh." I could think of nothing else to say. A moment before, I had been feeling thrilled that he had come back again; now I was filled with a cold feeling of disappointment. He hadn't wanted to.

He turned to face me and now he did look me in the eyes, but his expression was deadly serious.

"Look, Ghost, I'm not sure I'm doing the right thing. I'm not the best person..." He sighed. "You don't know what it's going to be like when it gets out, you know, that you've been living up here for years thinking it's World War Two. You probably won't even be able to stay here."

"Why not?" I demanded, with more indignation than I felt. The cold feeling was worse; it was a terrible numbing dread unfurling inside me. "This is my home."

"Because people are going to be interested. *Too* interested.

127

And even without *them*, there are all sorts of official people who are going to want to get involved. Your grandmother keeping you here like that, not letting you go to school, that was probably child abuse or something. They'll want to investigate. You need someone better than me to see you through all that. I'm not even sure I *can*. I mean, I'm not a relative. You probably ought to be with your family, if you have any anywhere."

"I don't have any," I said. "And even if I do have relatives somewhere, I don't want to go and live with them. I live *here*. At Langlands."

"You don't understand. When people find out, you won't be left in peace."

"Well, why do we have to tell anyone?" I said.

Tom gaped at me.

"Because...you can't stay here on your own forever."

"Why not?" I was feeling nettled now. "I don't know anything about your electromagnetic cooking machines, but I know how to run everything here at Langlands."

"Yes, but you can't grow everything yourself. You'd need things from the town, and if you go there..." His voice tailed off.

"They'd notice me, wouldn't they, because of these stupid clothes?"

Tom sighed again. "They do...stick out."

I knew he was right, and I'd practically forced him to say it, but still I felt stung.

"Look, you could help me with that. You could get me some different clothes, so I look the same as everyone else." He didn't say anything to that, so I pursued the point. "Please, Tom. *Please*."

He looked at me and I saw the ghost of a smile. "Yeah, I can just see myself going into Primark and buying girls' clothes." Then he shook his head. "I have to think about this, Ghost."

128

I remembered Grandmother talking about keeping me here at Langlands, whether she had done the right thing or not.

In two months' time you will be eighteen years old and no longer a child in anyone's eyes. A great many things will change then, Augusta, she had told me.

"Tom, you said they might think Grandmother not sending me to school was child abuse. Well, I'm eighteen in April. I'm not a child any more. So how can it matter?"

Tom was silent for a time after that but he looked unhappy.

"I'll be an adult," I said. "And then I can live here on my own if I like, can't I?" I looked at him pleadingly. "You just have to keep it secret until then. It's not even two months. *Please*."

And Tom nodded.

chapter twenty-nine

Tom

Bad news. I know this is bad news even while I'm nodding and Ghost is saying *Thank you, Tom, thank you so much.*

She does have a point, I guess. She *is* nearly eighteen. There's no point anyone screaming about the fact she isn't at school. All that'll happen if the whole thing gets out is that Ghost's life won't be her own any more.

It's not just about keeping my mouth shut though. She's going to need things – sugar, bread, milk, I don't know what else. That means borrowing Mum's car, and she's bound to ask questions. It's not going to end there, either. There's nothing magic about a birthday. Ghost is not suddenly going to be able to cope with twenty-first century life. She'd never even seen a can of Irn Bru before today. She's never seen a microwave. Is it even possible for someone to catch up on seventy-two years they've missed? I don't know.

I know this, though. I want to help her. Partly to spite the old lady, because whatever her reasons, she's done something bad here; she's fucked up someone's life. Mainly though, I'm going to do it for *her*. For Ghost.

I have to admire her. It's not long since she found out everything she's been told her entire life is a pack of lies, and it hasn't crushed her. And she had guts, coming down the stairs like that, that afternoon, thinking she was going to hold off soldiers with an ancient rifle.

It's more than that, though. She isn't like anyone I've ever known. Even with the shorter hair, she's different, different in a way that makes me want to keep on looking at her. That moment when I thought about kissing her comes back into my mind, more often than it should, considering that I've already told myself I'm not going to do it. And now she's asking me to do something for her, I want to say yes. Even if it *is* probably a bad idea.

Anyway, I promise to keep her secret, and then she says, "But what about the clothes, Tom? Will you help me get them?"

I think about that. "It depends what you want, Ghost. Buying sugar and tea, stuff like that, that's no problem, but I don't have enough to buy a whole new wardrobe. I'm supposed to be saving for when I go to university."

She looks at me calmly and says, "I have money."

"You do?"

"Well, Grandmother does. I mean, she did. I know where she keeps it."

I stare at her. I open my mouth to tell her that she really shouldn't be telling me this and that she *definitely* shouldn't tell it to anyone else who turns up at Langlands, but then it occurs to me that maybe she means a load of old coins like that 1944 penny I found on the windowsill.

"Okay," I say cautiously. "Maybe you should show me."

"Come with me," she says.

We go back down the passage to the hallway with the stuffed stag and then up the stairs to the landing where that room is, the one Dad and I worked on in the autumn. We go right past that, to a room I've never been into before, at the far end of the corridor.

Ghost grabs the door handle, and from the way she turns it, I guess that she thinks it may be locked. It isn't, though; it opens easily. The room inside is a bedroom, and you can tell right away whose it is – or was. It's an *old lady* room. There's even a trace of some kind of old lady perfume on the air, something a bit sweet and powdery.

It's full of stuff, but it's very neat and tidy. The bed has been made and there are cushions on it. The books in the little bookcase are lined up, with none of them sticking out or laid on the top. There are a lot of ornaments, china and glass ones, and all of them are carefully spaced along the shelves and the mantelpiece. Even the dressing gown on the back of the door is on a hanger.

Ghost goes straight for a desk under the window and starts pulling out drawers. There's a lot of paper in there, and she quickly loses patience and starts pulling it all out and dumping it on top of the desk. When it's all out she starts going through it. Pieces of paper flutter to the floor but she doesn't seem to care. Why should she? Old Mrs. McAndrew isn't going to come home and complain about the mess.

Whatever she's looking for, it isn't there, so next she tries the dressing table, and after that the bedside cabinet. There, she finally finds what she's after. She shows it to me. A notebook.

Ghost leafs through it until she finds what she's looking for. "Look."

There's a number written down there, in neat old lady handwriting.

"Is that her PIN number?" I say, feeling uncomfortable.

But Ghost says, "What's a PIN number?"

"Never mind."

"It's for the safe," she tells me.

We go downstairs again, and down a corridor I've never used before. The room we go into is a library: every bit of wall space is covered with glass-fronted bookshelves. All the books look ancient. There's a huge globe on a wooden stand and a cabinet in the middle of the room with big drawers that might be used to store maps. There are green velvet curtains at the windows and also on a narrow bit of wall between two of the bookcases, making a backdrop for a white marble statue. You'd think it was for decoration, but Ghost pulls it to one side and there's the safe.

"Grandmother never let me look in it," she says. "She had to write the combination down because she forgot things, but I could never get the book because she kept it in her room. But now..."

Now she's dead.

It occurs to me that if Ghost's never looked in there, there may not be anything in it at all, or at least, nothing valuable. But she's working her way through the combination and opening the safe, and then I see that I'm wrong.

There's quite a lot of stuff in there that she probably ought to go through, now that Langlands and everything in it has passed into her keeping: documents, bundles of letters, some flat boxes that look as though they might contain jewellery. There are also banknotes. Lots and lots of them. I'd say there are thousands of pounds in there.

chapter thirty

Ghost

Tom didn't seem very pleased when I opened the safe and showed him the money.

I had never seen any of it close up before; Grandmother wouldn't let me. I was fascinated to look at the notes. They all had the head of a man on them. At first, I thought it must be King George, which gave me a moment of confusion: in 2017 King George must be long dead, so how could he be on these crisp and new-looking bank notes? Then I saw that it was not the King at all, but a face I recognised from the frontispiece of one of the library's books: Sir Walter Scott.

The notes were of several different colours and there were a lot of them, mostly fastened into thick bundles. I had no idea however whether this represented a little money or a lot. I took one of the bundles out of the safe and showed it to Tom: the notes were a kind of lavender shade and had *20* printed on them.

He had a look on his face that I couldn't interpret – a kind of stillness. He looked the way he had felt to me when I ran into his arms – as though he didn't know how to feel.

"Is this good?" I asked him. "Is this a lot of money?"

Tom let out a long breath. "Yes, it's a lot of money, Ghost." He took the bundle carefully from my hands and turned it over. Then he put it back inside the safe and turned to look at me.

"Look," he said eventually, "This is too much. This is a fortune. I don't feel right about taking any of it."

"Why not?" I asked. "It was Grandmother's money, but it's mine now. If I say you can take some of it to buy things, I don't see why you can't."

"Yes, but...when you said you had money I thought you meant, I don't know, a jam jar with fifty quid in it, a week's food money or something."

"I don't see what difference it makes how much it is."

"Well, if your Grandmother had any other relatives, they might have a claim on some of it. The police are probably trying to trace them right now. How's it going to look if someone you hardly know has helped himself to some of it?"

That hurt. Maybe I did hardly know Tom; it was only months since I'd first set eyes on him, after all. But since Grandmother was gone, I knew him better than I knew anyone else in the whole world. I looked down at my hands, at the fingers tightening around each other.

"Grandmother didn't have any other relatives," I said in a low voice. "And even if she did, why would she leave any of her money to them?"

"I don't know, but I don't think you can just help yourself to everything. I think the will has to be read."

That was something I knew about. A lot of the novels in the library featured wills and their contents – old people hinting at what was in them or threatening to change them in favour of this or that person.

"Well, maybe the will is in here too," I pointed out. "All her other important things are in here. She kept her best jewellery in it."

Tom hung back, but I began to pull things out of the safe, piling them on the library floor. Before I was halfway through, I knew that there was a lot more here than money. There were things that I would need to examine. Apart from Grandmother's jewels in their little boxes with the gilded trim, and the fat bundles of bank notes, there were documents of various kinds: certificates with ornately engraved borders, official-looking letters, a single dark red passport with a gold coat of arms on the cover.

Grandmother's will was easily picked out, as it was bound in a thin cover with *Last will and testament* printed on the front. I opened it and read: *This will is made by me Rose Elspeth McAndrew born fifteenth of July 1935...*

I was conscious of Tom beside me, reading over my shoulder.

1935. So in 1945 she would have been just ten years old. It chilled me, reading that. I leafed through the few pages to the end of the will and there was her signature and the date the will had been made out, which was in 1999. This made it impossible that Grandmother herself could have been suffering under some kind of delusion that we were living in 1945. She absolutely *knew* the truth; she had signed her name to it. There were two other names, too, of people who had signed as witnesses. I did not recognise either of them, though the addresses belonged to the town. One of them was Fraser MacFarlane, the occupation given as solicitor, and the other was George Robertson, general practitioner.

The will, as I could quickly tell in spite of the formal legal language, left everything to me. If I died before Grandmother, or within 30 days of her death, all of it would go to what appeared to be a charitable organisation of some kind. I didn't recognise the name. There was no mention of any other relative. It was all mine. I was the mistress of an estate with a grand but dilapidated house, and in it, some old-fashioned jewellery and a lot of money in cash.

I didn't feel any joy at this knowledge. The grandmother I thought I knew had been drifting away from me since long before she drove into the town and failed to return; now I felt as though my own self was disintegrating too. *My granddaughter*

136

Augusta Elspeth McAndrew, the will said. That was me. Fraser MacFarlane and George Robertson knew that was me, too, in spite of everything Grandmother had drummed into me over the years about not letting anyone know of my existence. It was as though there were two of us: the Augusta who appeared in this formal document dated 1999, and the Augusta who had grown up believing it was 1945. Except the Augusta of 1999 really was a ghost, a nothing; she had no reality except on paper.

I closed the folder.

Tom said, softly, "You're right. It *is* yours, all of it."

"I know," I said, and we looked at each other. Tom was close to me, so close that I felt strangely nervous. "Share it with me," I said impulsively.

Tom's eyes widened. "I can't."

"Why not?"

"You don't know me," he said. "You can't share this with someone you've only just met. I might be..."

"Evil?" I said, holding his gaze. "Greedy, cruel?"

"No," said Tom levelly. "I'm not evil or greedy or cruel. But you don't know me, not properly."

"I don't know anyone else," I pointed out. "And I need to look like other people if I go out. You said yourself, looking like this I'd stick out. Just take some of it and get me the right things. Please. Just help me look like everyone else."

"You're never going to look like everyone else," said Tom suddenly.

I felt a brief moment of hurt at that. I thought he was saying that it was hopeless, that I was so out of step with his world, so clueless and strange and unable to adapt that I would never pass for one of the outside people, whatever I did and whatever I wore. It felt like a judgement falling. And then I discovered that that was not what he had meant, although certainly I had a long way to go before I understood how things were done in

2017, because he put his arms around me, pulled me close to him and kissed me.

It was unexpected and strange and wonderful. He bent his head and his lips touched mine, almost experimentally, and then his mouth was moving over mine caressingly, as though he wanted to drink the hot liquid feeling that seemed to be running through every part of me.

I was afraid that my hesitant attempts to kiss him back were clumsy, and I knew that I should have stopped him; Grandmother would have expected me to slap his face for insulting me. But I didn't want him to stop what he was doing. It didn't feel wrong. It felt – perfectly right.

It was Tom who broke the kiss. He drew away from me a little and we looked at each other. I could feel my heart thumping; the breath seemed to shiver in my throat.

"I'm–" began Tom, and I shook my head.

Don't say it.

I knew he was going to say that he was sorry for kissing me. But I wasn't sorry, not then, nor afterwards.

chapter thirty-one

We went through the rest of the contents of the safe after that. At first, we busied ourselves sorting through the papers, because it was easier than talking about what had just happened. If Tom regretted kissing me, I didn't want to hear him say so, and I couldn't think of anything to say about it at all. After a while, though, looking at all the things became so engrossing that both us forgot to be self-conscious.

"Look at this," said Tom, holding out a photograph. It was black-and-white, so old that the paper was yellowing. The subject was a little girl dressed in a short frock, ankle socks and patent leather shoes. She was squinting a little in the sunshine, and behind her was Langlands House; the stone porch was unmistakeable. *Me?* I wondered briefly. Then I turned the photograph over and saw the words *Rose, aged six* written on the back in pencil.

"That would be 1941," I said, staring at Grandmother's younger self.

"The War really was on then," said Tom.

That made me feel a little strange. So what Grandmother had told *me* had been true for *her*. She had been here at Langlands during the War. I was still staring at the photograph when Tom said, "There's one of you."

"There can't be," I told him. "Nobody's ever taken a photograph of me."

I took the photograph from him. Like the other one, it was black-and-white, the background plain, so you couldn't tell where it was taken. For a moment, I thought the girl in the picture really *was* me, the likeness was so strong. But I had no dress like the one the girl had on: made from a checked fabric, full-skirted and drawn in at the waist. I didn't wear my hair like that, either – the girl's hair was about the same length as mine now that it had been cut, but hers was neatly drawn back from her forehead, whereas I let mine frame my face. The longer I looked, the more I saw subtle differences in our faces: hers was a little wider than mine, her lips a little thinner. But still, the similarity between us was astonishing.

I turned the photograph over. *Rose, 1952*, I read, in the same pencilled handwriting. There was a stamp, too, from a photographer in the town.

Rose? I flipped the photograph over again and stared at it.

"It's not me, it's Grandmother," I said.

"No way," said Tom, looking over my shoulder.

"It is," I said. "It says so, on the back." I found it hard to believe too; I could only remember Grandmother as an old woman. In the photograph, she was about the same age as me. I wondered what had happened between then and now to make her do the things she had done – to spin that enormous lie. She looked happy and relaxed in the picture.

I wondered whether there were any photographs of my parents in amongst the heaps of papers. I knelt and began to sort through them, pushing aside bound documents and bundles of letters in my eagerness for more pictures. I found a large photograph of Grandmother on her wedding day, holding onto my grandfather's arm. She had on a simple white dress of heavy satin, and a veil held in place by a little diadem of sparkling stones. The veil was thrown back from her face and she was smiling. I looked from her to my grandfather with interest. I had never met my grandfather Angus McAndrew, who had died long before I was born. Would it have made any difference if he hadn't died, I wondered? It made me feel a little light-headed, thinking of all the different people Grandmother must have known, all the different relationships and influences which might have led to her doing what she did. To me, Grandfather looked kind but serious. But had he been strict, or even harsh? Had the obsession with 1945 come from him, or sprung up because he had gone? I gazed at his face for a long time, but Grandfather told me nothing.

I found three other photographs, which seemed to go together; they were all of a child, a little girl, and all of them were in colour. The colour wasn't as good as in the pictures in the magazines Tom had brought me; it had an oddly faded look. The girl was sitting in two of the photographs, standing in one of them, always in the corner of a room. *A child's room*, I guessed, looking at the patterned wallpaper and the tiny furniture – I had never had anything like that at Langlands. She wore a red pinafore dress with a cream-coloured blouse underneath it, and her chubby little legs were encased in ribbed stockings. Her hair was the same colour as mine but she had Grandmother's blue eyes. I turned over all three of the photographs; on the backs of two of them there was nothing written at all, but on the other one was inscribed: *Elspeth*.

"My mother," I said, amazed. It was the first time I had ever seen any picture of her. I felt a strange tightness in my throat, as though tears were going to come, but I fought the feeling down. I wanted to see whether there were any other photographs of her, taken when she was grown up – I wanted to see her as she was when she became my mother, not just as a child. I pawed through the documents and bundles of papers, spreading them out across the library floor until Tom and I were stranded on an island within a vast sea of paper, but I did not find a single additional photograph.

I did find my grandmother's birth certificate, and her marriage certificate, and a death certificate for Angus McAndrew, dated 1981. There was a dogeared medical card with Grandmother's name on it too. I also found a single gold-coloured key, shiny and quite new-looking compared to the ones on the bunch Grandmother had, but with nothing to identify it; another small mystery. I found no official documents for my mother, and nothing about me: no birth certificate, no health records. As far as the contents of the safe were concerned, I existed as the beneficiary of Grandmother's will, and otherwise not at all.

Langlands is a big house, I reminded myself, picturing all the cupboards and drawers, the bureaux and shelves, the trunks and cartons in the attic. There were hundreds, probably thousands of places where Grandmother could have stored things. I could search for years and even if I never found another photograph or document, it didn't mean there wasn't anything there, just that Grandmother had hidden it so well that I hadn't been able to find it. All the same, I had the nagging feeling that if there had been anything, it would have been here. To store all this money – a fortune, Tom had said – she must have thought it was the safest place in the house.

I picked up one of the photographs of my mother again and gazed at it, trying to imagine the adult features that would have grown out of the chubby child's face. It was horrible, feeling that she was just out of reach. It was one thing to grow up knowing that I had lost her, but it was quite another to feel that I was so close to seeing her, and yet somehow, she had slipped away. Why wasn't there more of her here, amongst the heaped papers? There wasn't even a certificate of her death.

A thought occurred to me then, an idea so surprising that for several moments I sat there on the library floor with the papers heaped up around me, not saying anything at all. Grandmother

142

had lied to me about the year, about the War, about the dangers outside Langlands. Perhaps she had lied to me about my mother, too.

I thought: *Maybe she isn't dead.*

chapter thirty-two

When Tom left that afternoon, I didn't try to make him stay longer. That may seem strange, because there was nothing I could think of that could be better than being with him, telling him things and watching him talk when he replied, and – maybe – being kissed by him again. But still, I wanted to be on my own for a while, to think. I couldn't tell him yet about my idea that my mother might still be alive. I didn't want to hear him ask the obvious questions, the biggest one being: *if she isn't dead, where is she?* She seemed more real to me than she ever had before, now that I had seen the pictures of her, and I wasn't ready to let her slip away from me again, not yet.

Tom took some of the banknotes with him in the end. I could see that the idea made him uneasy, but neither of us could think of an alternative. I couldn't go out into his world in clothes that were seventy years out of date, and I couldn't ask him to spend money he didn't have on me.

After he had gone, I went back to the library, where the safe still stood open, the contents spread out over the floorboards. I gathered it all up and packed it back into the safe: the documents and certificates, Grandmother's passport, the bundles of money. As I slotted them back into careful piles, I thought about the day Tom had come back to Langlands and I had stood on the stairs with the rifle clutched in my trembling hands, prepared to defend the house and all its contents. I supposed Tom was right; I wouldn't have handed over anything to anyone I didn't know. But Tom was not a stranger, not really.

What is he? I asked myself as the daylight streaming through the library windows turned to gold and began to fade, and the shadows lengthened. *Is he my friend?* I touched my lips with cool fingertips, recalling the feeling of Tom's lips on mine. The blood came into my face at the memory. I supposed that Grandmother would have said that what Tom had done had not made him my friend at all, but something much worse. But why should I care what Grandmother would have said? Why should I trust her? As I closed the door of the safe, I told myself that I did not care about that. I had only my own feelings to guide me now, and my own feelings told me that if Tom were to try to kiss me again, I wouldn't stop him.

Tom didn't come back for three days. He had to go to work with his father, and he had warned me too that it would take a while for him to get the things I wanted. I waited restlessly; I was impatient to see him, and impatient with myself. There was work to do – always work – but when the chores were done and I had time to spare, I sometimes found myself lingering in front of one of the great tarnish-spotted mirrors that hung in the house, trying to imagine how I would look in modern clothes. I made an unsuccessful foray up into the attic to look through the trunks for anything remotely like the things I had seen in the magazines, but it was hopeless. I saw now how limp and faded the fabrics were, how desperately old-fashioned the high necks and the rows of tiny buttons.

It was a relief on the third day when I heard the three blasts of the horn that meant it was Tom who had returned, and no one else. When I went out to him, he was already out of the car, and he had bags in his hands, flimsy shiny ones that showed interesting hints of the things inside.

We went into the house, to the kitchen, where Tom put all the bags on the table. I had given him some measurements but they were all in inches and Tom had said that there was another system altogether now. However, as soon as I started to lift the things out of the bags I could tell that most of them would fit. Whether I would feel comfortable wearing them was another question: they were quite unlike anything I had ever worn before, and most of them felt lighter too, because they were not armoured with thick linings and petticoats.

I hesitated, my arms full of clothes. "If I – if it looks all right, would you take me to the outside – I mean, outside Langlands estate – for a while?"

"Sure. Mum doesn't need the car today." Tom grinned. "She's being very understanding about me borrowing it. She thinks I've got a secret girlfriend I'm not telling her about."

You have, I thought, but Tom's words gave me another of those sudden cold feelings of doubt. Perhaps he didn't see what had happened between us the way I did; perhaps a kiss meant less to him than it did to me. Life outside Langlands was a mystery to me. Who knew how they did things out there?

I carried the new clothes upstairs to my bedroom, leaving Tom in the kitchen, warming his hands over the range. The room felt cold and neglected; I hardly spent any time here, hardly ever slept here anymore since the kitchen was so much warmer than the rest of the house, and there was no Grandmother to insist on any form of doing things.

It was hard to say which took longer: undressing myself or putting on the new clothes. My old things always took time to put on or take off: there were layers and layers of them, and nearly everything fastened with tiny hooks-and-eyes or buttons. The new things would probably take very little time to put on once I had got used to them, but they had fasteners of a kind

I had not used before, with two rows of miniature teeth that interlocked when you ran a tiny tab up and down them. It took me a while to work out how to operate it, and to feel confident that it would stay closed once I had fastened it.

There were a couple of white cotton shirts, and those were very practical and comfortable; they had no fasteners at all but could just be pulled on over my head. And there were trousers. I looked at those for a full minute before I tried putting them on, and when I did, I thought Tom had made a mistake about the size. They were too tight-fitting. I could get them on all right, and once I had the trick of it, I could do the fastener up, but they felt very strange, and they looked – well, I knew what I had seen in the magazine, but still I found it hard to believe that anyone walked about dressed like this, in things so closely fitting that they showed the entire shape of the hips and legs. There was nothing for it though; if I couldn't bear to wear modern clothes at all I couldn't very well go out.

Lastly there was a jacket, and that made things a little better: it was still a closer fit than I was used to, but it was made of soft leather and had a robust feel to it.

I put my own boots back on and laced them up, and then I found my hairbrush and brushed out my hair. After that, it occurred to me that perhaps I should add something – a necklace or a scarf, and I spent some minutes fruitlessly looking for something that seemed right, until I realised that I was simply putting off the inevitable moment when I would have to go downstairs and show myself to Tom. What would I do if he looked dismayed at the sight of me, or worse still, laughed? But there was nothing for it. I had waited a very long time to leave Langlands, and here was no other way of doing it than this. I left my room, closing the door carefully behind me, and went downstairs.

chapter thirty-three

Tom

It's hard to say what Ghost thought of the stuff I'd bought but she went off to try it all on. She's been gone longer than I thought she'd be, but now I hear her footsteps coming down the hall towards the kitchen. She pauses outside the kitchen door, as though she has to make up her mind whether to come in or not. I wait, and after a few moments she pushes the door open and comes in.

I don't say anything, I just stare. She looks like a twenty-first century girl. Well, not exactly like the other ones I know, because there's no fake tan and her eyebrows are all her own, but she looks modern. You wouldn't know she's just arrived here from living in 1945. It's almost impossible to remember that she isn't from now, that there are a thousand things she has no idea about.

She says, "Do I look all right?"

"Yes," I say. "You look great." *Understatement*, I think.

"Then can we go somewhere, Tom? Please?"

The way she says that, she sounds anxious, like she thinks she's going to lose her nerve if we don't leave right now, and maybe she's right. Even if we don't go any further than the main road, that'll be further than she's ever been from Langlands.

She wants to get on and do it before she gets too nervous to do it at all.

I say, "Sure. Where do you want to go?"

I think she's going to say she wants to go somewhere to choose some more clothes for herself, or maybe just drive around and look at the countryside if she can't face going anywhere with a lot of people. I'd understand that. But she looks at me hopefully and says, "Can we go and see the sea?"

I open my mouth to say *No, it's miles away, it'd take ages* and then I think, *why not?* We could get to Dundee in about an hour. Maybe not Dundee – too many people. Saint Andrews? Then I have a better idea. I'll have to use up the rest of the cash she gave me buying petrol, but there's no reason not to go.

So I say, "Yeah," and then I add, "It's going to be cold, though."

"I don't care," she says, and I think she really doesn't. What she cares about is getting moving before she chickens out.

We go back down the passage to the hallway with the stuffed stag's head. Ghost takes the key out of the inside of the door and when we are outside in the stone porch she locks up very carefully. I don't bother to point out that this is probably unnecessary because nobody ever comes up here.

When I open the car with the remote she looks startled, and I have to remind myself all over again that whatever she looks like on the outside, this isn't a twenty-first century girl. She stands and looks at the car for a few moments and I wonder whether she is waiting for me to open the passenger door for her. Then I realise she probably has no idea where she is supposed to get in anyway, not if the old lady never took her out in that vintage car of hers. I open the door for her, and when she's inside I close it.

When I get in, I have to show her how to put her seatbelt on, and that gives me a moment of doubt again about this whole thing. But I've said we'll go now.

"Ready?" I ask her.

She nods, though she looks a bit uncertain.

"Okay," I say. Then I start the engine, and we head off, over the gravel and onto the track which leads through the forest and to the world beyond Langlands.

chapter thirty-four

Ghost

When we got to the place where the track came out of the forest and into open land, the border of the Langlands estate, the car slowed down until it was going not very much faster than I could have gone on foot. I looked ahead, through the glass, and I could see the gate posts ahead. That was as far as I had ever gone before. Suddenly I began to feel a strange anxiety about what we were about to do. I had a terrible conviction that the car was going to stop altogether, before it ever crossed that limit – that it was a physical impossibility that I would ever leave Langlands. Some unseen force would prevent it ever happening, dragging me unwillingly back to the ageing house.

As the car slowed, the conviction became a smothering feeling. I could not move. I could not look at Tom, nor speak to him. The feeling of pressure on my chest grew until I could barely draw a breath and dark motes sparkled at the edge of my vision. I imagined the car stopping, refusing to move an inch further than the boundary of Langlands, or worse, the car gliding slowly over it and myself dissolving into the air like so much dust carried away on the wind. Panic boiled up inside me. The black sparkles on the air seemed to merge into one.

"Ghost? *Ghost?*"

There was an urgency in Tom's voice that brought me back to myself. I opened my eyes and saw sky, bordered by window frame. I was slumped in the seat, the belt Tom had fastened across me cutting uncomfortably into the side of my neck.

Tom was asking me what had happened, whether I was all right, but I didn't reply, not yet. I was pushing myself upright with my hands so that I could look out of the window properly.

It was bright out there, much brighter than it had been when we travelled through the forest. We were right out from under the canopy of trees. I twisted in my seat and peered out of the rear window. I could see the gate posts behind us, the opening into the forest a dark maw. They were far enough behind us that I could also see the metal grid that lay between them.

"We're out," I said.

"Yeah," said Tom. "What happened? Did you faint? You went a really strange colour."

"Why did we slow down?" I asked him.

"Because of the cattle grid." Tom sounded as though he was pointing out something obvious. "Did it make you feel sick or something?"

"No. I mean, maybe. I don't know." I turned back to face the front again, staring at the road that ran downhill ahead of us, the fields that flanked it, the great expanse of sky.

We were out. Outside the Langlands estate. And nothing had happened to me. The sky hadn't fallen on my head; I hadn't died on the spot. Tom had simply carried me across the line without hesitation, as easily as if he had taken me up in his arms and stepped across the threshold. The suffocating feeling had drained away. Now I felt a kind of wild exhilaration. We were out, in the world. I wanted to see *everything*.

I looked at Tom and said, "Can we go?"

He stared at me for a moment. Then he grinned. "Yeah."

Now that we were off the track with its deep ruts and mud, we were able to go more quickly. The car seemed to skim like a bird down the smooth road that led between the fields; the hedges on either side were a blur. At first it had a nauseating effect on me, but then I learnt the trick of it, to look a little ahead, rather than directly out of the side window. Even so, when we reached the end of the first road and turned left onto a wider one, the speed was alarming.

I sneaked a look at Tom, but he didn't seem concerned. Looking at him was a guilty kind of pleasure, and I would have carried on with it for longer, except that the background of trees and fields speeding past his window was too distracting; it made me feel dizzy again.

For a while, we passed through countryside with very few buildings in it. I saw one house at a distance, set back against the hill; it was not as large as Langlands, but it was still a good size. Then we passed two others that were so small that they seemed like dolls' houses to me, after having Langlands all to myself.

A little later we came into a village and here we saw a few people walking about the street. Several of them were old, like Grandmother, but I saw one woman who was much younger, perhaps not very many years older than I was, with a tiny child toddling along beside her. I turned my head to look back, but already they had dwindled to specks in the distance.

My mind went from that short glimpse of a mother and child to my own mother, and then to Grandmother and what she had done, and perhaps Tom's did too, because a few moments later he said, "I asked my Dad about Langlands." He glanced at me. "How long your grandmother had lived there, stuff like that. He grew up in the town so I thought he might know something."

"What did he say?"

Tom grinned. "He said not to go up there, if that was what I was thinking of, in case I ripped the exhaust off Mum's car on the ruts."

"You didn't tell him you'd been, did you?" I said, alarmed.

"Of course not. I said I was just curious because the old place was as creepy as – well, very creepy." He shrugged. "Dad said there were stories about it when he was a kid, and probably before that, too. He said he went up there once, when he was about my age. He'd just got his first car, and he took a girl up there. Not Mum – it was before he met her." Tom made a face. "He said it was empty. All the windows were boarded up. He wanted to break in, have a look around, but the girl he was with didn't want to."

"Did he do it?" I asked.

"No. They drove into the town instead and went to the chippy."

"Oh," I said, disappointed. "He couldn't really tell you anything, then."

"It's told us the house used to be empty back then," Tom pointed out. He thought for a moment. "I guess that would have been around 1980, 1985 maybe. But somebody was living there during the War, because there's that picture of your grandmother in front of the house, when she was a kid."

"I suppose she went away," I said, "And then she came back, later on."

"But why?" said Tom. He risked another glance at me. "What about you? Have you always lived there? Or can you remember living anywhere else – you know, before?"

I shook my head. "I've always lived at Langlands. Always."

"Well, where were you born? Did your Gran ever say?"

"At Langlands," I said.

"Really? Nobody gets born at home anymore."

Out of step with Tom's world again. Every time it happened it was a goad, like the sting of a tiny insect. Before I had thought it through I said, "Lots of people are born at home–" and then I stopped. *In 1945*, I thought. But it was not 1945.

Tom didn't contradict me. Instead he said, "What about your mum and dad? Can you remember them at all?"

I shook my head. I had asked myself that question so many times before. I had looked back into the past and strained to remember something, anything. But there was nothing – not even that strange feeling of not-quite-remembering. My parents existed in my memory only as a blank space.

"What did your gran say about them?"

I looked down, at my own hands entwined in my lap. "She said my mother was dead – in the War. If there's no War any more, I don't know what happened to her. But Grandmother said she was dead."

"It doesn't make sense," said Tom. "Even if it was 1945 right now, she couldn't have died in the War. I mean, it only went on for five or six years. If your mum died when you were a baby, well, that would be way more than six years ago."

I said nothing. This was worse than being out of step with Tom's time. Now I felt as though I had been ridiculously naive. Grandmother had talked of the War as something that had been going on all my life; she made it sound as though it had been going on forever. And I had not questioned that, not half enough. I felt angry at myself, and angrier than ever at Grandmother.

After a moment, Tom said, "What about your dad?"

I put my head up. "She would hardly talk about him," I said. "It was like he'd done something so terrible she couldn't even think about it."

"She never said what?"

I shook my head. "No." For a moment we travelled on in silence, past trees and fields and hedges. Then I said, "I've been wondering – about my mother. If she didn't die in the War like Grandmother said – I mean, if she couldn't have – then maybe –" I hesitated. "Maybe she isn't dead at all."

Tom said nothing for a while, and I began to wonder whether he had heard what I said. But then he said, "I guess it's possible. But then, where is she?"

Now it was my turn to be silent. I had had an idea about that question, but it seemed so tenuous that I was almost afraid to put it into words. But at last I said, "I thought maybe that was why Grandmother didn't like talking about my father. Maybe he was the one who took my mother away. I mean, she went with him."

My face was warm; it felt too intimate, sharing this idea I was nurturing, that perhaps my mother had left for love. The idea itself was no better than a sketch in my imagination. I did not know why my father would have had to go away, what urgent call of duty or obligation or emotion could have drawn him to itself. But to think of my mother following him for a love so great that it overwhelmed everything else was more comforting than imagining her dead. It was like the fairy tales in the books in the library, dramatic and beautiful.

In all those fairy tales there was always a villain: a spiteful stepmother, an evil gnome. In this one there was the poisonous little voice in my mind that said: *Why did she leave you behind?* It hurt to think that the all-consuming love I had imagined for her had left no room for me. But still, I preferred believing in love than in death.

chapter thirty-five

At least twice in the later part of that journey we went through built-up areas which I thought must be cities from the number of houses, although Tom said they were only towns. In these places there were more people on the pavements, and many more cars. Everything seemed chaotically busy. How did anyone ever cross one of these roads in safety? And how did the drivers find their way about, when everything went so fast and there was no time to read any of the signposts, let alone make a decision about which way to go?

The excitement I had felt earlier on, when we had made it out of the Langlands estate, was fading away. I began to think about what would happen if I were somehow separated from Tom out here, how I would never, ever be able to find my way home by myself. It was too far and too confusing. There was no reason to think that I could be parted from Tom, or that he would abandon me, and yet once the idea of becoming separated was seeded in my mind, it grew persistently, like ivy working its tendrils in between bricks. I had been chattering about what I saw from the window; now I fell silent. The streets that slid past me seemed as hostile as a desert, or the bottom of an ocean; I had no idea how to survive out there on my own. No matter how hard I tried to push it back, an oppressive sense of dread was creeping over me. I wanted to cry out, *turn around Tom, take me home now, please, Tom please*. The desire was so strong that I could almost taste the words in my mouth. I bit my lip to stop myself from blurting them out.

But now the car was slowing. Tom wasn't turning around; he was stopping. We slid to a halt and he did something that made the engine die. Then he turned to me with a grin, though the cheerful expression wavered when he saw the look on my face.

"Are you okay?"

I nodded, although my throat felt so tight that I couldn't speak.

"We don't have to get out. We can just go back if you want."

No, I thought. *I need air.* I pawed at the door but I couldn't work out how to open it, and the belt across my body was restricting me.

There was a click and the belt slackened. Tom had unfastened it. Then he was out of the car and opening the door on my side.

It was cold and windy out there. He had to hold the door to stop it swinging outwards, and the howling of the wind was instant and tremendous.

"Welcome to Elie," Tom shouted in my ear as I climbed out of the car. Oddly, as soon as I was standing there with my feet on the solid ground, I began to feel better. The cold wind braced me up. I was used to tolerating cold and bad weather; we had plenty of both during the winter at Langlands. It was green here, too, and that was better than the unrelenting grey of the towns, and there were no other people in sight.

Tom took my hand and began to pull me along. It was a good feeling, his hand in mine. His skin was warm; his grip was firm and reassuring. I stopped worrying about being somehow separated from him. I knew he wouldn't let me go. As we stumbled over the grass with the wind in our faces I felt my spirits lift. Then we came to the top of a piece of rising ground and I saw the sea for the first time in my life.

The sea. It was not blue nor green as I had read that it was in books, but a kind of slate grey colour, and it stretched so far into the distance that all perspective was lost: the faint horizon could have been two miles away, or twenty, or two hundred, or perhaps it was an illusion and there was no limit at all. Where the water met the land it foamed white, and sucked back and forth in restless motion. I could smell it, too; a subtle saline tinge on the air.

We went down onto the sand, which was damp and clinging even before we got close to the water's edge. The howling of the wind merged with the seething of the waves breaking.

I had to raise my voice to make myself heard. "I want to go in."

Tom looked astonished. "What, you want to swim? You can't, you'll freeze to death."

"No," I shouted back. "I can't swim." That was true; I'd never had the opportunity to learn. "Just my feet."

"You'll still freeze," he told me, but when I let go of his hand to bend and unlace my boots, he did the same.

When I stepped into the water it was a cold shock, but still I thought: *it's not so bad.* It was worth the chill to feel the new sensation of sand under my feet and the ebb and flow of the water. I moved my toes, savouring the feeling.

Perhaps a minute later I realised my mistake. The water was so cold that I didn't acclimatise. Instead of starting to feel warmer it simply felt colder and colder. My feet were already becoming numb. I ran out of the water and onto the sand and I was limping because I couldn't feel my feet properly. My trousers were wet to the middle of the calf too. The fabric felt strangely stiff and uncomfortable and clung unpleasantly to my ankles. Seemingly, modern clothes were a lot less practical than my old dresses, which could have been hitched up out of the way. Tom was no better off. The bottom inches of his trousers were dark with seawater too. He didn't seem bothered; in fact, he was grinning. The smile made him so handsome that I felt my cheeks burning and looked down hastily.

"Happy now?" he asked me cheerfully.

"I can't feel my toes," I told him, apparently studying them with great interest.

"I did tell you."

I picked up my boots and we walked to a large rock where we could sit down and do our best to dry our feet. It was almost impossible to get all the wet sand off; when I put my boots back on I resigned myself to feeling as though I was walking on grit for the rest of the day. I made a face and Tom laughed.

"Had enough?"

I shook my head, and pushed back the hair that was being blown across my face.

"Not yet." I pointed at the cliffs. "Can we go up there?"

"If you want. Aren't you cold?"

"No," I lied, trying not to shiver too obviously. Now that I was actually outside Langlands, I wanted to make the most of it.

There was a steep path zigzagging up to the clifftops. It took us a while to climb it, and by the time we got to the top I wasn't chilly any more, despite the wind; I was warm with exertion, and I felt hampered by my tight-fitting clothes. How did anyone do *anything* dressed like this? I was glad of my own worn-in boots. I'd seen some of the things girls wore on their feet in the magazine pictures, and I was convinced I wouldn't be able to walk in those at all.

Tom took my hand and pulled me up the last bit, and when we were standing at the top he didn't let go; we went on hand in hand. The clifftop was utterly unlike Langlands with its closely-packed trees. Up here there was grass but no trees; everything was flat and wide open, so that the wind could blast across it and the sky seemed to wheel above us, dizzyingly. I stopped walking, and Tom stopped with me. The wind was so strong here that I felt we could have taken flight altogether; I dared not go too close to the edge of the cliff in case it dragged me over. It was alarming but glorious too. From up here, where the view was not framed by the curves of the coastline, the sea looked truly infinite, as vast as the sky. As the sun pierced the clouds, the surface of the water shivered into a million sparkling fragments, too bright to look at.

It was cold here in spite of the winter sunshine. Tom pulled me into an embrace and his lips on my cheek, my mouth, made the only warm places on my exposed skin. The wind howled in my ears, drowning out everything: my breathing, the roar of the sea, Tom's words, if there were any. If someone had stood right beside me and said, *Turn back, don't do this*, I should not have heard them. I put my cold fingers into Tom's hair and kissed him back.

chapter thirty-six

Tom

You can't kiss someone for long in a freezing wind like that. Ghost can't pretend she isn't cold anymore; I can feel her shivering in my arms. We go back to the car, and as soon as the engine's running, I turn the heater on full blast.

We have to stop for petrol, so with the last of the cash Ghost gave me from her grandmother's safe, I pay for that and a takeout coffee for her. Then we set off again, and drive in silence for a few minutes while she sips the coffee. Then she says, "Tell me about 2017, Tom," so I do.

I tell her about modern medicine – how they can cure people of stuff that used to be incurable, and how they're starting to be able to make bionic arms that you can move by thinking about them. How they have running blades for people without legs.

Then I tell her about men landing on the moon, thinking that's going to amaze her, and I'm surprised when she doesn't seem that impressed. It takes me a while to realise that she doesn't believe me. She doesn't come out and say that. She just doesn't ask me much about it; she looks kind of distant while I'm talking about it. Maybe it's just too much for her to swallow, or maybe she thinks I'm just making it up.

I stop going on about the moon and tell her about ordinary

stuff instead. Things everyone has in their houses. She's seen some of it in the magazines I brought her: dishwashers, microwaves, washing machines. I do a kind of tour in my head of everything we have at home, and tell her about it. Old Mrs. McAndrew didn't have a freezer, not even a fridge, so Ghost is interested in those, in the idea of being able to keep things fresh for ages. Sometimes this look crosses her face, as though she's angry about something but keeping it down. She never loses it with me, though, so I guess it's the old lady she's cross with. Who wouldn't be, after spending years cutting logs and washing everything by hand when you didn't really need to?

Working out which things are new to her and which aren't is difficult. Langlands doesn't have any kind of power supply, but she's heard of gas and electricity and she knows what a phone is, even though the house doesn't have one of those either.

I nearly forget to mention the TV because it seems so obvious, but it's a totally new idea to her. "And everyone has one of those in their house?" she asks me, sounding like she can't believe it.

"Yes," I say.

She asks me questions about how it works that I can't answer, and that's frustrating for both of us. I suppose in her world things are simpler. The most complicated machine she's ever seen is probably Mrs. McAndrew's car, and that was ancient. Nothing fuel-injected under *that* bonnet.

It occurs to me that it would probably be easier just to take Ghost over to our place and *show* her all these things. But I've promised to keep her secret for now, and if we ran into Mum or Dad, that would be the end of that. Mum already suspects I've been borrowing her car to visit a girl, and we'd never get away without a million questions. Just one question, like "Are you still at school?" would be a disaster.

So I carry on doing my best to tell her how people live in

163

2017 – people who haven't been brought up by some mad old lady in a house in a forest. It's when I get on to explaining the internet that things really get complicated. I start trying to describe it, but the minute the word "computer" is out of my mouth I realise I'm going to have to go back and explain that, too. I'm halfway through doing that when I say the word "keyboard" and she says, "Like a piano?" and I get that feeling I've had before, like a kind of vertigo, realising there's such a big gap between what she knows and what I know, and she's relying on me to bridge it, and the job feels *too fucking big*. I'd have to be a human Wikipedia to do it.

We're only a mile or so from Langlands when I think, *even if I can't show her the house, I can show her the net.* I fish in my pocket for my smartphone and hold it out to her, keeping my gaze on the road ahead. "Here. It's a smartphone," I add, realising too late that she isn't sure what it is.

"A telephone?"

"Yes. But you can go online with it too. I mean, you can look at the internet."

"I don't know how to."

"I'll talk you through it. You see that button at the bottom of the screen? Press that first."

Silence. Then she says: "Nothing happened."

"The screen should light up."

Silence again, then: "No," she says.

We're at the edge of the Langlands estate; a moment later we rattle over the cattle grid.

"It's okay," I say. "I'll look at it when we stop."

"What is it supposed to do?" she asks me.

"Everything," I say, with a shrug. "You can go online with it, call people with it. Listen to music. Watch videos. I don't know. Take photos. Stuff like that."

I'm aware of her turning the phone over and over in her hands, as though it's a puzzle she can't begin to solve. We draw up in front of Langlands House and I turn off the engine.

"Here," I say, and she gives me the phone.

I thumb the *on* button confidently and nothing happens. The phone is dead. And then my mind skips back to this morning before I came to Langlands. I'd meant to put the phone on charge and then I never did it. I've been out all day, and there isn't even enough charge left now to turn the phone on.

Ghost is looking over my shoulder expectantly.

"It's no good," I tell her. "It's dead. It needs charging."

She doesn't say anything to that, so I glance at her and catch the sly grin that's gone almost as soon as it appears, the way she bites her lip before she turns her head to look innocently out of the window.

I slump back in my seat, torn between laughter and indignation. I'm holding the smartphone in my hand and it's nothing but a sleek piece of junk; I might as well be holding a stone.

"It does do all that stuff," I say lamely.

"Yes," she says, without catching my eye.

"I'll charge it up before I come next time." I pause. "It will work then."

"Yes."

"Stop laughing."

"I'm not laughing," she says, but now she is; the last word is lost in it. Ghost looks at me then, looks me right in the face, and her eyes are full of laughter too. She doesn't look like some strange refugee from 1945. She looks amazing. She looks like someone I could love.

chapter thirty-seven

Ghost

I was glad to get back to Langlands that day, the first time I ever saw the world outside. It was terrifying and exhilarating, knowing that I had crossed the border and nothing had happened; the sky hadn't fallen on my head. I saw the sea at last, and heard its whisper and felt its glacial coldness on my bare skin. I wanted to think about all of that, and about Tom's arms around me and the heat of his kiss.

I thought he would just leave me at the door of Langlands then and go, because it was getting late in the day. But he came into the house with me, standing at my shoulder as I unlocked the door. It took me a moment to manage the lock. My fingers were suddenly clumsy, and the light touch of his hand on my waist seemed to make it worse; I fumbled and almost dropped the key.

At last I managed it. Inside, the house was cold and rather dark. After the brisk wind and the sea air, the stillness had a dead quality to it. I imagined the dust drifting down and settling in layers over everything. Supposing I had left with Tom and never come back – what difference would it have made? Langlands would have decayed neither faster nor slower for my absence. I was not sure whether the thought was comforting or melancholy.

We went to the kitchen, where there was at least some warmth from the stove. I went immediately to stoke it up.

"Would you light the lamp, Tom?" I said over my shoulder as I knelt in front of the stove. There was an oil lamp on the table; I heard a rattle as he picked it up.

After a moment, I heard him say, "I don't know how to." And that was strange, finding out that growing up in the twenty-first century didn't mean you knew how to do everything people had done before.

I stood up and went over to where Tom was standing holding the lamp with a puzzled expression on his face, and held out my hands for the lamp and the matches. I showed him how to light it, and when I had replaced the glass I glanced up and found I was looking right into Tom's eyes.

He'd kissed me before of course, when we opened Grandmother's safe, and he had kissed me on the clifftop while the wind screamed around our heads. Now, even before he leaned in, I knew he was going to kiss me again and I felt a surge of something like vertigo, a sense of anticipation so sharp that it was almost like being afraid.

Afraid of what? That was the question. Not afraid of Tom. No. I was afraid of myself.

I *wanted* him to kiss me. The closeness, the feeling of his lips on mine, his hands in my hair – it was the most exciting thing I had ever felt, like falling and flying all at once, like being the falcon who cleaves through the air and then sweeps upwards without ever meeting the ground. I wanted it again, that feeling, so when Tom put his arms around me and pulled me towards him, I didn't resist. My lips parted naturally under his. My heart was thudding; I could hardly breathe. I put my arms around him, too, holding on, and I was astounded at my own daring.

Because it was daring. I knew I shouldn't be doing this. Spiting Grandmother was one thing; after her lies, there was no reason I should care what she would have said. But that didn't make it *right* to be here alone with Tom, clinging on to him as his mouth moved languorously over mine. I wasn't naive enough to think that because it felt beautiful it was good.

Tom was pressing against me; I took a step backwards, off balance, and felt the cool of the wall at my back. I tilted my head. My eyes slid closed; Tom's fingers snagged in my hair.

I knew I should push him away. Probably I should slap him around the face and tell him he had insulted me. We weren't engaged to each other, and these weren't brief decorous kisses behind a chaperone's back. These were *hungry* kisses.

I didn't do it, though. Tom's kisses were making me feel reckless. I didn't want him to stop. I wanted him to keep kissing me, to kiss me harder, to hold me more tightly.

Then his hand was inside the jacket he had bought for me, sliding under the soft shirt, and moving across my bare skin. I couldn't help it; I jumped. We broke the kiss. I turned my head aside and I was gasping.

I couldn't look Tom in the eyes. He leant his forehead against the wall, and I could hear the shuddering of his breath for a few seconds. Then he pushed away from the wall and stepped back.

Neither of us said a word. What could I have said? *I'm sorry?* I wasn't sorry. I was confused.

I straightened my shirt with hands that trembled and then I stepped past Tom and busied myself with the oil lamp, adjusting it unnecessarily until the flame flared up too brightly.

After far too long a time in which silence stretched out between us, Tom said, "I should be going. Mum needs the car this evening."

I wanted to say, "Don't go," or "Take me with you," but instead I said, "Yes."

I picked up the lamp and led the way back down the passage to the hall and the front door. Tom followed me closely, but did not touch me; nor did he kiss me goodbye as we stood at the door. He paused on the threshold though, and said, "I'll be back soon."

I had to be content with that. I watched him turn the car and drive off, and when the sound of the engine had died away I closed the door and locked it. Then I went upstairs. I meant to go to my room and change back into my old dress, but first I went along the length of the passage to Grandmother's room. My own room had a small mirror hanging over the wash-stand, but hers had a proper cheval glass in which I could see the whole of myself, from my new shorter hair to my boots. I put the oil lamp down on the dressing table and studied my reflection. As far as I could judge, I thought that I looked modern – at any rate, I wouldn't have stood out amongst the people I had glimpsed at the roadside today. It occurred to me that no girl or woman who looked the way I did had ever been inside Langlands before. It was a disturbing thought. Did I even belong here anymore? I turned away from the mirror. I didn't belong in the *outside* world either – at least, not yet.

I went to my own room and took off my new things. The trousers had dried during the drive back from the coast, but the fabric was stiff from the salt water. I would have to wash them, I supposed. For now, I simply folded everything carefully, as though I were a lady's maid putting away her mistress's clothes. It did feel like that – as though they belonged to someone else altogether.

I wished there *had* been someone else there – someone I could talk to. If, instead of Tom, it had been a girl of my own age who had come to the house that time, looking for the truth about the Langlands ghost, I might have made friends with her. I could have asked her so many things – except that if it had been a girl who had come that day, I wouldn't need to ask the most burning questions, which were all about Tom.

Was he angry with me when he left today?

That was one I wanted answered. He hadn't touched me

or kissed me again. We had hardly exchanged a word after I jumped and he stepped away from me. But he had said he would come back soon.

Did he really mean that? said the voice of self-doubt. Soon, that wasn't the same as saying *tomorrow* or *at the weekend*. It was vague; it might even mean *never*.

How is this meant to go on? That was the biggest one. I knew how it went according to the books downstairs in Langlands' library, books that had all rolled off the printing presses over seventy years ago. In those books, once the hero and the heroine had got over their dramatic misunderstandings (he too proud, she too idealistic), the gentleman would declare himself, first to the girl and then to her parents. A kiss might be exchanged. Marriage followed shortly afterwards, and if it didn't, the situation was considered disastrous.

I knew what happened after marriage, too, although Grandmother had never been explicit about that.

Another thing she was going to tell me one day in the future, and never actually did, I reflected grimly.

I might not have known at all, except that there was a book in the library about it. I had found it one rainy afternoon when I was looking for something new to read; I had climbed up the ladder to look at something on one of the upper shelves, and when I pulled out the book I wanted I saw that there was another one hidden behind it, placed flat to the back of the shelf. *Married Love*, it was called.

I had a feeling Grandmother would not approve of my reading that book, so of course I was determined to go through it from cover to cover, and I did. The critical information was in chapter five, which began with a quotation from Saint Paul: "Love worketh no ill to his neighbour." I read all of it very carefully, and I remember thinking that whatever it said on the cover of the book, there was nothing in the mechanics of it that absolutely required anyone to be married before doing it.

And that, I supposed, was the reason why people in books were always so eager to get married; otherwise, having once realised they liked each other, they might end up doing it without being married. Then the woman would be considered "fallen" – though not, apparently the man – and if there was a baby, it would be a "love child", which was a lot worse than it sounded.

I understood all of this, but it was as much use as having a map of Perthshire when you wanted to visit London. How did things work in 2017? I had absolutely no idea, and for that reason I could not guess whether Tom had been angry with me, or himself, or not at all.

It was a puzzle I was not going to solve that evening; the entire contents of Langlands' library couldn't have done that. Dressed once more in my old things, I went back down to the kitchen. I felt strangely flat, considering what a momentous day it had been: the day when I finally left Langlands and saw the outside world. I meant to make myself something to eat, but I had no appetite and it all seemed too much effort. In the end, I lay down on the bench with my blanket wrapped around me, and went to sleep with an empty stomach.

chapter thirty-eight

The next four days, Tom didn't come. He had not said that he would come back on a particular day, of course, and I had no idea what other things might affect his ability to come, but as time went on a deep gloom settled over me.

He is never coming back, I said to myself, trying to make myself believe it so that the disappointment would be less when he failed to appear the next day, and the next. I went about my daily tasks: chopping firewood, feeding the chickens. But all the time I was moving to and fro, carrying things in and out or pumping water, my mind was running over and over the events of that day.

Had Tom taken my behaviour as a rejection? Or perhaps he was just tired already of being with someone who knew nothing about his world, who had to be told everything, even how to turn on a telephone. It would be easy for him to abandon the whole thing as a bad lot. He had only to stay away.

I put the new clothes into the bottom drawer of a press in my bedroom. I would take them out again when I was finally forced to walk to the town for supplies, but otherwise I didn't want to see them. They were simply a reminder of a day that had ended in a way I didn't understand. It hurt me to think about it, although it was nearly all I *did* think about.

On the fifth day I woke up to a cold sunshine slanting blindingly through the kitchen window. I sat up and looked at the kitchen clock. The hands stood at half past three. I didn't think it was possible I had slept that long, and besides, the quality of the light pouring through the window said morning, not afternoon. The clock had stopped altogether; I had forgotten to wind it.

It occurred to me that not only did I not know what time it was, I didn't know what date it was, either. Somehow, I had lost track. Was it Tuesday, or Saturday? It was March now, I was pretty sure of that, but that was all I knew.

I went outside to fetch more wood for the stove and found the day was clear and bright. The air was very still and cool, and as I stood for a moment looking at the dark texture of the tree branches I heard faint sounds coming to me: the cry of a bird, the crackle of some wild creature in the undergrowth. And far off, an engine.

Hope didn't flare up right away. I'd heard such sounds before, when aircraft went over, or when work was going on in the fields beyond the forest. But as I stood there on the flagged path that led from the kitchen door to the back of the house, I realised that the sound was growing gradually louder. Someone was coming up the track through the forest.

I put down the basket I had been carrying for the chopped wood, and wiped my hands on my skirt. Then I walked slowly to the corner of the house, where I would have a view out onto the drive. I didn't run. It might not be Tom, after all; it could be those two people in the uniforms again. I pressed myself close to the stone corner, and waited.

I saw a flash of red between the trees before I saw the car properly. It was Tom's, all right, or at any rate, it was Tom's mother's. The sound of the engine swelled to a roar as the car laboured up the last part of the drive and crunched over the gravel. As the nose of it swung towards me, I stepped back behind the corner of the wall, out of sight.

I don't know why I did that. I should have been thrilled to see him after waiting five days; I should have run out onto the gravel with my arms outstretched. But I didn't. I hung back.

Five days, I thought. What good reason could there be for staying away so long? Perhaps he hadn't wanted to come back at all, and had only come now to say that he was sorry, he wouldn't be coming again. Or perhaps I was so much less important to him than he was to me that five days was nothing; it was not *soon* but *soon enough*. I wasn't sure I wanted to know which one of them it was. I was tempted to creep back into the house via the kitchen door, lock it up and hide until he had gone. At least then I wouldn't have to listen to what he had to say.

The car engine died and a moment or two later I heard the door slam. I stood with my back to the cold stone wall, biting my lip, not moving.

"Ghost?"

I heard him call me, and my heart sank even further. There was a hard edge to his voice. I thought he sounded angry. I had that impulse again, to run back into the house and hide.

Then I heard him call again, once, twice, the second time muffled because he had gone into the stone porch. The front door was locked, I knew that. In a second or two, he would be hammering on it.

I couldn't do it. I couldn't run away. I let out a long breath, and then I stepped out from behind the corner of the house and walked briskly around to the front, not letting myself think too carefully about what I was doing.

Tom heard my boots on the gravel and came out of the stone porch. His head turned towards me and I saw the scowl on his face, that barely flickered when he saw me.

I stopped where I was. It was impossible not to. It didn't matter that Grandmother had lied to me, that I was doing my conscious best to reject what she had taught me about the world. It was too ingrained – the suspicion of what lay outside Langlands, the threat of danger. Tom looked angry; my instinct was to keep my distance.

"Ghost?"

He strode towards me. I stood my ground, but watchfully. I struggled for something to say, but in the end, I didn't need to say anything. It all came spilling out of him.

"She wouldn't let me have the bloody car! That's why I didn't come. She had to prove a bloody point. Five days – five days it's taken to talk her round."

"She...?"

"Mum. I know it's her car but what does she expect me to do?" His brows drew together. "You know the day we went to Elie? She needed the car back for something she needed to go to, and I forgot. I just forgot. I didn't do it on purpose. I got home and we had this massive row and that was it. She says I can't use her car again." Tom let out a shuddering sigh of exasperation. "Fine, it's her car, but what does she expect me to do?" He shook his head. "I should have gone straight to uni instead of letting them talk me into working for Dad. Then I wouldn't be stuck there having to beg for the car when I want to go anywhere."

Then you'd never have come to Langlands at all, I thought. Perhaps the thought showed on my face, because after a moment Tom seemed to relax; the angry expression smoothed out of his face.

"Hey," he said, "I didn't mean to sound off at you. It was just I couldn't get back here and there was no way to tell you. And Mum was being..." He broke off, and didn't say what she had been. "She kept having a go at me, wanting to know where I'd been and who with. I didn't tell her," he added. "That's what's driving her nuts."

"I'm sorry," I said, because I couldn't think of anything else

175

to say. I didn't want to get Tom into trouble, but I was glad he had kept my secret.

"Forget it," said Tom. "Maybe we should get you a phone. Then if she goes off the deep end again and says I can't have the car, I can let you know."

I thought about that. "What if the phone dies, like yours did?"

He stared at me. "Of course. No way to charge it. There's no electricity anywhere here, is there?"

I shook my head.

"What were you supposed to do if there was an emergency?" Tom asked incredulously. "Like one of you got sick, or something? Didn't that ever happen?"

"I got very sick once," I said. "I don't know what it was. I just remember lying in my room on my own for a long time, and wanting Grandmother, and she didn't come. I think she went out somewhere, to a doctor, and brought something back for me."

"She didn't take you with her?"

"No."

Tom whistled. "She really didn't want anyone to know you were here, did she? I wonder what she would have done if you'd got worse – let you die?"

"Of course not," I said stoutly, but I felt uncomfortable. Grandmother had been so determined to keep me away from the outside world that she had kept up a lie for my entire life; she'd lied to everyone outside in a way too, by not telling them of my existence. If I had lain at Langlands dying, would she have made the decision to take me outside for help? I wasn't entirely sure she would have. What she had done was a bitter undercurrent to my thoughts; each time some fresh realisation broke upon me, the bitterness deepened. It made me want to break down the whole artifice, to trample on everything Grandmother had taught me. And it made me want to know more than ever: why?

chapter thirty-nine

Tom

Five days have made me angry, but they've also given me time to think. If there's anything to find out about Ghost's parents or why her grandmother did what she did, there's an obvious place to start looking. So that's where we go.

Is it possible the library smells dustier than it did the last time? I don't think it's possible – it wasn't that long ago – but I wonder whether Langlands has somehow given up the ghost without old Mrs. McAndrew presiding over it. The room feels dead, a tomb for books. I look at all those faded spines and wonder whether anyone will read any of them ever again. The sunshine coming in through the windows just shows up all the dust and the smears on the glass.

I leave Ghost to open the safe. The sight of all those wads of banknotes stacked up like bricks is kind of obscene. You can't see them without thinking about all the things you could spend the money on, all the things you've wanted for ages that you could just go out and *buy* with all that cash, and that feels like stealing. The money belongs to Ghost. I don't want to look at it.

I go over to that cabinet thing in the middle of the library and wait for her to bring the will. It doesn't take long for her to find it, and then she's standing next to me, turning over the pages until she finds the one with the signatures on it. She's so close to me that every time she turns a page her arm brushes against mine. I try to look at the typed words but my gaze keeps sliding around to the side of her face, the soft skin and the dark hair that she keeps absent-mindedly pushing behind her ear. I guess she isn't used to the new shorter length yet and it bothers her, the way it keeps falling forward. That makes me think of the day I cut her hair and how I suddenly wanted to kiss her. Then I want to stop messing about with old documents and just pull her into my arms and kiss her again, and I would, except I remember how she jumped last time. I don't want to mess this up.

I try to concentrate on the typewritten pages in front of us. There are the signatures: Fraser MacFarlane, solicitor, and George Robertson, general practitioner. I don't know either of them. I'm not surprised I've never heard of Fraser MacFarlane, because I've never spoken to a lawyer in my life, but I haven't heard of George Robertson either, and that *is* strange. There's only one doctor's surgery in the town and I think I've seen every one of them over the years because whenever I was sick Mum just wanted me seen to, she didn't wait for a particular person. Maybe he used to live in the town but he's moved away or something. I'll have to do some digging.

I slide my phone out of my pocket and take a photo of the two signatures so I won't forget them. I can feel Ghost leaning over to see what I'm doing, so I show her the snap. I could use the phone to Google the names right now, but it'll be easier on my laptop at home.

Instead, I take a step back. *Snap*. And there she is, captured on the screen: Ghost, half of her face pale in the sunlight coming through the windows, the other half in shadow, her dark eyes wide and serious. In that old-fashioned dress she really does look like a ghost, a beautiful one. I turn the phone so she can see the screen.

She doesn't react the way other people would do. She doesn't say, *oh, it's a horrible one of me*, or *do it again when I'm not making a face.* The way she looks at it is kind of sad.

"I've never seen this before," she says. "A picture of me. There aren't any."

"They had cameras in 1945 though, didn't they?" I ask her and as I say it, it strikes me that it's weird how I've fallen into the habit of thinking that's where she's from, 1945, like a time traveller instead of someone who grew up now but thinking it was another time.

"Yes," says Ghost. "But Grandmother never took any pictures of me. I've only seen myself in the mirror." She looks at the phone again. "I look – different. Still like me, only–"

"That's because you're used to seeing your reflection," I tell her. "Everything's the wrong way round. You know, a mirror image. A photo – well, if it's a good one – that's what you really look like."

"Oh," she says. She's silent for a few moments. Then, "I'd like a picture like this...of you."

"Don't you want one of yourself, if you don't have any?"

"No," she says. Then she thinks better of it and says, "Yes."

In the end, I make her stand next to me and I take one of us both. I can't text it to her because she doesn't have a phone, so I tell her I'll print it off at home and bring it next time. Then we mess about a bit, taking snaps of each other. Even if she'd never seen a smartphone before the other day, Ghost gets the hang of taking pictures with it pretty quickly. She takes some photos of me in the library and I take a few more of her, and then we go out into the hallway and open the front door to let in a bit of light, and she takes one of me standing underneath the stuffed stag's head.

I think about what my friends would say if they saw that one. If I told them I'd been at Langlands, that I hadn't just seen the outside but I'd been over the inside too. It would be the biggest story ever. It's impossible not to think about that, the same as it's impossible not to think about all the things you could buy with the money in the safe. I wouldn't do it – I'd never do it, any more than I'd pinch the banknotes. I think about it, though. If I showed my friends some of the pictures of Ghost in that old-fashioned dress standing on the staircase with the stuffed stag on one side of the picture, they'd probably think the same thing I did the first time I saw her. They'd think she was the Langlands ghost.

Ghost looks over my shoulder at one of those pictures. "I should have put something better on," she says wistfully, sounding like some of the other girls I know for the first time ever. Then she says, "There are better things in the attic."

I raise my eyebrows.

"Come and see," she says.

We go up the stairs, and past that bedroom where Dad and I repaired the ceiling. There's a scruffy-looking door at the end of the passage. Ghost opens it and we peer up a narrow set of wooden stairs towards a faint light at the top.

Ghost looks at me. "When you first came to the house, I was up there," she says.

I follow her up the stairs. I'm not sure what to expect at the top, and when we get there I just stare. It's *crammed* with stuff. There are crates and boxes and trunks, the sort people hide bodies in in films. There are square and rectangular things covered with sheets that are probably paintings or maybe mirrors, and a couple of marble statues. The light comes from a window at the far end, and as we pick our way towards it, I see that there's a bearskin spread out on the floorboards. An actual bearskin, with the bear's head attached.

Ghost doesn't seem bothered. She kneels on the bearskin so that she can open one of the trunks. It's full of clothes. I can see that straight off, because the thing on top is a heavy cape made of tweed, the sort of thing Sherlock Holmes would wear.

180

Ghost lifts that out and puts it on the floor. Then she pulls out a military jacket, bright red with blue cuffs and a lot of gold braid, but she sees the expression on my face when I look at that, and she dumps it on top of the cape.

The military jacket is followed by the ugliest pair of tartan trousers I've ever seen. Then she hauls out a tail coat, the sort of thing people used to wear in the evening. I laugh at that.

"No way," I say.

Eventually, though, she finds something that's okay – old-fashioned, but not so much that you'd feel really stupid putting it on: a dark suit, the sort of thing my great grandfather probably wore when he went out on a date with great gran.

Ghost looks at me, and I look back at her.

"All right," I say.

chapter forty

Ghost

I was happier that afternoon than any other time I can remember.

I found a dress in a beautiful shade of deep blue, with panels of gleaming satin overlaid with delicate net, and a shimmering silver trim. There was everything to match in the boxes: shirts, gloves, shoes, ties and cravats, stockings and petticoats. The previous owners of Langlands had parcelled up the costumes of their entire lives in the attic.

We carried everything downstairs and then I shut myself in my room to dress, while Tom went into one of the other rooms to do the same. I was quicker than he was, unsurprisingly, since I was used to tiny buttons whereas he had probably never seen collar studs in his life before. I waited on the landing, a little anxiously, for him to emerge.

When he did, I almost gasped aloud. It wasn't just that the clothes suited him. Tom was good-looking whatever he wore. No; it was because he looked so convincingly as though he came from 1945. It was as though instead of me trying to catch up with him in 2017, he had stepped back into 1945 with me.

I suppose he saw me staring because he looked rather self-conscious as he came up to me. He gave a half-smile that made my breath catch in my throat, and then he said, "I feel like we're going out for dinner at the Ritz or something."

I didn't tell him that those weren't dinner clothes. I didn't want to spoil the moment, and anyway, he looked so handsome that I didn't really care.

Tom looked at me, at the blue dress, and he said, "You look great, you look really..." and he hesitated, thinking of the right word, and I held my breath. "Right," he said in the end. "It suits you."

"Thank you," I said.

Tom came closer to me, and I thought for a moment that perhaps he would put his arms around me, and kiss me again. But instead he walked around me, studying me from every angle as though he were looking at something fascinating.

After a moment he said, "It's amazing. I don't know why but you don't look as though you've just dressed up. You really do look as though you've stepped out of 1945."

So he felt it too. It was almost – almost – possible to imagine that that was what had happened, that we belonged to what I now knew was the past.

Langlands did that to you. Of course, nearly everything in the house – apart from the few things Tom had brought in – was at least seventy years old. There was a confidence about the place, as though it were a grand old lady who simply refused to accept the passing of time and rejected everything new-fangled. Now that Tom and I were dressed to match the house, I felt the outside world fading away like a dream; it felt less and less probable when compared with the solid experience of me and Tom, here at Langlands, in our plundered finery.

We went downstairs after that, and took heaps more photographs with Tom's telephone. He took one of the two of us standing close together, and then he did something so that the colours drained out of the photograph and it became sepia, like the photographs in the library at Langlands.

"It looks really old now," he said, seeming pleased, but I said, "Turn it back the way it was."

"Why?"

"I like the colours better," I said. That was all I could think of to say. The fact was that it disturbed me somehow, seeing the photograph of us together, looking as though it had genuinely been taken a century ago. It made me feel a painful sense of yearning, as though I were far away from home.

Later, I took Tom all over the house, showing him the rooms he hadn't seen before, and telling him what I knew of the history of Langlands. We looked down from the windows at the gardens and the forest that fringed them. I made a meal with some of the things that Tom had brought with him, and we ate it in the dining room, laughing at each other from either end of the long table.

And Tom kissed me again.

He put his arms around me and bent his head and kissed me so tenderly that a soft and melting warmth seemed to run through my whole body. He didn't slide his hands under my clothes and across my bare skin as he had before. I think he understood that that day we had a few brief hours stolen from 1945, when love unfolded to a slow and formal timetable.

That day was beautiful, but it stands out in my memory for another reason: that was the day I first thought seriously that Tom might one day step into my world, instead of I into his.

chapter forty-one

The next time Tom came, he surprised me. Two days later, I was standing on the gravel outside the house, cradling a cup of tea in my hands and soaking up the late afternoon sunshine (still best enjoyed from the depths of a woollen coat, even in March), when I heard the distant sound of an engine.

Since so few vehicles ever came to Langlands, their different tones made a distinct impression on me, and this was one I did not recognise: it was thinner and more droning somehow than the engine of Tom's car. I stepped back into the shadows under the stone porch, and watched warily.

The droning sound swelled and then suddenly something burst out from under the trees. I knew what it was. I had seen illustrations of motorcycles in the books in the library and I had even seen one or two modern examples the day we had driven to the coast. Still, it was a surprise to see one come roaring up Langlands' drive. It stopped before the gravel, and the rider dismounted.

Tom, I thought, judging by the build and height, but with the helmet over his face it was impossible to be one hundred per cent certain, so I stayed in the shadows, waiting.

He did something to the machine to make it stand up on its own, and then he took off his helmet. Yes; it was Tom. I set down the tea cup on the edge of a stone planter and went out to meet him.

The leather jacket he was wearing suited him; he reminded me of the pictures I had seen of wartime flying aces. I remembered the terrible day he had told me that my life was out of time by seventy-two years, and I hadn't wanted to believe him. I had clutched at the thought that he might have reasons of his own for denying the War.

You haven't gone to fight. You might not be an objector – you might be a deserter.

That was what I had said, and I had offended him. Now that I knew him better, I didn't think he would run away from a fight. He hadn't tried to run that day I had confronted him in the hallway with a loaded rifle, although I had seen that he was afraid. He had stayed, and he had told me the truth.

Now I thought that *if* it had been 1945, he would have fought bravely. That was how I lived my life in those days: constantly in the conditional tense. *If this, then that...if only...*

Now, though, I smiled at Tom and he grinned back, pleased with himself.

"Surprise," he said. "I've been working on it for a while and I finally got it roadworthy. I can come up here when I like now – I don't have to rely on Mum lending me the car." He swung round to glance back at the bike and I looked too.

"It's lovely," I said, without the faintest idea of whether it was a very good motorcycle for 2017 or a very poor one, and Tom laughed.

"Mum doesn't think so. She thinks I'll have an accident on it, so she's keener than before to let me borrow the car."

We went into the house – to the kitchen as usual, since it was warmest there – and without preamble Tom said, "I looked for those two men, like I said I would. Fraser MacFarlane and George Robertson."

I just stood and looked at him, waiting.

186

"Fraser MacFarlane's dead," he said. He shrugged. "I'm sorry. I did an online search..." He must have seen the blank look on my face at that so he went on, "I looked on the internet. There are records on there, the same as paper ones, only easier to get at. There was an article in the local paper about him – *local solicitor remembered*, something like that. He died a couple of years ago."

"Oh," I said.

"George Robertson I'm not so sure about. He's retired, I know that. There was a thing about that in the same paper." He shrugged. "They don't get a lot of news. I couldn't find anything to say he'd died. That might not mean anything, though. I don't know what happened after he retired. If he stayed in the town, someone will know where he is. But if he died in some old people's home in England it probably wouldn't get into the paper here, and maybe not down there either, if he wasn't really known."

I looked Tom in the eyes, trying to read his expression.

"Is that the end? There's nothing else to find out?"

He shook his head. "No, it's not the end. It's a small town, Ghost. Someone will know where old Dr. Robertson went. I'll have to find out the old-fashioned way – by asking around." He grinned. "Cheer up. We'll find him in the end, if he's still alive and kicking."

And if he's not? I thought. *Then I'll never know why Grandmother did what she did. I'll never know...and I'll never, ever, stop being angry with her.*

I suppose my feelings showed on my face. Tom looked at me for a moment as though he was considering something, and then he said, "Look, let's not stay here this evening. Let's go out."

"How?"

"On the bike, of course. You'll have to change – you can't go out on it in that dress."

"Where will we go?"

187

"How about the town? The shops are nearly all shut so it'll be fairly quiet. We could get something to eat."

I thought about it. "What if we meet people – people you know?"

Tom shrugged. "We'll make up some story. We could say you're from England."

"Do I sound English?" I said.

"Well, you sound...different. Not in a bad way," Tom added hastily. "You just sound – I don't know – sort of formal."

"Oh."

"You could be here working. Maybe a gap year."

I didn't ask him what that was.

"We should probably think of a name," he added. "I mean, I don't think we'll meet anyone, but if we did, maybe it would be better to give some name other than Augusta McAndrew. Just in case."

"Isn't Augusta a usual name any more then?" I asked.

"Not really," said Tom gravely.

"Sophia?" I suggested cautiously, but Tom shook his head.

"Beatrice?" I hazarded.

I saw a muscle twitch at the corner of Tom's mouth. He said, "Not unless you're a big fan of the royals."

I didn't ask him why that would be a problem.

"Florence?"

At that, Tom gave a great shout of laughter. In fact, he laughed until he was wiping his eyes with the back of his hand, while I stood glaring at him with my hands on my hips.

"You choose then," I said crossly, when he had calmed down enough to listen.

"I don't know," said Tom. "How about Jess?"

"That sounds like a boy's name," I told him.

Tom started to laugh again, but stopped himself with an

effort. "At this rate we'll never go out at all. Let's worry about it later."

"All right," I said warily. "What should I put on?"

chapter forty-two

Five minutes later I came downstairs again wearing the trousers Tom had given me, and the leather jacket with a woollen jumper underneath; Tom had said it would be cold riding the motorcycle. I also had a pair of leather gloves that I had taken from Grandmother's room.

Tom unfastened the spare helmet from the back of the motorcycle and helped me to put it on. It was distinctly strange climbing onto the machine.

"Hold onto me," Tom said as he started the engine.

Riding down the track was unnerving. It hadn't rained the last few days so the ground was hard, but still the motorcycle seemed to bounce and judder alarmingly, and when we went over the grid at the spot where the track came out of the woods I thought I was going to be shaken to pieces. Once we got onto the proper road, though, it was wonderful – exhilarating and frightening at the same time, and totally different from being boxed inside the car. It felt *fast*. I could feel the wind rushing by and the vibration of the machine on the road and the delirious sense of skimming across a wide-open space with the sky wheeling above us. Where the road curved the sensation was terrifying. I was dizzy with it, gasping and holding onto Tom for dear life.

At last we came into the town, and as the fields and forest sliding past us turned into houses behind railed-off squares of garden my mood became suddenly sober. I imagined Grandmother driving along this same road into town in the shiny black car I now knew to be hopelessly old-fashioned. I imagined her gloved hands grasping the wheel tightly, her expression one of grim concentration. The places I now saw for the first time must have been as familiar to her as the rooms and corridors of Langlands were to me. Some of them must have had particular significance for her, and I had no way of knowing which. That house, for example, with all the woodwork picked out in a startling shade of crimson – that might have been the home of some great friend of hers, or simply a landmark on the way into town. I would never know. Did she even *have* friends here? I had no way of knowing that, either.

And of course, she had died here, in this world I hadn't shared with her.

My head was full of these thoughts as we came into the town centre. It didn't take long. I suppose the distance from the first house on the edge of the town to the square in the middle was less than from Langlands house to the edge of the estate where the grid lay across the road. Tom parked the motorcycle. I took off my helmet, feeling self-conscious as I did so. It was impossible to shake off nearly eighteen years of hiding myself – and yet who was going to recognise me, when there hadn't been so much as a single photograph of me in existence until a few days ago? And Tom was right, if anyone asked us, I could give a false name. There was really no risk. The unease I felt was like the residue of a bad dream, or the scar that itches long after the wound has healed.

I tried to concentrate instead on taking in the town. The street we had come down looked narrower and more closed-in than the towns and villages we had passed through the day we went to the coast. Some of the buildings were very plain and square; others had more elaborate – and I guessed older – architecture. It was fascinating to me to see the passing of time marked on the town: the garish-looking shop fronts grafted onto weathered-looking old buildings. There was a kind of memorial in the middle of the square, so I went up the steps to look and that and read the date: 1893. There was something reassuring in seeing that the past – a past that stretched back even further than 1945 – was still present here. Perhaps I was not so very far from home after all.

We walked about the town for a while. I found the shop windows fascinating, although I was not sorry that the shops themselves were closed. I imagined the town in the daytime being as busy as the city I had seen in the magazine Tom brought me. But the few people who passed us now took no particular notice of us.

Eventually, Tom dragged me away from the shops.

"We'll get a fish supper," he told me. "You can't live in the twenty-first century without having one of those."

I was bemused by the place he took me into, although the aroma of frying food was unbelievably good. We stood with our backs to the wall, waiting for our order.

"Where do we sit down?" I said to Tom in a low voice.

He glanced at me, amused. "We don't."

I was scandalised, but it wasn't until we were outdoors again and out of the earshot of the staff that I said, "We can't eat these in the street."

"Yes, we can," said Tom cheerfully. He held one of the paper-wrapped packages out to me. "We'll sit on the wall over there."

I followed him. The parcel was temptingly warm in my hands but I was still struggling with what he was suggesting.

"Tom," I said as we sat down on the wall, "Eating in the street – it's – it's not–"

Tom looked at me. "Let me guess. Your grandmother said it was bad manners."

"Yes."

Tom pulled back a fold of paper, extracted a large chip and put it in his mouth. When he had swallowed it, he said, "I don't know why she bothered, when she never took you out of Langlands anyway. What street did she think you were going to eat chips in?"

"She didn't like me wandering around with food at all," I said. "Not even in the garden." It crossed my mind that this prohibition had never stopped me from eating berries in the kitchen garden nor pilfering apples to eat in my room while reading a book, and I had never considered myself morally compromised by either of these activities. Still I hesitated. The smell of freshly-fried food that seeped out of the warm parcel on my lap was maddening. I could feel my mouth watering. And after all, why should I care what Grandmother would have expected me to do? But the lessons she had taught me about how to behave had been very soundly drummed in. *Just because something feels good doesn't make it good* – that was one of them, along with *handsome is as handsome does*. Just because the aroma of fish and chips was making me want to rip open the parcel and wolf the lot didn't make it a proper thing to do.

The paper rustled under my fingers but I didn't eat.

"Ghost," said Tom, "Eat something." He put his head on one side. "You're not going to be arrested for crimes against good manners, you know."

I stared into Tom's eyes. He didn't drop his gaze. He looked faintly amused, but he wasn't backing down. He was waiting for me to eat. It occurred to me that refusing the food he had bought me might be ruder than being seen eating in the street.

I opened the parcel and began to eat. The food was delicious. Once I had started I couldn't stop. I was ravenous, and anyway,

I had done it now, so I might as well enjoy it. I ate all of it, and then I crumpled the paper into a ball and licked my fingers.

I felt better after eating, warm and cheerful. Who cared if it was unladylike behaviour? I doubted whether the handful of people who had passed by while we were eating had even noticed me.

Grandmother was wrong. That wasn't just anger speaking to me anymore. Now I could see quite clearly that her way of doing things was irrelevant in Tom's world. I wondered if there had been any sense to some of those stuffy rules even in 1945. *Don't eat in the street; don't talk about money; tilt the soup bowl away from you; you must never be alone with a man.*

Later that evening, when Tom had brought me back to Langlands and kissed me goodbye, lingeringly, he paused, with his arms around me and his forehead resting against mine so that we were too close even to look into each other's eyes.

He said, "Ghost, you know...I'm not seeing anyone else. I mean, there isn't any other girl."

He was silent for a few moments after that, and so was I, but I could feel his fingers on the side of my neck, caressing my skin almost thoughtfully.

Then he said, "I don't know how this would have worked in 1945."

"How does it work in 2017?" I said softly.

Tom thought about it. "It goes as fast or as slowly as you want it to."

His touch was warm; my skin seemed to glow with it. When we were as close as this, I became dizzy; I couldn't think straight. I couldn't think what *fast* or *slowly* might be. All I could think about was Tom, the sound of him drawing breath, the way he was so close to me that when he blinked I felt his eyelashes graze my face.

At last Tom said, "It's going to get dark. I should go before it gets too dark to see the track."

"Yes," I said.

He kissed me again then, but briskly, his lips touching my cheek and not my mouth. Then he was walking towards the motorcycle, the helmet swinging from his hand, and I was watching him go, my hands clasped tightly together as though compensating for the loss of his touch.

After he left, I went back into the house and climbed the stairs to my own room. I had not slept there since Grandmother died. It was not just the cold – I was used to that, after all – it was the strange loneliness of being at Langlands by myself. The kitchen, warm and homely as it was, felt comforting. Sleeping on the bench or on the floor was a small price to pay.

Now, however, I went into the bedroom I had slept in since I was tiny, with its iron bedstead and the washstand with the little mirror hanging over it and its little bookcase stuffed with volumes in worn bindings. The bedstead was a double; the room had not been furnished with a single child in mind, but more probably for long-ago guests.

I took off my boots and climbed onto the bed. I didn't get under the covers; I simply lay on top of them, looking up at the ceiling with its ornate plasterwork, wreathed here and there with delicate cobwebs. After a while I turned my head on the pillow to look to my right, at the space beside me. I tried to imagine Tom lying there, next to me.

Rays of light from the dying sun slanted through the tall windows. The evening shadows were long now, and the light picked out everything with heightened contrast. It was too obvious that I was alone. I closed my eyes and tried again.

I could almost see him, his face turned towards me on the pillow. His blue-green eyes, his dark hair, the lines of his cheekbones. His mouth. I tried to make myself feel how it would be. Tom and I, lying here together. Tom rolling over to face me, touching my face, my shoulder.

I touched my fingers to my lips, feeling the soft pressure,

imagining Tom's mouth on mine. I traced the line of my collarbone, wondering how it would feel if it were Tom's hand caressing me and not my own. Would it be beautiful, or would it feel horribly, guiltily wrong?

I looked into myself, and all I felt was confusion. I couldn't tell where the sharp prickles of excitement ended and the searing stabs of guilt began.

Then a board creaked outside the bedroom door and I jumped as though a brand had touched my flesh. My eyes flew open. I was off the bed almost before I knew what I was doing, and now my heart was thudding so hard that I felt dizzy. I crossed the floor in a few paces and thrust the door wide open.

Nothing. There was nobody there. I went right out onto the landing and looked both ways, but I was quite alone. Of course I was. The creak I had heard was a board I had trodden down on my way into the room springing back into place, the sound amplified by my own guilt.

I sagged against the doorframe and put my hands over my face.

What's wrong with me? I thought. *Why don't I even know what I want?*

I stood there for a long time, until the last of the light had died and I had to creep downstairs to the kitchen in darkness.

chapter forty-three

Spring comes late in Perthshire; the trees are not yet green in March. Often, I would get up in the morning and be shivering with the cold as I banked up the fire in the belly of the kitchen stove. Still, sometimes the water in the chickens' enclosure was frozen solid when I went to feed them.

After the day Tom took me into the town on his motorcycle, he came again a number of times, sometimes on the motorcycle and sometimes in his mother's car. Once, he brought me a photograph of us together, the one we had taken the day we had dressed up in the things from the attic. I took a print that hung in my bedroom out of its frame and put the photograph in its place: me and Tom, smiling forever behind the glass.

My education in the ways of 2017 went in fits and starts. There were great gaps in Tom's knowledge of the history of the past seventy years. He did his best to fill the gaps by looking things up. He took to bringing a thing he called a tablet, that looked a little like the slate I had had when grandmother taught me my letters, only it had a kind of lighted rectangle on it instead of an area to write on. The tablet was unreliable for some reason related to the fact that Langlands House backed onto the side of a hill; when it worked, Tom could find out the

197

answers to things from it, but often it was slow, and sometimes it didn't work at all.

The other problem was that I found some things very hard to understand. History was less of a problem; once events were firmly in the past it was easier to trace the path of what had happened and what the outcome was. But I found it very difficult to make sense of some modern things. "Power" seemed to be a big problem because everything had to be run on gas or oil or electricity and there was never enough of any of these things, or else the wrong people had control of what there was, and when any of these fuels were used they did horrible things to the countryside.

"Why don't people just use less power?" I suggested.

Tom shrugged. "They need it for their cars and for aeroplanes and...well, just about everything in the house. Dishwasher, washing machine, TV..."

"They could use horses," I objected. "And they could do those jobs by hand – washing clothes and cleaning dishes – like I do here."

Tom shook his head. "People don't want to do that anymore. It takes up too much time. And anyway, if you have a couple, and they both go out to work, like Mum and Dad do, who's going to have the time and energy for doing all those other jobs by hand?"

"Your mother goes out to work? All the time?"

"Of course she does."

"But, Tom–!"

The discussion would go on from one incomprehensible circumstance to the next, as though we were passing through all the stages of an impossible quest without ever reaching the end.

In between trying to explain the main events of the last seventy years to me, Tom would take me out again – one evening we went for a walk on a path that ran alongside a river and twice passed under the remains of railway bridges, and one Saturday morning we went back into the town very early, before most of the shops were open. Sooner or later I should have to get used to busier places – I knew that – but not yet. The thought of so many people, of *crowds* of them, was dizzying. I had spent so long never seeing anyone but Grandmother, I could not imagine remembering dozens of faces – perhaps hundreds – of them, and recognising them when I saw them again. I would never forget Tom's face, I knew that – it was the one solid thing in a chaotic world, it was the eye of the storm. But all those others? I saw myself wandering through an endless multitude of strangers, every single one of them an unfamiliar face, every single pair of eyes turned towards me. No; I was not ready for busy places yet. Besides, it was Tom I wanted to be with, not all those unknown people.

Sometimes when Tom was telling me about the history that spanned the gap between his time and mine, and showing me pieces of his world, his words would fade away into the background as I lost myself in the pleasure of studying him. I liked the way his hair fell untidily over his forehead, the way he pushed it back without thinking about it; I liked the way his brows drew together when he was concentrating on something, as though the problem annoyed him. I liked the blue-green colour of his eyes, although now I had seen the real ocean I knew that it was not that colour at all, at least, not in Scotland – it was grey, silvery where the light touched it. Tom's eyes were the colour of the sea only in my imagination.

I liked to watch his hands, too, when he sketched shapes in the air with them, intent on describing things to me. The skin of his hands was roughened from working outdoors, but they were gentle when he touched my face or pulled me close to kiss me. I watched his hands moving and imagined their touch; sometimes I closed my eyes or looked away.

The hardest thing was that so much of my time was without

Tom: the long hours, days at a time sometimes, when I was utterly alone. I couldn't stop myself indulging in daydreams of Tom being there all the time. Without him, Langlands felt like a dead place, and I was the phantom who roamed through it.

I had to do *something* to stop the loneliness from becoming overwhelming, so when the day's chores were done, I spent my time trying to find out what I could about my situation. Tom had said he would ask around about Dr. Robertson, but surely there must be something to be learnt from the documents in the house?

Three times I took everything out of the safe in the library and sorted through it, document by document; I even riffled through the wads of banknotes, in case anything should be caught between them. I found nothing at all about Dr. Robertson. The second time I pulled the papers from the safe, out fell the gold-coloured key again. I picked it up and turned it over in my fingers but in the end, there was nothing to do with it but put it back into the safe.

I picked out the photographs again too, and stared at them as though if I looked for long enough they would come to life and tell me what I needed to know. The ones of my mother as a child I studied with yearning interest; I looked at the ones of Grandmother with mixed feelings. *Liar*, I said with silent bitterness. But the pictures of her at my age, and as a young bride, were taken long before I was born, long before she had started to tell me all those falsehoods about the War. Before it all went rotten. I put the photographs back amongst the other papers.

Then I tried the other places where I thought Grandmother might have stored papers. I went back into her room, where all the drawers were still pulled out from the last time I had been in there, looking for the combination to the safe. Well, why wouldn't they be? There was no-one to tidy the room if I didn't do it myself. All the same, it was strange seeing it like that, when she had always been so very neat in her ways. It gave me a pang of regret, which I squashed firmly.

At any rate, there was nothing about Dr. Robertson there, either.

I looked into drawers and bureaux and presses all over the house, but nothing came to light, and the search only served to show me that if there was anything, and Grandmother had really wanted to hide it from me, I would never find it. Langlands was simply too big, and there were too many places she could have hidden things. I couldn't take up every loose floorboard in every room or search inside every book in the library. I found nothing; it was Tom who made the breakthrough.

He came on a Tuesday afternoon, in the middle of a rainstorm. He brought the car, which was sensible, because even in the short distance from where he parked it to the door of the house he got a soaking. I hadn't heard the car coming for the drumming of the rain on the roof and windows, but I heard him knocking. When I opened the door he grinned at me, his eyes merry through the wet strands of hair that fell across them, and said, "Spring weather."

"Is it spring?"

"First day," he said, stepping inside and shaking his head to get rid of the water that dripped from his hair.

It was March 21st. In a little over three weeks I would be eighteen. I did not get far with that train of thought. Tom tried to kiss me and when I yelped at the water dripping off him, he laughed. He was so wet that I could feel the dampness seeping into my clothes from his jacket. When I stepped back, the fabric of my blouse had turned sheer with the damp and was sticking to my skin. I might as well have left the blouse off altogether.

I saw Tom looking and felt my face flame with a blush. I pulled the edges of my cardigan together over the damp fabric. For several moments silence stretched out between us.

In the end, it was Tom who spoke first. He cleared his throat, and then he said, "I've got some news. I've found something out."

I stared at him, uncomprehendingly.

"About Dr. Robertson. We may have found him."

chapter forty-four

It's strange how you can get used to *not knowing* something. When Tom told me he might have found Dr. Robertson, it was almost a shock. I didn't jump up and down with excitement; I just said, automatically, "How?"

Tom shrugged. "Like I thought I would, from asking around. First, I went to the address in your grandmother's will, but it's gone. There used to be a big house there, but they knocked it down. Now it's flats. I looked at the names on the doorbells but I couldn't see any Robertson. I checked in the phone book too, and he wasn't in that either, but maybe his number just isn't listed."

We began to walk down the passage to the kitchen.

Tom went on, "Then I went to the health centre, but they'd never heard of him. The woman on Reception said they couldn't give out personal details anyway, but she didn't know any Dr. George Robertson in the town." He shook his head. "She started asking me why I wanted to know, and I said he was an old friend of my Gran's. I don't think she believed me. Then she asked who my Gran was, so I said it didn't matter and left. I was thinking maybe he'd moved right away from the town."

"What did you do then?" I asked, thinking that it sounded hopeless.

"I was walking out and there was this notice on the wall

about when the centre was built, and I thought, *that's not all that long ago, maybe he moved on or retired before then.* When I got home, I Googled doctors in the town–" Tom saw my expression and added, "It's like looking them up." Then he went on, "But the only thing that came up was the health centre. I thought, there must have been something *before* that was built, so I tried looking for *old doctors' surgery* but there was nothing. Maybe if I'd had the name or address for it...but all I got was places in other towns." He grimaced. "I thought, *that's it, I don't know where to go from here.*"

Tom paused as I pushed open the kitchen door and we went inside. Both of us gravitated towards the stove; the outdoor temperature was no longer freezing but with damp clothing it was still unpleasantly cold.

Tom said, "Anyway, I got back from work last night and Gran was there, talking to Mum. She's eighty-six and she's lived in the town her whole life. I thought, *if anyone knows where Dr. Robertson is, it's her.* So I waited until Mum had gone off to make tea, and I asked her if she'd ever heard of a Dr. George Robertson."

"What did she say?" I was fascinated by Tom's narrative, and not simply because I wanted to know what his grandmother had told him. I couldn't imagine belonging to a family that had so many different people in it – mother, father, grandmother, probably cousins and aunts and uncles too. Some people had sisters and brothers too, though Tom didn't.

"She wanted to know right away why I was asking," said Tom. "She doesn't miss *anything*. After the woman in the health centre asked me that, I thought I'd better make up a story. I said someone Dad and I had done some work for had been asking, because they had something of his they wanted to return. Then she asked what."

Tom was grinning, as though his grandmother's persistence was funny. It made *me* unsettled; it seemed to me that sooner

204

or later someone was going to persist until they found out why he was really asking. Would he break his promise if someone pushed him hard enough? But Tom was unconcerned.

"I said the first thing that came into my head, which was a spirit level. That was what I was looking for that day I saw you, when Dad and I had just finished working here." He shook his head. "I don't think she believed me. She said it was an odd thing for someone to borrow from a doctor. But she said she knew Dr. Robertson. She said he was retired, but we knew that anyway, and he lives in the town. I asked where, and she said she didn't know, but probably one of the big houses on the north side of the High Street, because he'd always had money. And then," Tom concluded, "I could hear that Mum was coming back with Gran's tea, so I asked her about her indigestion, because she can go on for hours and hours about that."

I laughed in spite of myself. But then I said, "So we don't know exactly where he is?"

Tom shook his head. "But we know he's still alive, and he's living in the town."

"I suppose so," I said, but it was hard not to be disappointed. Nothing I had uncovered in the house had told me anything; I'd been relying on what Tom could find out.

"I'll keep asking," said Tom. "Someone will know. Someone always does."

He fell silent, and both of us listened to the rain rattling at the kitchen window. Even the light coming through it seemed to have a dismal grey tinge.

"How do you live here?" said Tom. "Most of the rooms are freezing, and it's so dark in here." He glanced at me. "I'm not insulting your house. I'd just improve a few things."

"Like what?"

"Electric lights, for starters. And central heating. Proper plumbing. And some of the windows round the back are boarded up. I saw that when we were here working. I'd get those replaced. I'd do that chimney properly, the one that fell through the roof. Yeah, I'd do the roof too. When we were up there you could see all the slates that were missing." He thought for a moment. "I wouldn't change the inside that much. I'd just restore things, like the broken bits of panelling. I'd get the ceilings and the wood repainted, and I'd get the whole place cleaned. Get all the cobwebs out."

"That sounds like a lot of things," I said. I should have liked listening to Tom talk as though he lived here, as though the house was his to work on as well as mine. But it made me uncomfortable, hearing him talk about the broken panels and the spiders' webs. Those were things I hardly noticed myself; there was no use in noticing them, since I couldn't do anything about them – I wasn't a carpenter and I couldn't reach the high ceilings to dust even if I wanted to. But Tom had noticed them.

Tom didn't seem concerned. "Probably quicker to build a new house," he said cheerfully. He looked up, away from me, gazing at something in his own mind that I couldn't see. He said, "That's what I want to do – build new things. I want to be an architect."

"Are you learning from your father?" I asked.

Tom shook his head. "Dad just does small jobs. Repairs, roofing, stuff like that. I said I'd work for Dad for a while to save up some money before I go to university. I think he's hoping I'll like it so much I'll take over the business in the end, but..." Tom shrugged. "I don't want to be mending roofs and laying patios for old ladies all my life. I want to design buildings." He grinned wryly. "Though it'll probably be supermarkets and blocks of flats."

"What if you could build *anything*?"

"Then I'd do something people would remember. Maybe a huge great tower in the middle of Glasgow. It would have an official name, but when people flew over the city they'd look out of the plane window and say, 'That's Tom McAllister's

Tower.' " He raised his eyebrows. "I don't know what's funny about that. I'm dead serious, you know."

"I'm sure that would be lovely," I said primly, doing my best to keep a straight face.

"Liar. You're laughing at me again."

"I'm not."

Tom folded his arms, but he was grinning. "Come on then, what would *you* do, if you could do anything?"

I opened my mouth to say something but no words came. What *would* I do? The world outside Langlands was too vast, too unfamiliar, too full of unknown possibilities. If I had walked down to the limits of the estate and stepped out into 1945, I would have known what to expect. But 2017 was an infinite realm of which only the tiniest part had been charted for me.

At last I said, "I'd find my mother. That's what I'd do." I looked at Tom. "I'd find out who I really am."

chapter forty-five

Tom

Someone will know, I told her, and sure enough, someone does. CCTV would be wasted in this town; it wouldn't tell you anything your neighbours couldn't. This time it's old Mrs. Campbell who knows.

Dad and I are putting down a new patio behind her bungalow. I don't know why she wants one – I can't see her spending the summer having barbecues. Most of the week it pisses with rain while we're working too. It reminds me why I don't want to do this forever. Mrs. Campbell's not bad though. She makes us cups of tea and piles the sugar in. I think she feels sorry for us, working away in her back garden with the rain dripping off our caps and running down the backs of our necks.

While I'm working my mind keeps drifting off to Langlands. I think how gloomy it'll be in the house, with the rain making that drumming sound on the roof. I think of Ghost moving about in there in the dark, looking like a real ghost in those old-fashioned clothes. It makes me feel bad for her, and uneasy. Going to Langlands is more than stepping back in time, it's like digging down into a grave.

We have to find the truth. Was there some good reason for hiding her away there? Because if not, I want to make her leave

Langlands now, right away. I want her in my world, not that creepy old place. It's on my mind all the time, what possible reason old Mrs. McAndrew could have had, but I can't puzzle it out. Maybe she really was just crazy, but she didn't strike me that way.

On the second day, Dad has go to the hardware shop to get something, so it's just me and Mrs. Campbell for a bit. Two minutes after he's gone, she's at the back door with a mug of tea and a piece of cake on a plate.

"Come in for a minute," she says. "You look frozen."

I reckon she picked that moment because she saw Dad going off. He always wants to get on with the work, not stand around talking. I guess she's lonely. There was probably a Mr. Campbell once but not anymore.

I look down at my boots but she tells me to come in anyway, and once I'm in, I'm grateful, because the kitchen is much warmer than the back garden. I sit at her kitchen table and eat the piece of cake, and she talks about the work and her daughter in Aberdeen and how the rain makes her joints ache. She's in the middle of telling me what the doctor said about that, when I think of asking her about Dr. Robertson. She's old enough to remember him for sure.

When I can get a word in, I say, "Mrs. Campbell, can you remember a doctor called George Robertson who used to work in the town?"

"Och yes," she says, and unlike the woman at the health centre she doesn't even ask why I want to know. She's too busy telling me what a handsome young doctor he was and how nobody could work out why he didn't marry – "broken heart, they said, only I don't know who broke it" – and how amazed they all were when he eventually married a girl with a lot of money. "He needn't have carried on doctoring at all, but he liked it that much – it's a vocation, isn't it?"

I keep an eye on the kitchen clock, wondering when Dad's

going to get back, while Mrs. Campbell gives me a rundown of all the major events in Dr. Robertson's life: the time someone got run over right outside the surgery and he ran out and saved their life; the son who grew up and moved down to London; his wife dying at sixty-two.

"Does he still live in the town?" I ask, thinking she's going to ask me for sure this time why I want to know all this. But she doesn't.

"Yes, he still lives in that place off Ferntower Road," she says. "The one with all the wood painted red. I can't think how he manages in it at his age."

She must be at least seventy herself, but I don't point this out. I let her finish talking, and then I thank her for the tea and cake and stand up. I'm back outside in the rain about two minutes before Dad turns up again.

"You've not got much done while I was away," he says.

I shrug. Nothing to say. I've already made my mind up. The first chance I get, maybe even tonight after work if it'll stop pissing it down for half an hour, I'm going to go down Ferntower Road and look for a house with the woodwork painted red. I'm going to find Dr. Robertson.

chapter forty-six

Ghost

The next time Tom came, he had something on his mind, something troubling him. I could see it in his expression; I was learning to read him the way I could read the changing weather in the skies over Langlands. This would have pleased me, except I could tell something was wrong.

He had brought me things: bread, milk, soap and some fruit I didn't recognise, strange, green things like mossy eggs.

"Kiwi," he said. "You don't eat the skin, just the inside."

I turned one of them over in my hands. "Are these a new thing?"

Tom shook his head. "I don't think so. I guess your gran just didn't like them."

After he had put everything on the kitchen table, he stood and looked at me, his expression grim.

"It's bad news. I found Dr. Robertson. But he won't talk to us."

I stared at him. "Why not? And how did you find him?"

"Mrs. Campbell. She's a woman Dad and I have been doing some work for. She's really old, so I thought she might remember Dr. Robertson, and she did." Tom scratched his head. "She loves talking. It's picking out the stuff you wanted to know from the rest of it that's difficult. I had Dr. Robertson's whole life story. Anyway, she told me where he lives – some big house off Ferntower Road, with the wood painted red. It wasn't difficult to find."

"You went there?"

"Yeah." Tom sighed. "Maybe that was a mistake. But I was there, outside the house, and I thought, why not? I thought I'd ask if he'd see you. Anyway, I wanted to make sure it was really him. Mrs. Campbell seemed sure about it, but she could have mixed him up with someone else. So I went and knocked."

"What did he say?"

"He didn't even open the door properly. He had a security chain on it. I said, 'Dr. Robertson?' and he said, 'Yes,' and then he said, 'What do you want?' I asked if I could talk to him for a few minutes. I said it was about someone he knew. He said, 'Who?' so I told him Rose McAndrew. He was quiet for a long time, and then he just shook his head and shut the door. I knocked again and he didn't reply. I called out, 'Can we just talk for a couple of minutes?' but...nothing. I couldn't think what else to do, so I kept knocking and then he opened the door a crack and said, 'Be off with you.' I could see he was going to shut it again so I said, 'Look, I just want to talk, I don't have to come in, and I wouldn't bother you if it wasn't important.' He stared at me for about two seconds and then he said, 'Go away or I'll call the police.' I had to go. He was going to do it."

I was silent when Tom finished explaining. I still had the funny green fruit in my hands; it felt rough, as though I were holding a fat little creature with a wiry pelt. I couldn't think what to say.

"I'm sorry," said Tom eventually. "I didn't want to push it. If he really had called the police, I couldn't have told them why I was there without mentioning you."

He'd remembered his promise. "Thank you," I said quietly.

Tom let out a long breath. "You know, maybe that's the

only way to get to the bottom of this. Talk to the authorities – the police, social services or whatever." He must have seen the alarm on my face because he hastily added, "We could wait until you're eighteen. It's only a couple of weeks. But look, they might be able to *make* him tell us what he knows. He can refuse to talk to me, but I don't think he can refuse to talk to them."

When he said that, I sat down on one of the kitchen chairs and put my elbows on the table and my head in my hands. Why was it so impossible to work out the best thing to do? Perhaps Tom was right, and we couldn't get to the truth on our own. It was true that I would be eighteen very soon. We could wait that little time and then ask for help. It wasn't as though I could hide from the outside world for the rest of my life anyway. So why did I feel so unhappy about the idea?

After a moment, Tom slid into the seat next to me. I felt him touch my hair gently, pushing it back behind my ear so that he could see my face.

I didn't look at him. Instead I looked down at my hands on the table top, turning them over so that I could study the palms, as if they were a map to somewhere I wanted to go. I struggled to find the right words to tell Tom how I felt.

"I wish–" I began, and hesitated. "I wish Dr. Robertson would have talked to you. Maybe we *can't* find the truth on our own, but whatever there is to find out, I feel like I want to know *first*." I shot Tom a glance. "Do you understand? I don't want to find out at the same time as a lot of strangers. If it's something bad, I don't want them looking at me, seeing how I react. And if..." I thought about it. "...if it was Grandmother who did something bad, I'd want to know that first, too."

I fell silent then. I couldn't explain my feelings about Grandmother any further than that. Thinking about her was like a dull dragging ache under my ribs. I couldn't imagine any reason big enough or urgent enough to justify what she had done. She had made me into an anachronism, a thing as out of place in the modern world as an Egyptian mummy or a knight in armour. In spite of that, I wanted time to think about what I would say to the world about her; how I should explain her to people who didn't know her. She wasn't just the person who had kept me away from the outside world, brought me up to a lifestyle that no longer existed, and lied to me for seventeen years. She was also the person who had taught me to read and write. She had braided my hair for me when I was too little to do it, and read me *Puss in Boots* and *The Tinder-Box* scores of times although she must have been horribly bored. She had made me cocoa when I had been out chopping firewood and my hands were frozen, and sometimes she had made me baked apples with cinnamon, which was one of my absolutely favourite things. I hated her for what she had done, and I missed her with all my heart, and I couldn't face talking to strangers about her until I had sorted it all out in my own head.

I suppose Tom was thinking too, because for a long while he said nothing either. In spite of the thoughts that swarmed in my head like angry wasps, I couldn't help but be aware of his nearness. No words passed between us, but I knew that his face was turned towards me. He sighed quietly, and I felt his breath on my skin.

When he touched me, I thought he just meant to smooth back my hair again, but he turned my face gently towards him. His gaze was intent, as though he were studying me. I would have blushed at the boldness of staring into each other's eyes at so close a range, except I could tell somehow that he was not thinking about kissing me; he had something else altogether on his mind.

At last Tom said, "I think there's a way to get Dr. Robertson to talk to us."

chapter forty-seven

"You know," said Tom soberly, "This is only going to work if the old man knew your grandmother back then." He glanced at me, then back at the road ahead. "If he met her after you were born, he'll only remember her as old."

"I know," I said heavily. When I looked out of the car window I could see a faint reflection of myself in the glass overlaid on the passing landscape. I thought I looked a lot like Grandmother when she was young; almost close enough that we could have been twins. I had dressed my hair the same way she had done hers in the photograph, drawing it back from my face and securing it at the sides with clips I had found in Grandmother's room. Of course, I hadn't been able to find a dress exactly like the one she had been wearing in the photograph we had found. The skirt was not as full as the one in the picture, and the fabric was better suited to summertime; I was shivering a little in it. But it was near enough.

Finding a suitable dress among the things stored in the trunks in the attic had probably taken less time than getting the right effect with the makeup. I had never worn it before, nor did I own so much as a powder compact. I had had to sort through the things on Grandmother's dressing-table and do my best with those. A good deal of trial-and-error had shown that the judicious application of one of her darkest shades of lipstick made my lips a little thinner and more like hers. I didn't like the effect; I thought it made me look older and somehow harder. It worked, though; it made me less like myself and more like her.

"Worth trying though," Tom went on. "There's a good chance he *did* know her when she was young. We know *he* was here then, because Mrs. Campbell said so, and we know your grandmother was, because of the photos." He gave a little grunt of amusement. "You know what Mrs. Campbell said about him? 'Nobody could work out why he didn't marry – broken heart, they said, only I don't know who broke it.' Maybe it was your grandmother. She was good-looking enough."

I smiled a little at that. It was strange to think of Grandmother breaking anyone's heart. She had rarely ever spoken of my grandfather, and not at all of my father, and I had read disapproval or distaste into her silence.

"Anyway," continued Tom, "She trusted those two – Dr. Robertson and the other guy, the solicitor who died – enough to let them know about you. I don't think she'd have done that if she didn't know them really well."

"No," I agreed. I shrugged helplessly. "She was so careful about it, all the time. It's still hard to believe she told them at all."

"Old friends," said Tom. "They had to be."

We were coming into the outskirts of the town now. I had been nervous before we set out; now I felt a little sick with it.

"He wouldn't talk to you before," I blurted out. "Why should he talk to us now?"

We turned right into a side road, and Tom let the car coast to a halt, checking that there was nobody behind us.

"This is what I think," he said, seriously. "Him saying no like that, it wasn't just because he didn't know me. Dad and I, we do jobs for older people and a lot of them have these stickers up by the door, saying *no cold callers*. He didn't have anything like that. And when I mentioned your grandmother's name he went quiet. He didn't say *who?* or *I don't know anyone called that*. He was thinking about what to do. I'm sure of it.

I think Dr. Robertson knew fine well what was going on, and he was protecting her. That's why I think the only person he'll talk to is her...or someone he thinks is her."

It all depends whether I can convince him I'm her, I thought. I looked at Tom and said, "Can we go? I think I want to get it over with before I lose my nerve."

I listened to Tom telling me that that wasn't going to happen, that I was going to be fine, that I looked so much like Grandmother that even if I spoke to Dr. Robertson in Mandarin Chinese he'd still think I was her. I l clasped my hands in my lap, but I could not make them be still; my fingers entwined restlessly. My mouth was dry. It was all I could do not to touch my hair; I felt exposed with it drawn back from my face so severely, but I dared not spoil the effect.

We were stopping again. "We're here," said Tom, unclipping his seatbelt. He tilted his head towards the street outside. "I'm not pulling into his drive because the less warning he has, the better."

"All right," I said, but it came out as a croak. I climbed out of the car and stood hugging myself in the chill spring breeze, my thin dress flapping around my legs. I had a pair of Grandmother's shoes on too, because all I owned were lace-up boots. The shoes were a half-size too small and the toes were pointed; they pinched uncomfortably.

Tom nodded towards a gateway framed with dense hedges, previously cut into neat rectangles but now rather overgrown. We had agreed that I would go to the door alone. If Dr. Robertson saw Tom, he might take fright and call the police as he had threatened to do before. I swallowed.

What's the worst thing that can happen? I said to myself. *Only that he won't speak to you.* But that was bad enough; then I might never know the truth about Grandmother and myself.

I picked my way carefully to the gateway and looked around the end of the hedge. I was used to things being old – everything at Langlands was old – but even to my eyes, the old doctor's house looked neglected. Weeds had sprung up everywhere, and while those flourished, whatever had grown in the planters at either side of the front door had long since died and shrivelled up. The only spot of colour was the bright red of the paintwork, and that had a sad, grimy look to it. There were blinds at the ground-floor windows, rendering them opaque. I supposed that since I could not see in, nobody inside could see out either, but still I had an uncomfortable feeling, as though I were being watched.

I took care to tread softly on the paving-stones that led to the front door, each of them surrounded by a bed of green moss, so that they looked more like stepping-stones in a scummy pond. Once I glanced back, looking for Tom, but he was wisely staying out of sight. I was on my own.

The house had a porch with an outer door that stood open, and an inner door that was resolutely closed. There was a doorbell at the outer door, but when I pressed it, it had a spongy feel to it and I could not hear it ringing inside the house. In the end, I did what Tom had done and knocked firmly on the inner door.

I listened, but all I could hear was my own breathing and the distant chirping of a bird. I knocked again, and this time I heard something inside the house: a slow shuffling. Dr. Robertson did not call out to say that he was on his way to open the door; based on Tom's experience, perhaps he hoped his caller would give up and go away before he got there. I did not say anything either, because I did not wish to give him the opportunity to tell me to go away without seeing me. I simply stood on one side of the door while he laboriously approached the other side of it. My heart was thumping so hard that I was beginning to be afraid that I would pass out.

There was a rattle on the other side of the door and then

suddenly it jerked open a little way, perhaps a hand's span, and I found myself staring at Dr. Robertson.

Since I had met Tom, I had been closer to many more strangers than I had ever been in my life before. I had passed them on the street, I had stood amongst them in the fish and chip shop. It was still a shock to be in such close proximity to somebody new – to be looking them right in the eyes.

Dr. Robertson was at least as old as Grandmother, and since I had never met my grandfather, that made him the oldest man I had ever seen. He wasn't handsome, either. Grandmother had been beautiful in spite of her age, or so I had thought, with her fine bone structure and clear blue eyes. Dr. Robertson carried every one of his years like a burden. The flesh of his face sagged, lapped in wrinkles, and his eyes had a filmy look to them, the whites as yellow as the leaves of an old book. He looked like nothing so much as an ogre from a fairy story.

My carefully-prepared words deserted me. Unable to say a thing, I lacked even the presence of mind to step forward to hold the door open, or step back to put space between us. I simply stood there, ramrod-straight and motionless, staring at him with round eyes.

Silence stretched out between us. I had time to take in the hand that gripped the door, its knuckles bunched and swollen to an angry shine. The quiff of hair that was now much more white than dark, but still held a little of its former colour, like a badger's stripe. The brown tweed tie, clumsily knotted by aged fingers.

"*Rose*," said Dr. Robertson in a voice that was corroded with an emotion I couldn't identify.

The next instant the door had closed smartly in my face and I was looking at its worn panels. I could not think what to do next. He had seen me, he had identified me as Rose McAndrew, and he had shut the door in my face.

I was still standing there wondering whether to try knocking

219

again when there was a rattle from the other side of the door as the chain was removed, and the door opened again, this time wide enough that I could see beyond the old doctor to a room at the end of the hallway where the bleak spring sunshine bleached everything to paleness.

"Rose," said Dr. Robertson again, and there was an almost pleading tone in his voice. "Is it really you?" He held onto the doorframe and the gaze of his rheumy old eyes moved over me restlessly, as though he could hardly believe what he saw, which I suppose was the case. "It can't be you," he said wonderingly. "You're as old as I am. They said you were dead."

Abruptly he turned away from me and sank into a chair that stood in the hallway, its back to the wall. The gnarled hands that curled around the arm rests were trembling, I saw.

I stepped into the house. Now he couldn't send me away without speaking to me; I was inside.

Dr. Robertson shrank back in the chair, as far away from me as he could, and I realised that he was actually afraid of me.

"Have you come to take me?" he quavered, and his gaze darted from side to side, seeming to stab the air.

I shook my head, and the ends of my hair, that I had curled so carefully to look like Grandmother's, bounced against my neck.

"I need to speak with you," I said gravely. I watched him lick his lips, considering. His eyes closed once, briefly, as though he wanted to clear his vision.

At last he put out a hand and pointed down the hallway to the coldly illuminated room at the end.

"We'll go to the sitting-room," he said. When I waited, he shook his head. "You go first. I'm not young anymore, I have to take my time."

I went down the hallway as he had directed. I did my best to walk naturally, although Grandmother's shoes pinched and rubbed with every step I took; I was reminded of the Little

Mermaid, who felt as though she was treading on upturned swords when she tried to walk like a human girl on her new legs. Behind me, I heard Dr. Robertson struggle to his feet with a grunt of effort, and then the sound of the front door closing. I thought about Tom waiting outside; it made me uncomfortable to think of him shut out.

There's nothing to be afraid of, I reminded myself. I could hear the old man's progress down the hallway behind me, and it was torturously slow, punctuated with grunts of effort. Even supposing he became furiously angry when he knew who I really was, I wasn't in any danger; I could be back at the front door and outside before he was a quarter of the way there. *All the same...*

I went into the sitting-room. The brilliant light came from large picture windows which ran the length of the room. In spite of its cold quality, it was the most cheerful thing about the room. It was very tidy, but it was the tidiness of a place that had no bustling life in it. There was a magazine lying on a little table, and it had been lined up so that it was perfectly parallel with the edge. Compared to Langlands with its panelling and wooden floorboards, there was a good deal of softness and comfort: a thick carpet underfoot, wallpaper with a velvety texture, thick drapes and plump cushions. All of it was in shades of light brown that somehow added up to an ineffably dreary effect. My eyes kept being drawn to the one visible spot of colour, a clump of yellow daffodils in the untidy garden outside the window.

A clock was ticking loudly in the stillness of the room. I looked for it and saw beside it on the mantelpiece a framed photograph of what could only have been Mrs. Robertson. She was smiling in the photograph and I thought that she had a pleasant face under her greying curls, but still it was just as depressing as the rest of the room; the photograph had faded with the passing of years, and you could tell that Dr. Robertson had been alone for a long, long time.

I heard the old man come into the room behind me and turned to face him. He shuffled forward a few steps, placing his hand on the back of a chair for support. The sunlight fell on my face, almost strong enough to blind me; it was a conscious effort to keep my eyes open, focussed on the old man's face.

He stared at me in silence for perhaps half a minute, his bushy brows drawn together in a frown.

Then he said: "Lassie, don't you think you'd better tell me who you are?"

chapter forty-eight

In the end we sat one either side of the little table, Dr. Robertson in a high-backed arm chair, and I on the overstuffed sofa. After telling me to sit, he fell silent, clearly waiting for me to explain myself.

I bit my lip. There was nothing for it, though, so I told the truth.

"I'm Augusta McAndrew. I'm Rose McAndrew's granddaughter."

"Oh," said the old man slowly. "That explains why you're so like her." He made a little grunt that might have been amusement or disparagement. "I've not seen any other lassies your age wearing a dress like that one, though, not for a very long time."

I said, "Are you the Dr. George Robertson who witnessed my grandmother's will?"

"I am," he said – just that, not giving anything away. The way he kept staring at me made me uneasy; I was not used to that kind of scrutiny. At last he said, "You're so alike, it's no wonder I took you for Rose. But she's dead, isn't she?"

I nodded.

The old man made a strange wheezing sound that I eventually interpreted as a chuckle. "I thought you were her ghost, come to tell me my time'd come. You're lucky I didn't have a heart attack and make it true."

I couldn't laugh at that; it struck me that perhaps he was right.

After a few moments, Dr. Robertson stopped laughing and looked at me very hard.

"You've come home from school to take over your inheritance, is that it?"

"I didn't go to school," I said.

"You've finished your studies, then?"

"No. I never went to school at all." I could feel the colour rising in my face as he stared at me. I had heard the way he said *to take over your inheritance*, his voice full of suspicion. "That's what I wanted to talk to you about," I added.

"Hmmm. I don't know what you think I can tell you."

"I want to know why she did – what she did," I said, the words coming out in a rush. "Why she told me all those lies. Why she let me go on thinking there was a War on when there wasn't. Why she made me think it was 1945 when it isn't."

Abruptly I stopped, realising that I was close to tears.

"I think," said Dr. Robertson into the silence, "That you had better tell me exactly what Rose did, don't you?"

It occurred to me then that he knew perfectly well what Grandmother had done; what he wanted to know was how much I knew. Anyway, out it all came – how I grew up believing there was a war on, a war so terrible that Grandmother and I had to hide from it; how I'd never even spoken to any person other than Grandmother until the day I came down the staircase at Langlands with a rifle in my hands and saw Tom in the hallway. How I never knew my parents, and didn't know whether what little Grandmother had told me about them was true or not. How Grandmother had said there were things she was going to tell me as soon as I turned eighteen – and how she herself had driven away one day and never come back, without ever spilling the beans.

I came to the bit where Tom and I went to the library at Langlands and hauled everything out of the safe, and I told Dr. Robertson how we found the will, with his name on the bottom of it, and how Tom had the idea of tracking him down to find out what he knew. When I got to that bit, the old man frowned, and I had the feeling he felt angry with Tom for having that idea. But I suppose he knew that it was no use being angry now, because he didn't try to pretend any more that he had nothing to tell me. He gave a great sigh, as though he were giving up on something, and sank back into the armchair. And then he began to talk.

"When I first met Rose, she was as like you as two peas in a pod," Dr. Robertson said. "That would have been in the fifties, probably before your parents were even born. She was a couple of years older than me and better off; her family owned the Langlands estate. I never dared ask her to come out with me. I think she knew I liked her, though, because she was always very kind to me, even though she probably thought I was a silly boy. Then she married Angus McAndrew and just about broke my heart. When he took her off down to England it was almost a relief, not to have to see the pair of them going about together."

The old man cleared his throat noisily. "I'm not telling you this because I'm sentimental. I just want you to understand why I helped her, later on."

I said nothing.

"Anyway, I got married myself a few years afterwards, and that was that. Just made our thirty-fifth wedding anniversary a little before she was taken." He nodded at the framed photograph by the clock. "We were very happy together," he said. "I wouldn't want you to think otherwise. But I did carry a torch for Rose. I don't think you ever forget the first person you love."

Dr. Robertson fell silent for a moment, thinking about this, before he went on. "Well," he said at last, "I suppose it would have been around seventeen or eighteen years ago when I got a knock on the door one night. It was around this time of year but it was already pitch dark, so it must have been late in the evening. Shelagh had gone to her sister's for a few days so I was on my own, which was just as well, all things considered. I was used to being called out at all hours of the day or night, being a GP, though normally it was a telephone call, not someone on your doorstep.

"Anyway, I opened the door and there was Rose. I knew her the moment I laid eyes on her. Sixty if she was a day, and still beautiful.

"'George,' she said, 'Thank God, thank God. It's me, Rose McAndrew. You remember me, don't you?'

"I started telling her of course I did, but she cut me off. She said, 'Is it true you're a doctor?' and she clung onto my arm when she was asking it, as though she was begging me to say yes.

"'Yes,' I said, 'I'm a GP,' and the next thing I knew she was just about pulling me off my own doorstep.

"'You must come with me,' she said, 'It's an emergency.'

"'I'm in my dressing-gown, Rose,' I said, as she didn't seem to have noticed. 'I'll need a couple of minutes. And what kind of emergency is it? You might be better calling for an ambulance.' I was having visions, you see, of a car accident along the road or some such thing. For a second she said nothing, as though I'd put her on the spot, and then she said, 'It's a young woman. She's pregnant.'

"Now of course, I did see expectant mothers in the practice, but mostly just for taking their blood pressure and telling them to take vitamins. This looked like something more serious, the way Rose was carrying on, so I started trying to ask her more questions, and all the while I was going over in my head which things I'd have to take with me.

"Rose wasn't having any of it. She started talking really wildly, saying I was the only person who could come and if I didn't then the consequences would be on my conscience.

"I wouldn't have done it for anyone else in the world. The sensible thing would have been to carry on talking to her, to try to get more information about what had happened, and then make a decision based on that. If she'd told me all the facts I might have gone with her anyway, but I'd certainly have called an ambulance. But..."

The old man looked up, spreading out his gnarled old hands as though to say, *what could I do?*

"It was Rose," he said. "I couldn't say no to her. I told her to come and wait inside where it was warm, while I went to dress myself properly and get my things together. She stepped into the house and stood there shivering. She hadn't even put a coat on. I pushed her towards this room and told her to warm herself in front of the fire until I was ready.

"I couldn't have been gone five minutes but when I came back she nearly dragged me out of the door – she was that desperate to be gone. She had a wee car parked outside the house – not that big black vintage thing she took to driving later, just some ordinary thing, a Fiesta or something. She said she'd drive and I could follow. She had a way with her, Rose did. If she told you to do something, you did it."

I smiled a little at that, in spite of myself. It was perfectly true.

"So I followed her," continued Dr. Robertson, "and she drove like a lunatic all the way up to Langlands House. I did my best to keep up, but it wasn't easy, with the car bouncing all over the ruts in the track. You could tell the road was hardly ever used. If it'd been later in the year and the plants had grown up higher we might not have got through. There was a tree trunk halfway up that had come down across the track and someone had pushed it out of the way, but not managed the job properly, so there was only just room to get past it. I had to slow right down as it was, and then I thought the car would never get up the slope. And by that time the lights from Rose's car were vanishing in the distance.

"And I was puzzled all the while, because so far as I knew, Langlands House had been shut up for years. Rose's relatives who owned it had died, I believe, and I suppose whoever inherited it, if anyone did, thought it was too much trouble and expense to modernise.

"When we got to the house, it was completely dark from the outside. Rose had a torch though, and once we were inside I could see a faint light coming from upstairs. If I was feeling puzzled before, now I started to feel anxious. The place smelled of dust and decay and you could see there were no electric lights; I guessed there wasn't any proper running water either, and that turned out to be right. It had to be pumped in the kitchen. If Rose's story about a pregnant woman was true, it was going to be hard to do much for her in all this mess. But I was starting to think that maybe there wasn't any pregnant woman at all. Maybe Rose was having some kind of delusion. I wasn't that kind of doctor–" The old man tapped his forehead, "– but I thought that was possible.

"And then I heard something, a sound from upstairs that I recognised at once. There's no mistaking it, the cry of a newborn.

Rose heard it too, and she just ran up the stairs. I couldn't keep up with her. I followed her into one of the bedrooms, and, well..."

He looked at me, raising his bushy eyebrows. "So we've met before, lassie, though you won't remember it." He sighed. "Your mother, poor soul, had done it all by herself while Rose was out fetching me. It was lucky for both of you that it was all straightforward. I checked you over, and her too, and then I begged the two women to go with you to the hospital. I couldn't begin to imagine why they thought Langlands was a suitable place to give birth, and if either mother or baby had taken sick afterwards – well, they'd have needed more than a country GP."

The old man shook his head. "They wouldn't hear a word of it. I tried to reason with them for a while but I could see your mother was getting distressed so I did what I could to make her comfortable, and then I took Rose away downstairs and had it out with her.

"I told her there could be a question of child protection – Langlands was practically derelict, it wasn't the place for a newborn baby. I could be in hot water myself if I didn't report my concerns to the proper authorities. I hadn't made my mind up to do that, not yet, but I wanted to shake her up a bit, get her to tell me exactly what was going on. Otherwise I could see her packing me off again without a word of explanation. She could be high-handed, Rose."

"What did she say?" I burst out, leaning forward. That was what I really wanted to know, after all: how Grandmother could possibly have explained herself.

Dr. Robertson shook his head resignedly. "The baby's mother was Rose's daughter. You'll have guessed that already. All three of them were hiding, and now you're going to ask me who from, and I'm sorry to be the one to tell you. It was your father they were hiding from.

"Rose told me a sorry tale, and you don't need to hear every single detail of it. Your mother was a lot younger than he was, and I don't think she knew what she was getting into when she married him, or perhaps she was already under the thumb, I can't say. He knocked her about and I don't know what else, and for a long time she was too beaten down to think of leaving. Rose was frantic, and desperate enough to stand up to him, but he wouldn't let her anywhere near your mother. He cut her off from all her family and friends.

"Then your mother became pregnant, with you. She knew

that if she stayed with your father, either he'd beat her again and maybe she'd lose the baby, or else the baby would be born and maybe he'd abuse it too. She found the strength to do for you what she couldn't do for herself, and ran away.

"She left with nothing but the clothes she stood up in. It was no use packing or anything, he'd have smelled a rat. She went straight to Rose. Your grandfather, Angus, had passed away by then, so it was just her and Rose. Rose knew your father would follow. He'd never let your mother go like that. In his eyes, she was his property. He'd probably have preferred to kill her than let her walk away."

The old doctor's face twisted in disgust. "I've seen it before. Patched it up a few times, too, even in a 'nice' town like ours. But your father was more dangerous than most, because he had resources – money, contacts. He's a very rich man."

He shook his head. "What was Rose to do? If she'd stayed where she was, down in England, it wouldn't have been long before your father caught up with them. She was determined that wouldn't happen. Oh, she knew there was a risk your mother would cave in and go back to him. I've seen that before, too: women so beaten down they don't have the will to escape any more. But Rose was tough, you know, tough enough for both of them. She packed up what she could, including all the valuables she could lay hands on, and drove all through the night to Langlands."

chapter forty-nine

I listened to Dr. Robertson speaking and pressed my hands over my stomach, afraid that the nausea roiling up inside me would tip over into actually throwing up. Every time I thought I was on solid ground, it seemed that things turned upside down and became worse than before. I was wrong about everything, I thought, sickly. *Grandmother really was trying to protect me and my mother. And the great love story I imagined between my mother and my father was a lie. I thought perhaps they went away together, that perhaps they loved each other so very much that there wasn't room for me, but now–*

It had been melancholy to grow up without my mother; it had been bittersweet to imagine her abandoning me for love. It was appalling to think of her leaving me to step back into the embrace of a monster.

"Don't cry, lassie," said the old doctor brusquely. There was nothing warm in his tone, but somehow the lack of sympathy braced me up. "Do you want to hear the rest of it?" he asked. "Because if you come knocking again, I'll not let you in, and if anyone else comes asking, I'll say I know nothing about it, you know."

And I nodded, looking him straight in the eyes, and said, "Yes, I want to know all of it. Everything you know. Tell me why she came to Langlands. Why did it have to be there? And why then – the Wartime, I mean?"

"Well, I didn't know she'd told you that about the War until just now, so I can't tell you exactly what was on her mind, but I can guess. Rose did spend the War years at Langlands, you know. The house had been inhabited up to that point; it wasn't derelict like it was later. She had relatives living there, and when the bombing started in the cities, her family took her to Langlands for safety. When I first knew her, when we were both young, she used to talk about it as a wonderful time. Her parents were very strict; their own parents were Victorians, after all. They had a lot of ideas about manners and upbringing and so on. Rose had more freedom there than she'd ever had before, running around in the grounds all day long. I remember her telling me once that even though it was Wartime, she'd never felt so happy or safe as she did then." The old man raised his eyebrows, looking at me down his nose. "So there's your answer. She wanted the same for you as she'd had for herself. Safety and happiness. Maybe she wished it really was still 1945, before everything went wrong."

"But what about my mother?" I said, trying to keep the tremor out of my voice. I knew I was on borrowed time with the old man; I had to know everything he could tell me. "Why didn't she stay at Langlands too? Did she go back to my father in the end? And why didn't she take me with her?"

"I can't tell you that, because I don't know. I saw Rose now and again in the town – not often, mind you, but I knew that she must still be staying at Langlands. She never came to me for doctoring. I suppose she thought least said, soonest mended. I never saw hide nor hair of you or your mother after that night she called me out.

"I spoke to her a few months after that night, one day in the street. I asked after the new mother and baby, and she said you'd both gone somewhere safe. I said that was just as well, because

Langlands was no place for a baby, considering the state it was in then, and she looked me in the eye and said I could come up there and see for myself whether there was anyone staying up there but her, if I liked. After that, I couldn't go without calling her a liar, so of course I didn't.

"All the same, I wondered about the pair of you. The last time I spoke to Rose was a few years back, maybe five years now. I asked after you and your mother again. She said your mother lived abroad now, and you were away at boarding school. I tried to say something about that night at Langlands, but she cut me off. She said the past was better left buried, and that was that."

You've come home from school to take over your inheritance, he'd said, when he first heard who I really was. I supposed the old man had believed what Grandmother had said.

I wondered what else I could ask him. Already he was stirring in his chair, gripping the arms with his gnarled hands as he prepared to stand up. *If you come knocking again, I'll not let you in*, he'd told me. This was my last chance.

I had to stand up myself, seeing that he was about to show me the door, but as I did so I thought of something.

"What was my father's surname?" I blurted out. "Can you tell me that?"

Dr. Robertson was on his feet now, and in spite of his age, everything about his posture showed an urgency to get me out of the house. "No," he said curtly, but even as my heart sank with disappointment, he added, "But I can write it down for you."

Without further explanation he stumped out of the room. I followed him into the hallway. There was a small table and on it an instrument that I recognised from photographs as a telephone. Beside it was a small notepad and a pen. After a moment's thought, Dr. Robertson wrote something, tore off the sheet and handed it to me.

I read what he had written and saw why he had said he couldn't tell me what the name was; I had no idea how to pronounce it. I opened my mouth to ask how he knew to spell it but he already had his back to me, making for the front door. The interview was over.

He waited for me, his hand on the door latch, and when I was near him, he leaned towards me, so close that I could smell the sweetish rot of his breath.

"I've told you all this for Rose's sake," he said. "But don't come back here, ever. And if you tell anyone else what I said, and they come knocking, I'll deny all of it. Understand?"

"Yes," I said. I realised that he was trying to be intimidating, and also that I was not afraid of him. I had lost the self-consciousness I had felt being confronted with a new face. When I looked back at him, I did not feel fear or anxiety or even surprise. I felt dislike. He could have helped Grandmother more than he did, knowing what he had. He could have asked more questions. Perhaps – just perhaps – things might have ended differently.

The old man opened the door, and as it swung back, I saw Tom silhouetted on the other side of it, his hand raised as if to knock.

He looked past Dr. Robertson, to me, and said, "Are you all right?"

"Yes," I said, stepping past the old man. I stood beside Tom, and both of us looked at him, framed in the doorway. He stared back at us, scowling, and I could see that he recognised Tom. For a moment I thought he was going to say something; his lips worked soundlessly, as though trying to frame words. But then he stepped back and closed the door so smartly that he almost slammed it. I heard the rattle as he attached the chain on the other side, and then the sound of a bolt being shot across.

Tom looked down at me. "I was starting to wonder if he'd

234

done something to you." His tone was light, but his expression was sombre.

I turned my back on the house. "I'm not too sure he didn't," I said slowly, as I moved towards the gate. "If he'd really cared as much about Grandmother as he said he did, he might have changed everything."

When we got to the gateway, I glanced back at the house, but there was no sign of life. After that I didn't look back again.

chapter fifty

The journey back to Langlands was a blur. I stared out of the car window without really seeing anything; to this day I could not tell you whether it was raining or there was dazzling sunshine. I told Tom all the details of what the old man had said, and the things he hadn't been able to tell me, too. But pressing in on me all the time were thoughts of Grandmother and how I'd wronged her.

I should have seen that she would not have done what she did simply to be cruel. After all, she had had to live the same life as I did, cut off from the world, without all the machines that made modern life so much more convenient. Perhaps it was harder for her, since she must have been used to those things beforehand.

I remembered the things she had said to me, the hints she had dropped in the last few months.

I want you to remember, whatever happens in the future, however things may seem, that I have always, always, had your best interests at heart.

She had said that to me, and later she had said: *There are certain truths that will be easier for you to cope with once you have become an adult.*

She had asked me to kiss her after she had said that, as though she foresaw my anger and bitterness when I knew the truth. It seemed a strangely vulnerable thing to have done. Grandmother had always been so strong; sometimes actually fierce, always dependable. Now I saw her as anxious and doubting, afraid of how I would react to what she would inevitably have to tell me, and going back over the past with feverish intensity, asking herself whether there had ever been a time she could have dared to let the pretence drop. If she had told me the truth when I was seven years old, or ten, or thirteen, would I have been content to stay at Langlands all the time, studying Greek and feeding the chickens? Or would I have given her the slip at every opportunity, and run down to the edge of the estate, where the gateway at the edge of the forest marked the beginning of the outside world? I knew the answer to those questions all too well, and she had too. So she had carried on with the pretence, and in her heart, she had said, *Forgive me.*

I do forgive you, I said silently, but it was too late.

As for my mother, I had no idea how to feel about her. Why had she not stayed with Grandmother and me? And where had she gone instead? Dr. Robertson had said that Grandmother had told him she had gone abroad; but then, she had also told him that I was at boarding school. So my mother might be anywhere; but she had never come back for me.

When we arrived at Langlands, Tom came into the house with me.

"Ghost? Are you okay?" he said.

"I feel so bad, Tom." I was fighting back tears. "I was so angry with Grandmother for what she did. I didn't even try to find out what happened to her – I mean, where they buried her. I felt like I didn't even want to know. But she was trying to *protect* me. She was trying to do the right thing for me."

Tom pulled me into his arms. "You couldn't know that. And you were in shock. You can't blame yourself for how you felt."

I shook my head. "I feel like I should have known. She *told* me she was doing it in my best interests." I looked up at Tom.

"Do you think it's too late now – to find out what happened to her?"

"I'm sure we *could* find out," Tom said. "We could go to the police. They'd know where to go – who to ask. But Ghost..." He hesitated. "There'll be questions, you know. A lot of questions."

"I'm her granddaughter," I pointed out. "Surely they'd have to tell me?"

"It's not as easy as that. I'm pretty sure you'd have to prove who you are, and you don't have anything, do you? No passport, no birth certificate, no school records, nothing. That means you'd probably have to tell them everything. And then a whole lot of people are going to get really interested–"

"*Too* interested," I said flatly, remembering what Tom had said when we discussed this before.

"Yeah," said Tom. He exhaled slowly. "It'll be a circus, Ghost. And you probably won't be able to keep your father out of it."

"Why not?"

"Because if you have to prove who you are – and I guess you'll have to, if you want to inherit this place – they might have to do a DNA test or something, and he's your only close relative, unless they can trace your mum."

"What's a DNA test?" I asked.

"It's just a kind of test to see who's related to who. But look, even if they don't have to do that, there's still no guarantee your dad won't find out. And if what Dr. Robertson said is true, he's not a nice guy."

I closed my eyes, resting my head against Tom's shoulder. "I don't know what to do, Tom. I can't just forget about Grandmother. I'd feel like I was abandoning her."

"You're not abandoning her," said Tom earnestly. "Look, it was really important to her that you stayed hidden until your eighteenth birthday, wasn't it? It's only two and a half weeks. We can keep trying to find out whatever we can. If we don't find anything, well..." He shrugged. "Then we can decide whether to go to the police. You'll be eighteen then anyway. If you don't want to see your dad, I don't think anyone can make you."

"All right," I said. I knew Tom's plan was sensible, but still I felt guilty. *Two and a half weeks*, I said to myself.

chapter fifty-one

Tom

I'm driving home now, but I'm hardly seeing the forest drifting past. I'm on autopilot, my head filled with what will happen if Ghost goes to the police. Or maybe *when*. She made me promise once that I wouldn't tell anyone about her, that I'd keep her secret, at least until her birthday. Now she's thinking about telling them herself, and I'm the one who's got cold feet.

I think about a scenario in which we don't tell anyone at all, not for ages. I keep on visiting her and teaching her about life in the twenty-first century. We buy her more modern clothes to wear so she doesn't have to go round looking like something from a history book half the time. She gets used to going out in places where there are lots of other people about. Eventually she learns enough to cope with life in 2017; people wouldn't notice anything odd about her at all. Then we go to the authorities and explain that there's a problem about paperwork, because her grandmother brought her up and home-schooled her and it seems as though the old lady never got around to registering her. It causes a bit of a flutter and a mountain of bureaucracy, but it gets sorted out in the end. It's a legal problem, after all, but it's not as though Ghost seems harmed or disadvantaged in any way. It's not as newsworthy as, say, a girl who was brought up entirely believing she was living in World War Two, and never seeing anyone from the outside world. It wouldn't make a really big splash in a newspaper. *Girl didn't have correct paperwork.* You'd need a dull week for news to run *that* headline.

This might work, this scenario. Except things have changed since she talked to Dr. Robertson. Ghost has stopped hating her grandmother. She wants to know what happened to the old lady, where they buried her – maybe she wants to put flowers on the grave. She might decide that's more important than staying hidden. It's not up to me to make the decision, but I don't think she really understands what it will be like if she tells.

All this is going through my head when I turn into the yard and stop the car. It's raining again as I get out of the car and lock the door. I have my head down, shoulders slumped with the weight of everything that's hanging over me, so I don't see Mum until she's right at my elbow, yelling at me.

She's holding her jacket across her chest, trying to keep out the rain, and she's furious.

"Where have you been all this time? I *told* you I needed the car this afternoon! I've missed my bloody appointment!"

Oh shit. I've done it again. I remember her saying that now, that I couldn't have the car all day. I just forgot. Too much on my mind, all of it stuff I can't possibly tell Mum.

I mumble something about being sorry, but I can see that isn't going to be enough, not by a long way. She's so angry she actually slaps me on the arm. I can't remember her slapping me since I was about ten.

"Bloody selfish!" she shouts.

That stings; it makes me start to feel a bit irritated myself, because okay, I forgot she needed the car, but I didn't *mean* to.

"You've got it now," I point out rashly.

"I needed it an hour ago!" she shrieks. "I'll have to pay for that appointment!"

I can see that anything I say is just going to make her even angrier, and I don't want to lose my temper myself because she's nearly given me a total ban on borrowing the car once already. So I say I'm sorry again, and then I head into the house, out of the rain.

I think she'll take the car and go but she doesn't; she follows me inside, still going on at me. Then I think I'll head for my room and wait till she's calmed down, but she's having none of it. Next thing you know, she's standing in my way with her hands on her hips and a face like fizz.

"Oh no, you don't," she says. "You and me are having a talk, Mister."

I put my head back and sigh. "Mum, I said I was sorry. I said it *twice*."

"It's more than the car," she says. "That's easily mended. I could tell your father to take the money I'll have lost out of your wages." She narrows her eyes. "I want to know what's going on with you."

"Going on?" I say. My heart sinks, but I try not to let it show on my face.

"Don't act the innocent," she snaps. She points at the kitchen, and as there's clearly no escape I slink in there. I try leaning against the cupboards but she says, "Sit down."

When we're sitting either side of the kitchen table, she folds her arms and says, "Right. What's going on?"

"I just forgot about your appointment," I say. "I do remember you telling me now. I just forgot. I'm sorry," I add, for the third time.

Mum leans towards me. "You're up to something," she says accusingly. "You never used to borrow the car as often as this, and I always knew where you were going. Now you've got it every other day and I never know where you are."

"I'm not a kid, Mum. I don't have to check with you every time I go anywhere."

"You do if it's my car you're taking."

"Okay," I say, stopping myself just in time from saying *sorry* again. "I get that now. I'll use the bike next time."

I start to get up but she's not having it.

"Sit down, Tom."

"Mum..."

"No, Tom. Sit down." She glares at me. "I'm not joking. I want to know what's going on. Where are you going all the time?"

We stare at each other in silence. All the possible responses to the question run through my head. I even have a mad impulse to tell Mum the entire story. But that doesn't last long. I've promised Ghost I wouldn't do that, and since she's the one it's all about, I don't think it's my secret to spill.

I sit and look at Mum and watch the angry shapes her mouth and eyes make, and try to zone out of the furious stream of questions she's launching at me.

It doesn't really work though. I can't help reacting when she says, "You're involved with someone, aren't you?" I guess she sees from my face that she's touched a nerve because she zooms in like a heat-seeking missile.

"Is it..." She pauses. "... a dealer?"

"*Mum!* I can't believe you even asked that." Now *my* arms are folded too. I'm so angry that I have to force myself to speak calmly. I say, "I've just been spending time with a – with friends."

"Friends," she says, flatly.

"Yes." My chin comes up.

"Friends I don't know?"

"I... guess not."

"Friends who never come here, either?" She shakes her head. "You've never been secretive, Tom. What's changed?"

"I told you. I'm not a kid. I'm nineteen. I have my own life."

"You still live here."

"Only until the summer. And I'd be at uni already if Dad hadn't talked me into taking a year out."

Mum stops looking angry when I say that and looks hurt instead: her only kid, dying to be gone. I relent, but I'm still not going to tell her anything I've promised not to.

"Look," I say, "It's nothing bad. I've met someone, okay? A girl. That's who I'm meeting."

Mum looks briefly relieved, but then she's back on the attack.

"And you can't bring her back here now and again?"

"No," I say, firmly.

"Why not? Are you ashamed of her?" Something occurs to her. "Are you ashamed of *us*?"

"No, Mum." Now I'm regretting telling her as much as I have, which is not much. I should have stuck to name, rank and serial number. "It's just not the right time," I say.

"Are you at least going to tell me something about her? What her name is, where she lives?"

"No, Mum."

We stare at each other across the kitchen table and I hold her gaze deliberately, not flinching, not giving in. At last she makes a small angry noise of frustration.

"You're not taking my car anymore," she says.

"Okay," I say calmly, though my heart sinks a bit. The bike is fine in good weather but not great when it's crap, which it mostly is around here.

Mum chews her lip. I can see she was expecting more of a fight about the car, but I'm not taking the bait.

"When?" she says at last. "When will you bring her over here, or at least tell me something about her?"

I push away from the table, getting to my feet. I'm ready for the conversation to be over now.

"Tom," she says.
I pause. "Soon."

chapter fifty-two

Ghost

Tom came back the day after, which was Sunday, but he came on his motorcycle, even though it was a cold day, and raining. He was grim-faced.

"Mum won't let me have the car anymore," was the first thing he said when he came into the house, his shoulders shiny with rain.

"Why not?"

"I forgot I was supposed to be home earlier yesterday. She missed an appointment because the car wasn't back, and she just flipped." Tom put up the hand that wasn't holding his motorcycle helmet and raked back the damp hair from his face. "Then she started demanding to know where I was going all the time in it."

Suddenly I was conscious of my heart thudding.

"What did you say?"

"I just said I was seeing a friend. She wanted to know your name, stuff like that, but I wouldn't tell her. I think she was madder about that than she was about the car."

A friend. When Tom said that, my heart misgave me. *Is that how he sees me?* I knew it wasn't, of course; I refused to believe that even in the twenty-first century anyone kissed anyone else the way he kissed me, simply out of friendship. He'd had to say what he did to his mother to keep my secret. I knew that. He was honouring his promise not to tell. It was entirely unreasonable to feel that he had in some way denied what was happening between us by not telling his mother, *there's a girl I'm seeing and I love her.*

Doubt came creeping in like a weasel, avid-eyed and furtive. *Maybe he's getting tired of this. Having to bring me things all the time. Explaining things to me that other girls he knows would just understand. Having to hide things from his own family...*

Just thinking like that made my head ache. It was exhausting, trying to understand Tom's world, trying to guess how I should act or be so that I wouldn't stand out or make myself ridiculous. And I thought too often of that day in the kitchen when we had been kissing, and Tom had slid his hand under my shirt, over my bare skin, and I had jumped like a cat. Sometimes I wished I had not jumped; sometimes I wished that it had ended differently. Then I would feel the hot sting of guilt, thinking that I wanted something that was wrong.

How does it work in 2017? I had asked Tom, and he had said, *It goes as fast or as slowly as you want it to.* But I supposed the end was always the same. I could tell myself that what was wrong for a girl in 1945 was perhaps not wrong for a girl in 2017 – but wouldn't that mean that there was no right or wrong at all, that everything depended on how you felt about it? Then I began to despair of making sense of anything.

"Hey," said Tom. I suppose I had drifted off into my own thoughts entirely because he passed a hand in front of my face, but he was smiling. Tentatively, I smiled back.

"Don't worry," he said. "I've still got the bike. She can't stop me coming. And look, I've started looking for information about your mum and dad."

He drew out some folded papers from inside his jacket. We

went through into the kitchen, and Tom spread them out on the table.

"I printed these off at home. I've brought the tablet but..." He shrugged. "...you know the reception's not great here."

I nodded solemnly, although I only had the vaguest idea what he meant.

"I started with your dad's surname. I reckoned if he's that rich, there has to be some record of him online. And there can't be many people with that name, not in Britain, anyway. I was right about that." Tom drew a deep breath. "Your dad's name's not just unusual, it's *rare*. I only got a tiny number of hits." He pointed. "This one's quite an old article about a company, However-you-say-it Commodities. They did importing and exporting. I tried the website address in the article but it came up 'not found' so I guess it doesn't exist anymore.

"Seems like it was run by two brothers of that name, one called Max and the other called Jacob." Tom glanced at me. "Max has to be your dad. I mean, there can't be *two* people called Max whatever it is. So that's him; that's how he made his money."

"Is there a picture of him?" I asked, craning to look.

"Not in that article," said Tom. He hesitated. "This is where it gets a bit weird. It's not really your dad we want to find, is it? It's your mum, and whether she's with him or not. So I tried searching for her married name and got nothing; tried *Elspeth McAndrew* – again, nothing. Then I looked for his name plus *wife*. If that didn't work, I was going to try it plus *divorced*. Only I got this."

Tom slid one of the printed sheets towards me. Even with the afternoon sun slanting in through the kitchen window, I had to squint a little to read the text; the letters were tiny.

"'Missing businessman declared legally dead'," I read aloud. There was a photograph, too, but it was small and very grainy, worse than the ones in the old magazines in the

Langlands library; it could have been anyone, really.

I looked at Tom. "What does this mean – legally dead?"

"It's when someone disappears and there's no body. After a few years they're declared dead, because they probably are. Then their family can inherit their money, and if they were married their partner is free to get married to someone else."

I looked at the photograph again but it was impossible to tell what my father had looked like; *I couldn't have said, I have his eyes or his hair is the same colour as mine.* If I stared for long enough, his face dissolved into a mass of little dots.

"Then he's really dead?"

"I guess so." Tom placed a finger on the text. "It says his brother Jacob was the one who applied to the court to have him declared dead. But look, this is the bit about your mother. 'Estranged wife.' They weren't together when he disappeared, and it seems like the family don't have any contact with her either. That's why it was his brother who went to the court."

I was silent for a little while. I stared at the picture with a strange mixture of emotions. I supposed this was good news. My father could not contact me; he could not try to claim me in any way. My mother had escaped him too. It was not as though Grandmother had brought me up to honour him; quite the opposite – she had seemed to shudder at the thought of him. But all the same: my father was dead. That was a very grave thing.

All the same, the fact that he had had to be *declared* dead in the way Tom had described bothered me. *They're declared dead, because they probably are*, that was how Tom had put it. That word *probably* was an uncomfortable one; it meant there was a chance, however tiny, that the person wasn't dead at all. If I had known my father, and loved him dearly, that might have been a comforting idea; I might have imagined him living a different life, in some far-off place. As it was, my father was a bogeyman, a threat hanging over my head. It made me uneasy to think that there was the slightest possibility that he might reappear. It wasn't as though I would even recognise him if he did. He could be anywhere; he could be anyone.

I shivered, and Tom put an arm around me.

"I'm sorry. I sprang that on you. I didn't think."

I shook my head. "It's not that. I just feel strange about him disappearing. It would be easier in a way if I knew he was really dead."

"He *is* really dead," said Tom firmly. "The court says so. His own brother says so. Anyway, look at the date of the article. That was 2007. Ten years ago. He'd been gone for seven years before they declared him dead, and there've been ten more years since then. If he was coming back, he'd have done it by now."

I still stumbled sometimes trying to orient myself in 2017, otherwise I might have seen it more quickly. As it was, it took me a few moments to realise what Tom was saying.

2007. And he'd been gone for seven years.

"So," I said slowly, "He disappeared in 2000." I twisted in Tom's embrace so that I could look up into his face. "When I was a baby. If my father vanished back then, why did Grandmother ever start lying to me?"

chapter fifty-three

I saw the shock seep into Tom's expression. His eyes widened, and for a moment he said nothing at all. Then he said, "Shit," which I knew by now to be a bad word. We stared at each other.

I can't bear it, I thought, remembering how I had hated Grandmother for what she had done, all the while I was mourning for her. I didn't want to be dragged back into that maelstrom of misery and resentment. There had to be a reason for this, and I had to find it.

"Maybe she didn't know," I said at last, dismayed at the pleading tone in my own voice. "She never brought any newspapers home and we don't even have a radio. How would she have found out he'd disappeared?" I studied Tom's serious face and thought that I saw doubt there. "She hardly talked to people in the town," I said. "We were *hiding*. Even Dr. Robertson said they hardly ever spoke, and he was the one who helped her when I was born." Something else occurred to me. "Dr. Robertson didn't know my father had vanished. He talked about him as though he was still alive. He said he was a very rich man. You wouldn't say that about someone if you knew they had been dead for over ten years. If Dr. Robertson didn't know, why should Grandmother?"

Tom was shaking his head. "It doesn't make sense though.

Wouldn't she have tried to find out what he was doing – like whether he was looking for you and your mum? I mean, deciding to hide you for eighteen years in a place like Langlands, without any electricity or even a phone, keeping all those lies going all that time, that's an extreme thing to do. Nobody would do that unless they were a hundred per cent sure there was no other option. Probably not even then. I mean, it's *insane*..." Tom's voice trailed off.

"She wasn't mad," I said stubbornly.

"I didn't really mean that," said Tom. "I just think she would have tried to find out. Anyone would have. And with a name like your dad's, it wouldn't be that difficult. I mean, look, it took me one evening to find that article."

"Where did you look?"

Tom shrugged. "Online."

"Well, Grandmother didn't know anything about looking online," I pointed out.

"She could have asked someone else to do it. The library has internet access. The staff would have helped her."

"But then they'd have known what she was looking for," I said. "She was so careful, Tom. I don't think she would have risked asking a stranger to help."

Tom sighed. "But – *eighteen years?* Even if she didn't dare try to find out at the beginning, you'd think she'd have tried later on, when your dad would probably have stopped looking for you and your mum."

I shook my head. "I don't think she did."

After that, we both looked at the papers laid out on the table in silence for a little while. I didn't want to argue with Tom about Grandmother; it gave me a horrible feeling inside, as though there was a hard knot inside my chest, being pulled tighter and tighter until I could barely breathe. I knew that there was sense in what he was saying, but if I accepted it I would be back where I had been before I talked to Dr. Robertson:

wondering whether Grandmother had had any good reason at all for what she had done to me – wondering whether *mad* was exactly what she was.

The other papers weren't as interesting as the one about my father being declared dead. One of them seemed to be about the brother called Jacob. *My uncle*, I thought. The idea was almost shocking. I had living relatives; if my father's brother were married, I might even have cousins. The text didn't say anything about that, though.

Tom saw me perusing it and laid a finger on the paper. "It says Jacob started up a new business in 2008. Maybe that had something to do with declaring your dad dead – he probably wanted to wind up the old one or something. Maybe he inherited from your dad."

None of that meant anything to me. "There's nothing here about my mother," I said, leaning over the papers.

"I'll keep looking," said Tom. "Dr. Robertson said she went abroad, right?"

I nodded.

"Well, even if that's true, it still shouldn't be a problem, if she has any kind of online presence as Elspeth McAndrew. If she's changed her name, though, that could be a lot harder."

"It sounds impossible," I said, beginning to feel really dispirited.

Tom considered. "Do you know what your gran's name was before she got married? If your mum's changed her name, she might be using a family one."

"Do you think so?"

"It's somewhere to start."

"I can't remember what it was," I said, "But there might be something in the safe with it on. I think her marriage certificate was in there."

The passage to the hallway was very dark when we passed through it. In overcast weather, the interior of Langlands was always very gloomy. I could hear the wind rattling the window frames, and the unmistakable sound of water gushing from a broken gutter, spattering onto the gravel outside the house. Moving confidently ahead of me, Tom seemed startlingly vital amid the dust and decay, like the single living creature in a world of ghosts and shadows.

In the library, I went to the windows and pushed back the heavy velvet curtains to let in as much of the dull grey light as possible. The fabric felt threadbare in my hands, and I felt a strange sagginess to one of the curtains. I looked up and saw that part of it had come away from the brass curtain rings altogether. Was it my imagination, or had the condition of the house worsened in the time since Grandmother had vanished?

Perhaps, I thought, *I'm simply noticing it more.*

I opened the safe and the two of us began to lift out the contents. Tom seemed reluctant to handle the blocks of banknotes. He piled them up carelessly on the floor, as though too lengthy contact between the notes and his fingers would somehow contaminate them.

I found the marriage certificate fairly quickly.

"Hepburn," I said, showing Tom the name spelled out in faded ink.

"Okay. I'll try searching for that."

We sat back on our heels, contemplating the papers scattered all over the floor.

"There were letters," I said. "I remember seeing them before. I didn't read them all because I didn't know who the people who wrote them were." I began sorting through the heaped documents. "I read one or two and they were pretty boring. But I think some of them had foreign stamps on, and Dr. Robertson did say my mother was abroad."

"Could any of the names have been Hepburn?"

I shook my head. "I don't think so, but I'm not *sure*."

"Well, let's look anyway."

Tom fished out an envelope bordered with red and blue stripes. "Was this one of them?" He drew out the letter, and turned it over, the paper crackling in his hands. "It's signed *Marion*. And... it's dated 1985." He read a few lines, his brows drawing together in a frown as he struggled to read the handwriting. "And you're right, it's boring." He stuffed the letter back into the envelope.

I picked up a little bundle of letters fastened together with a fraying ribbon. It took me a while to unpick the double bow that secured them. These letters weren't in envelopes, and although I riffled through them, looking at each one in turn, there was no address written at the top of any of them, and no year given in any of the dates, simply a month and day. They could have been written last year, or thirty years ago.

Out of time, I thought. *Like me.*

I was aware of a little prickle of excitement. I turned over the topmost letter and read the name *Edith* written at the bottom. That gave me a momentary pang of disappointment, but after all, anyone could sign any name they liked; it didn't prove the letters weren't from my mother. I turned over the whole stack and leafed through them again; all had the same signature.

"Tom," I said, trying to keep the excitement out of my voice. "Look at these."

I split the letters between us, and for a few minutes we both read in silence. *Dear Rose*, each of them began, and each of them ended with *Best wishes, Edith*. If I had been able to send and receive messages to my mother, I would not have been so formal. But perhaps that was on purpose; letters like these could not incriminate anyone, nor reveal their whereabouts. The contents were dull, too; the writer reported that she was well, and asked after Rose's health, and described excursions into 'the town' without ever naming it. Either 'Edith' was a very dull person indeed, or else she was deliberately keeping her communications safe. It was very hard to decide which, except that there were a very few lines that made me think that there was more to the letters than there seemed to be; there was something under the mundane surface, barely glimpsed, like a muculent creature moving beneath the smooth glassy waters of a pond.

Please write again soon; I'm dying for more news, I read at the end of one of the letters. Dying was underlined with a brisk slash of ink.

That's what I would say if I was desperate to know about someone I loved, I thought. The thin paper trembled in the grip of my fingers. Suddenly I was aware of the racing of my heart.

In a different letter, the writer said, *You asked how I am coping. As well as can be expected, is all I can say. The past is better left buried, I think.*

That was at the bottom of a page; I turned it over eagerly but there was nothing else in the same vein. 'Edith' had dropped the subject there, moving back onto more mundane matters.

"Listen to this, Tom," I said, and read the words aloud to him. It was hard to keep the tremor out of my voice.

"Let me see," he said, and I handed him the letter. He turned it over, as I had done. "That's all it says?"

I nodded. "But don't you think–" I stopped, hesitating to put my hopes into words.

"It could be your mum?"

I held my breath as Tom hesitated.

"Could be," he said at last. "It makes sense." Then he shook his head. "But none of the ones I've read have any date or address or anything. There's nothing to say where they were sent from. What about the others?"

"The same," I said.

Perhaps he saw my face fall, because Tom said, "The name could be useful, though. I'll search for *Edith* as well as *Hepburn*, and I'll try some other combinations, with *McAndrew* and *Elspeth*." He grinned reassuringly, and all of a sudden my

256

heart was racing again, but for quite different reasons. When Tom smiled at me like that, it was like stepping out of deep shadows into bright sunshine.

We went through the rest of the papers again after that, without finding anything more useful. I had looked at most of the documents before, and I didn't expect to find anything new. Gradually I became more interested in watching Tom's hands as he turned over sheafs of documents, or looking at his profile as he studied them – the straight line of his nose, the way he bit his lip when he was thinking. I wanted him to kiss me again.

Of course, he did kiss me again. After we had put everything back into the safe, we went back to the kitchen and Tom tried to make the tablet work, but he said it was useless; the heavy rain was making it worse than normal. He would have to carry on searching for my mother at home. The rain was expected to last until late in the evening, long after sunset.

"I should go before the track turns into a mudslide," he said, so I began to walk with him down the passage to the hallway, but before we got there he turned and pulled me into his arms and kissed me. It was so gloomy that I could barely see Tom's face. Emboldened by the darkness, I kissed him back, sliding my arms around his neck, my fingers in his hair. Clinging together, we stumbled back until my shoulder-blades touched the wooden panelling. My heart rate seemed to have accelerated to a dizzying pace. It was intoxicating, wanting something this much.

This time, it wasn't Tom sliding his hands over my skin that made me break the kiss and step back. It was me – me wanting him to do that so much that I could hardly bear it.

I drew away, my breath coming in sharp little gasps. I could feel the warmth as the colour rose into my face.

We looked at each other for a moment. Then Tom stepped

close to me again, but this time he didn't try to kiss me on the mouth. He touched my face, gently.

"Ghost, you know...I love you."

His voice sounded almost pleading. Suddenly all the breath went out of me; I didn't have enough left to say a word. If Tom had kissed me again then, I would not have pulled away, whatever happened. But he didn't. He said, "I'll come back soon," and then he walked away, down the dark passage, and when he got to the hallway he turned. In the light from the front windows I saw him smile at me, and then he was gone. I heard the great oak door bang shut.

I didn't try to follow Tom. I waited in the darkness until I heard the sound of the motorcycle engine starting up, and I listened as it crunched away over the gravel, and then grew fainter and fainter until the sound could no longer be heard at all.

I love you. I had not said it back, although I had thought it a hundred times.

I went back to the kitchen. The sheets of paper Tom had printed out for me were still scattered about on the big pine table. I collected them up into a neat little sheaf, the one with *Missing businessman declared legally dead* on it uppermost. My father's face, tiny and distorted by the mosaic effect of the photograph, stared up at me. I wished it had been a picture of my mother Tom had found, even if it had been as poor as this one. I wanted to see her face so much.

Declared legally dead. Perhaps it was the sinister meaning of those words that made me feel uneasy, as though there were something just outside the grasp of my conscious mind, a thought just out of reach, as a word may be on the tip of the tongue.

It was much later, when I was lying alone in my bed with the moonlight filtering in through the gap in the curtains and the wind and rain still clattering at the window, that I remembered.

The past is better left buried, I think. That was what the letter had said, the one written by a person calling herself Edith. Not such a very ominous thing to say in itself – just a figure of speech. But old Dr. Robertson, speaking of Grandmother, had told me, *she said the past was better left buried.*

It might be a coincidence, I said to myself. I turned over in bed, restlessly, turning my back to the silver streak of moonlight that bisected the room. It was no use; it gleamed off the glass in the picture frames on the opposite wall, too bright to ignore. I would have to get out of bed and close the curtains properly. Instead, I stubbornly squeezed my eyes shut. *Just a coincidence. People probably say that all the time.*

It was no use, though; the thoughts *would* come, welcome or not. *Legally dead. Left buried.* The shape of something was forming slowly in my mind, something as grim as the remains of a shipwreck seen through murky water.

My mother was gone; she had left me nearly eighteen years before and gone far away. Abroad, if Grandmother had not lied to Dr. Robertson and the old man had not lied to me. She had never come back for me, although there was nothing to stop her anymore.

My grandmother had hidden me, hidden all traces of my existence, until long, long after my father had vanished off the face of the earth and there was no reason to fear that he would claim me.

Dead. Buried.

Two women, one terrified and beaten down, the other afraid too, but fierce. A tiny baby, whom both of them were determined to protect. They would have done anything to keep that child out of the hands of the monster who came to claim it, anything at all. One of them might have done something so terrible that she had to go away – forever.

Dead, I said to myself. I chewed my lip and rolled around restlessly in the bed, willing myself to stop thinking, willing

259

myself to drop into welcome unconsciousness, but the question *would* come.

What if my mother killed my father?

chapter fifty-four

The next morning, I woke very late to find that the rain had stopped and there was brilliant spring sunshine, bright enough to pierce the threadbare parts of the green velvet curtains. I sat up in bed rather gingerly.

The last thing I could recall was lying awake, staring wide-eyed into the darkness, convinced that I would never get to sleep. Thoughts of what my grandmother and mother might have done had run through my head with the sickly repetitiveness of a fever dream. I had imagined Grandmother, her face as grim as an inquisitor's, listening to the rumble of an engine outside, the crunch of tyres on the gravel, long-awaited, always dreaded. I imagined my mother beside her, and because I did not know her face I supplied it with my own, and I saw in the eyes of both her and my grandmother a savage light that seemed to illuminate their faces from within. I tried not to think of the rifle that I had aimed at Tom that day on the staircase, gripped in steadier hands than my own, of the fearful explosion as it went off. It was no use. If not the rifle, worse things suggested themselves: the axe that was even now standing, blade down, handle up, in the chopping block at the back of the house. Grandmother's hands, the papery skin drawn tight over bunched knuckles that were red and slippery with blood.

I had been sure that unconsciousness would never come, but at some point, it had, and I had slept until my limbs were heavy and my head was foggy, the thoughts unravelling slowly and unevenly. I felt as though I should make my first movements with care, as though I were recovering from a bout of fever and unsure of my own strength. After a few moments, I slid my legs over the edge of the bed and stood up, the floorboards cool under my feet. Then I went to the window and recklessly yanked the curtains apart.

The sunlight was blinding but it seared away the horrors of the night before. I put up my hand to shield my eyes. It was still too early in the year for the green of springtime, but even the bare tree branches and the desiccated remains of brambles and the balding patch of grass visible from my window looked better in sunshine. I watched a flock of starlings poking about, their plumage iridescent in the light, and smiled to myself.

Bad dreams, I said to myself. *Just bad dreams. You never even knew your mother. How could you imagine her a murderess? And how could you ever think that Grandmother would help kill someone?*

It all seemed so stupid now, like something from the pages of one of the lurid old romances in the library. The sunlight streaming into the bedroom showed up every sign of wear and neglect: the floorboards worn smooth by the passage of feet over many years, the chips and scuffs in the paintwork, the little clouds of dust under the iron bedstead and the festoons of cobwebs that looped as gracefully as Christmas garlands in the upper corners of the room. All of it was old and decayed, but there was nothing sinister about it. I could not imagine murder taking place here; I could hardly imagine anything taking place here anymore. Langlands had a faded quality, as though it were the painted backdrop to a drama that had long since played out.

I dressed quickly, putting on some of my old clothes; the new things Tom had bought for me were not to be ruined with chores. Then I went downstairs to the kitchen to make tea. I filled the kettle with water, put it on the range to boil and made myself some bread and jam. The bread was home made, but the jam came from a jar Tom had brought me. It still seemed strange to me that Tom could just go and buy so many things that I would have made for myself; it seemed oddly helpless somehow, to get everything ready-made. But there was no doubt that the jam was good; it had set to a beautiful consistency that I didn't always manage with my own efforts, and the explosion of sweetness in my mouth was wonderful.

Tom loves me.

That was the sweetest thing of all. Now that the dread of the night time had evaporated, the thought had room to blossom extravagantly, as though it were a flower opening up to the sun. Nothing seemed too difficult anymore. We would find out what had happened to my mother, and we would lay Grandmother to rest, and we would face all the questions together.

I smiled to myself as I went about my morning tasks: washing up my breakfast things, feeding the chickens, carrying in more wood for the range. There were fresh eggs today; I decided I would make an omelette later if I could find mushrooms to put in it. At this time of year, I might hope to find morels. As I fetched a basket, I wondered whether Tom bought mushrooms from a shop too. But surely not? Keeping hens was certainly a nuisance sometimes, but mushrooms were simply there for the taking, so long as you knew which ones were good to eat.

I put on a coat against the cold spring air, picked up the basket and let myself out by the front door. There was a place that I knew, halfway up the hillside behind the house, where a stream flowing down over a rocky outcrop cascaded into a little pool. The water was freezing pretty nearly all the time, even in the middle of summer, but I loved to watch it foaming down over the rocks. I thought that I would go there now, and hunt for the morels on the way.

The forest was shot through with overgrown tracks, some of them paths used by former inhabitants of the estate, and some of them nothing more than rabbit trails. I followed one of these now, picking my way along as quietly as I could. There were rabbits and foxes and deer in the forest, as well as game birds, but there was never any hope of seeing any of them if you blundered through the undergrowth snapping twigs and splashing in puddles.

Very quickly, I ran into a place where the track was impassable; during the winter a tree had come down, and the way ahead was a mass of protruding branches. I turned right, aiming to make a wide loop around it. The detour took me to within sight of the old mausoleum, where the former inhabitants of Langlands lay buried. There was no discernible path leading to it anymore. The stone building was surrounded by a tangle of brambles, as impenetrable-looking as the hedge of thorns that surrounded Sleeping Beauty's castle. I was not tempted to try; my skirts would have stuck fast to the thorns. All the same, the old mausoleum was on my mind as I circled the fallen tree and began to make my way uphill.

Supposing Grandmother had not been buried or cremated yet? I wondered if it would be possible to bury her in the mausoleum. The ground would need to be cleared, of course; at the moment it was not only inaccessible but neglected. If the place could be made tidy, it would be a beautiful thing to do. Grandmother had spent some of the happiest times of her life here at Langlands. She had never forgotten that. In her deepest crisis, she had fled here. Even the deceit she had woven about our lives at Langlands had grown from the desire to go back to those better times. I thought that she would have chosen the estate for her last resting-place. It was the last thing I could ever do for her; it would feel like making peace between us.

When I came to the pool, I found that the wild garlic which grew nearby was coming out; the air was heavy with the scent of it. I gathered some of the leaves and flowers to add to the morels. It was very pleasant to kneel on the ground picking the plants and feeling the aroma of garlic intensify as I bruised the leaves between my fingers, until my mouth began to water. Afterwards, I knelt by the pool and washed my hands in the glacially-cold water, watching the water foam white as it descended from the rocks.

By the time I came down the hill, the basket piled with mushrooms and garlic leaves, I was beginning to feel pleasantly tired and a little thirsty. Thoughts were going lazily through my head, of taking Tom to see the little waterfall, and of the things I was going to cook, and finally, as the mausoleum came into sight, of my idea that Grandmother might be buried there.

The sun had gone behind a cloud, but as I approached the part of the track that passed the mausoleum, it came out again, dazzlingly, its rays piercing the leafless branches above. At the front of the mausoleum, something – a metal tie embedded in the wall, perhaps, or a crystal in the stone – was suddenly lit up, a brilliant point of reflected golden light that blazed briefly like the heart of a tiny fire. Then I had moved forward too far to see it, or the light had changed, and it was extinguished.

I walked the rest of the way back to the house feeling somehow comforted. I didn't really believe in *signs*; Grandmother had brought me up in too brisk and practical a manner. But still I felt as though the rightness of my idea about Grandmother's resting place had been confirmed by that brief moment of beauty. That day, all was right with the world.

chapter fifty-five

Tom

It's half past twelve at night and dark outside. It's dark in here, too, with just the bluish light from my laptop screen. I'm hoping Mum won't notice the light under the door. It's difficult to do anything in peace right now. Dad's taken on a job in Dunkeld, a customer who moved there last year, so we're getting back later than normal anyway, and then Mum wants us all to have dinner together; there's no sneaking a plate of food upstairs. Even when dinner's finished and I can escape, she keeps coming up on any excuse. I've never had so many hot drinks. I think she's hoping to catch me Skyping the mystery girlfriend or something, which is ironic really since Ghost is probably the only seventeen-year-old girl in Scotland who isn't online.

I yawn, a great big yawn that ends in a sigh. I'm not getting anywhere with this. I've tried every combination of Elspeth or Edith and Hepburn or McAndrew or that name neither of us can pronounce. There are a few Edith Hepburns and McAndrews on social media sites but none of them looks like the right person, which is no surprise really. If you went off to start a new life you wouldn't put it all over Facebook, not without changing your name. I haven't found anything on any of the news sites either, which might mean something or nothing. It looks like nobody reported *her* missing. On the other hand, she never came back for Ghost.

I have a bad feeling about this, a feeling that won't go away. Nobody is going to go off and leave their kid in a place like Langlands with one crazy old lady who pretends it's still 1945 and won't call a doctor when the kid is sick – not if they can help it. *Unless...*

Unless she had *to stay away, because the guy's disappearance was down to her.*

That was the first thing that came into my head. She wouldn't have been the first person to stick a knife into a man who'd been beating them up.

And then other things started to occur to me. *Maybe what old Mrs. McAndrew said was right all along and Elspeth's dead.* It would make sense. The dead don't leave a trail, online or anywhere else.

That still leaves the question: *if she's dead, how did she die?*

I think about that again as I scroll down another page of useless search results, mostly genealogy sites full of Hepburns who died in the 1800s.

Maybe she did do something to Ghost's dad, and then she killed herself afterwards. Maybe they fought it out, and they both died. Maybe she did go back to him, and wherever he went, he took her with him.

No, I think. *This is nuts.* All of it sounds over the top, like I'm trying to work out the plot for a TV series. But is it any crazier than keeping someone hidden for nearly eighteen years, and telling them it's still World War Two?

There's an opened can of Relentless sitting by my laptop. I upend it over my mouth, but there's nothing left in it.

Maybe she just...died, I think to myself, helplessly. *Natural causes. People do.*

It's useless. I'm never going to solve this. I rub my face, as though I can massage my overloaded brain back into life.

267

Natural causes, I think, and then: *Childbirth. People used to die of that all the time.*

I think that one through. Langlands House, eighteen years ago. Cold and dirty, with no running water or light. No way to keep things properly clean. And the old lady had had to go off for help, leaving Ghost's mother on her own.

Maybe it took longer to persuade the doctor to come with her than she thought it would. Longer than *he* said it did, anyway. Maybe they got back to Langlands and it was already too late.

That would mean Dr. Robertson lied about that bit, about making sure the mother and baby were both okay. And it would also be a lie about him meeting old Mrs. McAndrew in the street later on, and her telling him Ghost was at boarding school and her mother abroad. He could have been covering his own arse, knowing there wasn't anybody to call him out on it. Even for a retired doctor, it wouldn't be great for it to come out that he'd been involved in something like that – someone dying from lack of medical care in an abandoned house, and someone else helping themself to the baby, even if it was their own granddaughter...

And just like that, it comes to me. The most monstrous idea of all. *All of it was a lie. All of it.* Not just the bit about it's-1945-and-World-War-Two-is-still-on. *Everything.* Ghost's mother, and her husband, the bastard she had to run away from. The long drive up from England in the dark. The late-night call on Dr. Robertson. The birth of a baby in a huge old derelict house in the middle of nowhere.

Supposing, I say to myself, *Rose McAndrew took a baby. Not her granddaughter. Just someone else's baby.*

If it wasn't so late and I wasn't so tired maybe I wouldn't even be considering such an insane idea, but the more I think about it, the more it takes shape in my head.

There's the *why*, but that's not too difficult to guess. I remember when I was a little kid, there was a woman in the town who used to push around a big old-fashioned pram with nothing in it. I asked Mum why she did that, and Mum said she wasn't well in her head, and maybe she'd lost a baby of her own and had never been able to have any more.

But Mrs. McAndrew did have a kid, I think. *There was a photo of her, with Elspeth written on the back.*

And then right away I think: *Maybe she died.*

I think about the stuff we found in the safe. There was that one photo of Elspeth as a little kid, but nothing of her when she was older. Maybe she never got any older. Maybe she never got old enough to marry or have a kid of her own.

In that case, who married Max?

Estranged wife, that was all it said in that newspaper article about the guy who was supposed to be Ghost's dad. It didn't say *Estranged wife, Elspeth.* Max, the guy with the surname none of us can say, might not be Ghost's dad at all, and his ex-wife might not be Ghost's mum.

I slump back in my chair, rubbing my hands over my face and my hair. It all fits. It's scary how neatly it fits. It would explain why I can't find Elspeth McAndrew online, if she's been dead for forty years.

Ghost looks like Rose did when she was young, I think. *They have to be related.*

But then I wonder about that, too. If you grow up with someone, you pick up some of their expressions, their body language, all that stuff. Mum says that sometimes – *I sound just like your Gran.* If you grew up with just one person, if you spent seventeen years basically just with them, wouldn't you get to be a *lot* like them?

If I'm right, Rose McAndrew was – what? Criminally insane? An evil monster? Pitiable? Maybe all of those things. Dr. Robertson isn't innocent either – in fact, his part in it is starting to look worse and worse. He told Ghost he *saw* her mother, right after the birth at Langlands. Was he lying? And why did he give her Max's name?

I hear a creak from the landing floorboards outside my room. Mum on the prowl. I shut the laptop quickly, extinguishing the screen light, and wait in the dark for her to go away. Even after I hear her door close, I don't open the laptop again immediately. The darkness is comforting in a way; I can hide in it while I ask myself very seriously what the fuck I'm going to do about all this.

chapter fifty-six

Ghost

Tom came back late in the week, on a clear dry afternoon when the sound of the motorcycle carried to me through the cool air long before the machine burst out from under the trees.

I ran out of the house to meet him, and found that he had already dismounted and was standing bare-headed by the machine, the helmet swinging from the fingers of one hand. He encircled me with his arm, pulled me close and pressed his lips to my forehead. This was different from his usual greeting; it was more like something Grandmother would have done, somehow protective. I drew back a little and looked up at him.

Tom smiled at me. I still distrusted my own ability to read other people's expressions, but it seemed to me that there was sadness in his smile. Then he relaxed and the look was gone.

"Let's go somewhere," he said.

"Where?"

"Anywhere." I saw his gaze shift to the front of the house. "Let's just get away from here for a while."

I didn't point out that he had only just got here. A trip outside was exciting, although I hoped Tom wasn't going to suggest anywhere full of people.

I went back into the house to change my clothes; Tom stayed

271

outside. When I came out again, he was standing on the gravel staring up at the house again. Was it my imagination that there was something unfriendly in his gaze?

"A penny for them," I said as I went up to him.

He shook his head. "Nothing, really."

He helped me to put on the spare helmet and when I was settled behind him on the motorcycle we set off. I liked to travel this way, with the open air streaming past us like a torrent and my arms tight around Tom. The part down the track to the edge of the forest was unpleasant because of the ruts and bumps, but after that it was exhilarating. We sped past the fields and into the town and right out the other side, and then we turned up a lane flanked with hedges, that cut across the land towards rising ground and the hill beyond.

Tom parked the motorcycle by a gate that had been secured with a heavy padlock and chain. I took off my helmet and shook back my hair from my face. On the other side of the gate, a track led up into the forest between towering fir trees.

Tom was already scaling the gate with ease. He jumped down on the other side and waited for me.

It seemed to me that I could have climbed more easily in my old skirts than in the tight modern trousers Tom had bought for me, but I managed it anyway. Tom took my hand and we began to walk up the hill.

As we walked, Tom told me about the work he had been doing with his father, which had been some distance away in a place called Dunkeld. He told me a little about the town and about the job they had been doing, but the thing that interested me most was hearing him talk about his father – the things he had said and done. Tom's way of talking about him was far less respectful than the way I would have spoken about Grandmother when she was alive. He seemed slightly exasperated sometimes by his father's way of looking at things. And yet I thought there was real affection in his voice when he talked about the older man. It fascinated me to imagine all the relationships Tom had with other people – his father, his mother, his own grandmother, who sounded nothing at all like mine.

I asked him about his mother, but he seemed less willing to speak about her; when I asked, he looked away from me for a moment, into the forest. Then he made a little sound like a sigh.

"She's still annoyed at me because I won't tell her anything about you." He grimaced. "I'm not using her car anymore but I think that pisses her off even more, the fact that I've got the bike so I can go off without her knowing first."

"I'm sorry," I said. I couldn't think of anything else to say.

"I really haven't told her, you know. I haven't told any of it to anyone."

Before I had time to think of anything to say to this, he began to walk again, pulling me along with him.

I glanced at his set face, perplexed. Suddenly, Tom seemed to be angry, and I didn't understand why. It was weeks since he had first promised to keep my secret; now he seemed upset about it. I couldn't tell whether he was angry with me, or with his mother, or with the situation.

Tom's legs were longer than mine and he was moving more quickly than was comfortable for me; I stumbled, and then stopped, letting go of Tom's hand, and Tom stopped too. We stared at each other. I tried to read the expression in Tom's eyes.

"Tom," I said at last, "I believe you. I know you haven't told anyone. And I'm sorry about your mother, I really am. I don't want to get you in trouble."

For a moment Tom said nothing. Then, abruptly, he said, "I think we should go and see Dr. Robertson again."

"But he said not to come back. He said if I knocked again he wouldn't open the door."

Tom turned away and began to walk uphill again, and I had to follow him.

"Tom–"

"I know what he said. I still think we should speak to him again."

"But why? He said he wouldn't talk to me again, and he said if I told anyone else and they came knocking, he'd deny everything."

"Yes, but Ghost – how do you know that what he told you was true? Supposing it *wasn't* true? Or only part of it was true? Or he left something out on purpose, something important?"

I was confused, and slightly out of breath from trying to talk to Tom while hurrying to keep up with him.

"I don't know," I said, "But if we went back, why would he tell us anything different?"

"He might."

"But how would we make him?" A thought occurred to me. "You don't mean *threaten* him, do you? We can't do that."

"We have to do *something*," said Tom tersely.

"But why–?" I began to say, and then I stopped. I kept pace with Tom, but for a while the only words that came were the ones tumbling about silently inside my own head. Something was troubling Tom; I could feel it as plainly as walking with a stone in my shoe. There was something he wasn't telling me.

"Tom?" I said, and waited for him to look at me. "Did you find out anything new? About my mother, I mean?"

Tom shook his head. "No. I tried all the different names but..." He shrugged. "She wasn't there."

I waited for him to say more, but he didn't.

"Did you look for her with your– " I struggled to remember the right expression. "–online machine?"

Tom let out a sigh. "Yeah, I searched online. There was nothing."

"Not everything is – online – though, is it?" I persisted. I couldn't understand why Tom was being so reticent about it.

"No," said Tom. "But most people, you'd find *something*." He looked away, and kicked a loose stone across the track. "Like I said, I think we should go and see Dr. Robertson again. We've got more out of talking to people in the town than doing online searches."

"All right," I said doubtfully. I was remembering the old man's face as he had closed the door. *Don't come back here, ever*, he had said.

Tom took my hand again and we walked on for a while in silence. I chewed my lip, thinking.

Eventually, the track emerged from the forest and wound its way through banks of springy heather towards the top of the hill. Where the hillside fell away from us, there was an open view across the countryside. I stood still, pulling Tom to a standstill too, and stared out at the rolling landscape and the distant hills, at the silver sheen of a small loch. The view from Langlands House was always hemmed in by trees; by comparison, this was as breathtaking as the ocean had been when we saw it from the clifftops.

At the last section, we left the path and scrambled up through the heather to the summit, marked by a stone – a 'trig point', Tom said, though I had no idea what that was. I stood with my back to the cool stone and stared at the town in the distance. Tom stood close beside me and pointed things out, telling me which other things lay in different directions from the town.

I listened, but mostly I thought about how small and contained the town looked in the landscape. It was strange to be able to see all of it at once like that. When Tom told me that the city of Perth was in this direction or Stirling in that direction, I began to see the land as a kind of giant map stretching away into the distance on all sides, with the town an insignificant mark on it. It gave me a kind of vertiginous feeling, an echo of the slowly building panic I had felt the day Tom had driven me to Elie to see the sea and I had started to think of what would happen to me if we were somehow separated. The outside was so vast, and I felt as though all I understood of the geography of it was that it was *not* Langlands, where I belonged.

After a while, I turned my face away from the view and leant against Tom's shoulder, closing my eyes. Tom put his arms around me, and I put mine around him too. Sometimes when Tom held me, his touch was light, his hands moving restlessly over my face and hair. Now, we clung to each other as though we were afraid of being prised apart.

chapter fifty-seven

On Saturday Tom came again, just as fat raindrops were beginning to spatter the window panes. When I opened the front door to his knock, I felt the clammy coolness of the air.

"I thought we could go to Dr. Robertson's," was almost the first thing he said, after stooping to kiss me.

"Now?" I looked past him, at the rain slanting into the stone porch.

"Yeah."

I looked down at the motorcycle helmet dangling from his fingers. "We'll get soaked," I pointed out.

Tom shrugged. "I know. But it's important."

I bit my lip. "Tom, tell me *why* we have to go and see Dr. Robertson again."

Tom looked at me and I thought I saw a ripple of something – dismay or guilt – pass across his face. Then he said, "Because he might not have told us everything. He could have forgotten something, or left it out on purpose, or–" He stopped, shrugging his shoulders.

"What do you think he left out?" I said, boldly.

Tom hesitated. "I don't know."

I looked into his eyes, holding his gaze. "Tom, *tell* me."

He held out his hands, placating me. "I told you, I don't know anything for certain."

"You've got an idea though, haven't you?" I persisted. I went up very close to him. I was always very conscious of Tom's physical proximity to me; my skin seemed to tingle with the sense of it. Now it was as though sparks were arcing through the air between us. I felt he *must* tell me the truth when we were so close that I could see every individual eyelash, when I could smell the cologne he wore. "Tell me."

He thought about it for too long. "Ghost – it isn't really an idea. It's just something that..." He shook his head. "It might just be completely random."

"Tell me anyway. *Please.*"

"I–" He thought about it. "I don't think I should." Tom saw me open my mouth to say something and he went on, "Look, okay, something did occur to me. But it might be completely wrong. What would be the point of getting upset about something that might be nothing at all?"

"So it's something bad," I said.

"I didn't say that."

"Well, why won't you tell me, then?" I was struggling to keep my voice level.

"Let's just go over there," said Tom. "We can talk to him and... yeah, I know he said he wouldn't talk to us again but we can try to persuade him. What's the point in speculating about what he's going to say beforehand?"

"Maybe there isn't any point," I said, "But I want to know. *Tom.*" I saw his gaze slide away from mine and forced him to look at me again. "Just say it, whatever it is."

"Ghost, believe me, you *don't* want to know."

"I do." I couldn't help it now; my voice was rising. "Tom! I'm not a child!"

"I know you're not–"

"And I'm not stupid! I know I don't know all the things

about the outside that I ought to, but that doesn't mean I'm an idiot!" My hair had fallen over my eyes; I shook it back. "So just *tell* me, Tom."

And he did. We didn't even go through to the kitchen, where it was warmer and lighter. We stood there in the hallway on the dusty chequered tiles and Tom told me the idea that had come to him – an ugly, horrible idea that slowly took form as I listened to his words, as grotesque as a gargoyle. Tom thought Grandmother had made *everything* up: my father's cruelty, my mother's flight, the dangerous birth alone at Langlands, and not just those things but my parentage too. He thought that my mother and father weren't my mother and father at all. He thought that Elspeth McAndrew did not even exist anymore. Worst of all, he thought Grandmother had stolen me from someone – just taken me from my real parents when I was a tiny baby because she was sick inside her head. If what he said was true, I wasn't Augusta McAndrew. I didn't know who I was; maybe I wasn't anyone at all.

I listened to everything he said in horrified silence, corked like a bottle of poison by the stunned disbelief I felt. Then, when he was standing in front of me with his head down and regret in his eyes, I found my voice again.

"No." My throat was dry and the word came out like a croak. "No," I said again, more loudly. And then I was shrieking it, and I was flailing with my hands, trying to shove Tom away from me as though I could push away the thoughts he had put into my brain too. Tom took a step back, involuntarily, and then he grabbed my wrists, trying to stop me from shoving him. I wrenched myself out of his grip, and we parted, glaring at each other, both of us breathless.

"Ghost–"

"I don't believe it!"

"You don't *have* to believe it. It's just an idea. It's probably totally wrong. We'll just talk to him and he'll probably say it's all crap."

"I'm not talking to him!" I was really shouting now. "I'm not going. It's just a pack of lies, all of it!"

"I'm sorry–" Tom began, but I cut him off.

"I don't care. I'm not going." There were hot tears in my eyes now. I blinked them back, angry at myself for crying. "You shouldn't have said those things about Grandmother, Tom. Those lies. Grandmother wouldn't ever do a thing like that."

Tom turned away from me, putting his hands to his head, grasping his hair as though he meant to pluck it out in great handfuls. He took a few steps, almost stumbling, then turned back on himself as though pacing out the limits of a very small cage. I think he was as full of savage feelings as I was, but for a few moments he said nothing.

When he did speak, there was a strange tension in his voice. "I'm really sorry I upset you. But we have to know what happened. Look, it's just an idea I had, and you're right, it's probably crap. But don't you think we ought to talk to Dr. Robertson anyway? Even just to rule it out?"

"But it's not true. I know it's not." The blood seemed to be thrumming through my body so violently that I was afraid I would faint. I put out a hand and touched the wall, steadying myself. "I can't believe you would say that about Grandmother."

"It's not just about her," Tom burst out. "Can't you see that? Both of us are in trouble: you *and* me." His blue-green eyes were wide. "I want to know what I'm involved in. I know you don't want to believe your gran did anything wrong, and believe me, I really hope she didn't. But if she did, if she did something *criminally* wrong, I've been helping to cover it up for the last two months. I could be in really deep shit for that and...I want some warning."

"You go, then," I retorted. "You talk to him about your horrible idea."

"He won't talk to me."

"I don't care. I don't believe it and I'm not going."

"Ghost–"

"Tom, just go." I drew breath. "Go!"

I ran away from him, towards the stairs, and before I came to the turn in the staircase he had already reached the door. For a moment I paused in my flight and we stared at each other, me with my hand on the worn bannister, Tom with his on the door handle. Then I fled up to the first floor, and as I reached the spot where the stuffed bear stood snarling his eternal snarl, I heard the door bang closed.

I ran to my room. The anger and misery I felt were so terrible that I stumbled over to the bed and punched the mattress until I was too worn out and breathless to do it anymore. Then I collapsed onto it, curling myself into a ball, and cried until I felt sick. Outside the rain and wind had worked themselves up into a storm; I heard the distant rumble of thunder over the hiss of the rain.

At last I sat up, the tears drying on my face, and thought of Tom, riding back down the track and the rest of the way home in this weather. I was not angry enough to wish that he would come to grief. I looked at the rain-streaked window and the tree branches tossed in the wind beyond it, and my conscience pricked me.

When I went downstairs again, the house felt somehow emptier than before. I stood on the bottom step for a little while, looking around me as though I might find Tom still here, though I had heard the door close when he left. Then I went across to the door myself, and opened it to look out.

There was something sitting on the flagstones at the mouth of the stone porch. I went out to see what it was, shivering a little in the damp air. A little stack of groceries; Tom must have left them there before he rode away, not wanting to come back inside to give them to me after the way we had parted. There was a container of powdered milk, the seal intact, and a mesh bag full of oranges, their dimpled skins gleaming with wet from the rain, and a box of little cakes that looked as though it had probably been ruined; the cardboard was soaked and almost fell apart in my hands. In addition, there was a bag of sugar that was also spoiled; the paper had some kind of shiny coating but the rain had still got in. I carried everything indoors as best as I could.

I was right about the cakes. They were disintegrating into a kind of mush. After I had taken them out of the remains of the box I looked at them for a while, wondering whether to put them out for the birds, but in the end, I could not bear to waste food. I ate all of them, though the texture was soggy and unpleasant.

The sugar I took out of the bag and warmed in the oven in a roasting-pan. A whole two-pound bag of sugar was certainly too valuable to throw away, especially if I wasn't sure how or when I would get any more...

It was dawning on me uncomfortably that Tom might not come back. I had been so angry that we had almost fought, physically, and he... I remembered how wild his eyes had looked when he blurted out the things about getting in trouble because he had helped me. He knew the world outside Langlands; if he was afraid of that, perhaps he was right to be. Perhaps now that we had argued, he would decide that he had to stay away for his own self-preservation.

When I drew the roasting-pan out of the oven with gloved hands, the sugar was dry and brittle, and I wetted it all over again with the tears that dripped from my face into it.

chapter fifty-eight

Tom

I suppose Ghost was right about one thing: it was nuts to think of going to Dr. Robertson's house on Saturday during that rainstorm. By the time I'd got down to the cattle grid at the bottom of the drive, there was mud all over me and the bike. A soaking on the way home didn't help much either. Not the best way to persuade someone to let you into their house, turning up looking like a drowned rat.

When I got home, Mum followed me up the stairs complaining about the dirt I'd tracked into the house.

"I wouldn't be covered in mud if you'd let me have the car," I pointed out, which was stupid. If I'd ever considered discussing the mess I'm in with her, the idea was buried in the row that erupted after that. It ended with me slamming my bedroom door and not talking to her until the next morning.

So now it's Tuesday afternoon, and I'm standing outside Dr. Robertson's house on my own. Ghost isn't here. I haven't been back to Langlands since Saturday, but it's pretty clear how she feels about my idea. If I'm honest, though, that's not the only reason I haven't been back. I'm not saying I'm *never* going back. I just want to get my head straight first. And I want to know whether my idea is right.

The first thing I notice is that the old man's house looks more neglected than before, if that's possible. I mean, it's not been that long since we were here before. There are a bunch of those free leaflets that people put through the door heaped up in the porch and the rain has got them, so they're a soggy mess of wet paper right where you'd tread when you went in or out. I step over them, so that I'm standing right up close to the front door. Then I open the letterbox, being really careful not to make any noise, and look through, thinking maybe I can catch the old man unawares before he hears me knocking.

It's dead quiet in there, and dark, too. The blinds must be down on the back windows as well as the front ones.

Not good, I think. It's too late for him to be having a lie-in and too early for him to have gone to bed. Maybe he's sick, or gone away. *Or lying dead on the floor*. That's an option too, with someone that old.

I press my face close to the slot and breathe in through my nose, hoping *not* to smell the aroma of dead old man, and in fact all I can smell is slightly stale air. It's not bad enough to be offensive. It's more like the smell of old clothes in a charity shop, or the cupboard under the stairs in Gran's house.

Unloved, I think. Well, that's probably about right.

I wait for a bit, but it's absolutely silent in there, so if Dr. Robertson is at home at all, he's probably having a nap. There's no other option now but to knock, and if he answers the door, hope that I can talk him into speaking to me.

I knock several times, as loudly as I can, and then I wait. Nothing. I look through the letterbox again. Still dark, still nobody stirring.

"Dr. Robertson?" I shout as loudly as I dare through the letterbox. Then I try knocking again. After that, I stand back from the door, thinking about what to do next. If he's gone away, can I find out where? Eight more days, that's all I have.

When someone clears their throat behind me, I almost jump

out of my skin. I look round and there's a woman at least as old as Dr. Robertson, wearing a tweedy-looking hat and carrying a huge pair of garden shears. Her face under the hat is so wrinkly that it's like being stared at by a tortoise, and the way she's holding those shears makes me take a few steps backwards.

"Can I help you?" she says – well, that's what she says in words. Her tone says, *I can see you're up to no good, laddie.*

"I'm looking for Dr. Robertson," I tell her.

"Why?"

It's on the tip of my tongue to tell her to mind her own business, but this is not the time to start a row. In fact, I've thought about what to say if this happens. I slide a handful of Dad's business cards out of the back pocket of my jeans and show them to her.

"We were hoping to give him a quote for some work," I say.

"Really?" she says. "What work?"

I give her a look. "I'm afraid I can't discuss our clients' confidential business," I say. "Unless you're a member of the family?"

"Humph," she says, squinting up at me. "I'm his neighbour. I'm keeping an eye on his house," she adds, meaningfully. Like I'm a burglar and that's going to scare me off.

He *is* away. My heart sinks.

"Can you tell me when he'll be back?" I ask her. "I want to make sure he gets his quotation."

"You're wasting your time," she tells me. "He had a heart attack. He's in hospital. He has better things to worry about than your quotation."

"I'm sorry to hear that," I say, and I really am, though not for the reasons she thinks.

She stares at me, waiting for me to go, and there's nothing for it.

"Thank you very much, you've been very helpful," I say, managing not to make it sound too sarcastic. Then I walk out of the garden, taking a wide course around the garden shears, and back to the bike.

So that's it. Dr. Robertson might die, or he might get better and come home again, but whatever happens, it's unlikely I'll be talking to him any time soon.

I sit on the bike for a few moments before starting off, wondering what I'm going to do, and resisting the temptation to put my head in my hands. Then I glance around and the old lady's standing by Dr. Robertson's gate, watching me. I start the bike and drive home.

chapter fifty-nine

Ghost

Days passed, and Tom did not come back. There had been other times when he had not come for days and days, like the time when his mother refused to let him have the car, and he hadn't got the motorcycle working yet. I reminded myself of that, and yet it was impossible not to consider very seriously the possibility that he would never come back, ever.

"Just go!" I had shouted at him, and he had gone.

He had said *I love you*, not so very long ago, but I had never said it back to him.

I thought about those things, and I also thought about what I would do if my eighteenth birthday came and went, and I was alone. I knew my way to the town now, and I knew that I could walk there; it would take a long time, but the distance was not impossible. I could go to the police station, and tell them about myself, and ask them about Grandmother.

If I did that, I thought, I needn't tell them about Tom at all. Then he would never be in the terrible trouble that he thought was hanging over our heads. Nobody would ever point the finger at him for keeping my secrets.

I can do that, I said to myself. The idea filled me with dread, as though I were facing my own execution without even one friendly face in the crowd to look for, but it seemed like a *right* thing to do. It was in my power to protect someone I loved.

On Friday evening, the end of a lonely week, I was crossing the hall, intending to take some things upstairs, when I froze, hearing the sound of the motorcycle approaching.

Tom.

In a couple of minutes, he would be knocking at the front door. For a moment, hope flared up. Then I thought: P*erhaps I shouldn't let him in. Perhaps that would be the right thing for Tom, to make him go away again.*

Suddenly I was conscious of the rapid beating of my own heart. In my imagination I saw myself go over to the door and stealthily turn the key in the lock; I saw myself sink to the floor, hugging my knees, ducking my head and making myself as small as possible, so that if Tom tried peering in through the windows he would not see me. I would wait until he had exhausted himself knocking and I heard the motorcycle start up again, and then I would go upstairs to the turret window from which I had seen the men in uniforms. Once again I would be a silent, unseen observer, as Tom rode away into the forest.

In my mind's eye I saw all of this happening, and I went so far as to go over to the door and turn the key as carefully as I could. Then I stood there irresolutely, until I heard Tom's footsteps on the flagstones inside the stone porch. Now it was too late to move, or escape to another part of the house, or even crouch on the floor; he might hear me.

The first time he knocked on the door, I jumped; now my heart was really pounding. There was a pause, and in the silence I could hear my own breathing. I tried to hold my breath.

More knocking. Then, "Ghost! Ghost!"

I was facing the door. I placed my palm on it, feeling the polished wood cool under my skin, wanting to make contact with the thing that separated me and Tom. Then the door handle turned, vigorously, as Tom tried to get in. He rattled it, evidently not believing that the door was locked against him.

I took a step backwards, the hand that had touched the door going instead to my mouth.

"Ghost?"

I knew I shouldn't open the door. The questioning tone in his voice meant that he had started to doubt that I was there. The kitchen door was locked, too; he couldn't get into the house. I had only to wait long enough, and Tom would go away.

He might be relieved.

It was that thought that did it. Once I had thought that Tom might be glad to have an excuse to go, I wanted to *know*. There was no time to think about it; if he left I had no way to call him back. I turned the key and opened the door.

"You're here."

Tom stepped into the hallway. He didn't look any of the ways I had thought he might – not disappointed I was here after all, not contrite about the argument we had had, not bursting with vehement things he had wanted to say about that argument. Instead there was a brisk energy radiating off him. He plunged in with no preamble.

"I've found something out."

I stared at him.

"About your dad. You were right – about your gran, I mean. I'm sorry I said the stuff I did. It just seemed to fit at the time but I guess it was a crazy idea."

"Tom...I don't understand. Did you go to see Dr. Robertson?"

"Yes, but he wasn't there."

I shook my head, unable to make sense of what he was saying.

"Come through to the kitchen, and start from the beginning."

We went through, and I sat at the table. Tom leaned against the sink, seemingly too restless to sit.

"I went back to his house," said Tom. "Dr. Robertson, I

mean. Not on Saturday. I was soaked to the skin – you were right about that, too. I reckoned I'd never get him to talk to me, looking like a drowned rat. So I went back on Tuesday."

"But he wasn't there?"

"No, he's in hospital. His neighbour came out and told me." Tom made a face. "He had a heart attack. Even if he gets better, he won't be talking to anyone for a while."

"Oh, Tom." I couldn't think what to say. I hadn't liked the old man but the thought of his old heart stopping was too terrible; it made me think of poor Grandmother, collapsing in the street.

"Yeah." Tom let out a long breath like a sigh.

"But how did you find anything out if you couldn't talk to him?" I asked.

"By accident." Tom leaned forward. "It had nothing to do with Dr. Robertson. I had to leave his place right away because his neighbour was watching me, and then I couldn't think what to do next. I mean, there's nobody else to ask. In the end I decided to carry on with the online searches." He shrugged. "I didn't really think I'd find anything new, but what else could I do?" Tom looked at me a little warily. "I know you were angry with me for suggesting your grandmother took you when you were a baby, but don't get mad at me again. I just thought I'd look and see if there was anything online to prove it, and – there wasn't."

I said nothing.

"There was an article about a woman who took a baby from a maternity ward about the same time, but they got the baby back and arrested the woman. That was all. I didn't find anything else. No babies that disappeared altogether. Not even any pregnant women who vanished. I mean, *no proof* is not the same as *definitely didn't happen*, but still." Tom shrugged. "It makes it a lot less likely, right?"

"So that's what you found out?" I asked. I was perplexed; it sounded as though he hadn't found out anything at all.

"No," said Tom quickly. "I kept looking. But it was difficult because I've been working with Dad during the day, and in the evening Mum's still bugging me all the time. I did a lot of it late at night, when she and Dad had gone to bed. Then I got tired, and typed stuff wrong a few times. That's basically how I found out. I thought I'd try another search for your dad, and I typed the name wrong; I got the s and the z the wrong way round. And up came this article from ten years ago, with the same typo in the name."

"Typo?"

"The same spelling mistake," said Tom patiently. "That's why I hadn't found it before."

I stared at Tom. The feeling of excitement I had was not entirely pleasant. "Did it say what happened to my father?"

"No – I mean, it said the same as before, that he disappeared and was declared legally dead in 2007. They still don't know where he went. But they found his car."

"Where?"

"That's the thing. They found it in a glen over by Aberfeldy. That's maybe twenty, twenty five miles from here. Someone had driven it up there and dumped it. It's not near anything, not even somewhere walkers go. It'd been there for years, covered up with stuff growing over it. The only reason they found it was the Mountain Rescue were doing a search for something else, a missing person."

Tom was looking at me expectantly. "Don't you see? It proves he was here. He *disappeared* here. That's too much of a coincidence. He came up here after you were born, and then he vanished. Those things *have* to be related."

I chewed my lip, looking at Tom doubtfully. "It doesn't say what happened to him," I pointed out. "It could be anything."

"Yeah, in theory," said Tom. "He could have gone somewhere lonely and killed himself. People do that. But it's not likely that out of all the places he could choose to do it, he'd pick on one that's twenty miles away from Langlands, just by some kind of random coincidence."

Tom looked almost eager. He was convinced he was solving the puzzle, I could see that. But it was not just a puzzle to solve, a riddle like the ones in books. It was my family.

I looked down at my own hands, not wanting to meet Tom's eyes as I asked the question.

"What do you think happened?"

"I think he came here," said Tom. He pushed himself off from the sink and came to sit by me. He looked right into my face, his gaze searching mine, his expression serious. "I think he tracked your mother to Langlands. Maybe it took a while to work out where she was, but in the end, he cracked it. Then he turned up and...maybe he tried to get your mum to go back with him and she wouldn't, so he threatened her. Or maybe he didn't even try to persuade her, he tried to hurt her or your gran. Ghost...if they hurt him back, it would be self-defence."

"Hurt him?" I repeated, and I could hear the tremor in my own voice.

"Yeah." The corner of Tom's mouth puckered in a grimace of regret. "They probably just wanted to frighten him off, and maybe he wouldn't go and it got out of hand..."

"You mean murder," I said.

Tom shook his head. "Self-defence."

"It still means killing someone," I said in a very low voice.

"It's not the same," said Tom, firmly.

"But if it happened here, why was the car in that glen?" I asked, and Tom had an answer for that too. He had it all worked out.

"It's not difficult. Your grandmother knew the area from when she was growing up. She could have chosen a really quiet spot where the car wouldn't be discovered for ages and driven it there herself. Then she could have walked into Aberfeldy and caught a bus back, or gone back to the main road and hitched a lift back or something. It's twenty miles, not a hundred miles. She could have done it. And then if anyone found the car, there would be no way of connecting it with Langlands."

I looked away, biting my lip.

"So where is my father?" I asked unsteadily. "You said they don't know where he went, so he's not in the car, is he?"

"No," said Tom. He hesitated, and it was his silence that told me what I needed to know.

"You think here, don't you? At Langlands?"

Tom sighed. "I've been trying to think what I'd do if it were me. Driving twenty miles with a body in the car could be risky. Okay, those roads are pretty quiet, but if you *did* get stopped..." He shrugged. "And supposing someone found the car straight away? Instead of him being missing and it taking seven years to decide he's dead, there'd be a murder enquiry."

"It doesn't seem real," I said. "Thinking of Grandmother doing something like that. My mother too. I can't believe it." I looked at Tom boldly. "You must be wrong."

Tom said nothing.

"Tom, you *must* be wrong. There couldn't be a dead body here. What do you think they did – buried him in the garden? Wouldn't I know about it?"

Tom was shaking his head. "It was seventeen years ago, Ghost. You were a baby. You wouldn't have known anything about it."

"But I've been living here all that time. I've been everywhere in the house and grounds. I'm telling you, Tom, I'd *know*."

The words were barely out of my mouth before something occurred to me. *There's one place I haven't been.*

I pressed my lips tight shut, not trusting myself to say anything else. I had told an unintentional untruth, but I didn't want to unsay it. I wanted time on my own to think about it before I did that; I wanted time to talk myself out of the ideas

293

that were slinking like grim wolves through the darkest parts of my imagination.

I listened to Tom as he tried very kindly and patiently to convince me that we should search the house and as much of the grounds as we could. At last, I said, "Come back tomorrow."

It made sense. Who wanted to go hunting for such a grisly hidden treasure as a dead body, as twilight closed in and the shadows lengthened and merged until all was darkness? Tom said yes.

After he had gone, I went to the overgrown patch of lawn at the side of the house. I stood with my back to the grey stone wall of Langlands House and stared at the encroaching forest. A little way into the undergrowth, not visible from where I stood, through the tangled growth, was the old mausoleum.

I stood there until I began to shiver in the cool evening air, and then I went indoors, taking care to lock up behind me.

chapter sixty

On Saturday morning, I rose early to find the day grey and damp. I fed the chickens and made tea for myself. I had the end of a loaf of bread and a couple of eggs left, but I felt too restless to eat anything. The unease was like a sickness; it made me want to pace like a trapped animal.

I took the tea with me and made my way down the passage to the library. Then I set the cup on top of one of the cabinets, where its steam rose into the cool air, and set about opening the safe. I had to take nearly everything out again to find what I wanted: the bundle of letters signed *Edith*.

If I can just find something to tell me... What? I wasn't sure. Something to prove, absolutely, that my mother and grandmother had had nothing to do with my father's disappearance? I had read the letters before; I knew there was nothing in them that could give me that assurance. In fact, the few times the writer strayed away from dull, ordinary topics her words were ominous. *The past is better left buried, I think.* I stared at that sentence for a long while. *Literally buried?* I wondered, and shivered. The paper crinkled in my fingers, brittle and yellowed.

There is nothing to prove that these are from my mother, I reminded myself. *'Edith' may really be Edith, some friend of Grandmother's.* These letters prove nothing.

I began to stuff all the papers and boxes back into the safe, not caring how untidily I did it. One of the blocks of banknotes had broken apart and the notes had fluttered everywhere, like leaves torn from a book I did not know how to read. Most people kept their money in banks, I knew that now, thanks to Tom. When had Grandmother taken all hers out, and how, and why? It came to me again that I could never ask her anything now. Some things would never be known.

I gathered up all the notes into an untidy stack and as I picked up the last one, I saw something gleaming on the floorboards, a small fragment of gold against the dusty brown wood.

That key again.

I put out my hand and picked it up, turning it over in my fingers.

Gold.

Something was prickling in the back of mind. Even in the poor light of a grey morning, the key was very shiny, and as I turned it over the light hit it, so that it briefly flashed gold.

All of a sudden it came back to me, the moment when I came walking down through the forest towards the old mausoleum and saw a flash of gold at the front of it. I remembered the bright sunlight, the cool bite of the air, the crackle of twigs under my feet, and the scent of the wild garlic in the basket I was carrying. I remembered how it had made me feel to see that tiny flare of gold: that something was right, that it was a kind of sign. Now I thought it was telling me something very different indeed.

A loud knock at the front door made me jump almost out of my skin.

Tom.

I had not heard the motorcycle coming, so engrossed was I in contemplating the key and its probable meaning. All of a sudden my heart was beating with a guilty wildness, as though I had been caught in some terrible act. I shoved the key into the bodice of my dress, stuffed the last few notes into the safe and swung the door shut. Then I ran for the front hall. My cheeks were burning and I prayed Tom would not see from my face that something was amiss.

When I opened the door, he was standing there with his arms full of supplies he had brought for me, and a wary smile on his face, as though he was not entirely certain how he would be received. He needn't have worried; I was so concerned not to give anything away that I greeted him overenthusiastically, flinging my arms around him. A box of tea he had balanced on top of the other things hit the black and white tiles and crumpled.

"Hey," said Tom, but he looked pleased. When he had taken the things into the kitchen and put them down on the table, he pulled me into his arms and kissed me. I kissed him back, feeling the familiar heat that seemed to run through me whenever we touched each other, an almost painfully intense sensation that made me feel reckless when I was with Tom, and restless when I wasn't. But as I leaned against him, I felt something cold pressing into my flesh over my heart.

The key.

The realisation had a dampening effect. I drew back a little. We broke the kiss; the moment was gone.

I had forgotten about the cup of tea I had taken into the library. By now it would be stone cold anyway, exhaling all its heat into the frigid air. I brewed some more for me and Tom, and finally forced myself to eat a slice of bread and jam. We talked a little, Tom about his parents, I about the jobs I needed to do around the house and the vegetable garden, but the talk was half-hearted. We both knew what we were going to do that day. It was a strange thought, that we would be searching so carefully for something we desperately hoped not to find.

All the time, the key lay in the bosom of my dress, over my heart. Even after it had warmed to body temperature from contact with my skin, I imagined that I could still feel it, corpse-cold, pressing into my flesh. I said nothing about it to Tom.

And so began a very long day. Tom suggested that we begin in the attic and work downwards, which seemed as good an idea as any – assuming that you were not hiding a key to somewhere else entirely. I was hideously conscious of that as we climbed the stairs. Why didn't I say anything then? I considered it, and I didn't decide *not* to tell him, but I wanted to think about it a little longer. I suppose I was already convinced in my own mind that we would find my father there, in the mausoleum. Perhaps I wanted to steel myself to find out, or perhaps I simply wanted to put off having to face the truth.

Tom was carrying a lantern so that we could get into the very darkest corners. If I had thought that we might really force open one of the locked trunks and find the decomposed remains of a human being curled up in it, I would have drawn back from the task. But in my heart, I was sure we wouldn't. I probably amazed Tom with my boldness, the way I went about pulling the dust sheets off mirrors and paintings, opening boxes and looking inside the larger pieces of furniture, seemingly unafraid of what I would find. Soon my hands and my dress were grimy with dust, and I suspected my hair was powdered with it, too.

It took a long time to cover the whole attic. We found two locked trunks that had never been opened in all the time I could remember, and we had to go downstairs to look for tools so that Tom could break the locks. One of them proved to be full of monogrammed bed linen that smelled so musty that I would as soon have wrapped myself in someone else's winding-sheet as use it on my bed. The other contained furs. I plunged my hands in amongst them, and the feeling of the dead fur against my skin was strange, almost caressing. I burrowed down as far as the bottom of the trunk but there was nothing else in there.

Eventually we decided that we had spent enough time in the attic; there was nothing to find. We descended a floor, and I showed Tom the entrance to one of the servants' staircases.

After that we spent an hour going up and down all of the hidden staircases and along the passages. Tom was fascinated by the idea of being able to move about the house unseen, and wanted to see every inch, but the passages were very cobwebby and I soon became tired of picking the gossamer strands out of my hair. We found nothing, of course. I had been through these passages myself before and I knew we would not find anything.

Then we began on the first floor rooms. By now it was afternoon, and more overcast outdoors than before; the windows showed a grim vista of grey sky and dark clouds.

"We should have done the gardens first," said Tom, looking out. "It's going to rain." He made a face. "It's going to rain tomorrow, too. Dad was moaning about it this morning."

I went and stood by him. He was right; already the first drops of rain were landing on the glass. I thought to myself that perhaps we might not look outdoors at all, not if it settled in to rain for days on end.

It won't rain forever, I reminded myself. But it would be a reprieve.

Still I kept my own counsel. By late afternoon, we were both too tired to carry on. If it had been up to me, we would have given up hours before, but Tom was still tormented by the urgency to know the truth. It was not unreasonable for him to want to know what he had become mixed up in, I thought, but still I did not tell him about the key. I was acutely aware of it, still tucked down inside the bodice of my dress.

I don't need to tell him I hid it, I said to myself. *If I told him my idea tomorrow, or some other day, I could say I had only just come across it.*

I knew that would be lying but still I comforted myself with the thought.

When Tom left, he promised to come back the following afternoon. He looked so discouraged that it was on the tip of my tongue to say: *If my father is anywhere at Langlands, I know where it will be*. But I didn't say it. I kissed him goodbye and clung to him for a moment, and then I let him go and stepped back, and the key was still hidden in my dress.

After the sound of the motorcycle had diminished in the distance until it merged with the hiss of falling rain, I went indoors. I walked down the passage to the kitchen and sat down at the scrubbed pine table where I had sat so many times in the past, watching Grandmother make pastry or slice vegetables. I slid my fingers into the front of my dress and retrieved the key, now blood-warm. I put it down on the table top, the blade pointing dagger-like towards me, and stared at it for a long, long time, as the sun sank in the sky.

chapter sixty-one

The following morning it was raining heavily when I got up. It was late; when Grandmother was alive we had always risen early, but now it was nearly noon. I dressed hastily but instead of going straight downstairs, I went down the passage and into one of the other bedrooms, the one whose ceiling had been damaged that night the storm brought down the chimney. I went over to the window and looked out. With the rain running down the glass in streams, it was difficult to see anything clearly, but I knew what lay in the direction of my gaze: the old stone mausoleum. I stood there for a while looking out and chewing my lip.

I could go by myself. The key was still on the kitchen table. I had not put it back inside my dress; somehow, I did not like the idea of it next to my skin again. I could very easily pick it up, slip on a coat, let myself out of the house and go to look at the mausoleum. If I was wrong about the key, I would not have raised Tom's hopes of finding something.

In the end, though, I didn't do it. If the truth was buried out there, did I *want* to know? I walked around in a dream, thinking about that question. When Grandmother had left me and never returned, I had known that something must have happened to her, but there had been a very great difference between believing that and knowing it for certain. Now I thought perhaps there was a limit to the amount of truth that any one person could stand.

I put my hands to my head, which was beginning to feel as though it would split open with the terrible thoughts that throbbed through it. I had no answer to any of the questions that tormented me.

I was still thinking about it when Tom arrived in the afternoon; in fact, I had not come to a decision. But it was taken out of my hands. Tom came into the kitchen to warm himself up, water dripping from his clothes, and the first thing he saw was the key, still lying on the kitchen table. I had forgotten to hide it.

"Is that the key from the safe?"

I nodded, my throat suddenly too tight to speak.

Tom leaned over the table and picked it up. Then his blue-green gaze was on me, serious and urgent.

"Why is it here? Did you remember what it was for?"

"Yes."

"To do with your dad?"

I looked at him in silence for a moment, struggling within myself. I didn't want to say *yes*, not while I didn't even want to think yes. "Maybe," I said at last. "There's a place in the grounds. A sort of...it's a mausoleum. You know, a burying place. I think the key is from that."

Tom was staring at me. "Why didn't you say before?"

"I only thought of it today," I said, and felt the blood come to my face at the lie. "I've never been inside. I've hardly even been near it, my whole life. Grandmother didn't like me to – she said it was disrespectful to the dead."

I stopped, realising what I had said. Tom saw it too; I could tell by the expression on his face, the reaction that rippled across it. The next thing that he would say for sure would be: *Let's go and look, right now.*

302

"Tom," I blurted out, "I'm not sure I want to look."

Tom must have seen the anguish on my face. He put his arms around me, pulling me close, and held me for a little while. It would have been comforting except he still had the key in his fingers; I felt it pressing into me. "You wouldn't have to look," he said, into my hair. "I can go."

"But I don't know if I *want* to know," I said.

"I think..." He paused. "I think we *have* to know, Ghost."

I pushed my head against his shoulder, feeling the dampness of his jacket against my cheek. It was made of leather, for riding on the motorcycle, and it felt like cold wet skin.

"It's pouring with rain," I said.

"I know," said Tom. "It's only water."

He gave me a little squeeze, and then he let me go.

I watched him refasten his jacket.

"Is it far, this place?"

"No," I said.

He looked at me. "Will you show me?"

I let out a long breath like a sigh. "Yes."

I went to the peg by the back door and took down a coat, a long one made of waxed cotton that would keep off the worst of the rain. I didn't look at Tom while I put it on, my hands trembling a little as I did it up, taking my time as though I could put off what was to come.

Tom came over. "I mean it," he said. "You don't have to go. I can do it."

I shook back the hair that had fallen over my face and made myself look him in the eye.

"I'll come," I said. I took his hand, and his skin was as cold as the leather of his jacket had been. It was like holding someone who had drowned. I shivered.

Tom slipped the key into his pocket and together we left the house. I could hear the rain before we even stepped out of the front door and into the stone porch. Over the hissing of its falling there was the more intrusive sound of water pouring out of a broken gutter and spattering onto the gravel. I didn't bother suggesting we waited for it to stop. I knew this kind of rain; it would keep coming down for hours.

The moment we stepped out of the shelter of the porch it was like being pelted. Neither of us had a hood and before we had crossed the gravel both of us were blinking water out of our eyes, our hair plastered to our heads. I could taste it on my lips.

We rounded the corner of the house and crossed a patch of lawn that was becoming smaller every year as the overhanging trees encroached. Then we stepped into the forest, and the hiss of the rain became a rattle as it hit the trees above us.

We had to move slowly. I was used to going about in the forest; I stepped high over tangled brambles and my tread was light. Tom stumbled over knots of undergrowth, and his progression was accompanied by a percussion of broken twigs. We said very little to each other.

I saw the mausoleum before Tom did. The day was so dismal that its grey walls almost faded into the gloom under the trees.

"There," I said, and I heard Tom swear under his breath. Then we began to clamber over fallen trunks and the damp and rotting remains of weeds, until we were almost close enough to touch the cold grey stone.

Now we could see that there was a grey metal door set into the front of the building. The metal was dimpled and speckled with darker patches so that from a distance it blended into the stone around it. The only thing that stood out to the eye was the gold-coloured padlock that fastened it. Today there was not enough sunshine to make it flash out golden fire as it had the day I had gone hunting for mushrooms, but it still gleamed.

Tom had the key in his fingers. I wanted to say, *stop, wait a moment, let me think about this*, but he had already taken the padlock in his other hand and was trying to fit the key into it.

The lock was modern, unlike the rest of the mausoleum, but it had hardly been used in however long it had been there; I could not remember Grandmother ever going to the old mausoleum. Tom struggled for what seemed a very long time, while I bit my lip and my heart began to gallop in my chest. *Perhaps it won't open. Perhaps it isn't even the right key.* But at last he managed to get the key into the lock, and turn it. Even then, the padlock didn't spring open; he had to prise it open with his fingers. Carefully, he detached it from the door and offered it to me, the key still protruding from the lock. I shook my head. Tom looked at me for a moment, and then he slipped it into his own pocket.

He didn't ask me whether I was ready. It would have been pointless; I would never be ready. Instead, he seized the metal door handle and tried the door to see which way it would swing. There was no inward movement at all. He tried to pull it towards him, and it stuck on the tangle of plants and soil at the foot of it. Tom began to drag his heel along the ground, carving a furrow so that the door had room to swing out.

I watched him with a cold feeling of dread. I wanted to grab his arm and pull him away from the door, to stop him carving a path for it in the earth. I did nothing. I was paralysed. A sick horror throbbed through me with the pulsing of my blood; I could not even say, *stop*.

At last Tom stopped hacking at the ground and tried the door again. This time it swung towards him with a brittle complaint from the rusted hinges. For a moment we stared together at the gloom within.

What had I expected – that a grinning skeleton, propped against the inside of the door, would tumble out onto the wet ground and grin up at us with its lipless teeth? As my eyes adjusted to the dim light I saw nothing alarming, just grey stone walls and the rectangular shapes of two stone sarcophagi, one either side of the small room.

I stepped inside. The air in the room was several degrees colder than the air outside but the floor and the walls seemed perfectly dry; I saw the wet marks my boots made standing out clearly against the floor before Tom followed me through the doorway, momentarily blocking out the light.

I inhaled very cautiously. I could smell the damp forest outside and when Tom moved close to me I could smell his cologne. I could also detect a faint mineral tang from the cold stone. Was there something else, something sweetish, underneath? I wasn't sure.

Tom moved past me, and the pale light streamed in again. I watched him go down on one knee between the two sarcophagi, examining the left hand one, running his fingers along the seal between the coffin and the lid.

"Cemented," he said, glancing at me. "I could break the cement pretty easily but I'm not sure there's much point. It's been sealed a long time. More than, you know."

"Seventeen years," I said in a low voice, and he nodded.

Both of us looked at the other stone coffin. My eyes had fully adjusted now and I saw that there was something lying on top of it, something withered and unidentifiable.

Tom saw it at the same time, and put out a hand, touching it gingerly with his fingers.

"I think it might have been roses, once," he said. He ran his hands along the rim of the stone lid, testing it, seeing whether it would move. Then he looked at me, holding my gaze, his face serious. "I'm going to open this. If you want to go outside, now's the time."

I stared back at him. My heart was hammering so fast that I was afraid I would pass out. Terror swarmed through me, to my very fingers' ends. I wanted to scream at Tom that he shouldn't open the stone casket, that we should not have come here. I wanted to go backwards, to be back in the kitchen at the moment when Tom said, "Will you show me?" I would scream,

306

"No, no!" I would fling the key into the deepest part of the forest or the depths of the waterfall before I would let him use it. I wanted to squeeze my eyes shut and make it have happened that way.

But it wasn't possible, any more than it was possible for me to go back in time to when Grandmother was alive. I could not make myself believe any more in a War that had long since ended. I could not bring Grandmother back.

I looked at Tom and very slowly shook my head. *I'm not going outside.*

Tom paused for a second, studying the stone slab that formed the lid of the coffin. He put out both his hands and gripped it by opposite edges, adjusting his grip until it felt right. Then I saw his arms and shoulders strain as he heaved at the stone. There was an ominous grating sound and Tom gave a gasp. He pressed his lips together in a hard line and heaved again. I broke from my paralysis and squatted on the cold floor so that I could help him.

It was not the weight of the stone that made it hard to move; it was the rough stone surfaces which caught together and would not let the slab slide freely. When it began to move, it did so all at once, and both Tom and I had to move back sharply to avoid it landing on us. I sat back with a jarring impact that sent pain through my tailbone, and at the same moment I heard the slab hit the floor with a grinding thump.

Tom was up before I was, peering inside, and he began to turn towards me, his eyes wide, his mouth beginning to open to tell me to *look away, don't look*, but it was too late.

I looked into the sarcophagus and there was the ugly thing I had expected to see, brown and yellow and withered, the mouldering remains of clothing tented by the sharp outline of bones underneath, the eye sockets dark and corroded craters above the grim ivory smile of naked teeth. There were thin hands folded over the bowl of the pelvis, but they were more like the talons of birds, with the flesh gone and the length of the bones exposed.

I had expected to see something like this – yes, I had known I would see it, and had steeled myself for it. But I had not expected it to be female.

Because it *was* female; I saw that at the first glance, even though the soft parts of the body had long since rotted away. The stained and spotted covering was the remains of a dress, with tiny buttons and delicate pintucks on the bodice. A slender chain with a pendant on it, both tarnished almost black, encircled the vertebrae of the neck. And there was hair. *Lots* of hair. The browning skull nestled in it, like the great round body of a spider crouched in a cloud of spun gossamer.

I could not breathe. There was a scream building up inside me but it would not come out; I was choking on it, my chest hitching painfully. I kept looking at that dreadful head, the grisly brown remains of the face. The hair. It was *familiar*, that was the terrible thing. The more I looked, with eyes that felt as though they would start right out of their sockets, the more I could see the lines of the decayed face in the contours of the bones.

I know you.

Something broke inside me. The scream erupted at last, it burst out of me, scouring my throat, raw and hot as blood. It raged through me like a storm; my whole body shook with it, my hands clenched into fists. I could not see Tom, I could not see anything but the horror. It was as though I was being dragged over the edge of a great black pit.

Tom grabbed me by the shoulders, his face pale and set, his eyes wide.

"Ghost–"

I tried to wrench myself away. "It's me!" I screamed. "It's me!" I struck at him wildly. "Can't you see? It's me in there!"

"No – Ghost, it's not–"

Tom spoke to me earnestly, trying to make me look back

at him, but I was past listening. I raved and struggled in his grasp, and all the time I kept seeing it: myself, lying there in the stone coffin, crumbling into a brown and disgusting heap of decay.

At last Tom put his arms around me and simply held me as tightly as he could, turning so that I could not see the sarcophagus and its ugly contents.

"No," he kept saying into my hair, "It's not you, Ghost. It's not you."

When I had worn myself out, he half-dragged, half-led me out of the mausoleum. The rain was still coming down heavily; when he took my face in his hands and turned it up to his, I could feel the raindrops running down my cheeks like tears. I blinked against the drops in my eyelashes, gasping as I pushed back the wet hair from my face.

"Ghost." Tom made me look at him. "It's not you in there. Understand?"

"The hair..." I wanted to explain properly but I was suffocating, the tightness in my chest seeming to crush all the air out of me.

"I know. I saw it too."

"My hair."

"Not your hair. It's your mother – it has to be. That's why the hair is like yours."

I stared up at him dully. *It can't be her*, I wanted to say. *She's not dead*. But the words wouldn't come. The rain streamed down our faces as we stared at each other.

"Can you stand here for a minute?" said Tom. He pushed me gently back a step or two until my shoulders touched the wall of the mausoleum and I sagged back against it. He brushed a strand of hair out of my eyes with cold fingers. "I have to go back – inside. Just for a moment, okay?"

I nodded, swallowing. Nothing would have induced me to go back in there at that moment. I turned my head to watch him, the stone wall cold and damp against my cheek.

Tom ducked inside the doorway again. He was gone for no more than a few seconds, and when he came out again, pulling the door closed behind him, he was holding something. There was a tight, revolted look on his face. He said, "Let's go."

The ground was spongy now with the rain. Tom did his best to support me as we made our way back to the house. It was not easy; there was barely room for one person to make their way along the route we had trampled down through the undergrowth, let alone two, one supporting the other. Wet branches slapped at us. Our feet slipped in mud turned almost liquid by the water running off the hill. Rain was running down inside the collar of my coat now, and my clothes were sticking clammily to my back.

When we came out from under the trees it was easier going underfoot but there was no protection at all from the rain. The full fury of the skies was poured out on us. Tom dragged me bodily across the lawn and the gravel and into the stone porch. By now he was breathing hard and both of us looked as though we had been hauled out of deep water; our skin and hair were shining with wet.

When we got into the hallway, Tom helped me take off the waxed coat. I dropped it on the black and white tiles and together we stumbled down the passage to the sanctuary of the warm kitchen. I sank into a chair and stared at the room as though I did not know it. Nothing was as I thought it had been. Lies were piled on lies, deceit on deceit. I could not believe that I had been living alongside the mausoleum and its grisly contents without knowing, without ever suspecting. *Disrespectful to the dead.* I remembered Grandmother saying that, and I wanted to be sick, to scream, to beat my own head against the wall until I had beat the memory out of it. But I had no energy to do any of it. I was dropping down into a deep, dark well inside myself, and I would never stop falling.

Tom put something down on the windowsill, something that made a brittle little click as he put it on the hard surface, and then he came over and squatted down by me, trying to look into my face.

I knew the expression he wore. *Worried*, that was it. It didn't seem to mean anything to me; I couldn't understand why he looked like that.

He took my hand in his and said, "You're freezing," and I just looked at him. After a moment, he let go of my hand and got up. I suppose he went upstairs to one of the bedrooms then, but I barely noticed he was gone. I stared ahead of me, and my teeth chattered, and I dared not close my eyes because of what I saw when I did. After a while Tom came back with a bedspread and put it around my shoulders. Then he made tea, exclaiming impatiently over the length of time it took for water to boil on top of the kitchen range. I said nothing. I did not want the tea, but when it came I drank it anyway. There was no milk – Tom had not found the powdered stuff – and he had heaped in the sugar so that it was unbearably sweet. All the same, I began to feel a little better, and my hands were less numb after they had cradled the hot cup for a while.

Tom sat next to me, his own cup in his hands. He had taken off his jacket and there were dark patches on his shirt where the rain had run down inside it. For a long while neither of us said anything. The rain still rattled at the windows. Tom's jacket, hanging over the back of a chair, dripped water onto the kitchen floor.

"Tom?" I said at last. "Do you really think that was...? I mean..." I faltered, not wanting to say, *my mother*, not when I was speaking of the brown and foul thing in the mausoleum.

Tom nodded. "Yeah." He looked down, at the floor. "I think that was your mum." He paused. "I'm sorry."

"Do you think...?" I hesitated. "Do you think my father is in the other one?"

"I don't know. I don't think so. I mean, the other one was all cemented up. Look, I took something out of the coffin. Maybe we should look at that."

I watched as he got up and crossed the room to the window. When he came back he was carrying something. I saw that it was a rectangular tin with a lid, the kind that might have been used for biscuits or sweets; it had been embossed with a design that might have been flowers or ferns.

Tom held it out to me, but I hesitated to take it. "This was in the coffin?"

"Yeah. By the feet."

"Can *you* open it?"

"Are you sure?"

I nodded. "Yes."

Tom sat beside me again and I watched as he struggled to open the tin. At last he managed it. The lid came off, and we both peered at the contents of the tin.

Paper. Folded paper. A letter.

Whoever had placed it in the tin had folded it very carefully so that the words at the beginning of the top sheet were clearly visible.

To whom it may concern.

"That's Grandmother's writing," I said.

chapter sixty-two

Rose

Christmas Eve, 1999
To whom it may concern:

I, Rose Elspeth McAndrew of Langlands House, Perthshire, wish it to be known that I am of sound mind and that the contents of this document are as accurate a representation of the facts as possible.

If you are reading this, then the body of my daughter Elspeth Janet McAndrew has certainly been discovered. I killed her on November 29th, 1999. I did not report her death to the authorities. Owing to the frozen earth and winter weather I was unable to bury the body by myself, so I placed it inside the Langlands mausoleum, in an unused stone coffin.

These bare facts will be obvious if Elspeth's remains have been discovered. However, if my granddaughter Augusta Elspeth McAndrew is alive at the time when her mother's body is found, I would like her to understand the circumstances of what happened, in the hope that she may find it in her heart to forgive me.

I was born in Edinburgh in 1935, four years before the War broke out. During the war years, when it became dangerous to stay in the cities, my parents sent me to stay at Langlands House with relatives. I am an old woman now, but in all my long life I do not believe there was ever a time when I was happier. For a city child, the Langlands estate was a wonderful, exciting place to explore. We ate well too, in spite of rationing, because of all the space given over to growing fruit and vegetables, and the abundance of game in the forest.

I do not suppose that an old woman's memories are of interest to anyone else. I mention them simply to explain why I came back to Langlands later.

Father was killed in 1944, and after the War, my mother moved to Perthshire permanently, to be closer to her relatives. So I ended up within a few miles of Langlands, although I never lived there again until a long time afterwards. Mother's relatives were growing older, and as it became harder for them to maintain the house and grounds, they welcomed visitors less often. After their deaths, the house was closed up, although by then I had moved to England with my new husband.

Angus died in 1981, aged only 50. The marriage was a successful one, I think, and I grieved very sincerely for him. We had only one child, Elspeth, then in her teens, and she became the centre of my life after that.

I have asked myself whether it was my fault that Elspeth became entangled with such an unsuitable man. Was she overprotected? Perhaps. I had nobody but her. Angus left me well off, so there was no reason for her to be exposed to the harsher side of life, and having lost him so early, I was determined to look after her and protect her as best I could.

Of course, losing her father must have had an effect on her, too. It may be part of the reason that she fell for a man so much older than she was, although Angus was never so arrogant nor such a bully. Elspeth could not see these things; she thought he was "tough" and "confident". But I could see them. I was suspicious from the beginning, and of course he saw that. He kept his cloven hooves well-hidden until after the wedding, and then he did his best to keep us apart. I don't think what he felt for her can be called love. He simply wanted someone to tyrannise.

The first time she left him, I remember her huddled in my sitting-room with the bruises still fresh on her arms where she had pushed the long sleeves back, and telling me with tears in her eyes that he hadn't really meant to do it. She said he wasn't cruel, he couldn't help himself; he was like a little boy inside.

I agreed with her, but I didn't think he was a nice little boy. I thought he was like one of those boys who tortures animals for fun.

She went back to him that time. I begged her not to, but she went almost before he had had time to notice that she had gone. I think that's what she hoped, that he would not know she had come to me.

Later that night, the telephone rang it and was him. He said terrible things about what he would do if I tried to lure his wife away from him. I threatened to call the police and he hung up. After that sometimes the phone would ring and when I picked it up, there would be silence at the other end, and I knew it was him.

That was only the first time. There were other times, of course, and it got worse, and it became harder too for me to see Elspeth at all. When she became pregnant, she had to telephone to tell me when he was out; she went out to a call box to do it, so that he wouldn't see the number on the telephone bill. She was crying all the time she was telling me, because she knew he wouldn't let her see me. I didn't hear a thing for months after that. I was worried sick.

Then one evening the doorbell rang and there she was on the step, and a taxi was disappearing off up the street. She was big by then, because the baby was nearly due, but the first thing I noticed was that she had a black eye.

Of course, I knew he'd come after her, and he did. An hour and a half later he turned up, and I let him in so that he could see for himself that she wasn't in the house. He broke a few things searching for her, and he gave me a few bruises too. I pretended to be terribly frightened and promised to persuade her to go back to him if she came to me. In truth I was actually frightened. He wasn't like an out of control little boy, he was an ogre. But I had no intention of telling Elspeth to go back to him.

I hardly slept that night. I had too much to do. The following day I liquidised as much of my money as I possibly could, picked Elspeth up from the hotel I had sent her to, and we left London for good. The house could be sold later; I dared not make it obvious that we had left, so we simply took the things we needed immediately.

We drove north for a long time, and then we stopped for a while because I was too tired to drive anymore. I slept for a few hours and then drove on through the night, until we reached Langlands.

I was shocked when I saw the house again. It wasn't the way I remembered it – of course it wasn't, because nearly six decades had passed since then. But it was an ideal hiding place, and I thought we could make do for a little while.

Elspeth's baby, my granddaughter Augusta, was born in the house. I suppose people will be shocked by that. But when I was young, it was common for babies to be born at home. I went for a doctor, someone I had known myself when I was younger, but when we got back to the house the baby had already arrived.

I am not going to name the doctor in question. If his identity is deduced anyway, I wish it to be known that he is entirely blameless. He tried to persuade me to take Elspeth to the hospital in Perth for the birth, and when we found that the baby had already arrived, he tried to persuade me to take them there to be checked over. I refused. I accept responsibility for that too.

The baby was born healthy, and gradually Elspeth recovered physically from the birth. I hoped to persuade her to start divorce proceedings against her husband, but she put me off; she said she wanted to think about it a little longer. I think she was not well – in her mind, I mean. She found living at Langlands difficult. Elspeth didn't love the place like I did, and she hated having to look after the baby without any of the modern things she had come to rely on. Her moods became unpredictable. Sometimes she would be silent and low in spirits for hours; at other times she would lose her temper at the slightest thing. Once I found her crying bitterly over the baby in her lap. She said it was terrible to think that Augusta would never know her father, and that he had never seen his daughter. I was angry then. I know I was wrong, but it was too much to listen to her talking as though her husband was some poor misunderstood creature. We quarrelled, and then we didn't speak for a whole day.

It came to a head when Augusta was seven months old. I suppose the prospect of an entire winter in Langlands House made it worse for Elspeth. We argued more and more frequently. And then on the night of 29th November, she tried to leave with the baby.

I only heard her because the baby cried out. I always woke if Augusta cried in the night. I left my room with a lamp in my hand and found Elspeth on the landing, with Augusta in her arms and a bag on her back.

It was the very thing I had been afraid of: she was going back to him. I was appalled, and terrified for her and the baby. I was too upset to speak calmly, and a huge row erupted, both of us shouting at each other. Augusta became frightened and began to cry loudly. Elspeth was screaming at me, saying awful things, telling me I had no right to stop her going anywhere, accusing me of interfering. I couldn't think clearly with both of them shrieking. I was so afraid for them, but I was angry with Elspeth too. How could she even think of going back, and taking the baby with her?

I saw that she was going to turn away and go downstairs. I put down the lamp and reached out to grab the baby from her arms. If I couldn't stop her going back to him, I could stop her taking the baby with her. I could save Augusta. That was what I was trying to do.

I almost managed it. I had Augusta in my hands before Elspeth knew what I was doing. She gave a great scream of rage and lunged at me, and I–

I pushed her.

We were both so upset and angry. Neither of us really knew what we were doing. It was too easy to push too hard, to use more force than I meant to. I didn't mean to push her down the stairs. I'm almost certain of that.

I pushed her, and she screamed as she went backwards down the first flight, and for a moment her eyes met mine as I stood there at the top of the stairs with the baby in my arms. Then she turned over and there was a crunch as she hit the bannisters at the turn of the stairs. The scream stopped abruptly.

I didn't trust myself to walk down the stairs with the baby in my arms. I was trembling too violently. I stood there holding Augusta and waiting for Elspeth to move, to sit up and shout at me again for pushing her. But she didn't move. She lay there, perfectly still, but in a way that looked as though it would be painful, with her head bent at that angle, pushed up against the wood.

I called her name twice but she did not move nor reply. Augusta's shrieks ran down, as though she were running out of energy. I looked at her, because I wanted to look somewhere else other than at her mother lying there on the landing on the stairs, so silent and still. Augusta's eyes were very round, and her face was flushed from crying.

"It's all right, dear," I told her. "Mummy's resting."

I took up the lamp again and carried her back to the room she shared with Elspeth. We had never found a cot in any of the rooms at Langlands, only a cradle that Augusta had already outgrown, so she had a kind of bed made up on the floor. I tucked her in again, and made sure to close the door on the way out of the room. Then I went back to the staircase.

I suppose I knew what I would find. Elspeth was warm and her blue eyes were open, but she was stone dead. Her cheeks were still wet with tears of rage. I wiped them away with my fingertips and she never moved, never blinked. My daughter was gone.

I couldn't leave her where she was because I would have to bring Augusta downstairs in the morning. It wasn't something she should see. So I dragged Elspeth down the rest of the stairs as carefully as I could, and shut her in one of the downstairs rooms. Then I went to the kitchen, where there was a bottle of cooking sherry, and poured myself a glass for the shock.

According to the strict letter of the law, I should have gone to the police to report Elspeth's death. It was an accident, after all. I hadn't meant for her to die. But in the first moments I was afraid of being arrested, and when I had calmed down enough to think the situation through, I began to see other implications.

Elspeth and her husband were not divorced; they were not even officially separated. Augusta was his daughter. He would want to claim her.

I didn't deceive myself that he would do it out of love. He hadn't laid eyes on his daughter, after all. He would do it for the same reason that he wanted Elspeth back when she left him: because he would see her as his property. As for me, he had resented me before, but now he must hate me; he must have known that I had helped Elspeth to vanish. When he found out that I was responsible for her death, he'd probably be writing to the papers demanding the return of the death penalty. In no conceivable set of circumstances would he let me keep Augusta.

319

I suppose it will be said that I should have reported the death anyway, and that I should also have reported my concerns about Augusta's father having custody; I should have let the authorities make the proper decisions. But Elspeth had never been to the police when her husband beat her, not even once. It would be my word against his, and I was sitting here with her blood on my hands, at least figuratively.

I went to listen for Augusta's crying a couple of times, but she had fallen asleep again. I returned to the kitchen and sat there for most of the night, thinking about what to do. The lamp went out in the hours before dawn and still I sat there in the dark, until at last the first grey light began to outline the familiar objects all around me.

It seemed to me then, as it still does now, that I had never been as happy as I was during those early years at Langlands. Father had not died yet, and although Mother was strict, she was not as grim as she later became, nor was money so scarce. I remembered sunny afternoons exploring the grounds, and the intensely sweet taste of berries gathered in the kitchen garden, and the cosy feeling of sitting in the library with a book open on my lap while rain pattered on the window panes. Is it strange to have loved the wartime? I did, because the War kept me at Langlands, and Langlands seemed like a kind of Paradise back then.

I said to myself that I would forget about all the troubles that came later: Angus dying before his time and Elspeth getting mixed up with that man, and the years when I worried about her and hardly ever saw her, and could count the bruises on her when I did. I would wipe away the argument I had had with her, and when I had laid her to rest, I would try not to think about how her life had ended. I would go back to the war years, and I would take Augusta with me. I would give her the happiness I once had.

I am giving her the War too. I remember how Elspeth was

as a child: curious and impetuous. As my granddaughter grows, there has to be some bogeyman to keep her away from the edges of the estate – some reason to make her hide herself if anyone comes to the house. It will be easy, after all, because there is virtually nothing in the house that dates to later than the 1940s.

Sometimes I have a kind of waking dream that it really is 1940 again, and that Augusta is my own infant self, and I her elderly relative, and with enough loving care I can make the future different. The years stretch ahead like a ladder to be climbed: 1950, 1962, 1999. At the end there should be something better than an old woman dragging the body of her only child through the undergrowth to a stone mausoleum.

Augusta will have to know the truth one day, of course, and I do not know when that day will be. When she is eighteen, and an adult in her own right, nobody can compel her to do anything. Her father cannot insist that she lives with him. She will be safe from that, at least. But eighteen years is a very long time to persist with a world and a time that exists only at Langlands. I will have to hope that Augusta's father never finds us here. I will have to hope that I can find answers to the questions Augusta will inevitably have as she grows older, each more perceptive, more insistent than the last. I will have to hope that I can be anything and everything she needs me to be, for all that time.

Dear God, help me.

Rose Elspeth McAndrew

chapter sixty-three

Ghost

I read the letter through from beginning to end and Tom read it too, looking over my shoulder. Since that day, I have read it again, many times, trying to understand more, and better. I have tried to suck the marrow from the bones of her words. But that first time, all that I could think, all that ran through my brain with throbbing insistence, was: *Grandmother killed my mother*.

Knowing is *always* different from believing. Grandmother had always told me that my mother was dead; she had not lied about that. But it had never been real to me. When I found out that Grandmother had deceived me about so many other things, I hoped that perhaps my mother's death was a deceit too, that she was out there somewhere in the world outside Langlands. Now I knew that she was dead because I had seen her pitiful remains, brown and crumbling. I had *smelled* her, the faint lingering scent of her decay. And Grandmother had done this. *Grandmother killed my mother*.

I did not scream, or faint, or cry. I simply sat there, with the letter on my lap, walled up inside my own horror. Tom very gently took the pages out of my hands. He sat beside me, re-reading it, and I heard him curse under his breath, but it was like listening to something through glass or water; it did not touch me. I had turned to stone.

Tom stopped reading and folded the letter up again. He put it back into the tin and replaced the lid, as though he could seal up its contents again. Then he sat beside me for a while, with his head in his hands. Rain rattled at the window, and the kitchen clock ticked, but otherwise there was silence.

At last Tom said, "We have to go to the police." He looked at me. "Ghost? Do you understand? We have to tell someone about this."

His face was very close to mine.

"Ghost?" Tom touched my shoulder.

I stared back at him. "Tom..."

"We have to go to the police," he said again.

I shook my head, and it felt strange, as though the room were swimming past me, then reversing and flowing back like a tide.

"We have to lock it up again," I said. "I don't have the key."

"Ghost—"

"It's all right, Tom. We just have to put that tin back and lock the door."

Tom's eyes widened. "But we can't—"

"I don't have the key," I said again. I patted at my pockets, and ran my fingers over the surface of the table as though the key were there somewhere if only I could find it. "I don't have it. Where is it? I need the key, Tom."

"Ghost!" Now Tom was really gripping my shoulder, hard enough to get my attention. "We can't just lock the place up again. We have to tell someone."

"No," I said, and this time when I shook my head it was like shaking a snow globe; a blizzard of fragmented thoughts seemed to whirl around inside my brain. "No, we can't tell anyone."

"Ghost, there's a *dead body* in there. We have to."

I put up a hand and rubbed my face. "No, Tom. Grandmother will get in trouble."

"She's dead," said Tom. "Your grandmother is dead."

Tom didn't seem to be making any sense at all. "No," I told him. "My mother is dead. It's my mother in there, and we have to lock the door again."

Tom sat back and stared at me. His face looked strange: the eyes round, his mouth open, as though he had seen something terrible.

I looked at him, and then I began to look for the key again.

After a moment, Tom spoke in a choked voice. "Ghost, don't." He grabbed my hand and pressed something into it. "Look, here's the padlock, and the key." The muscles of his face were twitching.

I took the padlock and key from him and held them in my hands. I turned the key and with a tiny *click* the lock sprung open; I pressed it closed again with another *click*. It had been as easy as that to unlock the truth that I did not want to know.

I cried then. I cried for my mother, and for Grandmother, and for all the things that were wrong or ruined; I cried with great sobs that made my whole body clench like a curled fist.

Tom put his arms around me and held me. He did not say, "We have to go to the police" again. For a long time, he said nothing at all. At last, when I had cried until my eyes were red and sore and it felt as though there were no tears left to cry, I heard him say, "I don't know what to do."

I had been leaning against his shoulder; now I pulled back and looked into his face. *Do I look as drawn and shocked as that?* I wondered. We stared at each other.

"What–" When I tried to speak my voice came out as a hoarse croak. I cleared my throat, wiping my eyes with the heel of my hand. "What will they do when they come, Tom? The police, I mean? They'll take her away, won't they?"

Tom nodded reluctantly. "Yeah."

"I don't want to call them today. Please, Tom. I want some time – with her."

"You don't want to go back there?" asked Tom. He looked horrified.

"No." I shook my head. "I don't want to see – that – again. I just want some time."

Tom let out a very long sigh, but he did not say *no, it has to be today*. I suppose he thought, as I did, *what difference can it make?*

chapter sixty-four

Tom

How is it possible to try really hard to do the right thing, and end up doing the wrong thing? Old Mrs. McAndrew thought she was doing the right thing helping her daughter run away from her husband, and look how that ended up. Then she decided it was better for the baby to stay with her than go to her bastard of a father, even if it meant bringing her up in 1940.

And then there's me. So desperate to know the truth that I couldn't wait a second longer. *I think we have to know*, I said. I couldn't even wait for the rain to stop. I hacked lumps out of the ground so I could open the door to that place. That's how keen I was. And thanks to me, Ghost got a really good look at the seventeen-year-old corpse of her own mother. Well played, Tom.

I put my head in my hands, digging my fingers into my hair. *What have I done?* I ask myself. *You idiot*, I think. I keep thinking about what happened when we were in that place, the way she kept screaming *It's me! It's me in there!* For a moment I almost believed her. Anything seemed possible, after seeing something as horrible as that. It made me feel cold inside, looking from the dead body to the girl screaming her head off, and both of them with the same hair.

She shouldn't have seen that thing. And it's down to me.

I look at Ghost. She's sitting beside me, leaning back in the chair with her head resting against the wall and her eyes closed. She's so pale she really does look like a ghost. It's late in the afternoon now, and the shadows are getting longer. If we don't light one of those old lamps soon I won't be able to see her at all, she'll just fade into the darkness.

I think about what happened after she read the old lady's letter. She wasn't making sense – saying all we needed to do was lock that place up again, so her gran wouldn't get in trouble, like she'd forgotten old Mrs. McAndrew is dead. I felt...Okay, I'll admit it to myself. I was afraid. Afraid that something inside her had just...broken. Afterwards, after she'd been crying, she seemed calmer. She sounded like herself again. But I think the cracks must still be there.

I think about a lot of things. There's nothing to do *but* think, as the sun sinks in the sky and the room becomes colder.

I think about that car, abandoned in the glen near Aberfeldy, with plants slowly growing all over it. Where did Ghost's father go? Maybe he did kill himself. Sometimes people do that in lonely places, and it's ages before the body is found. But it was true what I said to Ghost before, that it's too much of a coincidence that it happened so close by. Did he come to Langlands house after all, and did the old lady deal with him? There's no way to know.

And I think about home. Mum will be making the dinner right now. The kitchen will be warm and full of steam. Dad will be sorting out stuff for the week, maybe loading things into the van. We're supposed to be doing some work for a customer over near Comrie tomorrow. Nine o'clock sharp on Monday morning, that's when they're expecting us; that's where Dad thinks we'll be. Except we won't. I don't even know where we will be. The police station, maybe, or driving up to Langlands together while Mum shouts at me, wanting to know why I never told her any of this before.

Nine o'clock tomorrow morning: I have no idea how we are going to get there, either. I've been thinking about that other time here in this kitchen, when I brought those magazines to prove to Ghost that it really is 2017. She went over to the drawer at the other end of the room and got these scissors out, great big kitchen shears with points on the end of them. I thought she was going to do something a lot worse than cut her hair with them. It seemed possible – she'd totally lost it, she could have done *anything*. I wonder what she might do now, if she comes out of the trance she seems to be in. Is it even safe to leave her here on her own tonight?

"Ghost," I say. I have to say it two or three times before she looks at me. It's like looking at a sleepwalker. She has a slow, loose way of moving that makes it look as though she wants to slip back into sleep. I don't think it's any use asking her how to do anything.

"Do you want some food?"

She just looks at me. I get up anyway and do the best I can. I open the stove and put some more firewood in. There's a lamp on the dresser, so I light that the way Ghost showed me once before. Then I look for something to eat. I find some bread that's just about edible, and some jam. There's no butter. I have a good look through all the shelves and cupboards in case old Mrs. McAndrew still kept cooking sherry, but there isn't anything. It has to be more tea, with no milk again. While I'm waiting for the water to heat up, I get my phone out and text Mum. *Will be back v late sorry T.* I think about other things I could add to that but in the end, I press *send* and then I turn the phone off so she can't call me.

We eat side by side at the kitchen table. The food's not great, and Ghost picks at it. I don't eat much either. I keep thinking: *What am I going to do? Am I really going to leave her here on her own tonight?* The place has never seemed so grim. Cold, dark, dusty-smelling. I've never been here at night before and the thought of it gives me the creeps. Then I think about the thing we found in the mausoleum and get a cold feeling at the base of my spine, thinking of it out there in the dark and the rain. We didn't even padlock the door shut again.

It's dead, I remind myself. *The dead don't get up and walk except in crappy horror films.*

Maybe some of these thoughts are occurring to Ghost too, because she shivers. I put out my hand to pull her close to me and when I touch the skin of her face and neck she's so *cold*.

"You're *freezing*." I put my arms around her, trying to warm her up.

"I'm so tired, Tom." It's the first thing she's said in ages.

I think of the things that would be good right now: a hot bath, an electric blanket, a heater. None of those things are at Langlands. There isn't even an electric kettle, for fuck's sake.

"What can I do?" I ask her.

"I'll light a fire in my room," she says. "You could bring some firewood up."

"Is that a good idea?"

"It's how we heat the bedrooms all the time in the winter," she says. "Only not normally in April, because Grandmother says—"

And then she stops, because it doesn't matter what her gran thinks about it anymore.

"Okay," I say quickly. "We'll make a fire."

She takes the lamp, and I pick up the basket of firewood that's by the stove. I follow her along the passage and up the stairs, past the stuffed bear at the top, and along the landing to her room.

I shouldn't be surprised. I've seen most of Langlands, I know what it's like: a museum. But still, it's strange, seeing Ghost's room. No IKEA furniture, no posters or mobiles or strings of fairy lights or any of the other stuff I've seen in girls' rooms. No laptop of course, no phone, no sound system – not

329

even an iPod. There's an iron bedstead and an old-fashioned washstand with a jug and basin on it.

I head over to the fireplace, put down the basket and squat down. I'm relieved to find matches; I was half-expecting to have to rub two sticks together or something. There's some paper to start the fire with, too, only it's not newspaper; it's thicker, in smaller sheets. It looks like it's been torn out of a book – not a printed book, one with blank pages to write on.

It's harder to make a fire than you'd think. After a while Ghost kneels beside me and gently takes the matchbox out of my hand. Then she does something with the grate and the trickle of smoke rising from my efforts is drawn up the flue. Pretty soon she has the fire going, though I'm not convinced it's ever going to warm the whole room up properly.

Then she sits back with a sigh, gazing into the heart of the fire. The light of the flames gilds her face and makes her dark eyes shine. She looks as though she is hypnotised by the tongues of fire that flicker in and out of the wood.

If I left now, would she just sit here for hours, perhaps even all night, staring into the flames until the fire burnt down and went out and the room turned cold around her? I think maybe she would.

I make myself get up, though it means moving away from the pitiful heat from the fireplace. There are blankets on the bed, so I strip two of them off it; one each. I drape one of them around her shoulders, and then I wrap myself in the other one and sit beside her.

It seems to me that living at Langlands must like being on some kind of survival course, only it never stops, you never get to go home and stick a ready meal in the microwave or put your feet up and watch TV. It just goes on and on being gloomy and cold, and everything takes three times as long as normal. It has to change. Nobody can go on like this, especially not when they're on their own most of the time. Even if we hadn't found that thing in the old mausoleum, even if Ghost didn't care about what happened to her gran, she would still need to get away from here. It's a creepy old dump. If you ask me, it even smells of death.

I put an arm around Ghost and pull her close. *I hate this place.* And you know what? I think it hates me too. The way the cold and the dark and the damp press in on us, like it wants to keep Ghost all for itself. But that just makes me more determined to get her out of here. I'm dreading tomorrow, but it has to be done, like a bloody and painful operation you have to go through.

Between then and now though, are hours and hours of darkness, and even though the trouble I'm already in is going to get even worse if I don't go home tonight, I don't want to leave her. I have this feeling that if I leave her alone here this one last time, the house is going to do something to get at her. Crazy? Maybe. But so much crazy shit has happened here already that anything seems possible.

And maybe Ghost can tell somehow that this is what's on my mind, whether to stay here or go home, because she stirs and looks at me. Her face is only centimetres from mine and I see the reflection of the dancing flames in her dark eyes, and her lips part and she says, "Don't go, Tom. Please. Stay here with me. Stay with me, Tom."

chapter sixty-five

Ghost

Stay with me, Tom, I said, meaning *Stay with me forever, live my life with me, love me* but mostly *Stay now. Don't leave because I can't bear it.*

I had never dared say it before. Now I couldn't not say it. It felt like survival.

That day was like being in a great fire. I can't describe it better. It felt like everything I had known, everything I had ever believed, had gone up in one huge raging conflagration, and when it was all seared away and I was crouching in the blackened ruins, there was nothing left of me at all but the blind need not to bear it alone.

Stay with me, Tom.

And Tom said, "Yes."

We sat for a long time, not speaking, watching the flames dance on the hearth. I leaned against Tom and felt his arm around my shoulders, and that was real, the warmth of his body and the pressure of his hand. Everything else was a nightmare I wanted to forget.

I kissed Tom first. I turned and kissed him softly on the mouth, letting my lips linger on his. I felt him hesitate before he kissed me back very gently, as though he thought he might hurt me, as though the wounds I had received that day made me too fragile to handle. But what hurt me was remembering. I wanted to blot it all out.

I put my arms around Tom and kissed him again. I curled my fingers in the fabric of his shirt and I could feel the tension of his body underneath. I kissed him because talking and thinking were no use anymore; it was like having to leap from a great height to save myself from fire or murder – there was no way to do it except simply to close my eyes and jump.

For a moment it was like embracing a statue. Then cold marble became warm and living; Tom dipped his head and kissed me back, kissed me properly.

I could feel the hunger in his kiss now. It was startling and exhilarating; it was the vertigo in the leap. His arms tightened around me, pulling me closer. He was holding me now, really holding me, and the energy shuddering through him was like a trap waiting to spring shut on us.

Then he broke the kiss, and I heard him gasp. He held me a little apart from him, his hands on my shoulders, his own head down; I felt the chill air flow in between us.

Last chance to stop. I sensed that as clearly as if it had been a sign that we had sped past on the motorcycle, a warning glimpsed briefly before it was far behind us.

I didn't want to stop. The desire to feel *this* and *only this* was savage in its intensity. I put up my hand and clasped Tom's fingers. My heart was racing and there was a strange tight feeling inside my chest. One afternoon long ago I had lain on the bed in this same room, imagining that Tom was there with me, imagining his hand on my face, my shoulder, then tracing the line of my collarbone. I swallowed. I moved his hand very deliberately, over my collarbone and down. Then I looked up, into his eyes.

For one breathless moment – nothing. The possibility hung between us, suspended like a sparkling drop about to fall.

Then we fell upon each other. My lips parted under his; I felt his hands on me and pulled him closer, recklessly. My fingers were in Tom's hair; his lips were on my face, my neck, my shoulder. The longing was unbearable; I shook with the agony of it.

Boards are too hard to lie on for any length of time. Tom stood up, pulling me with him, and walked me backwards to the bed. I felt the edge of it at the back of my legs and then we fell onto the mattress. The cold of the sheets was as brisk as a slap, but I was past caring.

I had never undressed anyone else in my life before; I struggled at first with the buttons on Tom's shirt. Then Tom helped me and we shed all the things that made us belong to 1945 or 2017, so that we were just ourselves, together.

It didn't hurt, like I half thought it would, though it was strange at first, to feel part of him inside me. I didn't look down. I kept my gaze on his face above me, half of it lit by the flickering fire, the other in shadow. His blue-green eyes.

Stay with me, Tom.

I pulled him down to me, my mouth under his, my fingers tangled in his hair. We moved together, tightly together, holding each other, and it was good, it was beautiful, it blotted out everything else, now and forever.

chapter sixty-six

Tom

I open my eyes and for the first few moments I see nothing. It's dark. Then my eyes begin to adjust to the faint glow of the firelight and the room takes form around me. I'm not at home, in my own room. I'm in one of the high-ceilinged rooms at Langlands House. I'm lying on my side in bed under a sheet and a blanket I don't remember spreading over myself. Under the sheet and blanket I'm naked.

I blink, remembering.

Ghost—

I roll over, propping myself up on one elbow, my mouth opening to say something though I have no idea what, and—

I nearly jump out of my skin. She's kneeling on the other side of the bed, hands clasped in her lap, perfectly still and silent. There is a blanket wrapped around her but her shoulders are bare, tendrils of hair falling over them. Her eyes gleam in the firelight like dark jewels. She watches me, calmly.

I stop myself swearing just in time, but my heart is thumping.

"You made me jump," I say, flopping back onto the mattress. "What are you doing? I thought you'd be asleep."

"Thinking," she says.

"Thinking," I repeat. I put my hands over my face and try

to rub some sense into my brain. I'm groggy with sleep. "What are you thinking about?"

"About you. About everything. We'll be happy, won't we, Tom?"

"Yeah." I put out a hand, wanting to pull her back down with me again, but she's just out of reach. Instead, I touch the sheet under us, and it's cool under my fingers. She hasn't been lying beside me for a while.

She's speaking again. "There are so many things I couldn't do by myself. It takes me ages just to do the things I already do, like chopping firewood and looking after the chickens. And there are things I don't know, which you'd know about. Do you think we could ever have electric lights at Langlands, Tom? Maybe not all over the house, but in some of the rooms? Could you do that?"

I can't keep up with this, but Ghost doesn't seem to notice.

"There's the water, too," she says. "It has to be pumped and then you have to heat it up on the kitchen stove if you want to have a bath or wash things. Could we have a water heater?"

"I guess so," I manage to say. "You'd need power first though, and Langlands isn't connected to the grid. But Ghost–" I pause, struggling for the right words. "I don't think you should be worrying about those things right now."

She looks at me doubtfully.

"You...we...have other stuff to deal with. What happened today and...what we have to do in the morning."

Silence. Ghost's dark gaze is fixed on me. I can feel my conscience poking me with sharp sticks.

"Look, I'm really sorry about today. You shouldn't have had to see that. I shouldn't have insisted on going and looking in that place, and I feel like a shit for doing it."

"You don't have to be sorry, Tom," says Ghost, quite calmly.

I shake my head. "Yes, I do. It was wrong. We should have

waited, and got the police to do it. Whoever it was in there, you didn't need to see it."

"It's all right now though," she says, and something about the way she says it sends a prickle down my spine. She's looking at me but there's a faraway look in her eyes, as though she isn't really seeing me or the room around us.

She says, "It was a terrible shock when I read Grandmother's letter. *I killed her*, she said. I remembered that thing in the stone coffin, and I thought: *Grandmother did that*. And I felt as though something inside me, not my body but the inside me, was being torn apart. Do you understand that? Grandmother, who loved me, and brought me up and cared for me for nearly eighteen years, did *that*. I saw it written in her own handwriting. It was like there were two Grandmothers, the loving one and the killing one, and I couldn't make them into one person, Tom. I thought I would go mad trying."

She smiles, and the smile is stranger than the calmness was. "You remember, Tom, the day you brought me all those magazines with the coloured pictures? The world out there seemed such a beautiful, wonderful place, with all its bright colourful things and all the machines that make life so much easier. I was really shocked that Grandmother had shut me away from it, and furious too, so furious that I hacked off my hair. I felt like I hated Langlands, and my whole life here. But now I can see that was all wrong. It's the world out there that's bad and rotten.

"The bad thing we saw today, it was the Outside that did it. Grandmother knew that, don't you see? She wanted to go back to the time before everything was poisoned by it, and she wanted to take me with her. Back to Langlands in 1940, before the War took her father, before she was widowed, before my mother met my father. Before the Outside made everything bad. And when she and my mother came back to Langlands, it was the Outside that crept in after them and ruined everything.

337

It was the Outside that tried to call my mother away, and caused the row that made her die. The Outside killed her, Tom."

My mouth is dry. "Ghost...you can't think like that. There are people out there who are going to help you. I know it's going to be tough, but when we tell them..."

Ghost is shaking her head. "We aren't going to tell them, Tom. Why would we tell them? They'll come here and ask thousands of questions, and they won't leave my mother in peace, they'll want to look."

I sit right up in bed and stare at her. I was dreading tomorrow myself, and the shitstorm that was going to break over both our heads, but it never occurred to me not to do it, not to tell anyone. There's a dead body out there in the grounds. I don't think you can just *ignore* that.

"Shit," I say before I can stop myself. "Look, you can't go on living here pretending nothing happened."

"Why not?" she says, calmly. "When Grandmother was here, she used to go out and get things when we needed them, and I used to stay here, at Langlands. We can do that. If we run out of anything, you can go into the town and I'll stay here. It's worked so far," she adds, sounding a little defiant.

"But–" I'm actually lost for words for a moment. Does she really think it could go on like that, forever? "What about when I go away to uni?" I say.

Ghost is very still, her expression neutral. The expression of someone who has to deliver bad news without losing her cool. "You won't go," she says.

It takes a moment for what she just said to sink in. *Is she joking?* But I can see she isn't. She's deadly serious.

"Hold on a minute," I say. My throat is suddenly dry and I'm struggling to sound calm and reasonable when inside I'm sliding up the panic scale, from nought to sixty in about two seconds. "I can't *not* go to uni. It's all planned. I've got my place."

I see the look on her face when I tell her this, and it isn't disappointment as you might expect. She looks shocked, as though I've just said something outrageous.

"You have to," she says.

"No, I don't," I say, horribly aware that we suddenly sound like two little kids fighting. "Look," I say, "I'll come back whenever I can. It's not impossible. And in the holidays, I'll be here a lot. But I can't just give it up. I need a degree for the job I want to do afterwards. I don't want to work with Dad forever. I hate it."

"You could do something else," she says stubbornly.

"I won't get a well-paid job without a degree. And anyway–"

"I have money," she says. "There's a whole safe full of it downstairs."

"That's not the point," I say, desperately. "And however much there is of it, it won't last forever. You must see that."

Her face crumples. I can see she's holding back tears, and I feel like a total bastard. Whatever I do or say, I make things worse for her. But I have to stand firm. I can't give up my whole future.

"You said you'd stay," she says. "You said you'd stay here with me. You gave your word."

"What? I didn't. I mean–"

Then at last it dawns on me, and I could slap myself for not seeing it before.

Stay here, Tom, she said. *Stay with me.*

"Oh God," I say, putting my hand over my eyes. I thought she was asking me to stay with her now, this evening. Tonight. But actually, she was asking me to stay – forever. *At Langlands*. She wants us to play house in this creaky, cold, cobwebby old heap with its overgrown gardens and creepy stuffed animals, not to mention the matter of the dead body in the mausoleum. The worst of it is, she's sitting there thinking this is a real possibility, that I'll do this, it's just a matter of getting over my objections about uni and the little matter of my future. And I'm sitting here in a state of blank horror at the whole idea. I'd die before I'd come and live at Langlands. I don't even understand how she can do it.

"Ghost," I say carefully, "I didn't realise what you meant when you told me to stay. I thought you meant tonight. I can't live here. And you shouldn't live here, either."

"Langlands is my home," she says, fiercely, her eyes glittering with tears.

"I know," I say. "But you can't spend your entire life here."

"I could if you stayed with me."

I shake my head. "I can't do that."

"Why? You said you loved me."

"I do." It's true, but still it feels like a lie when I say it, because it isn't going to get her what she wants.

"Then you'd stay. You *would*, Tom. You *would*." Now she's really crying, and I feel horrible, I feel sick inside for what I am doing to her, what I've done without meaning to.

"Ghost...it's not that easy..."

"Why not?"

"Because I have a life out there. In the real world. I have plans."

"Plans without me in them?"

"I didn't say that." I'm slightly nettled now. "I told you, I'll be here some of the time, during the holidays. It's not like we wouldn't ever see each other. But you have to see – living here at Langlands, pretending it's 1945 for ever, that's not real life."

"It's been my life for eighteen years," she says.

"I *know*. But look, how could you go on living here, chopping up firewood to keep warm, and pumping all your own water, when you know there's a whole different life out there? There are all these things to make life easier, so nobody has to do those things the hard way. You'd be wasting your life if you did."

"It's not wasting if that's what I want to do," she says stubbornly.

"Yes, but I *don't* want to do that. I *can't* do that. Can't you see?" The words sound so brutal, like a bitter medicine on my tongue. I hate arguing like this. I hate hurting her. But what else can I do? I can't agree to live at Langlands to spare her feelings. I feel sick at the thought of it.

Ghost is silent for a moment. She looks down, her hair falling over her face so I can't see her expression.

Then she says, very quietly, "Why did you stay tonight then?" Not looking at me. Regretting. Maybe actually ashamed.

Guilt claws at me.

"Because I love you," I tell her. "I wanted to be with you because I love you."

Another silence. Then: "Not enough," she says, in a low voice.

"Ghost–"

"Not enough!" she says, her voice rising. Her head comes up and through the tangle of hair falling over her face her eyes blaze at me. "You don't love me enough!" She's screaming at me now, tears running down her face.

I can't help it. I flinch back. At that moment I'm not exactly sure what I feel. Maybe fear. I think again of the scissors in her hand that time. She's so desperate I don't know what she might do.

She forces the hurt back down again, though. She's shaking with the effort, but she makes one last attempt to regain control. Her hands are curled into fists, the tendons in the wrists standing out.

"Please," she says. "Please stay with me."

That moment of silence between us is a tiny piece of eternity, a pendulum swing between what might be and what must be. I have to say it in the end, though.

"I can't. Not the way you mean."

341

I think she'll rage at me, but she doesn't. When she speaks, her voice is very low; I barely hear what she says.

"Then go away."

"Ghost–"

"Go away," she says again, and this time her voice is louder, her tone firmer. Ghost climbs off the bed, pulling the blanket close around her. Then she shakes back her hair and looks at me with a kind of grim dignity. "Just go," she says, and I hear her voice crack.

I get off the bed too. It feels weird having this horrible conversation while I'm stark naked except for a sheet. I start picking up my things and putting them on, because I can't think what else to do, how to stop this happening. She's so upset and angry I can't try to talk to her. There's a vacuum between us, bleak and ominous. I can't promise to do what she wants, either. I button my shirt and buckle my belt and wonder how it all went so wrong; when I took these things off I thought I was about to die of happiness.

When I'm dressed again I make one last hopeless attempt.

"Ghost, don't make me go like this. *Please*. Let's just talk."

But she's shaking her head, her lips pressed together in a hard line to stop herself sobbing again.

"Come on," I say. "It's pitch dark out there. How am I even going to find my way out?"

I've wasted my breath with that line of argument. It's too easily solved. The oil lamp is sitting on top of a chest of drawers and it takes her a matter of moments to light it from the fire with a taper. Her hands are trembling as she does it.

I feel like crying myself now. I pick up my jacket, but I hold it in my hands, not putting it on, not wanting my leaving to be final. There is nothing to do, though. She holds out the lamp, and I have to take it.

"I'll come back," I say. "Tomorrow. We'll work something out."

"No," she says.

"I can't just go like this–"

"Just go!" She practically screams it at me. "*Go!*"

So I do. I don't know what else to do. I walk out of the room and down the passageway and the yellow glow of the oil lamp goes with me, lighting the space around me but never really reaching into the depths of the darkness. Down the passageway, past the stuffed bear, down the creaking stairs.

When I get to the hallway below, I set down the lamp on the floor and I'm straightening up when I hear it. A terrible cry, full of anger and pain; a scream of agony, hacking raggedly through the air.

I was not meant to hear it. Nobody was. I stand in the hall in my tiny sphere of golden light, frozen with the horror of it.

Then I go. I walk away from the light, to the front door, which I prise open making as little noise as possible. Outside I can barely see where I'm going. I stumble away from the door. Towards the bike, and home.

chapter sixty-seven

Ghost

When Tom left, I broke. The agony was too much to contain. It burst out of me in a scream that burned my throat; I threw it up like poison. I had never known pain like it. The sharp grief of losing Grandmother, the slow dragging melancholy that came after it, the horror of the day, were nothing to what I felt now. I stumbled about the room, and when I ran into things I felt nothing. If dashing myself against the walls could have blotted out the misery I felt inside, I would have done it.

He said no.

The dreams I had had, of us both here at Langlands, spending our days and nights together, no longer seemed like a beautiful possibility. They were a torment, a gorgeous illusion kept forever out of reach by gibbering demons. Images flashed through my mind, tauntingly. Tom, opening the safe with me, taking the block of banknotes reluctantly from my hands. The day I ran out of the house and threw myself into his arms, before we had even kissed. Tom, in the clothing of 1945, the day we had dressed ourselves from the things in the attic. He had looked so handsome, so perfectly suited to the house, that I had really seen him living here; I had felt the potential of it within my grasp. And it was all nothing. It was dust and ashes.

The love we had made was nothing. It meant nothing. Tom had said he loved me, but he wouldn't stay and I couldn't go with him, into the abyss of the outside world.

I beat my fists on the mattress where we had lain together. I grasped the sheets with hands like claws and dragged them off the bed, panting and sobbing as I did it. I would have ripped them into flinders if I had had the strength. Instead I trampled them, dragging them across the dusty floorboards.

I tore down the framed photograph of me and Tom from the wall and threw it across the room. I heard the glass shatter. I threw other things after it – the brush and mirror from my dressing-table, a china trinket box, anything within reach.

It was no use. There was no-one to hear my screams, no-one to care about the mess but me. No-one to tell me how to begin to endure the terrible swamping agony that was erupting inside me. My screams echoed through the house and in all of Langlands there was nobody to reply. The rooms were dark and empty. The former inhabitants of the house in their gilded frames were still and silent. The books in the library, slowly crumbling into dust, had nothing to teach me.

I began to see how stupid I had been, how pathetically naive. I had thought myself so daring, hiding in the attic and spying on Tom and his father that first day. Taking risks, later, and letting myself be seen. Tom had been horrified the first time he saw me properly, only a few feet away from him, but I had let myself forget that in my great desire to be loved by him. I should have known that that first reaction – the recoiling from something so different to himself, the strange unnatural girl from the past – was the true one. He could never give up his own world for someone like that. Someone like me. Me, with my stupid name and my old-fashioned clothes and my ignorant questions.

Stupid, stupid.

And I had given myself to Tom. I had fallen back on this

very bed and let him undress me. I had lain there shamelessly naked and let him explore every part of me with his eyes and hands and lips. He had made love to me and I had exulted in it, thinking that this was love. And perhaps it *had* been love, but it was true what I had yelled at Tom; it was not enough.

Remembering how it had been, I blazed with shame. I thought of myself lying under him, gazing up into his sea green eyes, feeling the rhythm of our bodies moving together, and I put my hands over my face as if I could shut out the images that ran through my head. As if my own screams of furious misery could drown out the memory of his groans, my sighs.

Something was breaking inside me. I couldn't make sense of anything, I couldn't see any way for any of this to become right again. Everything was wrong, everything was rotten.

Grandmother had taught me that there was a War on outside the borders of Langlands, a great and terrible War with the capacity to turn living human beings into a mist of blood and bone fragments, a machine with no purpose but to destroy. She made me fear invasion, even here at Langlands – the crunch of booted feet on the gravel outside, the thunderous battering at the door, rough voices in the hall, the brutal savagery of soldiers.

And she was right. The Outside had invaded Langlands and laid everything waste. It took Grandmother first, spirited her away and never gave her back to me. It even defiled my memory of her; it told me that she was wrong to try to protect me from what was out there. It told me that she was a liar.

And then, when I was alone here, isolated, the War came to me. Tom came to the house. I met him with a loaded rifle but no shot was ever fired. He disarmed me with words, with stories. With the propaganda of his time. I saw that now. He invaded my home, and at last he invaded *me*, my body, naked and shuddering.

That wasn't the worst, though. The very worst thing was knowing that he had taken over the *inner* me. I had told him I loved him; I had craved his love in return. I might just as well have been a cringing prisoner of war, kissing the hand that held the bloody sword and begging for my life.

The rage that possessed me then was terrible. It was as though a demon had slipped inside my skin. I was angry at Tom for infecting me with such savage pain; I was angry with myself for being so stupid as to let him into my heart and my body. I could not tell where the anger against Tom became rage with myself; I could not see which one had the upper hand. I blazed with a fury so white hot that it seared away everything that was human in myself.

And then – Tom came back.

chapter sixty-eight

Tom

I'm sitting astride the bike, about to turn the keys in the ignition, when I realise I can't do this. I can't just walk away like this.

I know I could go back in the morning, in daylight, when Ghost has had a chance to calm down and things may not look so desperate to either of us. I could do that, yes. Part of me wants to do that. But it doesn't feel right.

She was so upset that I'm afraid of what she might do. It's not like I can kid myself there's anyone else there for her. She's completely alone. Even if she wouldn't purposely harm herself, she might neglect herself. She's hardly eaten a thing all day and the house is freezing cold and dark. Am I really going to leave her there like that?

I let go of the keys.

Am I the kind of person who sleeps with a girl, and then, when she's crying her eyes out, just walks away without a backward glance? I think about this. She told me to go away, but I'm not sure I can.

In the end, there's a kind of inevitability about it. I get off the bike and trudge back to the house. What am I going to say? I don't know. I just don't want to leave it like this.

The oil lamp is still burning in the hallway, its faint yellow light visible through one of the front windows. Otherwise the place looks grim.

I crunch over the gravel and enter the stone porch, my footsteps ringing on the flagstones. When I get to the great oak door I hesitate for a moment before knocking loudly, twice, to let her know I'm back. Then I push open the door a few inches and call her name.

"Ghost?"

Silence. I hear the wind sighing through the trees that press close around the house, and nothing else.

The door creaks dismally as I push the door right open and step inside. The first thing I see is the lamp, exactly where I left it. That blaze of gold in all the gloom draws the eye. Beyond it, the staircase, empty.

I turn and shut the door, cutting off the cold draught and the sound of the wind. In that moment, when the door closes and silence descends, I hear it: the tiniest creak; someone putting their weight on a loose board. I look up, towards the sound.

"Ghost?"

And then I see her, emerging from the black shadows at the corner of the staircase, where the light from the lamp can barely reach. She is wearing a nightdress that reaches almost to her ankles and as she comes forward it makes a light patch in the darkness. She is silent, staring at me with those big dark eyes between the curtains of dark hair that hang limply, as though wet. Her beautiful face is streaked with tears, giving her a faint resemblance to a damaged waxwork, gorgeous but tainted. I notice all of this, but then my gaze drops from her face to her hands and I see something else, something that makes my stomach turn over with cold terror.

She's holding the rifle.

Ghost stares down at me, and her face crumples, her lips twisting as she tries to stop herself crying. She raises the rifle and aims it at me with trembling hands; I can see them shaking from here.

"Ghost, don't shoot."

I can hear the tremor in my own voice. The gun could go off in her hands without her meaning to do it, the way her finger is dancing all over the trigger.

"I came back to talk," I call up to her. I can't tell whether she's taking in what I'm saying. She begins to descend the stairs, moving slowly, still keeping the rifle trained on me. I hear the treads creaking under her feet.

"Please," I say. "Put the gun down."

For a moment, I really think she's going to do what I say. She lowers the rifle a little, but then she wipes her eyes with the back of her hand and I see that she was only clearing her vision. Up comes the barrel again, a movement as grim as the swing of an executioner's axe.

My mouth is dry, my chest tight as though all the air has suddenly been sucked out of the room. My heart is pounding in my chest, pumping blood to my muscles, telling me to *run, run, run*. But the door is closed behind me. I can't just run away. If the rifle is loaded, if her aim is any good at all, she'll have dropped me before I can get it open.

Down the stairs she comes: another step, and another. With each movement she comes a little closer, her aim a little surer. Still she says nothing to me, nothing at all.

"Don't shoot me," I beg her. "I'm sorry. I came back to talk. Can't we sort this out? *Please?*"

Her head moves from side to side, slowly and deliberately. *No.* She gives a great sob but she doesn't lower the rifle. She keeps on coming down the stairs. A tremor runs through the barrel of the gun, as though it is sniffing the air. The way her finger flutters on the trigger makes me feel sick.

"Ghost, please," I say. "I love you."

And the gun goes off.

I see the look of shock on her face. I feel an impact that nearly takes me off my feet. I stagger and I look down and I see red I see red oh God I see red Ghost I

chapter sixty-nine

Ghost

Tom fell, and I stood frozen with the rifle in my hands and the crash of the gunshot still echoing in my ears. I waited for myself to wake up, for it to be a bad dream, for it not to be so. But it was so. I had shot Tom.

I dropped the rifle. I wanted to walk over to where he lay on the black and white tiles, but my limbs didn't want to obey me. My legs trembled under me, and then they wouldn't support me at all. I crumpled onto the floor.

I didn't seem to be able to think properly about what had happened. After a little while I crawled over to where he lay, because I didn't feel as though I had the strength to stand up.

Tom was very white and silent. The blue of his shirt was stained a deep purple and all around him there was a spreading film of red on the tiles. He was absolutely still. I watched but I could not see his chest rising and falling. I think I knew then that he was gone.

Still, I thought perhaps there might be something someone else could do, someone armed with all the modern things Tom had told me about, the medical advances. If there were some spark of life there, they might bring it back. I felt in his pockets until I found his telephone, thinking that I might somehow call for help. I turned the thing over and over in my hands, trying in a confused way to remember what Tom had told me about it, but I was unable to make it do anything at all. I pressed the button that should have brought it to life, but nothing happened. In the end, I put it back into his pocket. It seemed wrong for me to have it.

Then I tried shaking Tom. I tried putting my ear close to his pale lips to hear or feel his breath. There was nothing. At last, shuddering, I laid my head on the purple-dyed shirt, feeling the damp sticking to my skin, and listened for a heartbeat, but there was silence.

I had no energy to move. I lay like that for a long time, until a dull unconsciousness that passed for sleep came over me.

When I awoke, it was light outside. Sunlight came through the window. I saw it through a red film; my eyelashes were full of blood.

My head was still pillowed on Tom's chest, and even through his clothing I could feel how terribly cold and stiff he was.

I sat up, recoiling in horror from the bloodless face, the eyes staring into nothing. I could not stand up. Instead I scrabbled away across the tiles, moving backwards, eyes wide, until my back touched the wall. I put my arms around my knees, hugging myself. I stared at Tom lying on the tiles.

I don't know how long I stayed there after that. The sun coming through the windows was very bright at first, and then it moved and changed. There was light coming from the upstairs windows too, and that waxed and waned with the passing day. Eventually the light began to fade altogether.

I don't properly remember what I did all that time. I might have talked to Tom, even sung to him a little, or I might have done that in my head, or dreamed it. I think I cried some of the time. Sometimes I seemed to go away altogether, to be absent from myself even though my body was still sitting there on the floor of the hallway. Whenever I came back to myself after those times, I would glance at Tom and he would still be there, so cold and white on the floor, with his own blood congealed all around him.

I didn't feel hungry, even after so long with so little food, but at last it was thirst that compelled me to move. I was so stiff after sitting on the floor that the first time I tried to get up I simply fell over. Eventually I managed it. I staggered down the passageway to the kitchen, where I found a jug of water I had pumped the previous morning. When Tom was still alive. I poured myself a glass of it and drank, then I poured another and drank that too.

I sat at the kitchen table in the gathering dark and wondered what I should do. There was a tin of oatcakes on the sideboard; I opened it and ate two of them. They were dry, and filled my mouth unpleasantly, but I could not think of looking for anything else.

The kitchen stove was out. More from habit than from any real motivation, I lit it again. It would take a long while for the kitchen to become properly warm, but now that night was coming on, I could not imagine going back through the hallway where Tom lay. In the end, I spent the night in the kitchen, doing my best to keep warm by wrapping myself in Grandmother's old coat, that still hung by the back door. I did not sleep very much.

All that night, one thing ran through my head. Did I mean to shoot, or not? I was so angry, so full of pain. The whole world seemed like a war to me, and Tom was the enemy. My own body had been the collaborator. I was sick with myself and sick with him, filled with fury and shame so intense that it was like madness. When I heard him coming back, I had taken up the rifle, and in the extremity of my agony, I had pointed it at him. But had I meant to pull the trigger? I remembered the gun shaking in my hands because they would not be steady whatever I did. I remembered my finger hovering tremulously

354

over the trigger, risking at any moment the convulsive motion that would set the gun off. So easy for an accident to happen – the merest unintentional twitch of the finger would be enough.

I don't know why it seemed so important to decide whether I had done it on purpose or not. The end result was the same. Tom was lying dead on the floor of the hallway, and nothing could change that. I had shot him. My hands had killed him, no-one else's.

Still, it seemed to me that his death would be easier to bear if it were an accident, and not intended. Surely it *had* been an accident? My hands had been shaking so much I could hardly say that I was in control of them. Sometimes I really believed that it was accidental, but at other, bleaker, times I was afraid that I was simply deceiving myself, that underneath all my protestations and denials, I had really meant to do it.

At some point in these terrible deliberations, I finally fell asleep, slumped over the kitchen table, wrapped in Grandmother's overcoat and my blood-stained nightdress. I had not even washed Tom's blood off my face.

chapter seventy

When I awoke the next day, I was stiff again but a strange calm had descended on me. All the savage emotions had drained away. I felt hollow. It was hard to imagine that I should ever feel anything again. Nevertheless, I began to think what I should do, in a curiously detached way, as though the situation had nothing to do with me.

Tom was lying dead in the hallway of the house in a large pool of blood that had probably dried by now. His motorcycle was somewhere outside the house. I had blood on my clothes, and my skin, and in my hair. And my bedroom upstairs bore what only the dullest wit could fail to interpret as signs of a struggle.

What would happen if someone from the Outside discovered any of this? I supposed they would hang me, unless they had thought of something worse since 1945. I supposed that I deserved it, and yet – I saw no particular reason to offer myself up to it. It wouldn't bring Tom back.

The first thing to do was to put on some working clothes. I couldn't sort anything out dressed in the impractical combination of an outdoor coat and a nightdress with long sleeves and a trailing hem. I steeled myself to go back along the passageway and through the hall so that I could climb the stairs to my own room.

It was not as bad as I expected. I knew what I should see.

Tom did not look as though he was asleep, as people in books were sometimes supposed to do. He did not even really look like Tom. Something essential had departed; what was left was a shell. I had never seen anyone look as inert as that. There was no mistaking death. I could not even say sorry to him; he had gone, completely.

I went upstairs to my room, stripped off the coat and the nightdress, and dressed quickly in some of my oldest things. I took care to put on boots; there was a quantity of broken glass lying around from the shattered picture frame, and I had no desire to cut myself to ribbons on it. I caught sight of myself in the little mirror over the washstand and had to stare. There was dried blood on my face, like war paint, and parts of my hair were stiff with it. I poured some water from the jug into the basin and rinsed as much of it off as I could. I would have to bathe properly later, when the work was done, but there was something horribly grisly about going about with Tom's blood on my face.

I swept up the broken glass. The sheets I bundled up to take downstairs for washing. Once the bed was made again, the room would look much as it had before. Then I went downstairs, carrying a few things with me.

I tried to do my best for Tom. I couldn't leave him in the clothes that were dyed in his own blood. The horrible stiffness had gone now, so I was able with some difficulty to undress the body and wash it. I did my best not to look at the wound. It made his death too brutal, and I wanted to think that he was at peace now.

I cleaned as much of the floor around and under his body as I could, and then I dressed him in the clothes we had chosen together from the trunks in the attic. It took a long time. I had never had to dress anyone but myself before, and certainly not a male body. I knew what the collar studs and other things were, but it took me a while to fit them.

357

Mostly I was calm while I did this. Only once, when he was naked, an image flashed across my mind of the two of us in bed together, of his warm body moving together with mine. Then I ran outside, my hand to my mouth, and threw up helplessly onto the gravel.

I made myself go back inside and finish the task after that. There was no other thing I could do for Tom now.

When he was washed and dressed, I wrapped him in the largest sheet I could find. There was no other way to drag the body outside without making him just as dirty as before.

Only when Tom was secure in this makeshift shroud did I feel I could take a break. I stumbled down the passageway to the kitchen and drank as much water as I could. I scavenged some other things – biscuits, a withered apple – and made myself eat them. And I picked up the padlock from the mausoleum, with the key still sticking out of it, and put it into my pocket.

I opened the front door and propped it with a wooden wedge. Then I went out to look at the ground. I had no idea when the rain had stopped, but now the sun was shining and much of the water had evaporated or drained off. That was good; the grass and the soil would still be damp but I hoped I wouldn't have to drag Tom through actual mud. I went back to the hallway to fetch his body.

I made fists of my hands in the end of the sheet, and dragged it out of the house. There was no other way. I could not have lifted him. By the time we got to the corner of the house, my arms and hands and back were aching, and I was sobbing aloud. The sheet slid over the grass at the side of the house with a sound like a harsh whisper, and a bird, disturbed by the noise, fluttered out of the undergrowth and flew away. Other than myself and the bird, no other living thing stirred.

It took me a long time to drag Tom's body to the mausoleum. In places where tree roots or fallen branches crossed the path, I had to haul him over them bodily. Often, I had to stop and rest, and I leaned over the bundle, whispering *I'm sorry, I'm sorry*, crying at the final indignity being wreaked on him.

At last, I was able to drag him into the cool gloom of the mausoleum. I did not look at the contents of the open stone coffin. I knelt on the floor and uncovered the dead face; I kissed the dead lips, but already he was hard to recognise as the Tom I had loved. I covered his face carefully and stepped back out into the daylight.

Then I went back into the house, cleaned my hands and face as best as I could, and went to the library. There I selected a small volume bound in dark leather with the title picked out in gold on the spine: *The Book of Common Prayer*. I had no idea what Tom believed in, but it seemed the decent thing to do.

I carried the book out to the spot where he lay, and went through it until I found the order for the burial of the dead. I read all of it aloud. My voice wavered and cracked, and I dug the nails of the hand not holding the book into my palm, but at last it was finished. It was faintly ludicrous to observe formalities after I had killed someone, but it was also strangely comforting in a way. I couldn't make things right, but I didn't have to make them anymore wrong by disposing of Tom's body without dignity.

Afterwards, I closed up the mausoleum and locked it with the padlock. Then I walked wearily up through the forest to the place where the stream cascaded down the rocks into a pool, and I threw the key into the deepest part of the water.

Tom's motorcycle caused me some trouble. He had parked it at the far edge of the drive, where it was sheltered from the torrential rain by the overhanging tree branches. I went and looked at it for a long time. The keys were in it, but I did not dare to try and ride it anywhere. I was not sure I could have remembered the sequence of things Tom did with his hands and feet to start it, even if I had been relaxed and well rested; now I was miserable and exhausted. I did remember the power of the machine, how it had rumbled and throbbed when the engine was running, and I mistrusted it; I might as well have tried to ride a fire-breathing dragon.

In the end I pushed the bike over into the undergrowth. I fetched an old tarpaulin to conceal the bright metal, and then I did my best to conceal the whole thing under broken branches and handfuls of mulch. The effect was not entirely satisfactory but so long as nobody went right under the trees and actively searched, I thought it might escape notice. I hoped so. So long as it was never found, and Tom's body lay safely hidden in the mausoleum, his family need never know what had happened to him. They might imagine that he was still out there somewhere, skimming along the open road with the wind in his hair. I wished that were true myself. As I walked back into the house, I began to weep.

The next day was my eighteenth birthday.

chapter seventy-one

Ghost: some weeks later

They come, as I thought they probably would: two of them, in black uniforms. A man and a woman this time.

I've thought about it a lot. I could lock the doors and pretend there is nobody here, like I did the last time. They might just go away, but supposing they don't? They might decide to walk around the side of the house, to see if there is any other way in, and if they do that, there is just the remotest chance they might see that place under the tree, where the motorcycle is hidden. Or they might come back later and search properly. Better to give them some answers and let them go away for good.

I could tell them the truth, of course.

I killed Tom McAllister. He's in the old mausoleum in the grounds.

But I don't want to be hanged, or whatever else they do to people now. I know I don't deserve to live, since I've taken someone else's life, but still I want to hang onto my existence, haunted though it is.

It's Tom who haunts me, or at least, his absence does. Wherever I go in the house – the window where I stood and gazed at him, the attic where we chose the clothes together, the bedroom where we made love – I remember him. It's almost as though he's still there. But I never see him, even though I long to. The pain of his not being there is indescribable. I wish I still had something of him, however insubstantial.

I shan't ever leave Langlands. Oh, I suppose at some point I shall run out of things and I shall have to make the trip into town, travelling wearily by foot since there's no longer a car. But I shall keep my contact with the outside to a minimum. There *is* a kind of War going on out there, for me at any rate.

I shall stay here forever, with the ghosts of what passed and the ghosts of what might have been. *Forever* may not prove to be so very long after all. There's something wrong with me. I'm sick all the time; the last three days I've thrown up my breakfast. It's not like anything I've ever had before; perhaps it's something I caught from the Outside. Supposing it never gets better? Then maybe justice will be done after all.

In the meantime, I have to think what to say to these people. When they knock at the front door, I open it. I see surprise on their faces; I see them look at each other. They didn't really expect anyone to be here. I suppose I'm not looking my best, either. I'm pale and tired because I didn't manage to keep my breakfast down. I try to look presentable though, even though I'm alone here. I'm wearing a clean dress and stockings and shoes. Old things, but neat. I may let my hair grow again too in time.

"Good morning," I say, politely.

"Good morning, miss," says the man. "We didn't know there was anyone living here."

"Yes," I say. Just that.

They look at each other again. I suppose they are wondering who I am, and whether I was here before, and perhaps whether I have a right to be here at all. But that isn't what they have come for at this time.

"We're making enquiries about a missing person," says the woman. She holds something out to me.

Before I've even looked at it, I guess what it is. This is the moment I have to steel myself for. I mustn't react when I look at it. I mustn't give myself away.

It's a photograph of Tom. Handsome, kind, dead Tom. I take it from her fingers and look at it gravely, as though considering whether I might ever have seen this person before. I hear the woman talking, saying that this is Tom McAllister, aged nineteen, missing since, motorbike also gone, family grieving. All those things.

I shake my head. "I've never seen him before."

"Are you sure?" she says.

"He and his father did some work up here during the winter," says the man. "You weren't here then?"

"No," I say.

"And you haven't seen him around here at any other time when you've been here?"

I shake my head.

"This place has a bit of reputation locally," says the man, looking at me. His gaze is not unfriendly, but I am still on my guard. "Tom McAllister's family thought there was a small chance he might have come back up here. Dared himself, or something. They seemed to think the place was empty, now the previous owner has died." He shrugs. "Derelict buildings are dangerous. Break in, have an accident..."

"It's not derelict," I say. "I live here now."

"And you are?" says the woman.

"I'm Augusta McAndrew."

"A relative of the previous owner then? It's a shame you weren't here before," she says. "I heard it took them a while to find her next of kin."

"Yes," I say. I wish I could ask them about Grandmother, if they know where she is buried. But I stop myself. I've told

363

them I wasn't here when Tom and his father worked here last winter. It's best to leave it there. It's something, to know that they did find some of Grandmother's family – someone to take care of her.

"It's not possible the missing man could be here and you wouldn't have found him?" asks the man. "Any disused parts of the building, outbuildings, anything like that?"

I shake my head again. "I don't think so. You can look if you like."

I lead them into the house, down the passage and into the kitchen, where they can plainly see that there is only one set of everything left out from breakfast; I'm not hiding a living person in the house. Then we go out of the back door and I show them the henhouse, and the outbuilding where Grandmother used to keep the car. There's nothing untoward, though the woman wrinkles her nose at the smell of chickens.

I can see they're going to leave. They don't suspect the truth. If anything, they are more interested in how self-sufficient Langlands is, and how anyone can live up here, all by themselves. But that's not what they're here to investigate.

Of course, there may still be trouble. If they think to go back to the distant relatives they have found, and ask them about me, there will be questions. Will they do that? I don't know. It's Tom they're looking for now, after all, not Grandmother's next of kin. I may be safe.

I'm so tired, and I still feel nauseous.

Please let them go soon.

They do go, and on the way out, the woman says to me, "Don't you get nervous, up here on your own?"

"Why?" I say.

She looks a little embarrassed then. "Well," she says, "They used to say this place was haunted. The ghost of a girl who died here a long time ago."

"Oh, that," I say. "That's rubbish. That's completely wrong."

"Yes, well, just a story," she says. "Kids' stuff."

I watch them get back into their car. I keep watching as the man turns the car, and they drive off down the track, disappearing under the trees.

"Completely wrong," I say, although I know they can't hear me now; they're too far away. "It's not the ghost of a girl who died here. It's the ghost of a young man who died here."

And I pray, as ever, for it to be true.